CRITICAL ACCLAIM FOR
LEN DEIGHTON AND HIS
BERNARD SAMSON ESPIONAGE NOVELS

FAITH

"What raises Deighton's genre fiction to art is not only his absorbing characters but his metaphoric grace, his droll wit, his command of technical detail, and his sure sense of place."

—*The Washington Post Book World*

"With imagination, scrupulous attention to the punctilio, the manners and mores of the British Secret Intelligence Service (SIS), a chorus of grace notes, and a rare ability to keep us caring, Deighton serves up his seventh Samson with absolutely no diminution of style. It's Deighton's way and his strength."

—*Los Angeles Times Book Review*

"Those beginning the new year with thoughts of auld lang syne can welcome back at least one old friend. . . . There are enough surprises in this tale to keep readers intrigued and waiting for more."

—*The Orlando Sentinel*

"Among the heavyweights in the spy-thriller field, Englishman Len Deighton occupies an uncontested niche. . . . [Bernard] Samson remains his cool, cynical, impudent, defiant self, a loose cannon on the SIS deck who marches to a different drummer. . . . One can barely wait for the two books that will conclude the Samson saga."

—*The Buffalo News*

HOPE

"Does not disappoint . . . Samson has the shrewdness and intelligence of James Bond, without the fancy weaponry, expense account, wardrobe, or lifestyle. . . . His instincts are razor-sharp. . . . [And] Deighton keeps the tension building at a steady pace. By story's end, the reader's pulse has quickened."

—Associated Press

"Master espionage writer Len Deighton takes another sure-footed walk through territory trembling with uncertainty and change. . . . Many will find this richly textured novel so absorbing they will want to pick the series up at the beginning and revel in each book."

—*The Washington Post Book World*

"Deighton is the master of the corrupt and cynical politics practiced by the moles, spies, turncoats, and fall guys. . . . It's a complex story with ever-shifting loyalties, and Deighton sets some deep hooks before he discloses one more surprise."

—*New York Daily News*

"Terrific . . . *Hope* may restore your faith in spy novels."

—*Detroit Free Press*

"[A] remarkable series . . . the best of its kind ever created . . . Deighton's genius is his ability to revisit the same incidents and settings . . . and recreate them from a fresh perspective. The humor is dry, and the violence, it occurs, very, very convincingly."

—*Minneapolis Star-Tribune*

BERLIN GAME

"Each scene in this story is so adroitly realized that it creates its own suspense."

—*Newsweek*

MEXICO SET

"An author at the height of his power."

—*Chicago Tribune*

LONDON MATCH

"Taut . . . splendid . . . first rate."

—*The Wall Street Journal*

SPY HOOK

"Mr. Deighton's touch is unfailing. . . . Never a false note."
—*The New York Times Book Review*

SPY LINE

"Deighton is a master."

—*Los Angeles Times Book Review*

Books by Len Deighton

FICTION
The Ipcress File
Horse Under Water
Funeral in Berlin
Billion-Dollar Brain
An Expensive Place to Die
Only When I Larf
Bomber
Declarations of War
Close-Up
Spy Story
Yesterday's Spy
Twinkle, Twinkle, Little Spy
SS-GB
XPD
Goodbye Mickey Mouse
MAMista
City of Gold
Violent Ward

THE SAMSON SERIES
Berlin Game
Mexico Set
London Match
Winter: A Berlin Family 1899–1945
Spy Hook
Spy Line
Spy Sinker
Faith
Hope
Charity

NONFICTION
Fighter: The True Story of the Battle of Britain
Blitzkrieg: From the Rise of Hitler to the Fall of Dunkirk
Airshipwreck
ABC of French Food
Blood, Tears and Folly

CHARITY

LEN DEIGHTON

HarperPaperbacks
A Division of HarperCollinsPublishers

HarperPaperbacks
A Division of HarperCollins*Publishers*
10 East 53rd Street, New York, N.Y. 10022-5299

This is a work of fiction. The characters, incidents, and dialogues are products of the author's imagination and are not to be construed as real. Any resemblance to persons, living or dead, is entirely coincidental.

A hardcover edition of this book was published in Great Britain in 1996 by HarperCollins*Publishers.*

ISBN 0-06-109602-4

HarperCollins®, 👑 ®, and HarperPaperbacks™ are trademarks of HarperCollins*Publishers,* Inc.

Cover illustration by Danilo Ducak

First HarperPaperbacks Edition: November 1997

Printed in the United States of America

Visit HarperPaperbacks on the World Wide Web at
http://www.harpercollins.com

❖ 10 9 8 7 6 5 4 3 2

AUTHOR'S NOTE

The first three books of the Bernard Samson story, *Game*, *Set*, and *Match*, are set in the Cold War period from spring 1983 to spring 1984.

Winter: A Berlin Family 1899–1945 was the next in order of writing. The same places and the same people are to be found in it.

Hook and *Line* take up the story from the beginning of 1987 and through the summer of that same year. *Sinker* uses a third-person narrative focusing on Fiona Samson. It tells the story from her point of view and reveals things that Bernard Samson still does not know.

Faith, *Hope*, and *Charity* continue the story. *Faith* starts in California as Bernard's terrible summer of 1987 turns cold. *Hope* follows it into the last week of 1987. *Charity* begins in the early days of 1988.

Like all the other books, *Charity* is written to stand alone, and can be read without reference to the other stories.

I thank my readers for their kindness, their generous encouragement, and their patience. Writing ten books about the same group of people has proved a demanding labor but certainly a labor of love.

—Len Deighton
Portugal, 1996

ONE

JANUARY 1988. THE MOSCOW-PARIS EXPRESS TRAIN

A bloated vampire moon drained all life and color from the world. The snow-covered land came speeding past the train. It was gray and ill-defined, marked only by a few livid cottages and limitless black forest grizzled with snow. No roads; the railway did not follow any road, it cut through the land like a knife. I had seen enough of this cheerless country. I tugged the window-blind down, grabbing at a brass rubbish bin to keep my balance as the clattering train argued with a badly maintained section of track.

Sometimes, at night, people also succumbed. Jim Prettyman's complexion, which had always been pale, was ashen under the dim overhead light. Inert on the top berth, a rosary dangling from his white-skinned hand; on the other a gold wedding ring and a massive gold Rolex wrist watch indicating 9:30 in the morning. It wasn't 9:30 here for us. His watch had stopped. Or perhaps that was the right time in Moscow. We were a long way from Moscow, and for us it was still night.

Jim stirred, as if my stare had disturbed his sleep. But his eyelids didn't move. He made a noise; a deep breath and then a stifled groan that ended in a subdued nasal snort as he snatched his arm down under the blanket and resumed his sleep. Jim was tough and wiry but his appearance had never been athletic. Now his white face, with the vestigial eyebrows, made him look like a corpse prettified and readied for the relatives.

Jim had picked up some kind of infection of the liver, or maybe it was the kidneys. The Russian hospital doctors said they could treat it, but, since their diagnosis varied from day to day according to what they were drinking with lunch, no one believed them. Some doctor the American embassy had on call wouldn't give a diagnosis; he just advised that Jim shouldn't be subjected to a plane trip. Rather than have him face any more treatment by Moscow's medics, Jim's American wife had wired the money for him to be evacuated by train and attended by a nurse. Jim's wife was a woman with considerable influence. She had arranged that her father in the State Department send a night-action fax to make sure the embassy people jumped to it. She wasn't with us; she had to host a Washington dinner party for her father.

Although the paperwork for Jim's passage was being handled by the Americans, someone in London Central ordered that I should accompany him as far as Berlin. I was in Moscow at the time, and their message said it simply meant delaying my return by twenty-four hours. But going from Moscow to West Berlin by air was quite different to doing the same trip by train. By train I was going to encounter whole armies of nosy customs officials, security men and frontier police. Jim had a U.S. passport nowadays, the nurse was Canadian, and I was stuck with the German passport that I had used for my entry. With this cosmopolitan party I would have to cross Poland, and then travel across a large section of the German Democratic Republic, before getting to anywhere I could call home. Perhaps the people in London didn't appreciate that. There was sometimes good reason to think pen-pushers in the Foreign Office in Whitehall were still using nineteenth-century maps.

I was looking at Jim, trying to decide how ill he really was, when there came a sudden sound, like a shovelful of heavy mud hitting a wall. The compartment rocked slightly. With no lessening of speed, the express thudded the air and sped between some empty loading platforms, leaving behind no more than an echoed gasp and a whiff of burned diesel. The train was packed. You could feel the weight of it as it swayed, and hear the relentless pounding of the bogies. The compartments of the wagon-lit had been booked for weeks. The cheaper coach seats were all filled and there were people sleeping amid the litter on the floor and propped between baggage in the corridors. Five rail cars were reserved for the army: hardy teenagers with cropped heads and pimples. Their kitbags and rifles were under guard in the freight car. Returning to training camps after playing the sort of war games that didn't include time for sleep. Exhausted draftees. The fighting battalions had forsaken rifles long ago. Rifles were only for clumsy youngsters learning to drill.

Further back in the train there were East European businessmen in plastic suits and clip-on ties; shriveled old women with baskets heavy with homemade vodka and smoked pork sausage; stubble-chinned black market dealers with used TV sets crammed into freshly printed cardboard boxes.

Coming half awake, Jim stretched out a red bony foot so that his toes pressed upon the metal divider that formed the side of a tiny clothes closet. Then he grabbed the edge of the blanket, turned away, and curled up small. "Don't you ever sleep?" he growled drowsily. So he wasn't asleep and dreaming; he simply had his eyes closed. Perhaps that was the way Jim Prettyman had always fooled me. Long ago we'd been very close friends, one of a foursome made up with his petulant first wife Lucinda and my wife Fiona. We'd all worked for the Department in those days. Then Jim had been selected for special jobs and sent to work in corporate America as a cover for his real tasks. He'd changed jobs and changed wives, changed nationality and changed friends in rapid succession. He was not the sort of wavering wimp who let a good opportunity slip past while worrying who might get hurt.

"There's someone standing outside in the corridor," I told him.

"The conductor."

"No, not him. Our bad-tempered conductor has assumed tenancy of compartment number fifteen. And he's stinking, falldown drunk and will soon be unconscious."

"Slide open the door and look," Jim suggested. "Or is that too easy?" His voice was croaky.

"You're the one who's dying," I said. "I'm the security expert. Remember?"

"Was there someone at the railway terminal?" he asked, before remembering to try and smile at my joke. When I made no move to investigate the corridor noise he repeated the question.

"Yes," I said.

"Someone you recognized?"

"I'm not sure. It could be the same goon I had sitting in the lobby of my hotel."

"Go man!" said Jim wearily. He closed his eyes tight, and, with a practiced gesture, bound his rosary round his wrist in some signal of benediction.

I went to the door, undid the catch, and slid it open, unprepared for the bright moonlit countryside that was painted like a mural along the uncurtained windows of the corridor. There was a man there, standing a few steps away. He was about five feet six tall, with trimmed beard, and neat moustache. His woollen Burberry scarf struck a note of affluence that jarred with the rest of his attire: the trenchcoat old and stained, and a black military-style beret that in Poland had become the badge of the elderly veteran of long-ago wars.

We looked at each other. The man gave no sign of friendliness nor recognition. "How far to the frontier?" I asked him in my halting Polish.

"Half an hour; perhaps less. It's always like this. They are taking us on a long detour around the track repairs."

I nodded my thanks and went back into my compartment. "It's okay," I told Jim.

"Who is it? Someone you know?"

"It's okay," I said. "Go back to sleep."

"You may as well get some shut-eye, too. Will the Poles come on and question us at the frontier?"

"No," I said. Then, changing my mind: "Maybe. It will be all right." I wondered if the detour was really because of flood damage the way the press announcement said, or was there something at the frontier that the Soviets didn't want anyone to see?

I was regretting my ready agreement to take this train from Moscow back to my office in Berlin. I didn't have diplomatic status; they had wanted to supply me with a letter with the royal coat of arms at the top, asking everyone en route to be kind to us. That too was a legacy of the FO's nineteenth-century mentality. I had to point out to them that such a missive might look incongruous when carried by someone with a German passport accompanied by an American and a Canadian. I'd not objected to this task of escorting Jim, partly for old times' sake, partly because I'd heard that Gloria would also be in Moscow at that time and the delay would give me two extra days with her. That was another fiasco. Her schedule was changed; she was leaving as I arrived. I'd only had time for one hurried lunch with Gloria, and that was marred by her interpreter arriving to collect her half an hour early, and standing over us with a watch in one hand, a coffee cup in the other, warning us about the traffic jams on the road to the airport. My brief moment with her was made more painful because she was looking more alluring than ever. Her long blonde hair was tucked up into a spiky fur hat, her complexion pale and perfect, and her large brown eyes full of affection, and devoted to me.

Now I had plenty of time to regret my readiness to return by train. Now came the consequences. We were getting close to the Polish frontier, and I was not well regarded in the Socialist Republic of Poland.

I had recognized the man in the corridor as "Sneaky Jack," one of the hard men employed by our Warsaw embassy. I suppose London had assigned him to keep an eye on Jim. I had reason to believe that Jim's head was filled with the Department's darkest secrets, and I wondered what Sneaky had been ordered to do if those secrets were compromised. Was he there to make sure Jim didn't fall into enemy hands alive?

"Where's that bloody nurse?" said Jim as I locked the sliding door. He turned over to look at me. "She should be here holding my hand." The nurse was a pretty, young woman from Winnipeg, Canada. She was spending six months working in a Moscow hospital on an exchange scheme and had welcomed this opportunity to cut it short. She looked after Jim as if he was her nearest and dearest. Only when she was almost dropping from exhaustion did she retire to her first-class compartment along the corridor.

"The nurse has had a long day, Jim. Let her sleep." I suppose he had sensed my anxiety. Jim had never been a field agent; he'd started out as a mathematician and got to the top floor via Codes and Ciphers. It was better if he didn't know that Sneaky was one of our people. And it was bad security to tell him. But if Jim ran into trouble and Sneaky had to tell him what to do. . . ? Oh, hell.

"In the corridor . . . little fellow with a beard. If we hit problems, and I'm not close by, do as he says."

"You're not scared, are you, Bernard?"

"Me? Scared? Let me get at them."

Jim acknowledged my well-rehearsed imitation of my boss Dicky Cruyer by giving a smile that was restrained enough to remind me that he was sick and in pain.

"It will be all right," I told him. "With an embassy man outside the door they won't even come in here."

"Let's play it safe," he said. "Get that nurse back here and in uniform, waving a thermometer or a fever chart or something. That's what she's here for, isn't it?"

"Sure. If that's what you want." I felt that a man in Jim's situation needed reassurance but I was probably wrong about that as I was wrong about everything else that happened on that journey.

I went along to find the nurse. I needn't have worried about disturbing her sleep. She was up and dressed in her starched white nurse's uniform, to which was added a smart woolen overcoat and knitted hat to keep her warm. She was drinking hot coffee from a vacuum flask. Bracing herself against the rock and roll of the train, she poured some into a plastic cup for me without asking if I wanted it.

"Thanks," I said.

"I must look a sight in this stupid hat. I bought it for my kid brother, but I'm freezing cold. They don't have much heat on these trains."

I tasted the coffee. It was made with canned condensed milk and was very sweet. I suppose she liked it like that. I said: "I've done this lousy journey a million times and I've never had the brains to bring a vacuum flask of coffee with me."

"I brought six of these flasks," she said. "Vacuum flasks were about the only thing I could find in the Moscow shops that would make a useful gift for my aunts and uncles back home. And they all expect a souvenir. Can you believe that they don't even have fridge magnets? I was looking for something with the Kremlin on it."

"Moscow is not a great spot for shopping," I agreed.

"It's a not a great spot for anything," she said. "Lousy climate, stinking food, surly natives. Getting out of there early was the best thing that happened to me in a long time."

"Not everyone likes it," I agreed. "Personally there

are quite a few towns I'd be happy to cross off my itinerary. Washington, D.C., for a start."

"Oh, don't say that. I worked in Washington, D.C., for over a year. What parties they have there! I loved it."

"By the way, the comrades who come climbing aboard at the frontier can be difficult about jewelry. I would tuck that sapphire brooch out of sight, if I were you."

"Oh, this?" she said, fingering it on the lapel of her coat. "Mr. Prettyman gave it to me. I wanted to wear it, to show him I appreciated it." Maybe she saw a question in my face, for she quickly added: "It was a little present from Mr. and Mrs. Prettyman. His wife was on the phone. She asked him to give it to me. They are determined to believe I saved his life."

"And you didn't?"

"I stopped the night-duty man cutting his appendix out, that night when he was admitted. It was a crazy diagnosis but I guess he would have lived." She paused. "But that night doctor was very crocked. And he was going to try doing it himself. The things I saw in that hospital, you would never believe. When I think about it, maybe I did save his life."

"How sick is he?"

"He's bad. These kinds of infections don't always respond to drugs. . . . The truth is no one knows too much about them." Her voice trailed away as she fiddled with the pin of her brooch, concerned that she had revealed too much about her patient. "But don't worry. If anything had happened suddenly I could have him taken off in Berlin. The embassy people said Warsaw was not a good place." She held the brooch in the palm of her hand and looked at it. "It's a great keepsake. I like the kooky daisy shape; I've always loved daisies. I really appreciate it, but do you really think some Russkie is going to risk his career? He'd look kind of crazy, wouldn't he: snatching from a tourist like me a little silver-plated brooch with plastic sides and colored brilliants?" She grinned mischievously. "Want to look closer?"

"I don't have to look any closer," I said, but I took it from her anyway. "It's not a flower, not a daisy, it's an antique sunburst pattern. And that's not black plastic, it's badly tarnished silver, with yellow gold on the back. The big, luminous, faintly blue stone in the center is a top-quality sapphire; maybe thirty carats. It's been neglected: badly rubbed with scratches, but that could all be polished away. All those 'colored brilliants' that punctuate each ray of it are matched diamonds pavé set."

"You've got to be kidding."

"The fastening is a simple pin, without safety catches. It's antique . . . well over a hundred years old. It's worth a pile of money."

"Golly. Are you sure? Where did you learn so much about jewelry?"

"Back in the sixties, in Berlin, they were tearing down some old houses in Neustadt. The bulldozer pushed a wall down and found a secretly bricked-up part of the cellar. It was full of crates and metal boxes. My father was Berlin security supremo for the British. He had to take charge of it. He tried to get out of it but some of the valuables were marked with labels from the Reichsbank. That opened a whole can of worms . . ." I stopped. "I'm sorry, I'm being a bore." I gave her the brooch.

"No, you're not. I want to hear." She was examining the brooch carefully. "I don't know anything about the war and the Nazis, apart from what I've seen back home in movies."

"Gold, silver, coins, foreign paper money including pounds and dollars. And boxes of jewelry and antique cutlery and stuff; most of it solid silver. The Reichsbank labels made it political. The SS had stored their loot in the Reichsbank. So did Göring and some of the others. It could have been the property of the Federal Republic, or it might be claimed by the governments of countries the Nazis took over in the war. Some of the jewelry was thought to be part of the family jewels of the House of Hesse that were stolen by American soldiers in 1945. In other words no one had the slightest idea what it all was. The first job was to have it all listed and itemized, so the descriptions could be circulated. My father had three experienced Berlin jewelers going through it. It was in the old swimming hall in Hauptstrasse in Schöneberg. A big barn of a place, made of shiny white tiles, derelict at that time but still faintly smelling of chlorine and bleach. Folding tables from the army canteen were set up in the drained pool; the jewels and silver and stuff were all arranged on them and there were big printed numbers marking each item. I can see it now. There were cops sitting on the three-meter diving board looking down at us. My Dad told me to keep my eyes open and make sure the jewelers didn't steal anything." I drank some coffee.

"And did they steal anything?"

"I was very young. I'm not sure if they did or not, but in those days Germans were scrupulously honest; it was one of the aspects of Berlin I took for granted until I went elsewhere. These old jewelers showed me each piece before they wrote out the description. It went on for four and a half days. For me it was an intensive course in jewelry appraisal. But I've forgotten half of it. That stone is cut as *der Achteck-Kreuzschliff*. I only know the German word for it. I suppose it means an octagonal crosscut. The sapphire is a cushion cut; quite old."

"What happened to all the treasure?"

"I'm not sure. What I remember is having to decipher the handwriting—some of it in old German script—and type it out, with eight carbon copies. It took me a week. And I remember how happy my father was when he finally got a signature for it."

"That's quite a story," she said. "I've never owned real jewelry before. Now if you would kindly turn around and avert your eyes, I shall tuck my valuable brooch into my money belt."

The express slowed as we neared the frontier, and then, after a lot of hissing and puffing of brakes and machinery, crawled slowly into Soviet Russia's final western outpost, where floodlamps on tall posts swamped the checkpoint area with dazzling light. Like foamy water, it poured down upon the railway tracks and swamped the land. A freight train, caked in mud, was still and abandoned; a shunting engine was steamy and shiny with oil. At its shadowy edge I could see the barrack blocks of the local frontier battalion and their guard towers. Under the fierce lighting, starshaped shadows sprang from the feet of the sentries, railway officials, immigration, and customs men. The lights illuminated every last splash of icy sludge on the army trucks that were awaiting the Soviet draftees. The soldiers alighted first, in a frenzy of shouting, saluting, and stamping of feet. Then there came the noise of the army's well-used railway cars being uncoupled and shunted off to a distant siding.

☒   ☒   ☒

Inside the express train there was an almost interminable processing of paperwork by Soviet officials whose demeanor ranged from officious to witless. They gave no more than a glance at the paperwork for our party. I got a mocking salute, the girl a leer, and Jim's inert form a nod. Eventually the train started again. It slid out of the brightly lit frontier area, and, with many stops and starts, we clanked across the frontier to where the Poles—and another checkpoint—awaited us.

Here the lights were less bright, the armed soldiers less threatening. I stood in the corridor watching the whole circus. Fur hats bobbed everywhere. The soldiers climbed aboard first. Then the ticket inspector came, and then the customs officer, and then two immigration inspectors with an army officer in tow, and a security official in civilian clothes. It was a long process.

An elderly English woman came shuffling along the train corridor. She was wearing a raglan-style camel hair coat over a nightdress. Her graying hair was disheveled, and she clutched a bulging crocodile-skin handbag tightly to her breast. I'd noticed her on the platform at Moscow, where she'd got into an argument with a railway official about the seats assigned to her and the teenage boy with whom she was traveling.

"The soldiers have arrested my son," she told me in a breathless croak. She was distressed, almost hysterical, but controlling her emotions in that way that the English do in the presence of foreigners. "He's such a foolish boy. They discovered a political magazine in his shoulder bag. I want to go with him and sort it out, but they say I must continue my journey to Berlin because I have no Polish visa. What shall I do? Can you help me? I heard you speaking Polish and I know you speak English."

"Give the sergeant some Western money," I said. "Do you have ten pounds in British currency?"

She touched her loosened hair, and a lock of it fell across her face. "I didn't declare it." She mouthed the words lest she was overheard. "It's hidden." She nervously flicked her hair back, and then with a quick movement of her fingers secured it with a hairclip that seemed to come from nowhere.

"It's what they want," I said. "Give them ten pounds sterling."

"Are you sure?" She didn't believe me. She had become aware of her unladylike appearance by now. Self-consciously she fastened the top button of her coat against her neck.

"Why else would they let you come here and talk with me?" I said.

She frowned and then smiled sadly. "I see."

"The sergeant," I said. "Take the sergeant to one side and give it to him. He will share it with the officer afterwards, so that no one sees it. If things go wrong the sergeant gets all the blame. It's the way it works."

"Thank you." With as much dignity as she could muster in a frilly nightdress and scuffed red velvet slippers, she hurried off back to her compartment. The door was opened for her when she got there and the sergeant poked his head out and looked at me. I smiled. Expressionless he drew his head back in again.

More uniformed officials came crawling along the train; resolute and unfriendly like a column of jungle ants. But the Polish security man who took me into the conductor's compartment at the end of the carriage was an elderly civilian, a plump man with untidy wavy hair, long and untidy enough to distinguish him from the soldiers. He was wearing a red-striped bow tie and belted brown corduroy overcoat. He scanned my passport with a battery-powered ultraviolet light. There was nothing wrong with my papers—it was a genuine German Federal Republic document—but he ignored the name in my passport and said: "Welcome to Poland, Mr. Samson."

If they knew who I was, they knew what I did for a living. So they were not to be persuaded that I was an advertising executive from Hamburg.

He didn't give the passport back: instead he put it in his pocket. That was always a bad sign. He questioned me in German and in English. He told me his name was Reynolds and that his father was English, and born in Manchester. The Poles all had an English relative up their sleeve, just as the English like to keep an Irish grandmother in reserve.

I pretended not to understand English. Reynolds told me all over again in German. He was very patient. He smoked cheroots and kept referring to a bundle of documents that he said were all devoted to me and my activities. It was a thick folder, and once or twice it looked as if the whole lot of loose pages would end up cascading to the floor of the train, but he always managed to save them at the last moment.

I told him that it was a simple case of mistaken identity. Mr. Reynolds lit a fresh cheroot from the butt of his old one and sighed. Another ten minutes passed in fruitless questions, and then they escorted me off the train. Sneaky Jack did nothing except stand around in the corridor, getting a glimpse of me through the door now and again, and overhearing as much as he could. I didn't blame him. He was no doubt assigned to look after Jim. Solving the predicaments of a supernumerary field agent like me was not something upon which his career would hang.

As far as I could see I was the only person being removed from the train. I jumped down and felt the chill of the hard frozen ground through the soles of my shoes. It was darker now; the moon was hiding behind the clouds. They didn't handcuff me. I followed the two soldiers—a sergeant standard-bearer and a trumpeter, if the badges on their arm were taken seriously. We crossed the tracks, stepping high over the rails and being careful not to stumble as we picked our way through piles of broken sleepers and other debris. Mr. Reynolds was breathing heavily by the time we climbed the embankment. We waited for him to catch up.

I looked back at the train. There was lots of noise and steam, and all the squeaky commotion that is the ritual of trains as they prepare to move. The yellow blind of Jim's compartment went up, and the nurse was framed in the window. There was condensation on the glass and she wiped a clear patch with her hand. She looked this way and that, but it was too dark for her to spot me. She wasn't a Departmental employee, just a Canadian nurse engaged to accompany a casualty to London. Having a traveling companion suddenly disappear was no doubt disconcerting for her.

I stood shivering alongside Reynolds and his soldiers and we all watched the train pull away slowly. When it had disappeared the night was dark and I felt lonely. I looked the other way: back across the frontier to the Soviet checkpoint half a mile distant. It was still bathed in light but all the frantic activity there had ceased: the army trucks and the officials had disappeared. The lights were still glistening upon the oval of hardened snow, but the only movement was the measured pacing of a single armed sentry. It was like some abandoned ice hockey stadium from which teams and spectators had unaccountably fled.

"Let's go," said Reynolds. He flicked the butt of his cheroot so that it went spinning away in red sparks.

Before I could react the sergeant hit me spitefully in the small of the back with the metal butt of his gun. Caught off guard, I lost my balance. At first I slipped and then, as my knees buckled under me, I tumbled down the embankment with arms flailing. At the bottom there was a drainage ditch. The thick ice cracked and my foot went through it into cold muddy water.

When I got back on my feet I was wet and dirty. There was a wind that shook the trees and cut me to the bone. I wished I'd put my overcoat on before leaving the compartment to go and answer their questions. After five minutes stumbling through the dark, there was the sound of a diesel engine starting and then the headlights of a dark green army truck lit up a narrow road and trees.

They didn't take me to Warsaw or to any other big town. The truck bumped along country roads while the crimson dawn crept out from the woodland. The sky was beginning to lighten as we arrived at the grim-looking castle in Mazury. Without anything much being said they locked me in a room there. It was not a bad room; I had endured worse accommodation in Polish hotels. The worrying thing was our proximity to Rastenburg, where I'd recently shot some Polish UB men and not gone back to feel their pulse. Thinking about that made it a long time before I went to sleep.

The man who liked to be called Reynolds was apparently in charge of me. He came to see me next morning and directly accused me of killing two security officials while evading arrest. Reynolds talked a lot, and continued talking even when I did not respond. He told me I would be held and tried here in the military district headquarters. In the course of the investigation, and subsequent court martial, the army witnesses, prosecutors and judges would go and visit the place where my crime took place. He didn't mention anything about a defense counsel.

The second day was Wednesday. He questioned me all the morning and into the afternoon, and accused me of not taking the charges seriously. I didn't admit to any of it. I said I was German but he didn't believe me.

"You think your government is now strenuously applying for your release through diplomatic channels, do you not?"

I looked at him and smiled. He didn't know much about my government, or its diplomatic service, or he would have known that having them do anything strenuously was far beyond reasonable expectations.

"You've nothing to smile about," said Reynolds, banging his flattened hand upon a dossier lying on the table.

How right he was. "I demand to see the consul from the embassy of the German Federal Republic," I said.

I'd made the same demand many times, but on this occasion he became angry and rammed his cheroot down hard so that it split apart in the ashtray. "Will you stop repeating that stupid cover story?" There was real anger in his voice. "We know who you are. The Germans have never heard of you." Perhaps it was because he'd missed lunch.

They had me in a rambling old fortress that Reynolds called the citadel. It was the sort of fairy castle that Walt Disney would have built on a mountaintop, but this was a region of lakes and marshland and the prominence upon which the castle stood was no more than a hillock.

The buildings that made up the complex provided a compendium of fortification history: twelfth-century dungeons, a keep almost as old, and a seventeenth-century tower. There were three cobbled yards, the one beneath my window crowded with ramshackle wooden huts and other structures that the German army had added when it became a regional school of military hygiene during the Second World War. The walls were thick and castellated, with a forbidding entrance gate that had once housed a drawbridge. The top of the walls provided a path along which armed sentries patrolled as they had no doubt done for centuries. To what extent the poor wretches slapping themselves to keep warm were there because the army thrives on sentry duty and guard changes, or to warn of approaching danger, was hard to decide. But in this eastern frontier region at that time, the prospect of a Soviet invasion was never far from anyone's mind. Some Moscow hard-liners were proclaiming that the Poles had gone too far with their reforms, and the only way to maintain communist power throughout the Eastern Bloc was by a brotherly show of Soviet military repression.

Whether they were reformers, communists, or khaki-clad philanthropists, the military government in Warsaw wouldn't welcome Soviet spearhead armor lunging across the border. Perhaps that was why this enlarged battalion of Polish infantry was garrisoned here, and why their day began at 5:30 with a flag-hoisting ceremony, accompanied by a drummer and that sort of discordant trumpeting that drives men into battle. And why the congregation that lined up at the subsequent Holy Mass was in full battle order.

They had brought my suitcase off the train. In my presence they'd unlocked it and searched through its contents and photographed selected items. Now the case was open and placed on a low table in my room. They found nothing incriminating, but I didn't like this development. The suitcase, the photos, the polite questions, and everything else they did, smelled like preparations for a public trial. Were you ill-treated? No. Were you tortured? No. Were you properly fed? Yes. Were you given a comfortable room? Yes. Were these answers given freely and without coercion? That's the sort of dialogue I smelled in the air, and I didn't like the prospect one bit.

My third-floor window looked down upon a small inner yard. Beyond it there was the main courtyard, where the morning and evening parade took place. My room wasn't a cell. They weren't giving me the thumbscrews, rack, and electric shocks treatment. They didn't take away my watch and seal off the daylight to disorient me, or try any of the textbook tricks like that. The only torture I suffered was when Reynolds blew cigarette smoke in my face, and that was more because it reminded me of the pleasures of smoking than because I was overcome by the toxic fumes.

The room they'd given me high up in the tower also smelled of ancient tobacco smoke. It smelled of mold and misery, too. Its thick masonry was cold like ice, whitewashed and glistening with condensation. On the wall a plastic crucifix was nailed and on the bed there were clean sheets; frayed, patched, hard, gray, and wrinkled. A small wooden table had one leg wedged with a wad of toilet paper. On the table half a dozen sheets of notepaper and two pencils had been arranged as if inviting a confession. Fixed to the wall above the table there was a shelf holding a dozen paperbacks; Polish best-sellers, some German classics, and ancient and well-read Tauchnitz editions in English: Thomas Hardy and A. E. W. Mason. I suppose Reynolds was hoping to catch me reading one of the books in English, but he never did. It took too long to get the massive lock turned, and I always heard him coming.

There was a water radiator, too: it groaned and rattled a lot, but it never became warmer than blood heat, so I kept a blanket around my shoulders. A great deal of my time was spent staring out of the window.

My small inner yard was cobbled, and in the corner by the well lay a bronze statue. The statue had been cut from its pediment by a torch which had melted its lower legs to pronglike petals. Face down, this prone warrior waved a cutlass in one final despairing gesture. I never discovered the identity of this twice-fallen trooper, but he was clearly considered of enough political significance to make his outdoor display a danger to public order. While only a small section of the main yard was exposed to my view, I could see the rear of the officers' mess where half a dozen fidgety horses were unceasingly groomed and exercised. Early each morning, fresh from a canter, they were paraded around the yard, snorting and steamy. Once, late at night, I saw two drunken subalterns exchanging blows out there. Thus the limited view of the yard and the exposed secrets of the officers' mess was like that provided by the cheap fauteuil seats, high up in a theater balcony, the obstructed view of the stage made up for by the chance to see the backstage activity behind the wings. I saw the padre preparing for Mass in the half-light of early morning. I saw two men plucking countless chickens so that the feathers blew around like smoke, and during mealtimes the mess servants would sometimes emerge for a moment to covertly upend a bottle of wine.

The bigger yard was equally active. For most of the daylight hours it was filled with young soldiers who jumped and ran and reached high in the air at the commands of two physical training instructors. The trainees were dressed in khaki singlets and shorts, and they moved furiously to keep warm in the freezing air. The instructors ran past my line of vision, shadowboxing as if unable to contain their limitless energy. When in the afternoon the final company of men had completed their physical training, the sun would come out of hiding. Its cruel light showed up the dust and cobwebs on the window glass. It set the forest ablaze and edged the battlements with golden light, leaving the courtyard in cold blue shadow, luminous and shimmering as if it was filled to the brim with clear water.

My room was no less comfortable than those assigned to the junior officers who shared the same landing with me. Often, when I was on my way to the washroom and toilet, or when Reynolds was taking me downstairs to his office, I caught sight of smartly uniformed subalterns. They looked at me with undisguised curiosity. Later I discovered that a security company used part of the "citadel" for training courses, and the officers had been selected for politically sensitive duties supervising municipal authorities. For Poland was a land governed by its soldiers.

I was punched and slapped a few times. Never by Reynolds. Never when Reynolds was present. It happened after he became exasperated by my smartass answers. He would puff at his cheroot, sigh and leave the office for ten minutes or so. One or another of the guards would give me a couple of blows as if on his own account. I never discovered if it was done on Reynolds's orders, or even with his knowledge. Reynolds was not vicious. He was not a serious inter-rogator, which was probably why he'd been assigned to this military backwater. He wasn't expecting me to reveal any secrets that would raise questions in Warsaw, or even raise eyebrows there. Reynolds was content to do his job. He asked me the same questions every day; changing the order and the syntax from time to time but not waiting too long for a reply. Usually the final part of the day's session would consist of Reynolds telling me about his sister Hania and his lazy, good-for-nothing brother-in-law, and the wholesale delicatessen business they owned in Detroit.

On Friday afternoon the wind dropped and the trees were unnaturally still. From under low gray clouds the sun's long slanting rays hit the battlements. A sentry stepped forward and stood fully in the light to capture the meager warmth. Watching him I noticed a flickering in the air. Tiny golden pinpricks, like motes of dust caught in a cathedral interior. Snowflakes: the winter had returned. As if in celebration, from one of the rooms along the corridor Tauber burst into a scratchy tenor ren-dering of "Dein ist mein ganzes Herz." He sounded ter-ribly old.

By morning the snow was no longer made of gold. It had spread a white sheet across the land, and my bronze warrior was dusted with it. It didn't stop. By Saturday evening the snow covered everything. I heard the grinding sounds of the trucks that brought sentries back from guard duty at the nearby radar station. They came in low gear, their engines growling and their wheels intermittently spinning on the treacherously smooth section of roadway that was the approach to the main gate. The snow had blown across my yard, to form deep drifts along the wall, and the bronze warrior was entombed in it. I opened the window and put my head out into the stinging cold. The world was unnaturally hushed with that silence that such snow always brings. Then I heard shouting and saw an agitated sentry aiming his gun at me. I pulled my head in and closed the window. Happy to see such a quick response he waved his gun and laughed so that his happiness condensed on the cold air.

On Wednesday night, after five days in custody, a soldier came for me in the middle of the night. I recognized him as one of the PT instructors. He was a wiry fellow with the inscrutable face that seems to go with gymnasts, as if prolonged exercise encourages the contemplative condition. He led me down the back stairs and through a part of the building I'd not seen before. We passed through the muggy kitchens and a succession of storerooms that had once been cellars. Finally he indicated that I should precede him.

As I bent my head under the low doorway, he hit me in the small of the back. He followed that with another punch that found the kidneys and sent a jolt of pain though my body from heel to head. It was like an electric shock and my mind blanked out as I contended with the intense pain. I fell like a tree.

It was dark, but there was another man in the darkness. He came from the shadows and caught me, giving me a couple of hard jabs in the belly that brought my supper up into my mouth. I tucked my head down and tried to cover myself from their blows but they weren't deterred, nor inconvenienced. These two were experts. They worked on me systematically as if I was a side of beef being readied for the stewpot. After a few minutes one of them was taking my whole weight, holding me up to be punched. When he let go of me I crashed to the stone floor only half conscious. I couldn't think straight. Every part of my body was singing with pain. Under me I could feel coarse matting, and, reaching beyond its edge, smooth pavement. I moved enough to press my face against the cold stone. I vomited and tasted blood in my mouth.

The two men stood over me watching; I could see a glint of light, and their shoes. Then they went away, satisfied no doubt with the job they'd done. I heard their footsteps fade but I didn't try to get up. I pressed my head against a bag of onions. At the bottom of the sack, rotten onions had fermented to become a foul-smelling liquid that oozed through the sacking. I blacked out and then came conscious several times. Despite the stench I remained there full-length for a long time before very, very slowly rolling and snaking across the floor, slowly getting my back against the wall and inch by inch sitting up. No bones were broken; no bruises or permanent marks on my face. Theirs was not a spontaneous act of brutality or spite. They had been assigned to hurt me, but not permanently cripple me, and they'd done their job nicely. No hard feelings, chaps, it's all in a day's work for a soldier serving in a land ruled by generals. Lucky me that they hadn't been told to tear me limb from limb, for I'm confident they would have done it with the same inscrutable proficiency. Having decided that, I lost consciousness again.

Someone must have carried me up to the room in

the tower. I don't remember anything of it but I certainly didn't get there unassisted. But why, after a week of Mister Nice Guy, suddenly take me out of my bed and beat the daylights out of me without interrogation or promises? There was only one explanation and it slowly became clear to me. Some higher authority had ordered my release. This was Mr. Reynolds's tacit way of protesting that decision, and saying farewell to me.

Higher authority was satisfied, I suppose. The generals in Warsaw were not trying to provoke World War III. They just wanted to show their opposite numbers in London that they didn't like nosy strangers coming into their territory and doing the sort of things I'd done last Christmas at Rastenburg. They didn't want me demonstrating short-take-off-and-landing aircraft after dark, and kidnapping useful Polish spies. They didn't like me torching shiny new government-owned Volvo motorcars which were in short supply in Poland in 1987. And they didn't like the way I'd shot and wounded Polish security men who, having failed to stop me, had made sure that arrest-and-detain notices were posted throughout the land.

Well, that was my mistake; I should have killed the bastards.

Reynolds put me on the train the next night. He took me to the station in a car, talking all the time about his sister in America and pretending not to notice that his men had almost beaten the life out of me. It was the same Moscow-to-Paris express train, on the same day of the week. They even put me back into a compartment with the same number. My overcoat—which I'd not seen during my incarceration—was folded and stowed on the rack. Pointedly my passport was balanced on the small basket the railway provides for rubbish. Everything was the same, except that Jim and his nurse were not there.

The train compartment was warm. Outside it was snowing again. Wet dollops of it were sliding down the window glass. I slumped on the berth and stretched out. The pain of my beating had not abated and my clothes still had the sickening odor of putrid onions. My bruises and grazes were at that stage of development when the pain is at its most acute. I closed my eyes. I couldn't even raise enough strength to get up and slide the door closed. From the compartment next door I heard the raised voices of a young American couple arguing with a soldier. "They say it's a political magazine," said the woman. She had a nice voice, with the sort of musical Boston accent that the Kennedy family made patrician.

"I never saw it before," said the man. Then he repeated his denial loudly and in German.

There was a moment of silence, then the woman coughed and the man gave a short angry laugh.

I heard my door slide open. I half-opened my eyes and a Polish officer stepped inside to stare down at me. Then the sergeant joined him and the two of them moved on along the corridor. I suppose the American couple had picked up the local traditions without my assistance.

Some extra railway coaches were shunted and coupled to our train with a rattle and a jarring that shook me to the core. Then, after a great deal of whistling and shouted orders, the train clattered forward. I pulled the pillow over my ears.

TWO

THE SIS RESIDENCE, BERLIN

That bloody man Kohl," said Frank Harrington, speaking with uncustomary bitterness about the German Federal Republic's Chancellor. "It's all his doing. Inviting that bastard Honecker to visit the Republic has completely demoralized all decent Germans—on both sides of the Wall."

I nodded. Frank was probably right, and even if he hadn't been right I would have nodded just as sagely; Frank was my boss. And everywhere I went in Berlin I found despondency about any chance of reforming the East German State, or replacing the stubbornly unyielding *apparatchiki* who ran it. Just a few months before—in September 1987—Erich Honecker, Chairman of East Germany's Council of State, Chairman of its National Defence Council and omnipotent General Secretary of the Socialist Unity Party, had been invited on a state visit to West Germany. Few Germans—East or West—

had believed that such a shameless tyrant could ever be granted such recognition.

"Kohl's a snake in the grass," said Frank. "He knows what everyone here thinks about that monster Honecker but he'll do anything to get reelected."

Kohl had certainly played his cards with skill. Inviting Honecker to visit the West had been a political bombshell that Kohl's rivals found difficult to handle. The Saarland premier—Oskar Lafontaine—had been misguided enough to pose with the despised Honecker for a newspaper photo. The resulting outcry dealt Lafontaine's Social Democrats a political setback. This, plus some clever equivocations, patriotic declarations, and vague promises, revived the seemingly dead Chancellor Kohl and reaffirmed him in power.

Those who still hoped that Honecker's visit to the West would be marked by some reduction of tyranny at home asked him to issue orders to stop his border guards shooting dead anyone who tried to escape from his bleak domain. "Fireside dreams are far from our minds," he said. "We take the existence of two sovereign states on German soil for granted."

"Kohl and his cronies have taken them all for a ride," I said. The "Wessies" viewed Kohl's political manipulation of the Honecker visit with that mixture of bitter contempt and ardent fidelity that Germans have always given to their leaders. On the other side of the Wall the "Ossies," confined in the joyless DDR, were frustrated and angry. Grouped around TV sets, they had watched Kohl, and other West German politicians, being unctuous and accommodating to their ruthless dictator, and blithely proclaiming that partition was a permanent aspect of Germany's future.

"It aged Strauss ten years, that visit," said Frank. I

could never tell when he was joking; Frank was not noted for his humor but his jokes were apt to be cruel and dark ones. From his powerbase in Munich, Franz Josef Strauss had proclaimed something he'd said many times before: "The German Reich of 1945 has legally never been abolished; the German question remains open." It was not what Honecker wanted to hear. He might have won Kohl over, but Strauss remained Honecker's most effective long-term critic.

We were downstairs in Frank's house in Grunewald, the home that came with the post of Head of Station in Berlin. It was late afternoon, and the dull cloudy sky did little to make the large drawing room less somber. Yellow patches of light from electric table lamps fell upon a ferocious carpet of bright red and green flowers. A Bechstein grand piano glinted in one corner. Upon its polished top, rank upon rank of family photos paraded in expensive frames. Playing center forward for this team stood a silver-framed photo of Frank's son, a one-time airline pilot who had found a second career as a publisher of technical aviation books. Behind the serried relatives there was a cut-glass vase of long-stemmed roses imported from some foreign climate to help forget that Berlin's gardens were buried deep under dirt-encrusted snow. All around the room there were Victorian paintings of a sooty and hazy London: Primrose Hill, the Crystal Palace and Westminster Abbey all in heavy gilt frames and disappearing behind cracked and darkening coach varnish. Arranged around a polished mahogany coffee table there were two big uncomfortable sofas in blue damask, and three wing armchairs with matching upholstery. One of these Frank kept positioned exactly facing the massive speakers of his elaborate hi-fi system, its working parts concealed inside a birchwood Biedermeier tallboy that had been disemboweled to accommodate it. Sometimes Frank felt bound to explain that the tallboy had been badly damaged before suffering this terminal surgery.

Frank was relaxed in his lumpy chair. Thin, elegant legs crossed, a drink at his elbow, and a chewed old Dunhill pipe in his mouth. From time to time he disappeared from view behind a somber haze, not unlike the coach varnish that obscured the views of London, except for its pungent smell. After a period of denial, which had caused him—and indeed everyone who worked with him—mental and physical stress, he'd now surrendered to his nicotine addiction with vigor and delight.

"I read the report," said Frank, removing the pipe from his mouth and prodding into its bowl with the blade of a Swiss army penknife. Seen like this, in his natural habitat, Frank Harrington was the model Englishman. Educated but not intellectual, a drinker who was never drunk, his hair graying and his bony face lined without him looking aged, his impeccably tailored pinstripe suit not new, and everything worn with a hint of neglect: the appearance and manner which knowing foreigners so often admire and rash ones imitate.

I sipped my whisky and waited. I had been summoned to this meeting in Frank's home by means of a handwritten memo left on my desk by Frank in person. Only he would have fastened it to my morning *Berliner* doughnut by means of a pushpin. Such formal orders were infrequent, and I knew I'd not been brought here to hear Frank's views on the more Byzantine stratagems of Germany's political adventurers. I wondered what was really in his mind. So far there had been little official reaction to my delayed return to Berlin, and the detention in Poland that caused it. When I arrived I reported to Frank and told him I'd been arrested and released without charges. He was on the phone when I went into his office. He capped the phone, mumbled something about my preparing a report for London, and waved me absent. I resumed my duties as his deputy, as if I'd not been away. The written report I had submitted was brief and formal, with an underlying inference that it was a matter of mistaken identity.

I was sitting on one of the sofas in an attempt to keep my distance from the polluting product of Frank's combustion. Before me there was a silver tray with a crystal ice bucket, tongs, and a cut-glass tumbler into which a double measure of Laphroaig whisky had been precisely measured by Tarrant. He'd put the whisky bottle away again, but left on the table a bottle of Apollinaris water from which I was helping myself. Shell-shaped silver dishes contained calculated amounts of salted nuts and potato chips and there was a large silver box that I knew contained a selection of cigarettes. Tarrant, Frank's butler, had arranged a similar array on Frank's side of the coffee table. Apart from Frank's expensive hi-fi, Tarrant had ensured that the household and its routines were not modified by advances in science or fashion. As far as I could see, Frank did the same thing for the Department.

On an inlaid tripod table, booklets and files were arranged in fans, like periodicals in a dentist's waiting-room. From the table Frank took the West German passport I'd been using when detained in Poland. He flipped its pages distastefully and looked from the identity photo to me and then at the photo again. "This photograph," he said finally. "Is it really you?"

"It was all done in a bit of a hurry," I explained.

"Going across there with a smudgy picture of someone else in your passport is a damned stupid way of doing things. Why not an authentic picture?"

"An identity picture is like ethnic food," I said. "The less authentic it is the better."

"Can you elaborate on that a little?" said Frank, playing the innocent.

"Because the UB photocopy, and file away, every passport that goes through their hands," I said.

"Ahhh," said Frank, sounding unconvinced. He slid the passport across the table to me. It was a sign that he wasn't going to take the matter any further. I picked it up and put it in my pocket.

"Don't use it again," said Frank. "Put it away with your Beatles records and that Nehru jacket."

"I won't use it again, Frank," I said. I'd never worn a Nehru jacket or anything styled remotely like one, but I would always remain the teenager he'd once known. There was no way of escaping that.

"You are senior staff now. The time for all those shenanigans is over." He picked up my report and shook it as if something might fall from the pages. "London will read this. There is no way I can sit on it for ever."

I nodded.

"And you know what they will say?"

I waited for him to say that London would suspect that I'd gone to Moscow only in order to see Gloria. But he said, "You were browbeating Jim Prettyman. That's what they will say. What did you get out of him? You may as well tell me, so that I can cover my arse."

"Jim Prettyman?"

"Don't do that, Bernard," said Frank with just a touch of aggravation.

If it was a chess move, it was an accomplished one. To avoid the accusation that I was grilling Prettyman I would have to say that I was there to see Gloria. "Prettyman was more or less unconscious. There was little chance of my doing anything beyond tucking him into bed and changing his bedpans, and there was a nurse to do that. What would I be grilling Prettyman about, anyway?"

"Come along, Bernard. Have you forgotten all those times you told me that Prettyman was the man behind those who wanted your sister-in-law killed?"

"I said that? When did I say it?"

"Not in as many words," said Frank, retreating a fraction. "But that was the gist of it. You thought London had plotted the death of Fiona's sister so that her body could be left over there. Planted so that our KGB friends would be reassured that Fiona was dead, and not telling us all their secrets."

Fortified by the way Frank had put my suspicions of London in the past tense, I put down my drink and stared at him impassively. I suppose I must have done a good job on the facial expression, for Frank shifted uncomfortably and said, "You're not going to deny it now, are you, Bernard?"

"I certainly am," I said, without adding any further explanation.

"If you are leading me up the garden path, I'll have your guts for garters." Frank's vocabulary was liberally provided with schoolboy expressions of the 1930s.

"I'm trying to put all that behind me," I said. "It was getting me down."

"That's good," said Frank who, along with the Director-General and his Deputy, Bret Rensselaer, had frequently advised me to put it all behind me. "Some field agents are able to do their job and combine it with a more or less normal family life. It's not easy, but some do it."

I nodded and wondered what was coming. I could see Frank was in one of his philosophical moods and they usually ended up with a softly delivered critical summary that helped me sort it all out.

"You are one of the best field agents we ever had working out of this office," said Frank, sugaring the pill. "But perhaps that's because you live the job night and day, three hundred and sixty-five days a year."

"Do I, Frank? It's nice of you to say that."

He could hear the irony in my voice but he ignored it. "You never tell anyone the whole truth, Bernard. No one. Every thought is locked up in that brain of yours and marked secret. I'm locked out; your colleagues are locked out. I suppose it's the same with your wife and children; I suppose you tell them only what they should know."

"Sometimes not even that," I said.

"I saw Fiona the day before yesterday. She annihilated some poor befuddled Ministry fogey, she made the chairman apologize for inaccurate minutes of the previous meeting, and, using the ensuing awkward silence, carried the vote for some training project they were trying to kill. She's dynamite, that wife of yours. They are all frightened of her; the FO people I mean."

"Yes, I know."

"It takes quite a lot to scare them. And she thrives on it. These days she's looking like some glamorous young model. Really wonderful!"

"Yes," I said. I would always have to defer to Frank in the matter of glamorous young models.

"She said the children were doing very well at school. She showed me photos of them. They are very attractive children, Bernard. You must be very proud of your family."

"Yes, I am," I said.

"And she loves you," he added as an afterthought. "So why keep stirring up trouble for yourself?" Frank gave one of those winning smiles that half the women in Berlin had fallen prey to. "You see, Bernard, I suspect you planned the whole thing—your train ride from Moscow with Prettyman. I think you made sure that there would be no one else available from here to do it."

"How would I have made sure?"

"Have you forgotten the assignments you arranged in the days before you went away?" As he said this he toyed with his pipe and kept his voice distant and detached.

"I didn't arrange their assignments. I don't know those people. I did as Operations suggested."

"You signed." Now he looked up and was staring at me quizzically.

"Yes, I signed," I agreed wearily. His mind was made up, at least for the time being. My best course was to let him think about it all. He would see reason eventually; he always did. No reasonable person could believe that I'd carefully plotted and planned a way to get Prettyman alone in order to grill him about Tessa's death. But if Frank suspected it, you could bet that London believed it implicitly; for that's where all this crap had undoubtedly originated. And, in this context, "London" meant Fiona and Dicky. Or at least it included them.

"Did you try one of those fried potato things?" he said, pointing to one of the silver dishes. "They are flavored with onion."

"Curry," I said. "They are curry-flavored. Too hot for me."

"Are they? I don't know what's happening to Tarrant lately. He knows how I hate curry. I wonder how they put all these different flavors into them. In my day things just tasted of what they were," he said regretfully.

I got to my feet. When the conversation took this culinary turn I guessed Frank had said everything of importance to him. He rested his pipe in a heavy glass ashtray and pushed it aside with a sigh. It made me wonder if he smoked to provide some sort of activity when we had these get-togethers. For the first time it occurred to me that Frank might have dreaded these exchanges as much as I did; or even more.

"You were late again this morning," he said with a smile.

"Yes, but I brought a note from Mummy."

Surely he must have known that I was going to the Clinic every morning; they'd found two hairline cracks in my ribs, and were dosing me with brightly colored painkilling pills, and taking dozens of X-rays. I shouldn't be drinking alcohol really, but I couldn't face a lecture from Frank without a drink in my hand.

"Stop by for a drink tonight," he said. "About nine. I'm having some people in . . . Unless you have something arranged already."

"I said I'd see Werner."

"We'll make it another night," said Frank.

"Yes," I said. I wondered if he'd taste one of the "potato things" and find they were onion after all. I don't know what made me tell him they tasted of curry, except in some vague hope that the hateful Tarrant would be blamed. Perhaps I shouldn't have mixed alcohol and painkillers.

By the time my official confirmation as Frank's deputy came through I was settled into my comfortable office and making good use of my assistant and my secretary, as well as a personally assigned Rover saloon car and driver. I'd often remarked that Frank had kept the Berlin establishment absurdly high, but now I was reaping some of the rewards of his artful manipulations.

Frank, having resisted appointing a deputy for well over two years, made the most of my presence. He attended conferences, symposiums, lectures, and meetings of a kind that in the old days he'd always avoided. He even went to one of those awful gatherings in Washington, D.C., to watch his American colleagues in CIA Operations trying to look cheerful despite the seemingly unending intelligence leaks coming from the top of the CIA tree.

Although in theory Frank's frequent absences made me the de facto chief in Berlin, I knew that his superefficient secretary Lydia never missed a day without reporting to him at length, even when this meant phoning him in the middle of the night. So I never emerged from Frank's shadow, which was perhaps something of an advantage.

My new-found authority granted me the chance to put my old friend Werner Volkmann on a regular contract. Werner was always saying he needed money, although the fees we paid him wouldn't go very far to meeting Werner's lifestyle. His business—arranging advance bank payments for East German exports—was drying up. Things were becoming more and more difficult for him because the bankers were frightened that the DDR might be about to default on its debts to the West. But being on Departmental contract seemed to do something for his self-esteem. Werner loved what I once heard him call the "mystique of espionage." Whatever that was, he felt himself a part of it and I was happy for him.

"Having you here in Berlin, on permanent assignment, is like old times," Werner said. "Whose idea was it?"

"Dicky sent me here to spy on Frank." I said it just to crank him up. We were sitting in Babylon, a dingy subterranean "club." It was owned by an amusing and enigmatic villain named Rudi Kleindorf, who claimed to come from a family of Prussian aristocrats, and was jokingly referred to as *der grosse Kleine*. We were sitting at a hideous little gilt table, under a tasseled light fitting. We had been invited for a drink and a chance to see how everything was coming along. Our inspection had been quickly completed and now we were having that drink.

The club wasn't functioning yet; it was still in the process of being redecorated. The workmen had departed but there were ladders and pots of paint on the stage, and on the bar top too. There had been stories that it was to be renamed "Alphonse," but the Potsdamerstrasse was not the right location for a club named Alphonse. Whatever name it was given, and whatever the color of the paint, and the quality of the new curtains for the stage, and even some new, slimmer and younger girls, it would never be a place that tourists, or Berlin's *Hautevolee*, would want to frequent, except on a drunken excursion to see how the lower half lives. I wondered if Werner had been enticed to put some money into Rudi Kleindorf's enterprise. It was the sort of thing Werner did; he could be romantically nostalgic about dumps we'd frequented when we were young.

Werner reached for the bottle on the table between us and poured another drink for me. He smiled in that strange way that he did when figuring the hidden motives and devious ways of men and women. His head slightly tilted back, his eyes were almost closed, and his lips pressed together. It was easy to see why he was sometimes mistaken for one of the Turkish *Gastarbeiter* who formed a large percentage of the city's population. It was not only Werner's swarthy complexion, coarse black hair, large square-ended black moustache, and the muscular build of a wrestler. He had a certain oriental demeanor. Byzantine described him exactly; except that they were Greeks.

"And Frank?" said Werner. There was nothing more he need say. Dicky was youthful, curly-haired, energetic, ambitious, and devious; while Frank was bloodless, tired, and lazy. But in any sort of struggle between them, the smart money was on Frank. Frank had spent a great deal of his long career being splashed in the blood and snot of Berlin, while Dicky was concentrating upon crocodile-covered Filofax notebooks and Mont Blanc fountain pens. Werner and I both knew a side of Frank that Dicky had never seen. Never mind all that avuncular charm, we'd seen the cold-blooded way in which Frank could make life-and-death decisions that would have consigned "don't-know Dicky" to a psychiatrist's couch in a darkened room.

"What's Dicky frightened of?"

"Nothing," I said. "I can truthfully say he's frightened of nothing except perhaps an audit of his expense accounts." There were voices from behind the tiny stage and then a man came out and played a few bars on the piano. I recognized it as an old Gus Kahn tune: "Dream a Little Dream of Me."

"So it was Frank's idea?" Werner asked. Werner was an impressive piano player; I could see he was listening to the music with a critical ear.

"It wasn't anyone's idea. Not the way you mean. The job was vacant; I came."

Werner said, "Frank has managed without a deputy for ages. Don't you need to be in London . . . somewhere near Fiona and the kids? How are they doing?"

"They are still with Fiona's parents. Private school with extra tutoring as needed, a pony for Sally and a mountain bicycle for Billy, evenings with Grandpa, and plenty of fresh fruit and vegetables."

"What are you going to do?"

"Do? I can't snatch them away from the bastard without providing something better, can I?" I said, curbing my anger and frustration. The piano player suddenly ended his experimental tunes, stood up, and shouted that the piano was no good at all. A disembodied voice shouted that there was no money to get another. The piano player shrugged, looked at us, shrugged again, and then sat down and tried Gershwin.

"Couldn't they live in London with Fiona?" said Werner.

"It's an apartment—not fifteen acres of rolling countryside . . . and Fiona works every hour God Almighty sends. How would we arrange things? I'd have them here if I could think of some feasible way of doing it." I looked down at my hands; I had clasped one fist so tightly that a fingernail had cut my palm, and drawn blood.

Werner watched me and tried to cheer me up. "Well,

you don't have to be in Berlin forever and I'm sure there's plenty to do here."

"Enough. A Deputy Head of Station is on the establishment. I suppose Frank was afraid that if the position remained unfilled too long it would be abolished. Anyway it gives Frank a chance to disappear whenever he likes."

"But it ties you down."

"The theory is: I get one long weekend in London a month."

"You'll have to fight for it," said Werner.

"That's why I'm going this weekend," I said.

Perhaps he was right to be skeptical. I could see that events were unlikely to make it possible for me to go across to London so regularly. With Frank's frequent wanderings, I would be snatching a day or two as and when opportunities came along. "This weekend I go," I promised him again, and in doing so promised myself, too. "I'm booked on the plane; I'm seeing the children. And if World War Three starts at Checkpoint Charlie, Frank will have to handle the opening moves all by himself."

"You don't think London might have put you on the shelf? Put you here so you don't get access to mainstream material?"

"I handle everything going through here. You need top clearance for that."

"Except the secrets that Frank handles and keeps close to his chest."

"Not Frank," I said, but of course Werner was right. I'd not seen any of the signals about Prettyman, and the questions about moving him, and the complications that arose from his U.S. passport, until I got to Moscow. Who knows if there were other signals expressing interest in my past friendship with Prettyman, or my sometimes indiscreetly voiced suspicions of his role in Tessa's death.

"Frank invited me for happy hour and then read the Riot Act to me. It must have been prompted by London."

Werner gave me a told-you-so stare.

"Is London sniffing at me? Why me? Why now?"

"Because you keep on about Tessa, that's why. London have sidelined you."

"No," I said.

"And this is just the beginning. They'll get rid of you completely. Firing you in Berlin makes sure you can't kick up the sort of fuss you'd be able to do if you were made redundant while working in London Central."

"Well I'm not going to just forget about Tessa."

"You said you had forgotten about it."

"When?"

"You just told me."

"Don't shout, Werner. I'm not deaf."

Slowly and with exaggerated pedantry Werner said, "You told Frank you were trying to put the Tessa death behind you. You said the whole business was getting you down. You told me that, Bernie, not half an hour ago."

"Yes," I said. "But I didn't mean I was going to forget about it."

"What did you mean, Bernie?"

"I mean I will put aside all my previous suspicions and ideas. I will start afresh. I'm going to look into Tessa's death as if I'd come to it for the first time. I'm convinced that Bret Rensselaer is behind it all."

"Now it's Bret. Why Bret? Bret was in California, wasn't he?"

"If I could get Bret in the right mood, I could get him to spill the beans. He's not like the others."

"But what would Bret know?"

"Bret had access to a big slice of the Department's dough. It looked as if he'd embezzled it and some idiot tried to arrest him, remember?"

"And you saved him. You saved Bret that time. I hope he remembers that episode when he came running to you in Berlin."

"He's not likely to forget it. That shooting at the station changed Bret. They thought he would die. His hair went white and he was never the same again."

"But Bret didn't steal any Departmental money?"

"Bret was up front in a secret Departmental scheme to siphon money away. By koshering a few millions aside they covertly financed Fiona's operations in the East."

"You told me."

"But Prettyman was on that committee too. He put some money into his own pocket. They sent me to Washington, D.C., to bring Prettyman back but he wasn't having any."

"That can't be true, Bernie. Prettyman is a blue-eyed boy nowadays."

"He did a deal with them. I'd like to know what the deal was; but they bury these things deep. That's why I would like to get Bret talking. Bret was on the committee with Prettyman. Bret was the one who planned Fiona's defection. Bret would know everything that happened."

"My God, Bernie. You never give up, do you?"

"Not without trying," I said.

"Give up this one now. The people in London are not going to sit still while you light a fire under them."

"If no one there is guilty they have nothing to worry about."

"You sound very smug. If no one there is guilty, they will be even more furious, more angry, more vindictive to find that an employee is trying to hang a murder charge on them."

"If you are right, Werner. If you are right that they have sent me here as the first step in a plan to get rid of me, I have nothing to lose, do I?"

"If you'd drop it, they might drop it, too."

"Yes," I said. "And everything in the garden would be lovely. But I'm going to find out who gave the orders to kill Tessa, and I'm going to find the one who gave the order to pull the trigger that night. I'll face them with proof: depositions and any other kind of evidence I unearth. And well before they pull the carpet from under me, I'm going to have them dancing to the tune I play on my penny whistle."

"You are just angry. You are just angry that Dicky got the job you should have had. You are just inventing the cause for a vendetta."

"Am I? Well let me tell you this, Werner. There was a Canadian nurse on that train with Prettyman. She might have been holding hands with him. She has spent many happy evenings in Washington; or so she told me."

"Prettyman was always like that."

"She was wearing a brooch that belonged to Tessa."

"She was what?" He gulped on his drink.

"Oh, I'm glad you still retain the capacity to be surprised, Werner. I was beginning to think there was nothing you wouldn't nod through. Yes, one of Tessa's favorite brooches: a big sapphire set in yellow gold and silver and studded with matched diamonds."

"How can you be sure that it's not just a brooch that looks like the one Tessa had?"

"It's antique; not a modern reproduction. The chances of finding another one exactly like that are pretty slim. It was Tessa's brooch, Werner. And the nurse told me it was a gift from Mr. James Prettyman. Oh, yes, and from Mrs. Prettyman, too. But nursie seemed to think it was just junk jewelery. Is that what they all thought?"

"Did you ask Prettyman about it?"

"Unfortunately no. I was lifted off the train before I got a chance to beat an answer out of him."

"Shall I chase it? Where is the nurse now?"

"I've no idea; home with her family in good old Winnipeg, I suppose. Let her be, Werner. She knows nothing. It might pay off better if I surprise Prettyman with the questions."

Werner looked unhappy. "Please, Bernie. You are going over the top. I know it's all going to end in disaster. What will you do if they fire you? I'll do anything you want, but please drop this one."

"You and Frank treat me like I've just got back from a drunken party to report a flying saucer. I'm not going to drop it until I'm satisfied." I gulped the rest of my drink, then got to my feet and looked around the room again. Werner was determined to play baby-sitter for me, and I wasn't in the mood to be babied. I got enough of that from Frank all week.

"Then don't talk to me about it," said Werner. "That's all I ask."

He didn't say it quickly and angrily; he said it slowly and sadly. I didn't give any attention to that fact at the time. Perhaps I should have.

"This smell of paint is terrible," I said. "When is this bloody idiot supposed to be opening this dump?" I noticed with sadness that the old mural had disappeared under a couple of liters of white paint. It had been an imaginative array of hanging gardens, the great ziggurat and naked women dancing through palm trees, done by a drunken artist who had never traveled beyond the Botanical Gardens in Steglitz. I wondered what would replace it.

"Next Tuesday the builders said, but now they are wavering. The carpenters haven't finished and the painters have hardly started. They will have to finish and clear up completely before anyone can start polishing the floor. It will all take quite a time. Rudi is looking for somewhere else to hold his opening party. Somewhere bigger. Maybe a hotel."

"I can't just walk away and forget about Tessa," I said. "I just can't."

Werner was closely studying some tiny spots of paint that had been splashed on the table lamp.

By the time I left, the pianist was playing a Bach partita in a minor key. It wouldn't be easy to dance to.

THREE

The North Downs, Surrey, England

When someone asks you to make an objective decision that will affect their future, you can confidently assume that they have already decided upon the course they intend to follow. So when my father-in-law phoned to be sure that I would be with Fiona when she visited the children on the weekend, I sensed that there was something else on his mind and I wasn't expecting to hear anything comforting.

But those vague forebodings had faded a little by the time I was with Fiona in her shiny new Jaguar. It was one of the perquisites of her new post. The Department frowned upon senior staff using foreign cars, and a Porsche like the one she'd previously owned would have earned a quiet rebuke.

Fiona was at her magnificent best. She liked driving. Her dark hair was shiny and loose and wavy, and she had let it grow, so that it almost touched her shoulders, and swung wide to frame her face as she turned to smile at me. Her relaxed grin, natural skin texture and rosy cheeks reminded me of the young girl with whom I'd fallen so desperately in love. There was nothing to reveal her long ordeal in East Germany or the demanding workload that she now took upon herself without respite.

Escaping from London's seemingly interminable squalor, and its brooding suburbs, is not easy. The beguiling villages that once surrounded the capital had become small plastic versions of Times Square. Even the snow could not completely conceal their ugliness. But finally we reached some stretches of open countryside, and eventually the lovely old house where Mr. and Mrs. David Kimber-Hutchinson made a home for my children. Set in a particularly attractive part of southern England, the house was secluded. There were trees on every side: pines and firs mostly, evergreens that ensured that the scene changed little in winter or summer. The house was Jacobean but successive wealthy owners, and acclaimed architects, had done everything possible to obliterate the original structure. Since my last visit David had squeezed permission from the local bureaucrats to further deform the property with a six-car garage. The new building had a lacquered brass weather vane on its red plastic roof, and automatic doors at both ends, so that he could drive right through rather than face the hazards and inconvenience of backing out.

Fiona turned off the road and drove through the entrance where wrought iron gates entwined the monogram of my in-laws. "What a horror," she said as she caught sight of the new garage. Perhaps she'd said it to forestall any rude reaction that might have been my first response. The concertina doors were pushed back far enough to reveal her father's silver Rolls, and the black Range Rover that was her mother's current car. Her mother got through a lot of cars because each time she dented one she "lost confidence in it." This latest one had been chosen by David and, on his specific instructions, fitted with massive steel crash bars at front and rear. As if in tacit warning to other road users, it was painted with a livery of formalized flame patterns along its side.

Fiona gave a toot on the horn and parked outside, alongside a battered little Citroën with Paris license plates and a TEACHERS AGAINST THE BOMB bumper sticker. We got out and went into the garage, which was wide enough to take half a dozen Rolls-Royces and still have room for workbench, sinks, neatly coiled hoses, and an air compressor. I inspected David's latest pride and joy, a 3-liter Bentley open tourer, one of those shiny green icons of the 1920s. Vintage cars had become his passion since a series of bad falls, and a bitter dispute with the master of foxhounds, had stopped him chasing foxes.

Her father was standing at the workbench when we arrived. He waved her forward, using both hands upraised as if marshaling a Boeing into its slot. He was wearing dark blue coveralls of the sort that garage mechanics favor, but peeping from the collar there was a yellow cashmere rollneck.

"You made good time, darling," he announced approvingly as Fiona scrambled from the driving seat and kissed him.

"We were lucky with the traffic," said Fiona.

"And Bernard . . . what have you done to your face, Bernard?" He was sharp, I must say that for him. My face was only slightly swollen and had drawn little reaction from others.

"I walked into a birdcage."

"Bernard, you . . ."

Fiona interrupted whatever her father was about to say: "Bernard fell down the stairs . . . in Berlin. He cracked a rib. He's not fully recovered."

Fiona knew where I'd got the bruises of course. We'd not spoken of it but she must have read my brief report about the Polish fiasco and guessed the bits I left out.

"Watch yourself, Bernard," said her father, looking from one to the other of us as if suspecting that the whole truth was being withheld. "You're not a youngster any more." And then, more cheerfully, "I saw you looking at the Bentley. She's one hundred percent authentic; not a replica or made up from new parts."

"It's cold, Daddy. Let's go inside the house."

"Yes, of course. I'll show you later, Bernard. You can sit in her if you want." He led the way through a doorway that had been cut through a side wall of the original house to gain direct entrance from the garage.

"That frost last night," he said as he opened the door into his carpeted drawing-room. "I think it may have killed the eucalyptus trees. I'll be shattered if they go—after all the love and labor and money I've spent on them."

"Where's Mummy?"

"I have a tree expert coming this afternoon. They say he's the man Prince Charles uses."

"Where's Mummy?"

"She's resting. She gets up in the small hours and does all that yoga malarkey. Huh! And then she wonders why she gets tired."

"She says it's doing her good," said Fiona.

"Six o'clock is far too early. She runs the bath and that wakes me up," said David, "and then I sometimes have trouble getting off to sleep again." He slapped his hands together. "Now for elevenses, or would you prefer a real drink?"

"It's too early for me," said Fiona, "but I'm sure you can persuade Bernard to join you."

"No," I said. It was a culture trap. England's holy ritual, of halting everything to sit down and drink sweet milky tea at eleven o'clock in the morning, would be marred by a dissenter guzzling booze, or even coffee.

"I'll order tea then," said David, picking up a phone and pressing a button to connect him to one of his many servants. "Who's that?" he asked, and having elicited the name of a servant he instructed, "Tell cook: morning tea for three in the Persian room. My usual—toasted scones and all that. And take tea to Mrs. Hutchinson: Earl Grey, no milk, no sugar. Ask her if she's going to join us for lunch."

"How lovely to be home again," said Fiona. I know she only said it to appease her father, but it made me feel as if I'd never provided a proper home for her.

"And you are not looking too well," her father told Fiona. Then realizing that such remarks can be interpreted as criticism added: "It's that damned job of yours. Do you know what you could be earning in the City?"

"I thought they were firing people by the hundred after the crash last year," she said.

"I know people," said David, nodding significantly. "If you wanted a job in the City you'd be snapped up." He leaned towards her. "You should come to the health farm with us tomorrow. Five days of rest and exercise and light meals. It would make a new woman of you. And you would meet some very interesting people."

"I have too much urgent work to do," said Fiona.

"Bring it with you; that's what I do. I take a stack of work, and my tiny recording machine, and do it away from all the noise and commotion."

"I have a meeting in Rome."

He shook his head. "The life you people lead. And who pays for it? The poor old taxpayer. Very well then, it's your life."

"The children are still studying?" Fiona asked him.

It was not just her way of changing the subject. She wanted me to hear the wonderful things her parents were doing for our children. On cue, her father described the highly paid tutors who came to the house to give my children additional lessons in mathematics and French grammar, so that they would do well in their exams, and be able to go to the sort of school that David went to.

When the tea tray came, everything was placed on the table before Fiona. While she was pouring the tea David divested himself of his coveralls to reveal a canary-colored cashmere sweater, beige corduroy trousers, and tasseled loafers. He spread himself across a chintz-covered sofa and said, "Well, what have you done with poor little Kosinski?"

Since David was looking at me as he said it, I replied, "I haven't seen him for ages."

"Come along! Come along!" said David briskly. "You've locked him up somewhere and you're giving him the third degree."

"Daddy. Please," said Fiona mildly while pouring my tea.

Pleased that his provocation had produced the expected note of exasperation from his daughter, he chuckled and said: "What are you squeezing out of the little bugger, huh? You can confide in me; I'm vetted."

He wasn't vetted, or in any way secure, and he was the last man I would entrust with a secret of any importance. So I smiled at him and told Fiona that I wanted just one sugar in my tea and yes, a toasted scone—no, no homemade strawberry jam—would be lovely and promised that it wouldn't spoil my appetite for lunch.

"I flew to Warsaw to see him," said David, flapping a monogrammed linen napkin and spreading it on his knee. "Just before Christmas; at five minutes' notice. No end of bother getting a seat on the plane."

"Did you?" I said, inserting a note of mild surprise in my answer, although I had been shown a surveillance photo of him and Kosinski there at that time.

"He told me that Tessa was still alive."

I watched Fiona's reaction to this startling announcement; she just shook her head in denial and drank some tea.

"It was a ruse," I explained. "He probably believed it but it was just a cruel attempt to exploit him."

"And exploit me," added David. He accepted a buttered scone from Fiona and nibbled at it as he thought about his visit to his son-in-law.

"Yes, and to exploit you," I agreed, although it was hard to imagine how even the wily tricksters of the Polish security service would find ingenuity enough for that. "Now he is working for us. I don't know any more than that."

"Don't know or won't tell?"

Fiona got to her feet, looked at the ceiling as she listened, and said, "I believe the French lesson is ending."

"Yes," agreed David, after punching the air in order to expose his gold wristwatch to view and see the time. "She doesn't give us a minute of extra time. The French are all like that, aren't they?"

Reluctant to censure French venality in such general terms, Fiona said, "I'll just go and say hello to her, and ask her how they are coming along." Clever Fiona; she knew how to escape. It must have been something she learned while working with the KGB. Or with Dicky Cruyer.

"Fifteen pounds an hour she costs me," David confided to me. "And she has the nerve to add on traveling expenses from London. The trouble is I can't get anyone from the village. You need the authentic *seizième arrondissement* accent, don't you, huh?"

I drank my tea until, from somewhere upstairs, I heard Fiona trying out her Paris slang on the lady teacher. She hit the spot, judging from the sudden burst of hearty feminine laughter that followed the next exchange.

I faced David and ate my scone, smiling between bites. We both sat there for a long time, silent and alone, like a washed-out picnic, under dripping trees, waiting for the thunder to stop.

Having finished my scone before my host, I got up and went to the window. David came and stood alongside me. We watched Fiona tramping across the snowy garden. The teacher was with her, and hand-in-hand with the children they inspected the snowman. The snow had retreated to make icy-edged white islands into which the children deliberately walked. Billy—coming up to his fourteenth birthday—considered himself far too old to be building snowmen. He had supervised the building of this one on the pretext that it was done solely to entertain some local infants who had been at the house for a tea party the previous afternoon. But I could tell from the way they were acting that both Billy and his younger sister Sally were proud of their elaborate snow sculpture. It wouldn't last much longer. A slight thaw had crippled it so that it had become a hunchbacked figure, glazed with the icy sheen that had formed upon it overnight.

"Everybody respects her," said David.

"Yes," I said. It was true that everyone respected Fiona, but how significant it was that her father should claim that. Even her mother and father didn't really love her. Their love, such as could be spared, had been lavished on Tessa, the younger sister, the eternal baby. Fiona had too much dignity, too much achievement, too much of everything to need love in the way that most people need it.

My memory went back to the day that I first met Fiona's parents, and to the briefing she provided for me as we drove down here to see them in my old Ferrari. It was my final outing in that lovely old lady. The car was already sold, the deal settled, and the first installment of the money deposited in my bank. The money was needed to buy Fiona an engagement ring with a diamond of a dimension that her family would judge visible to the naked eye. Tell them you love me, she had advised. It's what they will be waiting to hear. They think I need someone to love me. I told them that. I would have told them anyway. I did love and never stopped loving her.

"You love her," said David, as if needing to hear me say it again. "You do: I know you do."

"Of course I do," I said. "I love her very much."

"She bottles everything up inside," he said. "I wish I knew what went on inside her head."

"Yes," I said. Many people would have liked to know what went on inside Fiona's head, including me. From what I knew, even the KGB agent—Kennedy—who had been assigned to seduce her, and monitor her thoughts, had failed. He'd fallen for her instead. The wounding fact was that Fiona had taken that sordid little adventure seriously. She'd fooled him of course. She hadn't betrayed her role as a double-agent working for London because Fiona was Fiona—a woman who would no more reveal her innermost thoughts to her lover than she would to her father, her children or her husband.

I watched her with my children; this woman who had bowled me over and from whom I would never escape, this remote paragon, dedicated scholar and unfailing winner of every contest she entered. She might even emerge as the victor in the bitter contest for power in the Department. I suppose my feeling for her was founded upon respect as well as love. Too much respect and not enough love perhaps, for otherwise Gloria would never have turned my life upside down. Gloria was no fool but she was not wise; she was sizzling and street-smart and perceptive and desperately in love with me. I was torn in half: I found myself in love with two women. They were entirely different women but few people would find that an adequate explanation. I told myself it was wrong but it didn't make the dilemma less excruciating.

"That cloud base: it never gets really light these days," said David, turning away from the window and sitting down. "I hate winter. I wanted to get away to somewhere warm but there are things here that I must do myself. You can't trust anyone to do their job properly."

I chose a chair and sat down opposite him. It was a lovely room, the sort of comfortable family retreat that is only found in England and its country houses. So far this room had escaped the "face-lifts" that David had inflicted on so much of the house. The furniture was a hodgepodge of styles; a mixture of the priceless and the worthless. The Dutch marquetry cabinet, and the collection of Lalique glass displayed inside it, would have fetched a fortune at auction. Next to it there were two battered sofas that had only sentimental value. A lovely William and Mary marquetry mirror reflected an ancient stained and frayed oriental carpet. The log fire made crackling sounds and spat a few sparks over the brass fire-irons. The yellow light of the flames made patterns on the ceiling and lit up David's face. "He tried to murder me, you know," he said, and turned to look out of the window as if his mind was entirely given to his family in the garden. "George," he added eventually.

"George?" I didn't know what to say. Finally I stammered, "Why would he do that? He's family."

David looked at me as if declining to respond to a particularly offensive joke. "It makes me wonder what really happened to Tessa." He went and stood by the window, his hands on his hips.

"George didn't kill your daughter, David. If that's what you are driving at."

"Then why try to poison me?"

Again I was speechless for a moment. "Why do you think?" I countered.

"Always the police detective, aren't you, Bernard?" He said it with a good-natured grunt, but I knew he had long since categorized me as a government snooper. He said society was rife with prying petty officials who were taking over our lives. Sometimes I wondered if he wasn't right. Not about me, but about the others.

I made a reckless guess. "Because you suspected him? Because you accused him of being a party to his wife's death?"

"Very good, Bernard." He said it gravely but with discernible admiration. "You're very close. Go to the top of the class."

"And how did George react?"

"React?" A short sharp bitter laugh. "I just told you; he tried to kill me."

"I see." I was determined not to ask him how. I could see he was bursting to tell me.

"That's one of my walking sticks," he said suddenly. Following his gaze I saw that out on the snowy lawn Billy was patching up the snowman with fresh snow and had removed the snowman's walking stick while doing it. I wondered if David was going to lay claim to the snowman's hat too. "I didn't know they wanted my stick for that damned snowman."

Billy and Sally patted more snow on to the snowman's belly. I suppose the thaw had slimmed it down a little.

Turning back to me, David said, "In Poland, I complained of a headache and George gave me some white pills. Pills from a Polish package. I didn't use them of course."

"No," I said. "Of course not."

"I'm not a bloody fool. All written in Polish. Who knows what kind of muck they take . . . even their genuine aspirin . . . I'd sooner suffer the headache."

"So what happened?"

"I brought them back with me. Not the packet, he'd thrown that away; or so he said."

"Back to England?"

"See that little cherry tree? I buried Felix, our old tomcat, under it. The poor old sod died from one of those tablets. I didn't tell my lady wife, of course. And I don't want Fiona to know."

"You think the tablet did it?"

"Three tablets. Crushed up in warm milk."

"Did the cat eat them willingly, or did you dose it?"

"What are you getting at?" he said indignantly. "I didn't choke the cat, if that's what you mean. I was dosing farm animals before you were born." I'd forgotten how highly he cherished his credentials as a country gentleman.

"If it was a very old cat . . ."

"I don't want you discussing this with my daughter or with anyone else," he ordered.

"Was this what you wanted to ask me?" I said. "The dead cat and whether to report it?"

"It was one of the things," he admitted reluctantly. "I wanted to ask you to take a note of it off the record. But since then I have decided that it's better all forgotten. I don't want you to repeat it to anyone."

"No," I said, although such a stricture hardly conformed to the way in which he identified me with the powers of government. I recognized this "confidential anecdote" about his son-in-law's homicidal inclinations as something he wanted me to take back to work and discuss with Dicky and the others. In fact I saw this little cameo as David's way of hitting his son-in-law with yet another unanswerable question, while keeping himself out of it. The only hard fact I could infer from it was that David and George had fallen out. I wondered why.

"Forget it," said David. "I said nothing, do you hear me?"

"It's just a family matter," I said, but my grim little joke went unnoticed. He was still standing in the window, and now he turned his head to look out at the garden again. Fiona and the children were heading back. Seeing David profiled, and in conjunction with the snowman at the bottom of the lawn, I wondered if the children had intended it to be a caricature of their grandfather. Now that the belly had been restored and the shoulders built up a little it had something of David's build, and that old hat and walking-stick provided the finishing touches. It was something of a surprise to find that my little children were now judging the world around them with such keen eyes. I would have to watch myself.

"They're growing up," said David.

"Yes, I'm afraid so."

He didn't respond. I suppose he knew how I felt. It wasn't that I liked them less as grown-ups than as children. It was simply that I liked myself so much more when I was being a childlike Dad with them, an equal, a playmate, occupying the whole of their horizon. Now they were concerned with their friends and their school, and I couldn't get used to being such a small part of their lives.

"I've got two suitcases belonging to that friend of yours." David meant Gloria of course. "When she brought the children over here to us, she left two suitcases with their clothes and toys and things. Expensive-looking cases. I don't know where to contact her, apart from the office, and I know you people don't like personal phone calls to your place of work. I thought perhaps you would be able to take them and give them back to her."

"No," I said. "I don't go to the London office, I work in Berlin nowadays."

"I didn't want to ask Fiona."

He displayed characteristic delicacy in not wanting to ask Fiona about the whereabouts of my one-time mistress. He didn't really care of course. The question about the suitcases that Gloria had left with him was just a warning shot across my bows. Now he got on to more important matters.

"She's still not well." He was looking at Fiona and the kids.

"She's tired," I said. "She works too hard."

"I'm not talking about being tired," said David. "We all work too hard. My goodness . . ." He gave a short laugh. ". . . I'd hate to show you my appointments diary for next week. As I keep telling those trade union buggers, if I worked a forty-hour week I'd be finished by lunchtime Tuesday. I haven't got even a lunch slot to spare for at least six weeks."

"Poor you," I said.

"My little girl is sick." I'd never heard him speak of Fiona like that; his voice was strained and his manner intense. "It's no good the pair of you telling each other that she's just tired and that a relaxing holiday and a regime of vitamin tablets are going to make her fit and well again."

"No?"

"No. Tonight we have a few people coming to dinner. One of the guests is a top Harley Street man, a psychiatrist. Not a psychologist, a psychiatrist. That means he's a qualified medical man, too."

"Does it?" I said. "I must try and remember that."

"You'd do well to," he said gruffly, suspecting that I was being sarcastic but not quite certain. He moved away from the window and said, "He agrees with me; Fiona will never be fit enough to take charge of the children again. You know that, don't you, Bernard?"

"Has he examined Fiona?"

"Of course not. But he's met her several times. Fiona thinks he's just a drinking chum of mine."

"But he's been spying on her."

"I'm only saying this for your sake, and for the sake of Fiona and your wonderful children."

"David. If this is a prelude to your trying to get legal custody of the children, forget it."

He sighed and pulled a long face. "She's sick. Fiona is slowly coming round to face that truth, Bernard. I wish you would face it, too. You could help me and help her."

"Don't try any of your legal tricks with me, David." I was angry, and not as careful as I might have been.

With an insolent calm he said, "Dr. Howard has already said he'd support me. And I play golf with a top-rate barrister. He says I would easily get custody if it came to it."

"It would break Fiona's heart," I said, trying a different angle.

"I don't think so, Bernard. I think without the children to worry about she'd be relieved of a mighty weight."

"No."

"Why do you think she's been putting it off so long? Having the children back with her, I mean. She could have come down here as soon as she returned from California. She could have taken the children up to the apartment in Mayfair—there are spare bedrooms, aren't there?—and made all the necessary arrangements to send them to school and so on. So why didn't she do that?" There was a long pause. "Tell me, Bernard."

"She knew how much you both liked having the children with you," I said. "She did it for you."

"Rather than for you," he said, not bothering much to conceal his glee at my answer. "I would have thought that you would have liked having the children with you, and that she would have liked having the children with her."

"She loves being with them. Look at her now."

"No, Bernard. You can't get round me with that one. She likes coming down here to see the children. She's pleased to see them so happy and doing well at school. But she doesn't want to take on the responsibility and the time consuming drudgery of being a Mum again. She can't take it on. She's mentally not capable."

"You're wrong."

"I'm surprised to hear you say that. According to what Fiona tells me you yourself have said all these things to her . . ." He waved a hand at my protest. "Not in as many words, but you've said it in one way or another. You've told her repeatedly that she's trying to avoid having the children back home again."

"No," I said. "I never said anything like that."

He smiled. He knew I was lying.

David's dinner party seemed as if it was going to last all night. He was wearing his new dinner suit with satin lapels, and his patent Gucci loafers with red silk socks that matched his pocket handkerchief, and he was in the mood for telling long stories about his club and his golf tournaments and his vintage Bentley. The guests were David's friends: men who spent their working week in St. James's clubs and City bars but made money just the same. How they did it mystified me; it wasn't a product of their charm.

By the time the dinner guests had departed, and the family had exchanged goodnights and gone upstairs to bed, I was pretty well beat, but I felt compelled to put a direct question to Fiona. Casually, while undressing, I said, "When do you plan to have the children living with us, darling?"

She was sitting at the dressing table in her night-dress and brushing her hair. She always brushed her hair night and morning, I think it was something that they'd made her do at boarding school. Looking in the mirror to see me she said, "I knew you were going to ask me that."

"Did you?"

"I could see it coming ever since we arrived here."

"And when do you think?"

"Please, darling. The children's future is hardly something to be settled at this time of night, when both of us are worn out."

"You can't keep on avoiding it, Fi."

"I'm not avoiding it," she said, her voice raised a tone or so. "But this is not the time or the place, surely you can see that."

It was obviously going to cause an argument if I pursued it further. I was angry. I washed and cleaned my teeth and went to bed without speaking to her other than a brusque goodnight.

"Good night, darling," she said happily as I switched out the light. I shut my reddened eyes and knew no more until Fiona was hammering at me and shouting something I couldn't comprehend.

"What?"

"The window! Someone is trying to force their way in!"

I jumped out of bed but I knew it was nothing. I was getting used to Fiona's disturbed sleep. I went to the window, opened it and looked out. I froze in the cold country air. "Nothing here."

"It must have been the wind," said Fiona. She was fully awake now. And contrite. "I'm sorry, darling." She got out of bed and came to the window with a dispirited weariness that made me feel very sorry for her.

"There's nothing there," I said, and gave her a hug.

"I think I must have eaten something that upset me."

"Yes," I said. She always blamed such awakenings on indigestion. She always said she couldn't remember anything of the dream itself. So now I no longer asked her about them. Instead I played along with her explanations. I said, "The fennel sauce on the fish, it was very creamy."

"That must have been it," she said.

"You've been working too hard. You should slow down a little."

"I can't." She sank down at the dressing table and brushed her hair in a mood of sad introspection. "I'm directly involved in all the exchanges between Bonn and the DDR. Enormous sums of money are being given to them. I wonder how much of it is being pocketed by Honecker and Co., and how much gets through. Sometimes I worry about it. And they become more and more demanding."

I watched her. The doctor had given her some tablets. She said they were no more than pep pills—"a tonic." She had them on the dressing table and now she took two pills and drank some water to swallow them. She did it automatically. She always had the tablets with her. I had a feeling that she took them whenever she felt low, and that meant frequently. I said, "How do you pay them?"

"Depends. It falls into four categories: Western currency payments to the East German State, Western currency payments to private individuals, trade credits guaranteed by Bonn, and a hotchpotch of trade deals that wouldn't be done except that we—or more frequently Bonn—push them along. I don't have much to do with that end of it. We are only really interested in the money that goes to the Church."

"Is the Department involved in any of the money transfers?"

"It's complicated. Our contact is a man named Stoppl. He's a founder of 'the Protestant Church in Socialism,' a committee of East German churchmen who negotiate with their regime's leaders and do deals. Some deals involve the Western Churches, too—there is a Church trust which arranges the money—or sometimes Bonn. All of these deals are very secret, things are done but never revealed. Sometimes we have Honecker and Stoppl negotiating one-to-one, out at Honecker's Berlin home on the Wandlitzsee."

"So these deals must be common knowledge among the communist top brass?" Honecker's palatial dwelling was in the Politburo residential compound. The communist leaders had their luxury homes there, together with an abundance of capitalist luxuries from camcorders and laptops to soft toilet paper. The whole site was guarded by armed sentries and surrounded with a chain-link fence and razor wire. I knew that locale very well: it was an intimidating place to visit. The identity of visitors to the sanctum was carefully checked, and their names logged in a book held by the guard commander.

"Oh yes. They all share in the spoils. Our official

line is that they may steal a lot of the money but some gets through to Stoppl's people and that money is vital."

"Vital. Yes."

"In church halls and vicarages, and church premises of all kinds, ordinary people talk about local social problems, about environmental pollution and injustice. They talk about peace and human rights issues."

"I get the idea, Fi."

"The underlying theme is Christian protest."

"You're playing with fire," I told her.

"Christian values."

"You sound just like your father," I said.

"That's what you always say when you lose an argument with me."

"I shouldn't have said it."

She laughed derisively. "Is that a retraction or just an apology?" But Fiona *was* like her father, there was no denying it. Equally obvious, she didn't enjoy that resemblance. I think Fiona dearly loved her mother, but not her father. She was frightened of being too much like her mother; frightened of ending up bullied and silenced as her mother had been over the years. That determination to escape her parents was the key to Fiona's complex personality. For she was also afraid of becoming like her father. At least that's how I saw it, but I wasn't a psychiatrist. I wasn't even a psychologist. In fact I didn't even have a proper contract for my penpushing job in Berlin.

"And for how long will the West keep pumping money into Honecker's bankrupt regime?" I asked.

"The communists are extremely good at wining and dining visiting press and TV people. The Leipzig Fair is their showcase. Ill-informed newspaper articles in the West consistently say Honecker's economy is strong, and getting stronger. You must read the junk that newspaper feature writers produce in return for a first-class ticket and a couple of days of being feasted and flattered. Last month the World Bank had their resident half-wits putting out some crackpot statistics to prove that per capita income in the DDR was higher than in the U.K. Yesterday I saw a glowing press cutting from some journalist in Dublin telling her readers that the West could learn a lot from what the East Germans are doing. That sort of bosh is translated and circulated in the East, and it keeps the lid on things back home in Honecker's kingdom."

"Honecker is cunning. It's a police state, but the East Germans are sheltered from crime, given apartments, cheap food, and jobs—no unemployment in the workers' state—cheap holidays, free education, free medical care. It's no good saying it's lousy medical care, or that the jobs are poorly paid, or that the workers are crowded into nasty little apartments. Or that thousands die from the filthy pollution in the air and the rivers and canals are frothing with poisonous scum and belly-up fishes. The citizens of this gigantic prison camp have what the Germans call *Geborgenheit*—security and shelter—and they are not going to fight in the streets to get rid of the regime."

She sighed. She knew I was right.

"The DDR is bankrupt. The West must chop off all payments without warning," I said. "It's the only way to bring change. Let the regime collapse. Show the East Germans that they are living a lie; they are living on handouts from the West."

"But Washington and Bonn are afraid that Moscow will move in to prop Honecker up if we don't support him," said Fiona.

"Moscow? Don't start thinking that Gorbachev is some kind of freedom-loving capitalist. He's a dedicated comrade, making a few concessions to the West in order to preserve some semblance of what Lenin created. It will need a braver man than Gorby to reform the USSR. The whole Federation is on the slide. In a few years Moscow will be as bankrupt as Honecker."

"In a few years, yes. That's why Britain, and the Americans, refused to give Honecker a state visit even when Belgium, France and Spain agreed. How could they do that? And then that silly man Kohl invites him to West Germany. Honecker is shaky, but how long will he last? With such stupid leaders in the West to help him, no one can be sure."

"If Moscow goes bust, will the West cut Honecker off without a pfennig? That will be worth waiting for."

Fiona went over to the window. The sky was getting light now. When she spoke it was with a determination that she seldom revealed. "Yes, and the Honecker regime will collapse. And then the Church groups we've trained will be needed to hold things together."

"So that's the scenario?"

"It's what I've given half my life to," she said, as if she was now counting the depth of her sacrifice rather than its duration.

Gently she pulled back the curtain to see the early morning sky. There was a band of mist stretched across the horizon. Dark clumps of treetops floated upon it to make tropical islands in a luminous ocean. I didn't want to challenge her ideas, but every report we saw from agents on the ground said that the Stasi had increased in numbers, and increased in influence, month by month for the last five years. Maybe it was a reaction from a regime that was doomed, but that didn't mean it was less dangerous. The

Stasi were penetrating Fiona's precious East German Church groups. In Allenstein bei Magdeburg the pastor was working for the Stasi until, just before Christmas, someone put a bomb under his car. And every month the Stasi—self-styled "shield and sword of socialism"—tightened up security. They opposed all attempts to liberalize the regime. The Stasi stamped upon anyone who dared to ask for anything at all. Even Russian publications were banned as too liberal. Now, in what must surely be the ultimate echo of George Orwell's predictions, East Germans had been forbidden to sing the lyrics of their own national anthem, because its words "Germany united fatherland" might give loyal communists ideas about cooperating with West Germany.

Perhaps Fiona was thinking along the same sobering lines, for she didn't pursue the matter. "We mustn't leave too late," she said without turning round. "I hate driving in the dark, nowadays. It's a sign of growing old I suppose. And we're dining with Dicky on Monday."

"Do you know how to work this gadget?" I was turning all the knobs of the tea-making machine. David had installed them in all the guest bedrooms.

"It's easier to use the electric kettle," she said. She plugged it in and started it. She switched on the lights, too. Then she went back to bed. "It's too early to get up, darling."

"We'll have tea in bed," I said.

"Very well, but if I don't answer your next question for a long while, I may be asleep."

"I was thinking of ducking out of Dicky's dinner, but I can't think of a convincing excuse."

"We'll have to go, darling. Everyone will be there. It's not social and it's not optional. Dicky's dinners are just Departmental meetings in disguise."

"I don't feel strong enough for a whole evening of Dicky's imbecile chit-chat."

"You don't feel like it!" said Fiona with a sudden burst of resentment. "How do you think I will enjoy sitting round the table with them all?"

I leaned across and kissed her on the ear. She didn't have to draw a diagram for me. By everyone she meant that Gloria, my one-time lover, would be there. And everyone present would be watching with interest every glance, word, and smile that the three of us exchanged. It was difficult for her; but it was no picnic for me either. Maybe Gloria would think of a convincing excuse.

I looked round the room, waiting for the kettle to boil. We'd been installed in the best of half a dozen guest bedrooms. This one was "the Mozart room" and its walls were hung with framed music manuscripts and some early wooden musical instruments: a concertina, a violin, and a mandolin. To save on space, each instrument had been cut in half and mounted on a mirror. It saved on musical instruments, too, I suppose.

"Suppose George did try to murder him?" said Fiona calmly, as she sat propped up in bed watching me make the tea. "It can't be entirely ruled out, can it?"

"For what purpose?" I said, and for a moment regretted confiding the conversation to her. But I couldn't see any way I could avoid reporting it all to the office, and that meant Fiona.

"Does there have to be a purpose? You have always said that not every act has a purpose."

Actually what I "always said" was that people "go mad" or rather act in irrational and inexplicable ways. There was no evidence to suggest that her father was mad. At least no madder than I'd always known him. "I suppose we could provide it to the interrogation team at Berwick House and see if they can spring it on George to any effect."

"Felix was very old," said Fiona.

"Look, darling. If that had really been a lethal poison, the poor old tomcat would have died in style."

"What do you mean?"

"It would have shown symptoms of poisoning."

"How can you be so sure?"

"I've never come across painless poisons," I said, "except in books." I made the tea and took the tray, with teapot and cups and milk jug, to Fiona's bedside table. She was fussy about tea and liked to pour it herself.

"Never?"

"It would have to be from one of the major groups: arsenic, cyanide, or strychnine. Any of those would have caused Felix spectacular symptoms."

"Daddy is not very observant."

"After feeding it what he suspected was poison intended for himself? He'd be watching every move of that damned cat, you know he would."

"I suppose you are right," she said. "All poisons?"

"Cyanide brings on a desperate breathless choking spasm and convulsions. Strychnine brings even more violent convulsions. But the most likely poison would be arsenic, or one of the other metals. It's the poisoner's first choice."

"Yes, we had an arsenic case while I was in Berlin. I had to give evidence. It had no security dimension. It was a domestic quarrel—one of the clerks tried to murder his wife. One of the police pathologists told me that, of all the poisons, arsenic produces symptoms most like those of natural disease."

•

"Well that's because pathologists don't get to the scenes of crime until life is extinct. Next time you see him, tell him arsenic brings on vomiting, trembling, and bloody diarrhea. If your father had seen the cat succumbing to a lethal dose of arsenic he wouldn't have waited until our next weekend visit to mention it to me."

"I suppose you're right, you usually are." She meant of course that I was usually right about vulgar brutal matters that it was better not to know about. "The pathologist was a her," she added as an afterthought.

"Your father didn't really believe it was poison."

"Daddy's not paranoid," said Fiona, deftly avoiding the question.

No, I thought, he's just a megalomaniac. For people who think of themselves all the time, paranoia is simply a way of confirming how important they are. I said, "He only had to dig the cat up, and send it along to a laboratory."

"I think we should suspend judgment." Her slow smile revealed her true feelings: that my prejudice was unreasonable and unyielding. Of course she might have been implying that there were lots of painless poisons; exotic toxins that chemists concoct in secret government-financed laboratories. But that would have brought us into the world of officially authorized murder; and for the time being, neither of us wanted to believe George could ever have been a party to that kind of killing. "I'll pour the tea, shall I?"

"Lovely. What are you reading?"

She took her book from the table so that I could see its cover: *Buddenbrooks: Verfall einer Familie.*

"Good grief, Fi, you've been reading that same book for ages."

"Have I? What's the hurry? Is that enough milk for you?"

"Yes," I said, taking the tea from her hand. But in fact I don't really like milk in tea; it was one of the many English ideas I never properly adjusted to. "So Billy got on the football team at school. Well, well, well. I never saw him as an athlete."

"Yes, that's wonderful," said Fiona. She didn't like sport of any kind but she tried to sound pleased.

"There was no one trying to get in the window, Fi," I said.

"It was just the sound of the wind," she affirmed. "I don't know what came over me. Listen to it howl in the chimney."

"Yes," I said, although I couldn't hear the wind in the chimney nor anywhere else. The night was almost unnaturally calm.

FOUR

LONDON: THE CRUYERS' HOME

"Now that Bernard has finally joined us," proclaimed
Dicky Cruyer in a voice tinged with impatience, "we
can proceed with the ceremony."

Dicky was wearing a navy blue dinner suit. He'd
bought it back in the days when everyone said dark blue
photographed better on television. But Dicky had never
been on television, and now his suit just looked unusual.
In response to Dicky's urgent hand signals someone
reduced the volume of the hi-fi from which came Stan
Getz playing the "One-Note Samba."

I was the last to arrive only because Dicky had
dumped a file upon my desk just two hours before and I
had been working to complete it before leaving the
office. I caught Fiona's eye and she blew me a kiss.

Bret was there, wearing a new dinner suit. His slim
figure looked good in black. Together with the white
hair brushed tight against his skull, his angular face so

carefully shaved and dusted with powder, he looked somewhat menacing: the sort of gangster figure that Hollywood invented when George Raft and Jimmy Cagney stopped doing musicals.

Resuming his brisk parade-ground voice, Dicky said, "I know everyone here tonight will . . . give Bernard a glass, Daphne darling . . . will join me in offering Augustus my belated congratulations on becoming Operations supremo. Hurry, Daphne. We are all waiting."

Daphne Cruyer was pouring measures of champagne from a magnum bottle of Pol Roger. Daphne became nervous at these occasions when her husband brought his colleagues home to a little dinner party. She should not have distributed the empty glasses to the guests before going round with the bottle. Now, as they held their glasses out, she was finding it difficult to pour from the big bottle without spilling some wine each time.

"Thank you, Mrs. Cruyer," said Augustus Stowe, as the champagne overfilled his glass and ran bubbling down his fingers to drip on to his shoe. Stowe had never visited the Cruyers before, and judging by the distracted look on his face was wondering what he was doing here now. He was an efficient, outspoken, and extremely irritable Australian. As some of the messenger boys had demonstrated on the wall of the men's toilet, Stowe was remarkably easy to caricature because of the hair that grew from his ears and nostrils, and the fact that his head was shiny, pink, and completely bald.

It was of course a contrivance to call this dinner party a celebration of Stowe's appointment. That had all been celebrated, debated, and deplored many weeks before. Stowe was reassigned when Dicky was appointed to

"Europe Supremo." It was only a temporary arrangement. Augustus Stowe, who had held that Europe job for some time, was urgently needed to deal with one of the calamities that were a regular part of life in Operations. Stowe was still there but he wouldn't last much longer. No one held on to Operations for very long. Firing the chief of Operations was the standard act of contrition that the Department offered to the Joint Intelligence Committee each time the politicos lobbed a salvo of complaints at us. And lately those salvos had become a cannonade.

But Dicky was the deskman par excellence. By having my wife Fiona as his assistant, he'd kept a grip on both the German Desk and the Europe job, too. This dinner party was a way of saying to Augustus Stowe—and the world in general—that Dicky was going to fight to hold on to the Europe Desk. It was a way of telling Stowe not to come back this way.

"Now everyone has a glass, I think. So congratulations, Augustus!" said Dicky, holding his glass aloft. With varying measures of enthusiasm and gestures of good will, the assembled company complimented Stowe and then sipped their drink and looked around.

"That's not a ready-made bow tie, is it, Bernard?" said Dicky as he pushed past me to see why the girl with the peanuts and olives was not distributing them quickly enough. She was talking to Gloria and they were comparing the heels of their shoes.

"Come along," Dicky told the girl. "You should be doing the hot sausages by now."

"She forgot the mustard dip," Daphne told him. "We haven't used these caterers before. They sent six packets of frozen bite-sized pizzas without asking if we had a microwave. I was hoping they would thaw but they are rock-hard."

"I can't do the catering, too, darling," Dicky told her in distant tones. "It's not much to ask: just to make sure these catering people bring the right food. My God, we are paying them enough."

"It looks ready-made," I said, "but that's because I'm good at tying them."

"What was that, Bernard? Oh, yes. Well, be a good chap and take the olives round, would you?" Then he turned back to Daphne and said, "Put the pizzas in a hot oven, darling. I'll just keep on serving 'shampoo' until they are ready."

I found the table where Daphne had abandoned the magnum of champagne and poured myself another glass. Alongside the champagne there were two vases crammed with expensive cut flowers. I suppose the other guests had brought them as gifts. I felt guilty about not doing the same until I noticed that a tall bunch of dark red roses held a card saying FONDEST LOVE FROM BERNARD AND FIONA.

"We love that painting of Adam and Eve," I heard Dicky saying behind me. I turned and found he was confiding his feelings to Bret Rensselaer and Gloria. I offered them all olives but only Gloria took one. She bit into it with her amazingly white teeth and then handed the pit back to me. There was a certain intimacy to this action and I think she thought so too. I smiled at her. It looked as if this might be the most intimate thing to happen between us for a very long time. Dicky was telling Bret how Daphne had bought the painting cheap in a flea market in Amsterdam. I had heard the story a thousand times, and I clearly remembered Bret standing here in the Cruyers' drawing-room listening politely to Dicky's rambling and rather dubious account of this purchase.

Augustus Stowe was standing by a glass case in the corner studying the contents: Dicky Cruyer's valuable collection of antique fountainpens. It seemed an appropriate collection for a man who had climbed so far in the world of bureaucrats. Stowe perhaps thought so too, for he pulled a face and moved on to join two people from his Operations section who were talking with Fiona. It didn't really matter whether Augustus Stowe was the guest of honor or just an extra man. The evening had really been arranged so that Dicky could clarify his working relationship with Bret. This was a make-or-break evening. The work at the office might or might not be discussed, but by the time the evening ended these two men would have made their peace or declared war.

Dicky had found it difficult to adjust to the way in which Bret Rensselaer had unexpectedly arrived in London. Unrolled from the magic carpet and into the Deputy's office like Cleopatra for a startled Caesar, he had seized control of the Department. His only real superior, the Director-General, seemed to be giving Bret a more or less free hand.

"Europe can no longer be treated like an odd assortment of people with weird languages and funny costumes," Dicky was earnestly explaining to Bret. "Europe together musters more people, more talent, and more wealth than the entire USA."

Bret said nothing. And yet I knew from the long time I had spent with Bret in California that it was the sort of remark that usually produced an acid question about why Europe couldn't afford armed services to defend itself without American military help. Bret was an Anglophile, but that didn't mean he felt European. Bret's infatuation with England and the

English made him exceedingly skeptical about life lived by foreigners beyond the English Channel. He smiled at Dicky.

Dicky said, "Since moving into the Europe slot I have made it my business to visit every one of our European offices. I love Europe. In some ways I think of Paris as my real home."

"How are you managing to divide authority with Fiona?" asked Bret.

"She hasn't been complaining?"

"She's so busy running around the globe that I seldom get the pleasure of talking with her."

"She supports me in everything I do," said Dicky. "I hardly know how . . ." He paused and wet his lips. I suspect he'd been about to say that he didn't know how he would manage without her but it came out: ". . . how I would replace her."

"No need to worry about replacing her, Dicky," said Bret.

"No?" said Dicky nervously and drank some champagne. It was at a previous gathering like this—in Dicky's home—that Bret had announced that he was the newly appointed Deputy D-G. That traumatic experience had left Dicky nervous that Bret might choose this evening for another such bombshell.

But Bret didn't add anything more to this verdict on Fiona's security of tenure. Somewhat pointedly, he moved away from Dicky to speak with her. I heard him say, "You are looking ravishing tonight, Fiona." She was wearing a severely cut dark green dress with matching shoes. When Bret started talking to her she frowned and bent her head as if concentrating. Or perhaps she was looking at her silk shoes. She had told me many times that they were difficult to keep in good shape. She never wore them when driving, she slipped them off and operated the pedals in her stockings.

Everyone was in evening dress. Mine was creased in all the wrong places. I'd packed it carelessly when coming back from my weekend with my father-in-law and only got it out of my suitcase half an hour or so before arriving at Dicky's.

As if to cover any confusion he'd suffered at Bret's hands, Dicky turned to me and said, "Bret's a bit nervous tonight. There was a personal security alert for all senior staff this afternoon. I told Bret he should be armed but he said it would spoil the line of his tuxedo." Dicky laughed in a way that made it difficult to know if he was scoffing at Bret's foolishness, or memorizing the line for his own use.

"No one told me," I said.

Dicky sipped his drink and glanced around the room to see who was talking to whom. "Well, you are not exactly senior staff, old boy," he said with a boyish smile. Dicky was looking young and fresh and energetic this evening. And his hair had suddenly become almost unnaturally curly. I wondered if he had it permed from time to time. "It's nothing to be alarmed about. The embassy hoodlums have been ordered to provide some sort of back-up. And that's as much as we have discovered. I doubt if it's a hit of any sort. I suspect it's something to do with dissidents. It could be anything. It could be a break-in or a line tap."

Daphne came to Dicky's side. She was wearing a long, plain dress with large, embroidered flowers on it. Daphne had picked up a damaged piece of tapestry in one of the antique markets she frequented, and had removed the flowers from it. "Will you be able to carve the lamb?" she asked Dicky.

"I told you not to get a leg."

"A shoulder is so fatty," said Daphne.

"Get Bernard to carve it," said Dicky. "He's good at that kind of thing."

"Could you, Bernard? I've had the knife sharpened."

"Of course he can," said Dicky before I could reply. "He's my slave, isn't he? He'll do anything I tell him to do." He put a hand round my shoulder and hugged me. "Right, Bernard?"

"I'll carve it for you, Daphne," I said. "But I'm not an expert."

"Your poor face," said Daphne. "What happened, Bernard?"

"He applied the old powder-puff a bit too energetically," said Dicky.

"No, really," said Daphne, looking at me with sympathy.

"It's secret," said Dicky. "Let him alone. Bernard is paid to take a few knocks when the job calls for it."

I knew of course that Dicky was giving me the sort of treatment he would have liked to be giving to Bret. Although I hadn't followed the exact implications of his brief exchange with Bret, his subsequent irritation was enough to tell me that Dicky did not feel entirely secure in his Europe Desk job. I wondered if Bret was about to leapfrog Fiona into becoming Dicky's senior. It was the sort of device that Bret would use to shake up the Department. And Bret had been heard to say that a shake-up was exactly what the Department urgently needed. The trouble was that I was always the one who got Dicky's flak.

"It's mid-life crisis," said Daphne when we reached the kitchen and I was appraising the roast leg of lamb and putting an edge on the carving knife. "That's what my doctor says."

Daphne was wearing a professional cook's white apron of starched white cotton. Her name—Daphne Cruyer—was embroidered in red on its front, in the style of self-acclaim made famous by Paul Bocuse. "You're young yet, Daphne," I said.

"Not me; Dicky," she said, showing a flash of pique. "Dicky's in mid-life crisis."

"Your doctor said this?"

"The doctor knows how upset I am," she explained. "And he knows how insensitive Dicky can be. It's all those young girls he has around him all day. He has to keep proving his masculinity." She fetched a large oval plate from the massive shiny steel professional oven she'd had fitted since my previous visit. "You can carve it in advance, Bernard."

"I'll do it at the table, Daphne. I know that's how you like to serve dinner."

"You are a dear man," she said. "If all the girls were chasing after you, I would find it easier to understand."

"Yes, so would I," I said.

After that the guests sat down and the dinner party continued in the way that Dicky's dinner parties usually continued. Daphne made sure that Gloria and Fiona were sitting as far apart as possible. And for that I was grateful to her.

The next day I made a journey that took me into England's authentic countryside. This was a stark contrast to the cozy toyland which my father-in-law shared with London's stockbrokers, bankers, judges and gynecologists.

Visits to "Uncle" Silas had punctuated my life ever since I was a small child. I had always loved Whitelands, his rambling great farm on the edge of the Cotswolds. Even in winter it was magnificent. The house, built of local light-brown stone, its ancient carved-oak front door, and its mullioned windows, provided a perfect image of old England as the Christmas card industry chose to record it. Countless times I had hidden in the cobwebbed attic or sat in the paneled billiards room, on the bench under the cue-rack, looking at the doleful heads of assembled deer, now moth-eaten and threadbare. I couldn't think of Whitelands without smelling the freshly baked scones that Mrs. Porter brought from that temperamental old solid-fuel oven. Just as I couldn't remember exploring that vast stone barn without sneezing, or recall the chilly Sunday morning journeys to the church in the village without a shiver.

For me, the highlight of my visits to Whitelands was the perfect roast beef lunches cooked with loving care by Mrs. Porter, the housekeeper. On Sundays it was always local game: if not partridge or pheasant, then Silas would be carving and serving hare or rabbit. As I grew up and learned to count, I was permitted to supervise the billiards score-board. It provided an excuse to be there, an opportunity to watch my father, Silas and other luminaries of the Department, smoking Silas's Cuban cigars, drinking his vintage Hine brandy and arguing in a good-natured way about how the world should be arranged and exactly how and when they would do it.

Whitelands had been in the Gaunt family since one of his more affluent predecessors bought it from a beer tycoon who went to something more grandiose. Only after he retired did Silas come to live here all the year round, and his hospitality became legendary. All manner of weird people came here for the weekend; musicians—prominent or penniless—were especially welcomed, for Silas was devoted to music. They were seldom famous people but they were always convivial and interesting. The weekends were an unchanging ritual: a country walk as far as the river, church service, smoky afternoon billiard games for men only, and a formal dinner for which the guests were expected to dress in long gowns and penguin suits.

Silas was a distant relative of Fiona's family, and he became the godfather of my son. Friends became relatives, and relatives became friends. The Department had always been like that; a curious intermingling of bright boys from expensive schools and their otherwise unemployable male relatives. Perhaps it would have been better and more efficient if its personnel had been recruited from a wider spectrum of British life, but it wouldn't have been so amusing, or so frustrating.

Now Whitelands and all it represented was to end forever. Some of the rooms had already been cleared of Silas's more personal possessions. One capacious white dust sheet had transformed the chairs, and the long polished table of the dining room, into a wrinkled dirigible. The dining table, without extension panels, was shorter than I ever remembered it. I was saddened to think that I would never again see that table loaded under food, crowded by visitors, and noisy with arguments.

"I'll come back," said Silas firmly, as if reading my thoughts. "I'm only leasing this place ... short lease. And to people I know well. I've told them I will be returning. I'm even trusting them with the key of my wine cellar."

"I hope so, Silas," I said. "What about Mrs. Porter?"

"She'll be living nearby. I made that a condition. I need to know there is someone here, keeping an eye on things on my behalf. You'll come and see me?"

I nodded. We were sitting in what Silas called "the drawing room." Most of the light came from the big open fire upon which he had just placed a mossy log. This was the sanctum to which Silas had retired when he first became unwell. Around him he had arranged some of his most cherished possessions: his favorite lumpy sofa and an equally lumpy painting of his grandfather on a horse. Silas was lumpy too. Already big in frame, his indulgence in good food, and complete indifference to his personal appearance, had made him fat and unkempt. His remaining hair was fuzzy, his jowls heavy, his shirt frayed, and his woolen cardigan—like Silas himself—slowly coming unraveled.

"You put in the new trees," I said.

"It broke my heart to lose the elms."

"They'll soon grow."

"Canadian maples or some such thing. The forestry people said they grow quickly, but they are sickly-looking growths. I don't like the look of them."

"Give them a chance, Silas. You mustn't be impatient."

"An apartment," said Silas. "What will life be like in an apartment block?"

"I thought it was your idea."

"It was a compromise," he said. "At first it was only my local doctor threatening me. Then the Department joined in. They say it's all for my benefit, but I'd rather stay here and put up with whatever happens. We've all got to die sometime."

"You mustn't talk like that," I said. "You've got years of life and work ahead."

"What about my music?" said Silas. "I'm taking all my records and tapes. I hope I'm not going to have some wretch banging on the wall just because it's after eleven o'clock."

"Get well," I said. "That's the important thing. Get well and come home to Whitelands again." .

"I'm not sick," he declared. Although old and somewhat wheezy, he appeared to be in good health and quick-witted, too. "But the Department made me submit to a physical examination by their stupid doctor. It's some new rule about the pension funds. That's what started the fuss. Otherwise I wouldn't have agreed to go away at all. Before you go, you might like to take a last look around, Bernard?"

"Yes," I said.

"And I want you to take a crate or two of wine with you. Choose whatever you like." Before I could respond, he added: "I will never get through it all even if I live to be one hundred."

I looked at him and waited to hear the reason for him demanding my presence. Silas was a noisy extrovert, a blunt and yet devious old man, and certainly not likely to bring me down here without a specific reason. He got up and closed the door. Tall and plump and untidy, he had many weaknesses, of which gambling was the one most associated with him both at work and at play. "There are things that were never committed to paper, Bernard. When I go, the facts will go, too. You understand?"

"Of course."

"I've always been a gambler," said Silas. "Sometimes I've won. When I've lost I've paid up without complaint.

But in all my years in the Department I've never gambled with people's lives. You know that, Bernard."

I didn't answer. The truth was that I didn't know what was decided in the secret dialogues that men like Silas had on the top floor.

"When I thought we were going to lose Fiona last year, I was worried. They are not like us, Bernard, those people over there. They don't interrogate, explicate, and isolate." He smiled; it was one of the maxims of the Department. "If they had got wind of what Fiona was doing to their precious socialist empire her end would have been too savage to think about. They put that fellow ... what's his name ... into a furnace: alive. At first no one here would believe it, but then we intercepted the official account. It was done in front of witnesses."

"What is it, Silas? What are you trying to tell me?"

"I didn't know they would kill Tessa," he said. "All I was told was that there would be a faked identity. Her identity."

"Who told you that?"

"We handed the whole project over to the Yanks," said Silas. "We needed to be distanced from it."

"That doesn't fit with what I know," I told him. "It was done by a man named Thurkettle, wasn't it?"

"Thurkettle. Yes, an American."

"An American mercenary. The story I heard is that he was released from a high-security prison to do some dirty work for the CIA. Very dirty work."

"Perhaps he was," said Silas. "I thought he was a bona fide Washington man. I was persuaded to give him a free hand."

"To do what?"

"Certainly not to murder anyone," said Silas

indignantly. "I never met him personally of course, but I was assured that he could provide a smoke screen while we brought Fiona out."

"A smoke screen? What did you think he was going to do?"

"It was vital that the Stasi people, and Moscow, too, should think Fiona had died. If they had known that she was safe, and in California, giving us a detailed picture of everything they had done . . . well, they would have simply taken emergency action: changed codes, changed methods, changed agents, changed everything. Fiona's years of courage and jeopardy would have been in vain."

"But Tessa was killed. And her body was burned to help the deception."

"What can I say to you? I can't say I wasn't at fault, because I was. I trusted that swine. I thought it was going to be only a matter of paperwork."

"Without a body? How would that have worked?" I asked him.

"A dead body perhaps. A body taken from a hospital mortuary. That has been done before, and will no doubt be done again. It's not the use of the body, is it? It's the killing."

"Yes, it's the killing," I agreed.

"Tessa's death has brought terrible consequences," said Silas. "None of us will ever be the same again. Not you, not Fiona, not that poor husband of hers. And certainly not me. I haven't slept one full night since I heard the news. It was the end of my relationship with the Department, of course. The D-G wanted me to continue in my arm's-length advisory role, but I told him I couldn't. It broke my heart."

"Where is Thurkettle now?"

"He went to Oregon, the last I heard of him. But he may have moved on. Canada perhaps. The Americans had given him a new identity so he could do more or less as he wished. There was talk of having him face some sort of murder charge, but that would have meant negotiations with the Americans. And even if they had agreed we could hardly drag our covert actions through open court. Concealing the fact that Fiona was alive and well was exactly what we had started out to do in the first place."

"Yes," I said.

"And to some extent Thurkettle probably feels he did what had to be done."

"Yes," I said. "And to some extent I suspect that's how you feel, too."

Silas frowned. "I thought you would understand," he said. "Your father would have understood."

"He would have understood all right. He was accused of shooting some German named Winter back in 1945. He was innocent. But the Department let the charges stand because they didn't want him to face questioning by American lawyers in another jurisdiction."

"That's an oversimplification," protested Silas.

"It ruined his career, didn't it?"

"Your father understood that it was necessary."

"Very well. But don't expect me to go along with the kind of bloody nonsense my father put up with. My father is not me, and I am not my father. Time has moved on, and so has everything else."

"I hate rows," said Silas plaintively.

"Yes, of course you do. So do I, if I can get my way without having them."

When I left the room Silas leaned back and closed

his eyes as if in pain. I sought out Mrs. Porter to say good-bye. I was hoping to hear her confidential opinion about Silas and his plans. I found her in the kitchen, and she was determined to keep her own counsel. "I know what you want to talk about, Mister Bernard," she said. "But I know my place. It's not for me to have an opinion about anything." She took out her handkerchief and wiped her nose. "I can't seem to shake off this head cold," she said. "And there is so much to do in the house." She smiled at me. Mrs. Porter had helped to create the magical atmosphere of Whitelands. It was difficult to guess how much of all I loved would remain after new tenants moved in.

I got into the car and found myself trembling. I don't know why, perhaps it was due to anger and resentment, or the memories of my father's humiliation. I drove down to the village and stopped at the Brown Bess. It was an unfashionable little pub, sandwiched between a scum-encrusted duck pond and a neglected war memorial. Those villagers who could afford it, and the weekend inhabitants, kept to the other pub, the big multi-mirrored Queen Victoria that faced the village green, where the weekend cricketers and their adoring families could enjoy frozen food with foreign names, and champagne with a dash of blackcurrant juice. The Brown Bess was an intimate gathering place for dart-playing farmworkers. The landlord served me with an excruciating politeness bordering on hostility.

I took my beer and my cheddar-cheese sandwich and sat on the steps of the war memorial to eat it, scarcely noticing the cold. I wanted to think. To be subjected to the devious ways of my father-in-law, and then

Silas Gaunt, in close succession was more than anyone should be asked to endure. I rebelled. Afterwards— when it was too late—even my most loyal friends and staunchest supporters said my plan of action had been headstrong and ill-advised. The kinder ones said uncharacteristically so. They wondered why I acted impulsively without taking one of them into my confidence, or giving more thought to the consequences.

It was David's claim upon my children—and Fiona's apparent indifference to it—that worried me most. The problem and possible solutions went round and round in my head. That day, sitting on the war memorial with my pint of beer, I listed on a single page of my notebook every alternative open to me; no matter how absurd or impractical. I went through each answer one by one and rejected only those that stood no chance of success. It looked like this: arguing with David would get nowhere, while fighting him through Britain's expensive legal system would result in custody of the children for him and legal fees that would bankrupt me. With the conversation about arsenic fresh in my mind, I even considered killing him. I might have done it too; but I felt that even undetected it would provide the children with a legacy even worse than having David as a "father."

To add another dimension to my predicament, I couldn't forget the warning that an Englishman from the Warsaw embassy had given me recently. He thought the other side might take revenge on Fiona, for the way she had tricked them, by killing off her loved ones one by one and at unpredictable intervals. They had done that to a Russian defector named Simakaitis, and he'd ended up in a mental home. Well, Fiona's sister was dead, and her brother-in-law was in trouble that might

well have been contrived by Moscow. Fiona was far
from well; sometimes I thought she was on the edge of a
breakdown. Perhaps there was some diabolical scheme
to take revenge upon the whole family. And perhaps it
was working.

I made the most of my extended stay in London. The
next day I went to a rendezvous in the basement of
one of those secondhand bookshops that crowd the
Leicester Square end of London's Charing Cross
Road. The meeting was at my request, so I could
hardly argue about the venue. I had been to the shop
before. It was a useful meeting place—I knew them
all—and I picked my way down the narrow wooden
stairs to a cellar that became a labyrinth of small
rooms. Every room was crammed with old books.
Here and there, freestanding racks divided the spaces
so that it was a squeeze to get past them. There were
books piled on the floor, and more remained unpacked
in dusty cardboard cartons.

The subterranean rooms were damp, for London is a
basin and we were not far from the river. The books
gave off a musty smell. Encyclopedias of all shapes and
sizes shared the shelves with the refought battles of
wartime generals, the tarnished stars of yesterday's
show business, and the memoirs of forgotten politicians,
their perceptions polished by hindsight.

Books were scattered everywhere. Some had toppled over, some were pushed sideways on to the shelves,
and some were on the floor as if discarded. It was as if
an unexpected emergency had interrupted work here. As
I passed through the low doorways from one shadowy
chamber to another, I might have been exploring a

prehistoric tomb, and the depredations of robbers long since gone.

I recognized some of the books—they were positioned exactly as they had been when I was here a year or more ago. So was the Swede.

The Swede was a professional pilot. Physically powerful and unquestionably courageous, but by nature cautious. It was the perfect temperament for a man who had landed aircraft in total darkness on unfamiliar terrain, and flown out again. Systematic and serious, he was racked by the chronic backaches and hemorrhoids that went with the flyer's trade. Once he'd been a beautiful young man—you could see the traces of it—but neglected teeth, a roseate nose, and thinning hair now made him just another senior citizen.

He was wearing a new Burberry trenchcoat, a matching tweed hat, and tartan scarf: a totemic tribute to the British Tourist Authority. When I came upon him at the appointed spot in the cellar he was standing under a crudely lettered sign, BIBLE STUDIES. Although seemingly engrossed in a heavy leather-bound volume, he looked up and pushed the book back onto the shelf.

"Always Bible Studies, Swede," I said. "Why is that?"

One hand was in the pocket of his beige trenchcoat until he brought it out to flourish a huge Colt Navy revolver, an antique gun that I knew to be of lethal accuracy. "Grab air!"

"Don't be a tiresome fool, I'm not in the mood for jokes."

"Bang, bang. You're dead." He was short and weather-beaten, his spoken English marked by a nasal intonation that he had acquired in America.

"Yes, I know. Do that to one of our newer kids and they will waste you."

"It's a replica. I bought it in a store selling model cars and planes. It's a perfect repro. Isn't that neat? Exactly like the real thing. Look." He offered me the gun. It was a detailed reproduction. Only its light weight betrayed it. I gave it a glance and passed it back to him. I suppose it is in the nature of men who fly that they retain some childish faith in gadgets. Otherwise they might start believing in gravity.

"It went well . . . that pickup I did for you."

"Yes," I said. It wasn't like him to mention past jobs. What was he looking for: a medal? a commendation? a pension? By now he should have learned how much the Department hated anyone they termed "hangers-on," and that meant anyone who expected proper recompense.

"It was your brother-in-law, wasn't it? That nervous little fellow we brought out?"

"No," I said.

"That's what I heard."

"Heard? Heard from whom?" I asked. He played with the gun, aiming it at the light bulbs and at the door.

"We aviators get around." He looked at me. "Why all this special secrecy? Why London? Why not contact me through your man in Stockholm? Are you in trouble, Bernd?"

"Listen to me, Swede," I said, and told him briefly what I wanted him to do. A straightforward air pickup task, the sort of job he'd been doing for twenty years.

"Is this for the Department?"

"Do you think I'm going private?"

"It will cost a lot of money. Whatever way we do it, it will cost."

"I know."

"In the old days the Irish Sea was a milk run. But since your Irish rebels started bringing in their Armalites and Semtex, the British have pointed their low-level radar that way, and keep it manned day and night." He pushed his gun into his pocket. "Where do I pick up your people? England? Where do I tell flying control I'm going? Don't ask me to drop into some neglected little wartime strip by night, I've given up those jobs where you ground loop around some potholes a mile deep and then hit a combine harvester. Is it worth it, Bernd? I mean, there's no passport control between England and the Irish Republic. Immigration scarcely glance at you. I hear it's a walk-through. What are you doing smuggling people across the water by plane?"

"It's not so easy. Immigration is still intact. Boats are conspicuous, and as soon as you mention Ireland they think you are in the IRA, and get on the phone to the police."

"Bring a speedy little Irish boat over. No?"

"Even more conspicuous," I said. "Outboard motors and other valuable stuff are stolen, so these coastal communities are always watching out for passing strangers who might be about to rip off the boats."

He scratched his face. "The smaller the better then. It might be possible to rent a plane from one of those little flying clubs in East Anglia or somewhere. Cash, no questions asked. I don't know. I'll have to enquire into it. How soon are you wanting to set this one up?"

"Soon. As soon as possible."

"Then clubs are out. They don't get going until the weather brightens a bit. Even renting a decent commercial ship isn't easy at this time of year."

"Yes," I said. For him it would be complicated. He

would have to do it using bogus identification and all the fake papers needed in Europe to get and fly an aircraft. Lately some rumors had been circulating that the Swede was ready to do all kinds of things that once he would have declined—drugs, arms, and gold—and people were saying that he was becoming a lot less discriminating in his choice of clients. That's the sort of nasty things the rumors were saying. I didn't believe them of course, but when freebooters like the Swede grow old you can never be sure which way they will go. And the childish fascination he showed with his imitation gun was not reassuring.

He said, "It's not for the Yanks, is it?"

"No."

"Because I won't work for the Yanks anymore. They make their detailed plans and then, when the time comes, they turn everything on its tail. I don't work for the Yanks."

"Yes, I know," I said.

In fact the man everyone called the Swede was German, a Rhinelander named Franz Bender. In 1944 he was a young civilian pilot working for Messerschmitt at Augsburg. When the war ended, American air force specialists went and grabbed the Messerschmitt jet fighters, the engineers, designers, and the pilots, too. I can only guess what stories he told them, but the truth was that he was only qualified on light planes. But the Americans believed him. They found American army uniforms to fit them all and smuggled them back to the U.S. I don't know if he ever had to prove he could fly one of those wartime jets, but they kept him on. He lived on the American base at Wright Field for nearly three years, teaching what he knew about flying and servicing jet planes, and making up the rest. He was good at translating Luftwaffe training manuals into American-style English. They paid him a generous civilian salary; gave him a car and an apartment. He had lots of girlfriends. He was a good-looking kid and his accent delighted them.

Then one night, coming back from a party, a cop pulled him over for speeding. He had no driver's license, no social security card, and, when he admitted he was an alien, not even a passport to prove who he was. The cop was a tough vet from the 82nd Airborne and not sympathetic to Germans in any shape or form. Neither did much sympathy come from the other officials Franz encountered. The war was over and those American pals of his, who might have pulled strings to help him, had become civilians and disappeared. No one was prepared to help him. U.S. Immigration held him in custody for almost six months, but no lawyer stuck with him and he was deported to Germany. Although the charges against him were dropped he was banned from entering the States ever again. He'd never forgiven the Americans for what he regarded as an act of betrayal.

"Perhaps you are making a big production out of it," I said. "Couldn't we have a wealthy Swedish national, in a Swedish-registered aircraft, on holiday—flying here and there to amuse his friends?"

Still waving the gun around he suddenly said, "It's your kids, isn't it, Bernd?"

If he had shot a hole in the *Information Please Almanac* for 1965, and made it bleed, he could not have shaken me more. Was it that obvious? Did everyone know so much about my personal life that they could guess what I might do next? "Give over," I said.

"They will find them and send them back. It's the Hague Convention: custody hearings always take place in the jurisdiction where children are normally resident. What's more, those stupid judges always send the kids to the country where they have spent most time. I know, my cousin went through that stuff. The judge was a clown, and the social services led him by the nose all the time. They'll get you in the end like they did him."

"Do you charge for this kind of advice? Or does it go with the air ticket?"

He shrugged. "Okay. It's no concern of mine, but don't ask me to get involved."

"Just steer the big bird, Swede."

"Are you sure you are not in trouble, Bernd?"

"I told you, no," I said.

"With your people? Or the opposition? You want to disappear, I'll tell you many places a million times better than Ireland." I didn't answer. He stared at me while his mind whirled. "Or are you going to run across to Cork and climb aboard that Aeroflot connection that flies direct to Havana?" Slowly he smiled. "You cunning bastard. And from Cuba where?"

"Why all these questions?" The Swede had always been taciturn and positive, now he had become a garrulous fool.

"Because it all stinks, Bernd," he said feelingly. "The way you tell it, it stinks. I've never had worse vibrations than I'm getting now." He took off his new hat with a sigh, and rubbed the bright red line it had left on his forehead.

"You need a size larger hat," I said. "Or maybe a size smaller head."

He shuffled his feet, gave me a silly smile and then looked at his shoes. We both knew that he'd have to do it. I wouldn't have compromised myself in this way unless I'd been sure of him. Over the years the Department had given him a steady supply of well-paid jobs. Whatever he suspected about this being a private job, he wasn't likely to risk losing a contact like me. "Look, Bernd. We've known each other a long time and we've both done each other a few favors over the years, so I'm not sure which of us owes what to whom. But the only reason I am standing here indulging you in this mad idea is because I know there is not the slightest chance of your getting anyone else to even think about taking it on."

"Short takeoff and landing. Single engine I think; there's not much room at the Irish end. Grass, of course, but it's used by a club so there's no obstructions worse than hedges. I'll get someone to take a close look at its condition when we get nearer the time."

He didn't reply for a moment, then he said, "This is not Nintendo; this is not a computer game we are playing: zap the pixels and the screen goes dark. Putting an airplane down on to a garbage dump in pitch darkness is for keeps. Pilots don't benefit from their mistakes, Bernd. Pilots don't benefit from their mistakes because the poor bastards don't live long enough after the first mistake to benefit."

I'd heard it all before of course. These black-sky pilots liked you to know they were earning their fees. "Okay, Swede," I said. "Put away the violin."

"I can keep my mouth shut," he said. "I flew the plane for your friend Volkmann that night when it all happened. I kept that quiet, didn't I? You didn't know that, did you?"

"No," I said, and my ears were flapping. I was trying to remember if he had met Werner, and if so where and when. "Did Volkmann fly that night?"

"Not Volkmann. The plane wasn't intended for him,

he was just the one who sent me the order. The plane was for your buddy Prettyman."

"Prettyman?"

"Don't play dumb, Bernd. Jay Prettyman, the Department's arm's-length hatchet man. The white-faced one—the spooky guy with no eyebrows."

"Yes, Jay Prettyman. I know him."

"Of course you know him. He was one of your close buddies, wasn't he?"

"I don't have any close buddies," I said.

"And I'm beginning to understand why," said the Swede. "He briefed me. I was to wait for him to arrive no matter how long. I had a package for him. He was to climb aboard and I would fly him out to England. The timing was important. They found an early-morning slot for me at Gatwick. I didn't want to get there too early and attract a lot of attention with the flight control people. They are all Gestapo."

"Yes," I said. The Swede regarded all authority with contempt. Even the flight controllers were classified as mortal enemies rather than saviors. "Tell me more."

"It was almost light before anyone arrived. When the car came it wasn't Prettyman. The arrangement was that Prettyman would be riding a bicycle. I'd take the bicycle with us. It gave him a chance to hide the car away somewhere. I'd taken my seats out to make space for it. I'd even tried a bicycle inside to make sure there was no difficulty getting it through the door."

Good careful Swede. "But it was a car that arrived?"

"I guessed something had gone badly wrong. Your wife was being extracted by road, wasn't she?"

"Yes," I said. "And who was in the car?"

"A woman. She wouldn't fly with me. She just told

me to get out of there as soon as possible. She told me to go home and forget about it. She said I'd be paid a bonus for being kept waiting. I knew that was bullshit. Did you ever hear of those bastards paying a black-sky for being delayed?"

"Who was it? Someone you recognized?"

"I don't know," he said. "I gave her the package and I took off out of there."

"Don't start playing smart-ass with me, Swede."

"I said I don't know. That means I don't know. Got it?" He was suddenly aggressive as he perhaps realized that he was saying more than he intended.

"You are too old, and too goddamned scarred, and too poor to start handing over packages to people you don't know. How did she identify herself?"

He waved his long-barreled gun. "Passport. Mrs. Prettyman. Valid U.K. passport. What was I to do?"

"Don't whine. What was in the package?"

"I don't know. It was sealed. It was a locked case. It weighed a ton. I gave it to her and she beat it right away. Mrs. goddamned Prettyman climbed into her car without even a thank-you or good-bye. It was a long time before I got it figured out."

"What did you figure out, Swede?"

"It was some kind of hit. It was never intended that I should fly Prettyman out of there. What would I be doing with a package for him? Hell, we were on our way to Gatwick. What was in that package that he had to have it on the airplane? His makeup? His vitamin pills?" The Swede laughed. "No, Prettyman was involved in a hit. I was there to collect the corpse. My guess is that the case contained identity papers for the one they were going to kill. That's why it was all so secret. That's why Prettyman had to get it."

"Have you seen Prettyman since?"

"I never spoke about it from that day to this. I know how to keep my mouth shut."

"Until now," I said.

Swede seemed suddenly to regret his indiscretion. He drew himself up like a soldier getting ready to receive a medal, or be kissed on both cheeks. Or both. "I will need at least a month to make the preparations," he said. "I will need someone to help at the English end. Someone with a bit of authority."

"I brought some cash for you." I'd brought a sealed envelope containing two thousand pounds in twenties. Now I handed it to him.

He took the envelope and carelessly pushed it away in an inside pocket. "I'll need at least five grand up front and I won't be able to give you much of a refund if you cancel. It will have been used by that time. And once I deliver your passengers I take off and that's the end of our deal."

"Did I ever do it any other way?"

"You're crazy, Bernd."

"They are my kids," I said.

"Your passengers," he corrected me, determined not to be a party to my crime. "Have you told them what you intend? Don't surprise them at the last minute, will you, eh? I don't want to be struggling with unwilling youngsters. That could make for real trouble."

"Only four beats to the bar, Swede. You just drive the plane; leave the passenger manifest to me, right?"

"It's the best way," he said, with a silly smile on his face.

It was only then that it dawned on me. "You bastard. You're as drunk as a skunk."

"Naw, naw, naw," he said.

I stepped forward to slap him, or rattle him, I'm not sure what. He waved the huge replica Colt at me in a way more comical than threatening. "Don't shake the pinball machine, or you won't get your peanuts," he said.

"If you let me down, Swede, I'll kill you."

"Yah, yah. I know what you're like." It didn't sound like warm approval. "Gabrielle left me," he said sorrowfully. "A marketing development analyst, he calls himself. What's that? What the hell does a development analyst do? He's just a youngster. She says he makes a hundred thousand dollars a year. Can you believe it?"

"I can believe it," I said. I'd never heard of Gabrielle; I didn't know if she was his wife or his girlfriend, or his pet piranha. But whatever she was, I could easily believe she'd want to get away from him.

"Gabi! Gabi!" He said it more loudly to help me remember. "The one you borrowed the car from."

"Oh, yes." I remembered now. Gabi Semmler, a thirty-year-old Berliner who worked as a private secretary to an air charter company with which the Swede wanted to do business. I had in fact seen her in Berlin quite recently. I wondered if that was before, during, or after the breakup. But I didn't wonder about it very much.

"Don't worry, my old Bernd. Swede won't spill your beans. Swede never lets you down."

"Sober up," I said. "And make it quick."

"Yah," He put the muzzle of the long-barrelled gun against his own temple and shouted "Bang" loudly enough to make me jump.

"Come along, Swede. Time to go walkies. Put away your toys." It was terrible weather. We emerged into Charing Cross Road just as a thunderbolt ripped the dark sky apart with a jagged blue line. The crash of its thunder echoed all along the street. Cars, delivery vans, black taxis, and the red double-decker buses, glistening with rain, were suddenly frozen by the lightning's flash. Gutters, swollen and turbulent, swept fleets of litter to the maelstrom of the drain. The ferocious downpour made tall stalks on the pavement, and there was a clatter of noise as rain hit the shopwindow glass and drenched me. The Swede came into the street and we both huddled in the shelter of a shop doorway, trying to spot an available taxicab.

"Sometimes I wonder what goes on in that head of yours, Bernd," the Swede said. "Is this a dream of a new life far away?"

"Tell people your dreams, and they never come true," I said.

"Yah, yah, yah," said the Swede and laughed. He had an awful laugh; like the bray of an angry mule. Suddenly he spotted a cab. He ran into the street, dodging between the cars as they braked and swerved to avoid him, and all the time he bellowed "Taxi! Taxi!" to get the driver's attention. "Heathrow: terminal one," he shouted to the driver as he climbed inside. He gave me a brief salute of thanks—or was it mockery?—before sliding the cab window closed. I watched him go, suspecting that as soon as he was out of sight he'd tell the driver some other destination.

Then a white Ford Transit pulled away from the curb and into the traffic. It bore the lettering that proclaimed it to be from a supplier of luxury foodstuffs to restaurants. The driver's face was familiar to me but I couldn't place him. One of the Department's corps de ballet perhaps. If they were tailing the Swede, I wondered if I'd been logged, too. I preferred to believe it must be some sidekick of the Swede's. I told myself he was apt to be overcautious even when meeting old friends. Engaging a minder was usually a sign of bad conscience, or bad company, or carrying too much cash.

I finally got a cab. My next stop was Mayfair and the office of an estate agent. I told the cabdriver I was still looking for the precise address, and let him go round Grosvenor Square twice while closely watching the other traffic. That uncomfortable, unhealthy, and neurotic paranoia that had helped keep me alive so long, made me think I was being followed. I wondered if the Ford Transit had not been Swede's man after all, but rather the changeover vehicle for my tail. But if there was someone tailing me now, he was an expert. Or perhaps simply someone who knew what my appointments were, and got there ahead of me.

I was ten minutes late. One of my father-in-law's many lawyers was waiting too, and tapping his fingers on a thick bundle of papers. In 1983, when Fiona suddenly abandoned me and the children, and departed to East Germany, our home was rented to four young Americans. But now the Americans were moving out. Three of them were posted to banks in Singapore and Hong Kong, and the last remaining tenant couldn't find anyone to share the rent. The agent wanted me to sign papers reassigning the property to my father-in-law. I had little alternative, for the major financial investment in the house had been made by him: our investment had been no more than love and labor.

The agent's office was an elegant room furnished with antique furniture, with framed engravings, and maps of historic London on the walls. Maps are of course the décor adopted by men reluctant to display their taste in art. The only discordant note was struck by the gray plastic word processor that occupied a table in the corner and buzzed. "So good of you to be so punctual," said the estate agent, as if he'd been warned that I might not show up at all. He smiled reassurance and I smiled right back at him. My father-in-law wasn't a crook; Fiona and I would come out of it with reasonable compensation for our slice of the mortgage, but I hated the way he always did these things through his minions. Why the sudden summons to this office? Why couldn't he have discussed the Duke Street property with us when we were with him at the weekend?

I signed over the penciled crosses.

When I returned to work Dicky was waiting for me. He was sitting in his office, a large comfortable room with the skins of genuine lions stretched across the floor, and a view across the trees from the two windows. Between the windows he had positioned his lovely rosewood table. The top of it was virtually clear. It was Dicky's oft-stated belief that ordinary office desks, telephones, and word processors were not necessary for work, and for the sort of work that Dicky did, they weren't. He had only one telephone, and the only reason he had a fax machine here was because he had recently been deferring his choice of lunch place until he'd studied the faxed daily menus of his favorite haunts.

"Have coffee," he suggested. It was a significant offering, and demonstrated that Dicky had something important to ask me. The coffee appeared from the next room, where Dicky stored all the ugly office machinery and the pretty young girls with whom Daphne competed.

"You saw Uncle Silas?"

"Yes," I said. I was sipping coffee and sitting in the

soft, white leather armchair that Dicky had recently installed for his visitors. There were new curtains too, and the official sepia portrait of the sovereign had been put into a rosewood frame, so that it matched his table.

"He sent for you?" And in case I didn't understand. "Silas Gaunt sent for you?" Dicky sat behind his table with his arms folded. He was wearing a blue pinstripe suit of very ordinary style. I guessed he'd been with the politicians.

"There was a garbled message . . ." I explained. I thought he was going to complain about my taking time off to go there without asking his permission.

"He's been refusing to see anyone." Dicky touched his lips with his fingertips. It was a gesture he often used, but I sometimes saw it as some kind of unconscious fear that he was saying too much. "Silas refused to see the D-G last week. He said he was ill. When Bret tried to meet with him he was extremely abusive."

I savored the coffee. It came from the shop of Mr. Higgins. Dicky said it was the best coffee in England and Dicky was very fussy about coffee.

"Ye gods, Bernard. Don't just sit there drinking coffee and smiling at me. I'm asking you a question."

"What are you asking, Dicky?"

"Why you? Why would Uncle Silas send for you while he refuses to see anyone from the top floor? Even the D-G. He told Bret he wouldn't even let the prime minister into his home. He was swearing at Bret like a drunken sailor. Bret recorded the call. He was really insulting. So why you, Bernard? What's it all about?"

"He wanted to talk about my father."

"Is that all?"

"Yes, that was all," I said.

"All right, don't go taking offense at every little thing. No reflection on your father."

Dicky's phone rang. "It's for you, Bernard." He handed it to me. It was Bret on an internal line. With that brisk and unmistakable transatlantic accent he had no need to identify himself. "Bernard." The accent on the second syllable. "There's been an irritable female caller on an outside line. Desperately trying to reach Fiona."

"She's in Rome," I said. "The terrorist symposium."

"Sure, I know that," said Bret imperiously. "I sent her there. Do you want to talk to Gloria? She will tell you who took the call."

"Is it something for Dicky?" I said. I couldn't understand why I should be suddenly handling my wife's day-to-day workload.

"It's not work," said Rensselaer. "It's a family matter. Private." His voice was uncharacteristically concerned as he added, "You haven't got a car here, have you?"

"No."

"Take Gloria's."

"To do what?"

"If you need it, if you need it," said Bret, almost losing his cool. Then, more calmly, he said, "Gloria has her car here. She will sort it out, Bernard. She's good at this sort of thing."

At what sort of thing, I was about to ask, but he had already hung up his phone.

I made hurried excuses to Dicky and went to the office I was using. I was looking up Gloria's number in the internal directory when she put her head round the door. She was wearing a crimson suit. Her blond hair was drawn back and her forehead covered in a neat fringe. The change in her appearance was startling. "Bernard!" she said. "Where have you been? I've been phoning everywhere trying to locate you. You don't have a mobile phone; there was no contact number. You just disappeared. I had security go to every room in the building." She wasn't smiling; she seemed annoyed.

"I do that sometimes," I said.

She stepped into the room and pushed the door behind her closed as if about to confide a secret to me. "Did Bret tell you?" Now I could see her more clearly. She appeared to be brimming over with rage. Her face was full and rounded with it, her lips pouting, and her big brown eyes wide open and glistening with animosity.

"What? Tell me what?"

"The school phoned. I phoned them back. It may be nothing." She stopped before bringing out the rest of it in a rush. "The school minibus went off the road and turned right over. It's mostly just cuts and bruises but some of the children—five, the matron said—will be kept in the hospital overnight."

"Billy's school?"

"Yes. I'm sorry, I should have said that. Yes, Billy's school. A collision with a motorcycle . . . on the way to a football game with a school in south London. The driver's badly hurt and the motorcyclist is in intensive care. Oh, Bernard!"

"Where is he?"

She was trying to make it easier for me, I could see that. "We're not sure that Billy is hurt. There were several ambulances and the children were taken to different hospitals. One of the girls downstairs said it was on the radio. I phoned the BBC but they said it must have been some local news bulletin."

"Do you know which hospitals?"

"The school said they would telephone again as soon as they hear more about it. But I think it's best we go to the school. Other parents are there already. They will know everything that's happening."

"It's all right. I know the way."

"Let me drive, Bernard. Look, your hands are trembling."

"Don't be silly," I said, but I found myself pushing my hands into my pockets in case she was right.

"Your in-laws are away. Their housekeeper, or whomever it was I spoke to, said she didn't know how to contact them."

"They're at a fat farm. They don't leave contact numbers; they don't like to be disturbed there."

"I'll leave all this stuff; I'll get you to the school."

It was a nerve-racking journey, with Gloria driving like a Mexican car thief and the rain beating down, and the traffic jams that always result from such storms. Gloria was giving all her attention to the road as an excuse not to engage in conversation, but I couldn't mistake how much the news had upset her.

With other circumstance it might have proved a perfect opportunity to confide in her. I strapped in tight, sat back, and looked at her. It was no good denying that I needed her. I needed her now, when the news had brought me low, and I badly needed to hear her say she loved me. I wanted to hear her say that she would gladly exchange her life in England for some lackluster pennypinching life with me. A life in some distant foreign land without an extradition treaty. But I didn't broach any of these complex and far-reaching matters. I sat huddled in her car, an old Saab that she'd got ready for rally-driving but which had blown up on a reconnaissance trip before even starting the first rally. Now it had become her London runabout, a fierce roaring beast which called for endless tinkering and a driving technique that catered to its many vices.

Billy's private school was distinguished more for its high fees and exclusivity than for its academic excellence. It had been chosen by Fiona's father. The school had made its home in a fine old creeper-covered mansion long since adapted, subdivided and bent to the needs of academe. When we arrived its gravel forecourt was crowded with the hastily parked cars of distraught parents. The marques of BMW, Volvo, Mercedes, and Rolls measured the aspirations of parents whose faith in the government's oft promised meritocracy was less than absolute.

The school matron was a plump gray-haired woman in a high-necked white blouse, pleated tweed skirt and flat-heeled shoes. She had been assigned to greet with a weary smile, and copious sweet tea and biscuits, those relatives who had flouted the instruction to stay at home by the phone.

Gloria and I were sitting in the staffroom under a colorful poster depicting the fiercer members of various endangered species of the animal world. I was on my second cup of tea, and selecting a jam-filled biscuit from the plate Gloria offered, when a thin young man in a mauve track suit told us his name was Hemingway and that he was my son's house master, while studying a clipboard and avoiding our eyes.

"I don't think your son was on the bus," he said, still looking down at his paperwork. "He's certainly not on the football team."

When I replied that I thought he was, Mr. Hemingway ran a nicotine-colored fingertip down the typewritten list on his board and said, "His name isn't here. So he couldn't have been on the bus. No spectators went along; just the team and two teachers."

"If he's not on the team and wasn't on the bus, why did you phone?" I said.

"Phone?" He looked up at me.

"My wife's office. Someone called my wife and left a message."

"But not from here," he said, tucking the clipboard under his arm. "No one from here phoned any of the parents."

"But . . ."

"No one from the school phoned. We are responding to calls but we are not alarming people." He smiled. He was obviously selected as a man who would face irate parents resolutely. "The Head was saying to me—only half an hour ago—that it was incredible that the word got around so quickly. No parents or next-of-kin have been contacted by us. It was on the radio of course, and parents phone around their friends. It must have been a friend who phoned you, not the school. The Head decided to wait until we had a proper report from the hospital, and a list of who will be held there overnight. It still hasn't come, but as you see there are at least two dozen parents here."

"How can I be sure about Billy? That he's safe?"

"The little lad must be here. On weekdays no boys are permitted to leave the school grounds without written permission. Why don't I send one of the boys to find him? This afternoon he should be at the social awareness class . . . ah, no, Mrs. Phelan is ill. Wait a moment, your son's class were swimming . . . no, I tell a lie: current affairs . . ."

They found him eventually. Billy was in the library, sitting at the back near the heating radiator, memorizing the names of the world's highest peaks for a geography test. He was wearing shorts, long socks, and a T-shirt with the slogan BAD SPELLERS OF THE WORLD—UNTIE. He was a different child here in the environment of his school, his hair parted carefully and his shoes polished. And his movements were diffident and restrained. For a moment I found it difficult to recognize him as my little Billy.

"I'm sorry, Dad," he said.

"We were worried," I said, embracing him.

He kissed Gloria. She suppressed a little sob and then blew her nose loudly on a small handkerchief that, after some rummaging, she had tugged from her handbag.

"They said I could be a reserve. One of the halfbacks had a wisdom tooth seen to. But he got better too quickly."

"Would you and Mrs. Samson like to take your son off for the evening?" said Hemingway, patting Billy on the head and smiling at Gloria. "He could miss prep, I'm sure."

"Yes," said Gloria, assuming the role of Mrs. Samson effortlessly, "we'd like to do that."

"Wow. Thank you, sir. Would that be all right, Dad? There's a super new Chinese restaurant opened in the high street, where that rotten old secondhand bookshop used to be. It starts serving early: the Peking Duck it's called—but my friends all call it the Piping Hot."

"Sounds good," I said, looking quizzically at Gloria. She nodded. "It's Gloria's car," I explained to Billy.

"That great Saab. Yes, you can see where the rally numbers used to be. And a car phone antenna. It's super. What tires do you have?"

"Go and get your coat and a scarf," I said. "And a sweater, it's cold."

I looked at Gloria. I didn't have to say anything. It was clear that Billy had seen us arrive, and gone off to hide in the library. "Who cares if he's on the football team?" I said to Gloria.

"He wants you to love him," she said. "He wants to do something to make you pleased."

"I do love him," I said testily. Was I such an ogre? It was one of those days when everyone was speaking in riddles.

"And be proud of him."

"I hate football. I hate all games," I said, "even chess." Mr. Hemingway's hearing must have been remarkably acute, for I noticed him stiffen as I said this, although his back was towards me as he stood with other parents on the far side of the room.

"Billy doesn't really like Chinese food," said Gloria. "Insist we go to that place on the bypass, it's called The Old Barn or The Manoir or something phoney like that. He can have spaghetti and meatballs and that dessert with apples that they set fire to at the table."

"So why did he say Chinese?" I hissed. Perhaps I was speaking too loud; people were looking at us.

"You said you liked Chinese one day in Islington when it was raining and we were looking for somewhere to eat lunch before going to a matinee of *Hamlet*. Billy was doing it at school. Remember?"

"Oh, yes." What a memory she had. I would have given six months' salary to have been able to remind her of what she was wearing on that lovely, perfect, happy day that I'd entirely forgotten.

"If you two—you and Billy—would just stop trying to do nice things for each other, you . . ."

She never finished what she was about to say, for Billy had made a lightning change of clothes, and was now dressed in a gray flannel uniform with the school's Latin motto on the breast pocket. He was running down the stairs swinging his raincoat in his hand.

The fact that we took Billy for a dinner of spaghetti and meatballs did not deprive him of the chance to make jokes, and parade his learning, using the name of the new Chinese eating place. The jokes ranged from oodles of noodles to snub-nosed Pekingese poodles and on to Peking man, and if we didn't laugh enough, Billy explained the reference to us. And he did it in exhaustive detail. He was, in many ways, very like me.

With every last strand of spaghetti devoured and every crêpe flamed, folded, and eaten, with jokes all told and Saab tires examined, Billy was delivered back to his school dormitory. Gloria drove me back to London. It was a perfect opportunity to have the serious talk with her that I had been putting off so long.

Perhaps I didn't choose the most prudent way to begin. "I'm going to get him away from that bloody school. He'll grow up to be a detestable little snob if he stays there. Did you notice that joke about the slow-witted policeman?"

"Oh, Bernard! Whatever are you on about? You constantly make jokes about people—dim stockbrokers and greedy politicians. Don't be so captious. Billy will never be a snob like that. He is lovely and full of fun."

"Sometimes I feel like running off with him," I said, putting a toe into the territory as lightly as I knew how. Gloria Kent, of Hungarian extraction, immediately sensed the danger: you don't grow up a foreign girl in an English school without knowing there is a minefield on both sides of every English social exchange.

"He would never go," she said.

"You sound very certain."

"He'd be miserable. He doesn't know you well enough, Bernard." I could tell from her tone that she was expecting a rush of objections from me, but I let it go and waited. "He loves you, and he knows that you love him, but you don't know him really well."

"I know him."

"You know the child he used to be."

I thought of Mr. Hemingway. Billy had spoken of his house master several times over dinner. I don't say Billy hero-worshipped Mr. Hemingway, or even admired him, but any hint of praise from Mr. Hemingway was an accolade that Billy was keen to share with us. "That would come," I said.

Gloria wasn't so sure. "He has his friends and a set routine. You can tell that from everything he said tonight. You may regard that school as a factory producing Philistine, pin-brained Englishmen of a sort you heartily despise, but it's Billy's only reality. And he likes it."

"Thanks, Gloria."

"Did you want me to baby you? You waited too long. Take him back to your fancy Mayfair apartment, but he'll be a stranger. It will all take time, Bernard. Forget any idea about waving a magic wand. He's a young man. He has a mind of his own."

"I suppose you are right," I said through gritted teeth.

"Would your wife give her phone number to the school?" said Gloria suddenly, as if she'd been thinking about it.

"No," I said.

"And not to some other parent?"

"Especially not to some other parent."

"Then who phoned the office?"

"And why?" I added.

She controlled the car with a manic skill that never quite became frenzy. As we sped along the shiny suburban streets, the neon lights made halos of bright pink and blue and green around her blond hair and painted her face with savage patterns. It didn't seem like the moment to ask Gloria if she'd like to run away with me. But in the event I didn't have to; she read my mind. And she wasn't going to let me out of the car without telling me how well she read it. "You are not in Berlin, Bernard," she said as we pulled up in front of my apartment. I reached for the door catch but not too strenuously. "You can't handle two women in that psychotic way you run from one side of the Wall to the other."

I didn't answer. I could see she had something she had to say. "I know you love me, and I love you, too," she said in the speedy perfunctory small-print way that advertisers deal out the mandatory health warnings. "But you already have a wife and children. Now you must let me alone, and let me make my own life."

"But Gloria . . ."

She tapped the accelerator just enough to make the engine growl. "Let me alone, Bernard," she implored frantically. "For God's sake, let me alone."

She stared straight ahead as I climbed out of the car. "Good night, Gloria," I said. "I don't want to hurt you."

She didn't turn her head and she didn't answer; she just drove away.

FIVE

BERWICK HOUSE, ENGLAND

I resented being sent to London Debriefing Centre to squeeze some reactions out of my brother-in-law George Kosinski. He was being detained on a warrant: which was the Department's way of saying imprisoned without promise of trial. That he was held in a lovely old eighteenth-century manor house, and permitted to wander in its seven acres of lawns and woodland, to say nothing of its rose bushes, orchard and vegetable garden, did not alter the fact that Berwick House was surrounded by a high wall. Or change the fact that the innocuous-looking men working in the grounds were armed. My unease was of course compounded by the fact that I had personally brought George from Poland. And I had submitted a report that described his long-term service as an agent of its communist government. That had been acted upon immediately; my other suggestions were ignored. I'd put aside my personal feelings about George. My anger at his treachery and stupidity had abated. Of course he was small fry by some measures, but even a low-echelon agent such as George could, if handled skillfully, provide valuable information about contacts and safe houses and all the mumbo-jumbo of enemy activities here in Britain. George had not been handled skillfully: he'd been shelved. That was partly because any such vital information he gave us would have to be handed to "Five," the Department's rivals, and give them a chance to outshine us when the time came to boast to our political masters.

So I wasn't in a happy frame of mind as I turned into the gates of Berwick House. The tires scrunched on the gravel path as I stopped for the identity check. I pulled my card from my wallet but I didn't need it. The barrier was raised immediately and we went straight through. I suppose the two guards recognized the official car and driver, and one of them seemed to recognize me. He scowled.

There had been a drastic effort to clean the place up since my last visit. The ancient army huts, and their pervading smell of tar preservative, had disappeared from what once had been the croquet lawn. KEEP OFF THE GRASS signs were staked into the mud, erected there in the hope that summer would bring grass enough to hide the huts' broken concrete foundations which had resisted the drills and bulldozers.

The rain had stopped but water was dripping from the trees and there were deep puddles in the gravel drive. Two men in coveralls were fitting cables along the bed of the newly drained moat that surrounded the redbrick main building. The irises, lilies, and bulrushes had been ripped out and stacked along the path, ready for the compost heap. As we went over the redbrick bridge to the courtyard, I could see the way the under-water alarms were being replaced with new technology. I wondered what it was costing. It didn't seem as if the Foreign Office cashiers were betting on an early end to the cold war.

The dismal and draughty entrance hall provided more evidence of the many changes that Berwick House had undergone over the years. Its history was to be seen in the notices that defaced the lovely paneled walls. The earliest notice was poster-sized, protected by heavy glass, and framed in oak. It declared Berwick House to be a "prohibited place" by order of the Secretary of State (1911 Act, section three). The typography was Victorian, its style like a sedate theatre playbill. Amended and supplemented by the Official Secrets Act of 1920 and 1939, it must have been fixed to the wall soon after Berwick House was taken over by the authorities in that week after war was declared. There were other notices, of varying age, dealing with everything from fire precautions to the playing of transistor radios and not smoking. Now that so many Home Office employees, security men, and Special Branch officers were carrying handguns, there was a lock-up closet for guns, and bright new notices: STRICTLY NO FIREARMS BEYOND THIS POINT. On one of my previous visits they mislaid the Walther PPK I was carrying and tried to give me a nickel-plated Spanish Astra in its place. It took me an hour to sort it out. Since then I had always made a point of saying I was unarmed.

Having signed the book, and noted that the previous visitor's signature was dated four days earlier, I collected my "exit chit" and was taken up to see George. I was pleased to find that he had been assigned relatively comfortable rooms. Number five suite was one of the best accommodations, after the staff offices and Governor's apartment. It was large. Its position on a corner of the first floor provided two windows for the drawing room and extensive views of the grounds. The room was exceptionally tidy; neurotically so. His red velvet slippers were placed alongside his chair, cushions plumped and exactly positioned, even the newspapers were neatly folded as if ready for resale. The book he was reading—*The Last Grain Race* by Newby—had a page marked with a slip of newspaper. The book, and a case for his spectacles, were positioned upon the newspapers with care.

George Kosinski was standing at the window, looking out at the bare trees and the high walls that surrounded the property. He took off his heavy spectacles as if to see me better. "Bernard. They said you were coming." His accent—the hard high pitch of London's docklands—revealed his origins, despite his West End clothes.

George Kosinski was forty years old. A stocky, restless Londoner born of Polish parents, he had inherited all the moodiness and poetic melancholy of his forebears. He looked well but dispirited. He'd trimmed his mustache and cut his gray, wavy hair shorter. Now, despite the well-cut pants, monogrammed shirt, and soft Italian moccasin shoes, I did not see much of the flashy tycoon that I remembered from earlier days.

"I was ordered to come," I told him. "I knew that if you wanted to see me, you would have sent a message."

His quirky smile suggested that, should he ever find himself in need of help or sustenance, my name was not one that would naturally come to his mind.

"Shall we take a walk?" I said. He went across the room to get his coat. "Wrap up, it's cold outside."

"I haven't had a breath of fresh air for a week," he said. It was not true. I had asked that he should not be allowed his daily walk for the two days before I arrived simply because I wanted him to feel a bit cooped up. But I knew from the record that he normally spent an hour outside each day. I knew what he ate, and what he complained about. I even knew how many times a day he went to the toilet. Detainee reports are thorough in some respects. "I hate this place," he said.

"I know," I said. He could hardly hate it more than I did. There was never anything enjoyable about coming down here to hear the contrived fictions of men who saw the error of their ways only after getting caught.

Yet the deeper reason I hated it so much was because of the odor of despair that visits here brought to my nostrils. Berwick House was the end of the trail for the men locked away here. Even those released without officially ordained punishment did not go unscathed. No one escapes the discontent that pitiless self-examination brings to those who try to serve two masters. Of the men I'd seen here, at least four eventually took their own life. Then there were the tragic cases, like Giles Trent, murdered in error when a disinformation plan went wrong. And Erich Stinnes, a KGB man I killed in a messy exchange of rounds that sent his arterial blood gushing into one of my recurring nightmares.

George put on his coat and looked in a mirror to arrange his hat and cashmere scarf. It always encouraged a detainee to be taken away from the rooms where microphones could be hidden. London Debriefing Centre's handling of George had not been done properly. LDC staff never seemed to learn how important the preparation period was, and how much it affected the interrogation. George was not angry, he was not restless and he was not pacing up and down in frustration. It was too quiet and too comfortable here, and he had been given nothing to do. That gave him too much time to think. Thinking at night, when sleep is being lost, is good; but thinking in the daytime is bad. Opportunities for thinking were not desirable when you held a man such as George. Giving him time to reflect gave him time to reconsider, to invent cover stories, weave elaborate lies, suppress guilt and justify his treason. Furthermore I was not an experienced interrogator; I was just a member of George's family.

"I know why you came," he said. We had walked around the walled vegetable garden in silence, apart from George identifying the dead and dying herbs that had been planted in an elaborate cruciform pattern. "You want to know if Tessa was a part of it." He bent to pick some leaves.

"Was she?"

"You don't care about me. It's Tessa you are worried about. Tessa and what she might have been hearing from your wife over the years. What she might have told me and what I might have passed along the line."

"I can't say I've worried about that angle a great deal," I told him.

"No? Then you'd better start worrying about it. You can bet that's the part of it your masters are worried about." He threw away the leaf and pushed his glasses into place with his forefinger. They were always slipping down his nose. I don't know why he chose such heavy frames.

"Is that what they've been asking you here?" I said. I knew it wasn't; I'd seen the transcripts.

He pulled a face. "Yes, and no. They go around and around. Yesterday we were talking about my school-days. One of them is a psychiatrist, complete with a slide show. And even a book of those damned inkblot patterns. I thought those things were ancient history by now."

"Rorschach test patterns. Yes, well that's normal routine," I said, in case George had formed some kind of paranoid resentment about it.

"Tess was implicated right from the beginning," said George.

I didn't respond.

"Sorrel," said George reaching down to pluck a large green leaf, crushing it in his hand, and then sniffing at it. "I suppose it grows all the year round. I didn't know that. Not much aroma."

"Where were you at school, George? London I suppose, with an accent like yours. Was it a school in Poplar?"

He swung his head round to stare up at me, hardly able to believe that I was not going to follow up his tempting nugget about the treason of his wife Tessa, and the possible involvement of me and my wife, too.

"Yes, good old Poplar," he said, stressing his cockney accent. "You knew that of course. But they say a trial lawyer should never ask a question to which he doesn't already know the answer."

"I'm not a lawyer," I said.

"But you've done your homework, Bernard. And I admire the way you steer away from the subject of Tessa as if not interested."

"It's not a matter of being interested, George. It's simply that I recognize it as a bit of bloody nonsense. You'll have to do better than that to get my undivided attention."

"Will I, Bernard? Well, you deny it. You'll have plenty to deny by the time I've finished spilling my guts to them."

"For instance?" I said.

He was getting intense now. That was what I wanted. He pretended to be giving all his attention to the herbs. Upon his open hand he had laid out an array of them, some curled and brittle and blackened by frost, others hard and green and aromatic. He prodded at the leaves with a fingertip, as if giving them all his attention. "Mint. That one I don't recognize. Marjoram. Bay . . . but its real name is *Laurus nobilis*. Sometimes cookery writers translate it as laurel, but laurel leaves are a deadly poison."

"And taste like hell," I said affably, as if I didn't mind his absurd little herb recognition rigmarole.

He looked at me quizzically. "Like bitter almonds, at least that's what I read somewhere. It's the writers who make all the mistakes, Bernard. The people who worship little pieces of paper with writing on. The cooks and gardeners never get it wrong because they don't care what it's called."

I grunted. I suppose it was a spontaneous and clumsy attempt to show me how wrong it was to categorize him as an enemy. The truth, as he no doubt saw it, was that decent old George had tried to play some sort of game that wouldn't harm either side. I was able to guess the meaning underlying George's allegory only because nearly everyone locked up here persuaded themselves that the truth was something along those lines.

"'For instance,' you ask me," he said. "For instance, I could tell them about Tessa's relationship with that fellow Trent, the communist agent. He was one of your people, wasn't he? Then there was your meeting with that CIA maverick Posh Harry ... a meeting you arranged in my offices in Southwark."

"That was years ago, George." I said it as calmly as I could. Locked up here and brooding upon the way I had brought him to book, George had lots of time, lots of motivation, and all the necessary ingenuity, to weave a thousand unconnected incidents into a web from which I wouldn't escape. Perhaps his fabrications wouldn't completely convince the interrogators, the D-G or the Appeals Board that I was a traitor, but the result might give them an excuse to discharge me as unreliable without feeling guilty about it.

"These interrogators are not fools, George. They have come across spiteful nonsense before. Implicating friends and relatives—it's not unusual in our sort of business."

He threw the herbs away and rubbed his hands together and looked at me. "No? How often do you have a prisoner here revealing what he knows about relatives who have top jobs in your 'sort of business'? His sister-in-law? His brother-in-law? His wife? Tell me how often, Bernard. Oh, they'll listen. When I start talking, they'll listen. You can bet on that."

Now it was all coming out: overt threats delivered with malicious intensity. Concealed beneath George's assumed calm there was a desperate drowning man, one whose flailing would pull down with him anyone he could clutch. "Not often," I said. "You're a special case."

He nodded and smiled grimly. "Yes, I am. So if it's a servile confession you've come here for, forget it."

"I'm not your implacable enemy, George," I said. "Your wisest course is to tell the truth." I'd been sent here to Berwick House on Bret Rensselaer's instructions. Bret had told me to start him talking. Well, in that respect my visit certainly seemed to have been a success. The trouble was that George seemed to have focused all his animosity on me.

"You're right, Bernard. It's damned cold out here. Let's go back into the warm."

There was nothing to be gained from letting George use me as a punching bag for all his frustration and resentment. But while we were still in the garden and away from the microphones I tried to make my own position clear.

"Listen to me carefully, George," I said. "I came here today because I was ordered to come. But before coming I put away as much of my personal feelings as I could possibly repress. With great difficulty, I'm still doing that. But you choose to make it personal and threaten me. You threaten me with your lousy, rotten lies and fairy stories." George was looking at me with his eyes open. I think he had never seen me really angry before. "Listen to me carefully, George. When you face the interrogators you tell them the truth, the whole truth, and any excuses you can invent." I grabbed his upper arm and squeezed as tight as I could. This hurt him I suppose, for he pulled a face but didn't cry out. "But if you tell lies about me, I will beat you bloody. I won't kill you or even cripple you but I will hurt you, George." I shook him so that his teeth rattled. I hoped there was no one watching us. "Even if it costs me my job, my pension, or six months in the nick, I will beat the daylights out of you. And I'll get to you even if I have to break down doors."

As soon as I loosened my grip on his arm he stepped well back from me. My words had been mild enough, but he must have seen the rage that I felt brimming up inside me. He'd seen it in my eyes, and in my face, for now he stared at me as if he was frightened to look away lest I assaulted him. Behind his spectacle lenses his eyes were bright and his cheeks pinched and pallid. "You're a madman," he said in a breathless voice. "You should be put away in psychiatric care, Bernard. What's happened to you? I'm family; I'm family." He touched his face as if I had slapped him. It was as if the mere thought of the physical beating had brought him pain.

"Don't Bernard me, you bastard." I'd kept my anger under control for too long, and now I was on the verge of going wild. I took a deep breath and remained rooted there staring at him as I recovered my composure. I told myself that this wasn't the time and place; and that George wasn't really the enemy. George was a nothing, a delivery boy, a kid from the paddling pool who'd fallen into the deep end. George was a child on a visit to the zoo, prodding a finger through the bars of the cage to distinguish moth-eaten fur rug from bad-tempered gorilla. Now he knew. But it was too late to make much difference. I didn't say anything else to him. I returned him to his room, got a "body receipt" signature from the floor clerk, signed out, called for the car, and went home.

I went directly back to London, apart from a brief stop off at a big hotel on London's outskirts. It called itself an inn, and this deception was furthered by the way some architect, who had OD'd on Hollywood Westerns, had provided it with a shiny interior of fake Victorian advertising mirrors and plastic paneling. There were pinball tables, too: like glass comic books and flashing and clicking furiously, the sound echoing around the place that was empty of customers other than the driver and me.

The driver stuck to orange juice but I needed a whisky. A large single malt: a Laphroaig. The barman could only find Glenfiddich, so I had two of those instead. Fortified with the smoky taste, I made a couple of calls from the public phone in the lobby. I liked public phones, they were more private than private ones, and the calls more or less untraceable. But none of the calls got any response at the other end. The Swede had not gone home. It made me angry to think he had taken my money and continued his drunken spree. God only knows where he was. His answering machine at his home in Sweden was switched off. There was no answer from the airfield he used, and his contact number in London was giving out the shrill sounds of a line that has been disconnected. I cursed my own stupidity. I'd heard rumors that the Swede went off on melancholy bouts of drunken roving, but I'd not believed them. For years our assignments together had found him a model of competence and sobriety. It was the big bundle of cash that had tempted him of course. But why did it have to be my money?

I hung up the telephone and went into the toilet. The door banged behind me and I looked up. Two men— dressed in leather jackets and jeans—had followed me. Both looked like manual workers, but there was a marked age disparity. The elder man was about thirty-five. He stopped and stood with his back against the door to make sure we were not interrupted. He was a strong man, taller than me, and with calloused hands and battered face. A boxer, judging by the stance he adopted. Boxers can never get out of the habit of standing with their toes turned in.

The younger man was about twenty, with wavy hair and long sideburns. I'd only glanced at them. Now I went to the sink and turned both taps and took liquid soap into my hand as if I was about to wash. Keeping my head down over the bowl, I watched in the mirror as the younger man came up behind me. He thought he had me cold, so he was careless. I turned and slapped the liquid soap into his face. He must have thought it was ammonia or something harmful, for he reared away with his eyes closed and mouth open in a splutter of anger. I hit him hard in the belly, and gave him a jab in the nose as he bent forward. He dropped the knuckleduster he'd been holding and it landed on the tiles with a clatter. But the little guy was tough. He straightened up and shook his head and came at me again. He punched at me with the straight sort of blow that comes from a lot of time at the punching bag, and his fist connected with the side of my face as I ducked aside. It was lucky for me that he'd lost his brass knuckles, otherwise even that glancing blow would have sent me reeling. As it was, the pain of it rattled me. I grabbed at his jacket and held him as I tried to butt my head into his face, but the liquid soap I'd thrown at him was now all over the floor. I slipped on it and only kept my balance by hanging on to his jacket.

There was something absurd about the way we waltzed around the tiled floor, slipping and sliding and punching and clinching with neither of us able to land a decisive blow.

Under my coat, in a shoulder holster, I was carrying a sample of Heckler and Koch's best hardware. I'd been wearing it since the personal security alert. I had taken no notice of Dicky's taunts, figuring that the sort of hard men the other side were using lately might not accurately discern that I wasn't senior staff.

As my feet found a drier piece of floor, I was steady enough to get a better hold on him. I slammed him backwards, pounding him into his partner with enough force to knock the breath out of both of them. As the younger one turned his upper body to avoid my blows, I kicked his knee. The toe of my shoe found the right place, so that his leg buckled and he dropped full-length to the floor. I kicked him again and his face went bloody. It was crude stuff but these were crude people.

It gave me enough time to open my coat and get to my gun. Holding it tight I brought it round to slap the elder man in the side of the face. He was a tough old bird but the gun was heavy steel, and I hit him hard enough to cut him. He gasped with surprise as much as with the pain. It gave me a chance to knee him hard in the balls. As he went down I slammed him again with the gun and took a pace backwards to wave it at them.

The old one put his hands high enough to change the light bulbs. A VP70 is customarily carried with a round in the chamber, and you don't have to be Superman to fire off its eighteen rounds like a machine gunner.

"Keep still, old man," I told him. "I'll waste you and laugh."

He didn't answer. I frisked him and then bent down to the youngster on the floor and made sure he didn't have a gun. I took his knuckleduster from where it had fallen and stuffed it up his nostrils. "Next time I'll kill you," I promised cheerfully. "If not me, one of my friends will kill you. Either way, you wind up dead. You understand?" Neither of them replied, but I could see they got the idea. "I should put a bullet into both of you. There is a drain here, and tiles, so it won't make a mess." I let them think about it for a minute. "Scram—while I'm in a good mood."

The old fellow bent and effortlessly lifted his chum to his feet. He said, "Let me explain, old pal."

"Shut up."

"It's not you we are after. It's the Swede."

"Get out of here before I change my mind."

I wiped my face and straightened myself out. I put the gun into my coat pocket, so I could get to it quickly, and went back into the bar. I wasn't going to be driving, so I quickly downed another whisky.

Outside it was cold. I checked the car park for strangers but the cars were all empty. My driver was already at the wheel and waiting for me. "Is there some kind of trouble?" he asked when I got into the back seat of the car. I suppose I was trembling or hyped up or dishevelled. I'm not sure what it was.

"You stupid bastard," I said. "You'd sit drinking your bloody orange juice while the opposition wasted me, wouldn't you?"

"What happened?"

"Forget it," I said. "Next time stick to Scotch; that citric acid you are drinking is eating up your brain." The driver was an ex-cop. He was supposed to be guarding the passengers he carried. That's what he was paid to do.

Suddenly all the strength went out of me and I slumped back in my seat. Perhaps I had over-reacted to the two men. I often over-reacted. It was why I had stayed alive so long. But neither of the two had been armed, except for the knuckleduster. I wondered what they intended to do and who might have sent them. If they were really looking for the Swede, what sort of racket were they in with him?

We reached outer London as darkness came. The outward-bound traffic lanes were jammed with commuters going home. I spotted a flower shop still open. On impulse I stopped the car, went in, and had them send to Gloria a dozen long-stemed red roses. On the greetings tag I wrote "How can I thank you enough?" I didn't sign it. At the time it seemed like a tender, restrained, and appropriate way to say thanks.

The Department had a long-standing regulation about burglars. Any employee finding strange marks around the keyhole of their front door was obliged to call the Duty Officer before proceeding inside. Of course no one obeyed this inconvenient and draconian order. It had been drafted after a female typist left some official papers on the underground train, and invented a story about her apartment in Fulham being broken into. No one believed her story except a simpleton named Henry Tiptree, the investigating officer, who drafted the new regulation as a way to justify the time and money he wasted asking everyone working for London Underground a lot of stupid questions.

I didn't do anything like that when I got back home and found the door was not double-locked. I turned the key very quietly and opened the door very slowly. Poking my head inside the door, I heard a movement upstairs. I closed the door behind me and then tiptoed up the stairs. I moved along the bedroom corridor.

"Oh, you made me jump!"

"Jesus, Fi! I thought you were a burglar!"

"What a lovely greeting, darling. You always

know the right thing to say." Fiona was standing in the doorway of the tiny dressing room that had become a boxroom and storeroom, too. She was holding up a black cocktail dress, as if trying to decide whether to consign it to Oxfam. Behind her, our largest suitcase was balanced on the rollaway bed where her sister had often slept after fighting with her husband George.

I put away my gun and went and kissed her. She smiled and kissed me back, but she did it without relinquishing her hold on the dress. "Are you all right, darling?" she asked. "You look funny."

"I thought you were in Rome," I said.

"I was. Now I'm off to Düsseldorf. Dicky can't do the European Community Security Conference and Bret says someone has to be there to wave the flag." She leaned over her suitcase to count the packets of pantyhose and added an extra one.

"When do you have to be there?"

"I came back to get more clothes. And I'm having my rough notes printed out and spiral-bound, to look impressive. I'm going to the office to pick them up . . ." She looked at her watch. "My God! Is that the time? I'll never catch the plane."

"Did you hear about the bus accident? Billy's school? The football team."

"Yes. Billy sent me a fax, and the office sent it on to me. I had my girl phone the office and tell you. Why did you go rushing down there, darling? You had everyone at the office worried. And it's bad for the children if you make a crisis out of every little thing."

"You phoned?"

"No. I just told you: my girl phoned. I didn't want you to worry."

"A fax?"

"Billy sent Daddy a fax about the crash as soon as it happened. He often faxes them from the school office. Daddy fixed it up with the house master. And Daddy told Billy that unless he sent me a fax at least once a week he'd get no pocket money. It's worked wonders, I must say. Daddy's awfully clever with the children." She picked up a cobalt-blue party dress and held it against her, and then did the same with a dark green one. "Which one do you think, darling?"

"A bit formal, aren't they?"

"These European people always have a rather grand dinner and ball on the last night."

"The green one," I said. "You looked lovely in that at Dicky's the other night."

"It is pretty, isn't it? But the shoes that go with it are getting scuffed." She put the green dress back into the wardrobe and packed the blue dress in her suitcase. "When are you due back in Berlin?"

"They want me here in London for that meeting tomorrow and another on Tuesday."

"Unless George says something startling there will be very few items on the agenda," she said.

"The D-G will be there, and Bret is chairing it. It's a hot potato. I think they want to fix lead weights on it, and drop it into the archives. Dicky is encouraging the idea that the sooner the whole Polish fiasco is forgotten, the better it will be for everyone. And that means forgetting George's activities, too."

"You saw George? Will they release him?"

"Even the D-G can't make that decision alone, but yes I think they'll let him go. Five may guess we're holding him but they can't be sure. In any case they probably won't make difficulties, providing he comes clean and then goes straight back to Switzerland and keeps *stumm*."

"How can you be so confident that Five will agree?"

"I asked around."

"You know people at Five that well?" From her tone of voice it sounded as if Fiona disapproved of my having friends in the Security Service. I smiled and didn't answer. "Don't be disloyal to the Department, darling," she said in that throaty tone that I have always found so seductive. "Nothing is more important than that."

"No," I said. "Nothing is more important than that."

"I only asked," said Fiona quickly and defensively. "I'm not going to report you to the D-G, or Internal Security," she added sarcastically. "Why do they want you there? Doesn't Frank usually come over for those policy meetings? Something bad?"

"My role is to say yes to everything. Then, when it all goes wrong, Frank can say I never told him."

"And will it all go wrong?"

"I don't know," I said. "And I don't much care." I went into the bedroom where I had spotted a cup of coffee Fiona had abandoned. I sipped some of it. For the first time I could say "I don't care" with all my heart. I'd been suffering agonies of guilt about abandoning Fiona and taking the children with me, but now I shed those penitent feelings in a sudden joyful instant. I wouldn't be here to concern myself with how the review committee disposed of George Kosinski, and swept under the carpet their foul-ups in Poland and elsewhere. I couldn't any longer worry how Fiona, and her egoistic father, arranged their lives. I wouldn't be a part of their lives any longer, and neither would my children.

I know I shouldn't have felt resentment or envy that

Billy had been sending a regular fax letter to his mother, but couldn't it have been arranged without the threat of withdrawing his pocket money? And couldn't there have been a copy forwarded to me? No matter. When I had Billy and Sally to myself I'd make sure I did the right thing for Fiona, and even for her parents. And I would have Gloria, too, if everything went according to plan.

I looked at the next room, and at Fiona standing under the merciless bare bulb that lit it. She was trying to close the lid of her suitcase upon a tall pile of beautifully folded clothes interleaved with white tissue paper. She was kneeling on the rollaway bed, pushing down on the lid of the case with all her might, but she couldn't get it closed. Unaware that I was watching her, she gave a scarcely audible sob that combined anger with despair. There were tears shining on her cheeks and her eyes were bright and mad. Was she worn out, just frazzled, angry and bordering on the hysterical due to her worries about the work she did, and her unremitting schedule? Or was this a glimpse into her real mental state?

"Are you all right, darling?" I called from the bedroom without letting her know I had seen her break down and cry.

Slowly she got to her feet and came at snail's pace to the door. She leaned an arm against the door frame and whispered, "Would you mind helping me, darling? I never can seem to close it."

She never could seem to close it because she put ten times as many clothes into the case as it was designed to hold. And like all women, she thought that all it needed was a man's weight and muscle to shut and lock it. It never occurred to her that the hinges were being strained to the breaking point. I got the case and put it on the floor. After a struggle, I got it closed and locked. "You'd better put a strap round it," I said. "You've put far too much into it. One of these days it's going to burst open and scatter your silk panties across the carousel."

"Don't be silly, darling. I've cut back to the bare minimum; I should have my low-heel shoes, my new hat, and some more woolens really. Düsseldorf will be cold at this time of year," she added with unanswerable logic. Then, on the carpet at her feet, she noticed the fabric flower, a white camellia that must have fallen off her Chanel dress when I was trying to get the case closed. She picked it up, and as she pretended to smell it she looked at me and smiled. She had restored herself, wiped her tears, and polished her smile. She picked up a hairbrush and began putting it through her hair in a way she used to do every evening before she went to bed.

What had happened to her after she defected; during those terrible years when she was a double agent? She seldom talked of it, but once she'd confided that the worst part was the interrogation that took place when she first arrived over there. The Soviets have many skilled interrogators; it is a talent born of their sort of paranoia. And there would be no relaxation of their rigor even when they were questioning "a heroine of the battle for socialism." It was a lonely business, she said, and then changed it to being a solitary business. "But after surviving those endless questions I never felt really lonely again," she'd told me. "I often felt isolated and sometimes I felt forsaken, but I never felt lonely. I knew I was lucky just to have survived it." Poor Fiona.

"A penny for your thoughts, darling," she said.

"Nothing," I said, and before I had to invent a lie the phone rang. I was nearest, and when I answered it the night-duty clerk told me that the car was on its way.

When I relayed this message to Fiona she emphatically denied that it could be for her.

"I have no car. Bret's driver is taking me to the airport. I think I'll phone and ask him to bring the typed report with him from the office. No, it can't be anyone for me, darling."

"Who is the car for?" I asked the duty clerk.

"For you, Mr. Samson. Mr. Rensselaer and Mr. Cruyer will be collecting you in five minutes. Would you please go downstairs and wait for them. It's very urgent, they said. Very, very urgent."

SIX

MAYFAIR, LONDON

"Who is it? Bernard? Good! Put your skates on and hurry on down. I'm in a car at your front door and it's urgent. Urgent."

It was Dicky Cruyer's reedy voice on the apartment's doorphone speaker. I had only put the phone down two minutes before, and now he was at my door. He was taking no chances on my finding a way to escape him.

"What's happened?" I said into the door phone.

"Yes, I know you've had a long day, Bernard. We all have. Jump to it, there's a good chap."

I felt like pointing out that Dicky's long days were invariably punctuated by leisurely lunches followed sometimes by a postprandial doze in his office with the "meeting in progress" sign switched on.

Fiona was toying with the fabric camellia, wondering perhaps whether to ask me to open the case again.

She looked at me as I hung up. "Dicky," I said. "He's downstairs, waiting for me."

"It's late," she said.

"Do you know what it might be?" I asked. She shook her head. I unlocked my desk and got the VP70 pistol that had proved so useful against the hoodlums. It was a bit on the heavy side, but used with a soft holster it was a nice smooth gun that didn't rip the linings from my jackets. She watched me test it and check the magazine but didn't comment. Things had changed; there was a time when the sight of me packing a gun brought out all her anxieties. I said, "I'll be off then."

"Good-bye, darling," she said. "I'll miss you." She held her arms out to me.

We embraced and I kissed her. "Have a safe trip," I said. She shivered.

"Oh, I forgot," she said into my ear as if cooing songs of love. "That silly girl . . . the one Dicky has given me as a temporary secretary, opened one of your letters."

"Was it anything exciting?" I said, still holding her tightly.

"The bank. You were terribly overdrawn. Three thousand and something . . . and four hundred . . . I forget exactly how much. I transferred some money from my account to tide you over."

"You shouldn't have done that," I said. "I have back-pay due . . . overdue, in fact."

"We are not so rich we want to pay those bloodsuckers any more bank overdrafts," she said. "Or are we?"

"Thanks," I said.

"There's no need to give me so much housekeeping money. Not while you are in Berlin."

"You are my wife," I said doggedly.

"I worry about you," she said. "Daddy gives me more money than I need. And it must be terribly expensive for you in Germany with the mark going up and up."

"I manage."

"I wish I could be with you." Her fingers explored my waist. "You've lost weight." I turned my head and looked into her moist eyes. It was never easy to know exactly what was in her mind. Perhaps that was why she was able to hold her own among all those inscrutable public school ruffians. I was not convinced by her wish. Why should she want to be with me? She'd be confirmed as permanent Deputy Europe within a month or two. No woman had ever got that high on the promotion ladder. Perhaps she guessed what was in my mind, for after what seemed ages she said, "Do you love me, Bernard?"

"Yes, I love you." It was true. I loved her no less than I had always loved her. The only difference was that now I loved Gloria, too, and, no matter how I tried, I couldn't stop thinking of her. "Take care, darling."

Waiting for me in the street there was a black Rolls-Royce with three whip antennas. It was not a new car; it was tall and angular, built in those days before every Rolls wanted to squat down and look like a Mercedes.

The driver opened the door for me. "Jump in," said Dicky, indicating the little folding jump seat upon which he had been resting his boots. It was warm inside the car, the engine was purring away and the heater was on. Dicky slumped on the black leather back seat with Bret Rensselaer in the far corner.

Bret nodded to me. He was hunched stiffly against the arm rest in a dark suit, charcoal-gray tie, starched white shirt, and gleaming black Oxfords neatly laced.

His face was dejected and his hands clasped as if in prayer. The sleek Rolls belonged to Bret: elderly, respected, formal, and waxen, like the man himself. Like some other American Anglophiles I'd met, Bret had an obsession with renowned old English motorcars if they had an extra long wheelbase and elaborate custom-made coachwork with brass fittings and silk tassels.

Dicky was wearing scrubbed jeans, and a dark blue cable-knit sweater, the collar of his denim shirt just visible above the neck of it. The way he now rested one leg across his knee revealed the cleated sole of his stylish cross-country boot. Bundled alongside him on the seat he had his leather jacket. It looked as if Bret had picked him up from home at short notice.

"What's the problem?" I asked as the driver started the engine and pulled away.

"You'll see," said Dicky. "One of your pals is the problem . . ."

"We don't know," said Bret, speaking over Dicky's voice with an irritable tone that made Dicky dry up, look contrite, and chew a fingernail energetically, as if trying to press the words back into his mouth.

For a few minutes neither of them spoke.

"Are we driving around the park until the spirits try to contact us?" I said.

Bret gave his famous fleeting smile. But within a few minutes the car had emerged from Park Lane, passed Buckingham Palace, and was heading south.

"Special Branch are there. Five are there, too. It will be a Goddamned circus. I don't want any part of it, unless you need my clout. You and Dicky go inside and look. We'll park around the corner; I'll stay in the car."

"Look at what?" I said.

"A body," said Bret. "They are getting impatient.

They will move him as soon as you've had a chance to look. They will have made photos and taken all the measurements by the time we arrive."

"One of our people?"

"That's what Five claim," said Bret. "They say one of their people recognized him."

"He was carrying a gun," said Dicky.

"Maybe a gun," conceded Bret. "I had conflicting reports about the gun."

"A field agent?" I asked. I wondered why they wouldn't just tell me all they knew, but I could see they were both disturbed by it. Dicky was wringing his hands with occasional interludes while he chewed his nails. Bret looked drawn, breathless, and stiff. The desk people seldom came into contact with the blood and snot of the Department. Any sudden reminder that they weren't working in Treasury or Agriculture came as a nasty shock. "It's not Harry Strang, is it?"

"Harry Strang?" Dicky's cry was scoffing in tone. "Why should it be Harry Strang?"

"I don't know," I said.

"You do come out with some ideas, Bernard. Sometimes I wonder what goes on in that brainbox of yours." He gave a brief mirthless chuckle and glanced at Bret, who was looking out of the window. "Harry Strang," he said reflectively. "Harry Strang retired ages ago."

"They are holding someone," said Bret. "A youngster. He found the body."

"They will have to charge him or let him go," said Dicky. "We thought you might want to take a look at him. Just in case . . ."

"In case of what?"

"In case you recognize him," said Dicky. "You're

inside and outside, too. You are in Berlin and London. You're always on the go. You know everyone." He looked at Bret; this time Bret met his eyes. "Departmental people, I mean."

"Do I? Perhaps I do." What sort of people did these two know then? I had the feeling that they had brought me along for some other reason; for some reason they didn't want to admit.

Wimbledon. Once it had been a pretty little village outside London. But when this became the spot where the mighty South Western Railway touched the networks serving London's southern suburbs, Wimbledon ceased to be a village. A frequent train service, season tickets, and affordable housing had helped London swallow it up. The big lighted signs we passed offered Thai takeaways, Big Macs, unisex sauna, rented videos, and the brilliantly lit products of The Handmade Belgian Chocolate Shop.

Wide and tree-lined, the backstreet in which we came to a stop was quiet. The houses were large with fake-timber facades, front lawns, and wide gravel in-and-out drives. They were built for families who enjoyed Assam tea, and heather honey on Hovis toast, in front of a coal fire, until a nanny in a starched apron came and said it was time for the children to take their bath.

But they were no longer family homes, at least not many of them remained as such. Carefully painted noticeboards stared over the privet hedges to tell you that they were nursery schools or "residential homes." While in Catholic countries men and women selflessly shared their homes and children with their aged relatives, in Protestant countries equally selfless men and women spent every last penny to lock their aged relatives away to languish in such places as these. Here the warm and well-fed unwanted spent their final years seated side by side watching television with the volume very loud. They were plied with sweet tea and fruit cake and frozen dinners by nurses from the Indian subcontinent where the Assam tea comes from. And spent their final days in refined despair.

Bret remained in his warm car parked out of sight. Dicky walked ahead of me using his flashlight to find the gate of the house we were looking for. The building was dark, and encased in an elaborate builder's scaffolding, like an angular version of the bare trees that framed it. There was a man standing on the doorstep. He was in civilian clothes but his stance, and the quiet way in which he challenged our approach, revealed him as a policeman. When he'd seen our identity cards we went in. Just inside the door there was a uniformed cop who'd found a kitchen chair to perch upon. He was reading a paperback book—*Linda Goodman's Sun Signs*—that he pushed out of sight as we came upon him.

The whole house was in the process of being gutted by builders. Walking through it was precarious. At the front, a part of the floor was missing so that the cellar was visible. Only the staircase remained to show what a lovely old place it had once been. Dicky used his flashlight as we picked our way through the debris: a cement mixer, broken timber, ladders and bent buckets.

There were voices from the back of the house. I recognized the slight, notably refined, Edinburgh accent of "Squeaky" King of MI5, a prima donna of the Security Service. There were four of them there. The only one I didn't recognize was a tall pale-faced man wearing a soft felt hat, loosened silk scarf and ill-fitting fawn-colored overcoat. His stiff white collar and dark tie marked him as a senior police officer in improvised disguise. There was a police doctor with him, a man I knew from the old days. I recognized him because of his distinctively worn-out, capacious leather bag of the kind that doctors cart around. There was also Keith Golds of Special Branch, a wily old-timer. I winked at Keith. I could see he'd been here a long time putting up with Squeaky, who technically was in charge. Squeaky was wearing his usual winter outfit: a short sheepskin overcoat with its woolly collar pulled up high around his neck. On his head he had a close-fitting checked cap. With his flushed face and squinted eyes he had the look of a race-track tout.

"Hello, Bernard," said Squeaky with a marked lack of enthusiasm.

"This is Mr. Cruyer," I said, and introduced Dicky to him. Or maybe I introduced King to Dicky. I always seem to do it the wrong way round; and some people, including Dicky, sometimes take that as a serious blow to their pride.

"Show me," said Dicky, without spending too much time on polite exchanges of compliments. At the coal-face we always got along well with the workers from Five but Dicky and Squeaky conducted themselves like viceroys, charged with upholding the authority of their tribal chiefs. Squeaky didn't disguise his feelings about Dicky intruding into Five territory, while Dicky treated Squeaky like a judge censuring some pretentious traffic cop.

"Into the breach once more, dear friends," said Squeaky, leading the way.

Golds rolled his eyes. I suppose they'd all suffered quite a lot from Squeaky while waiting for us to arrive.

He led us into the garage, a separate structure which, until the construction work began, had been connected to the front drive by means of a tarmac area at the side of the house. Temporarily it had become a storage area. They'd taken one of the electric cables the building workers were using, and rigged a bare bulb to illuminate it. There were empty oil drums and some tea chests and wooden crates all stacked up as high as they could go, and throwing long shadows.

"Here we are," said Squeaky, like a stage conjuror bringing a rabbit from the hat.

The others had seen it before. They'd had a chance to get ready for it. But even I found it gruesome. Dicky looked away and made a retching noise that became a clearing of the throat and then a cough. He got out his little Filofax notebook and buried his head in it.

The body had been moved. A chalked outline showed where it had fallen to sprawl across an oily drip tray. Everything had spilled out; the dark ancient oil and fresh blood had grown tacky and made a strange pattern like a map of a mythical country drawn across the floor. The corpse was now laid out nearby, and we gathered round it like a funeral party. The upper part of the head was a bloody mess, wire-frame spectacles smashed into it, and the skull battered brutally. Only the lower part of his bloodied face was recognizable. His thin lips twisted in rictus mortis. "When a man is born, he cries and others laugh; when he dies he smiles and other cry," says the old German proverb. But there were no tears from these mourners.

"What's the score, Doc?" I said when no explanation was forthcoming.

"Nasty, isn't it?" said the doctor. "He took a dozen or more blows with a hammer."

"We have the hammer," said Squeaky.

"Cause of death?" I asked.

"The killer wielded the hammer with tremendous force," said the doctor. "Right-handed man. You can almost rule out a woman; not many women with that sort of strength."

"We're looking for a right-handed male tennis champion, are we, Doc?"

"I'm only trying to be helpful," said the doctor.

"Just tell me the cause of death," I said slowly and clearly. "Mr. Cruyer can write it into his notebook. Then we can all go home and get to bed."

"How can I be sure what happened or when?" They always start off with a disclaimer. "Elderly man, viciously attacked: could be heart attack . . ." He gave a quick look at me. "What the layman calls myocardial infarction. Or perhaps just old-fashioned shock. He has multiple skull fractures of course. One of the hammer blows made a deep puncture over the eye." He stooped to point. "That's probably the one that did it. His eye on that side has a blown pupil. That's usually a clincher. But I'm just a pill pusher. You'd better wait for the post-mortem."

"He was standing up?"

"Yes. He must have taken a gruesome amount of punishment before he went down. At least five blows. You can see from the blood splashes. More blows while he was on the ground. The top of the crown of his skull is intact."

"The hands?"

"Fingers fractured and deep cuts. He tried to fight him off. Look for yourself."

"Who found him?"

The doctor nodded to the police officer from whom

he'd heard it. "A sixteen-year-old kid . . . neighbor, lives three doors away. Kids come here and sniff glue."

"Where is the kid now?"

"He's with his parents and a woman police constable; he had to have a sedative."

"Time of death?"

"I've no idea, except that it was today rather than yesterday. It's damned cold in here. Sometime within the last eight hours."

"Okay," I said. Boxes and oil drums were splashed with blood. There was lots of blood but the stains had gone dark and brown like last night's dinner gravy. But most of the spattered stains formed a band of marks along the boxes; at what would have been head level when he was standing up being beaten to death.

"Bloodstains and hairs on the hammer," said Squeaky. "It's a straightforward killing. We've done all that Agatha Christie stuff before you arrived."

"What was in the pockets?" I asked.

"Someone had been there already," said Squeaky.

"Any idea who it is, Bernard?" Keith asked.

"No papers on the body? Nothing at all?" I asked innocently.

"Good God, Bernard," said Squeaky in an exasperated voice. "It's one of your people. Why the hell don't you admit it? Identify him and let these people start clearing up the mess. Try being honest and cooperative for heaven's sake. Bugger about here for another hour, and one of the newspapers will get hold of the story." He looked at me and more soberly added, "No, no identification papers on the body. Nothing of any significance on the body. Bus tickets, small change, fifty pounds sterling in tens. Keith is taking the wallet, and odds and sods for Forensic.

Whoever did it went through the pockets with great care and attention."

"Or maybe that was done somewhere else and then he was brought here."

"We can't rule that out," said Squeaky. "But you don't believe it and neither do I."

Dicky was writing in his notebook and didn't look up.

"It's a German national," I said. "About sixty-five years old. Not one of our people. A freelance commercial pilot. We used him from time to time for arm's-length jobs. I don't know his real name. Is that honest and cooperative enough for you, Mr. King?"

"It will do for a start," said Squeaky, appeased perhaps by my polite use of his surname. "So what do you make of it?"

"Some kind of meeting?" I offered.

"Obviously," said Squeaky. "Who? When? And why here?"

"A building site like this is not bad," I said.

"What about being seen by the workers?"

"British building workers?" interjected Dicky. "In winter? When did you last have any work done, Squeaky? These characters scamper off home right after lunch."

"But not premeditated," said Squeaky, ignoring Dicky's levity. "The killer must have got covered in blood."

I looked at him. Squeaky was a canny Scot. He might just be leading me on. I said, "I'd be more convinced it was spontaneous if we knew for certain the killer found the murder weapon here on site."

The short intake of breath from Squeaky served to indicate exasperation. "That's really baroque, Bernard. That would be quite a complicated scenario: killer comes along with the hammer, all prepared to get spattered with blood? Why not do it quickly and quietly. Silenced gun? Or a knife? Or bare hands? The victim wasn't armed."

"You're right, Mr. King," I agreed.

"Any next-of-kin, close friends or business associates that you know of? Wives? Girlfriends?" He smirked. "Boyfriends?"

"No one," I said. "He was a loner."

"So okay if we clear it all away?" asked Squeaky, looking around. "By the way, we found this over there in the corner. I don't think it has any bearing on the killing." He brought a transparent evidence bag from his case. Inside it there was Swede's replica Navy Colt. "I suppose one of the kids who come here lost it."

"Sure, clear it all away. That's okay with us, isn't it, Dicky?"

"We appreciate your prompt call to us," said Dicky, becoming suddenly diplomatic. "It wouldn't have been much fun having the D-G read it in the *Daily Mirror* and wanting to know what's what."

Squeaky gave a grim nod. It wasn't going to be in the *Daily* anything tomorrow morning, or any other morning. That was what Special Branch and the local law were sewing together when we arrived.

Dicky was very businesslike. He made sure they were not going to mess about and make us wait until the postmortem. Squeaky promised him a copy of the prelims, all the physicals—complete external exam, dental chart, scene-of-crime photos, fingerprints—and anything that Five's Coordination people came up with on their data base. And Dicky wanted it all by end of work the following day. "And the 'posting' as soon as it comes," Dicky added with an authoritative nod. It was almost as if he knew what he was talking about.

"You knew him?" the doctor asked me as the others turned and moved off, leaving me still staring at the body. I suppose he'd noticed I was a bit upset by the way I'd chewed into Squeaky, and then let him have it, too.

"Off and on over the years," I admitted. "In fact he got me out of trouble . . . a couple of times."

"If he'd been a bit younger he might have fought his killer off. He must have been a tough old bugger. But at that age the skull becomes thin and osteoporotic."

"Yes, we lost a tough old bugger," I said. "The best pilot in the world and as brave as hell."

That Bret was sitting in his Rolls and parked round the corner was no great secret. Squeaky was renowned as a rulebook man: not at all the sort of man who would forget to stake out his meeting place with two or three of his instantly recognizable heavy-glove squad. I had no doubt that they were watching us now, their eyes in constant movement and their chins drawn into the collars of their black trenchcoats as they chatted unceasingly into their phones.

"How did it go? Who was there?" Bret asked. He stopped reading his *Economist* and folded the corner of the page to keep his place. I could tell that all Bret wanted was a brief confirmation that nothing catastrophic had happened.

"Squeaky. With Golds to hold his hand," said Dicky. "And a doctor . . . one of Bernard's old drinking companions, I understand. So we have an inside line there if we need it."

"And what was the conclusion?" said Bret.

"It was the German pilot . . ."

"The Swede," Bret corrected him gently.

"They call him the Swede," said Dicky.

Having settled that misnomer, Bret's curiosity seemed to wane. "No problems?"

"I told you there was no need to come, Bret. They will fax all the medical junk tomorrow if you want to go through it."

"If there are no problems I don't need to see any of it," said Bret emphatically. "I've got a desk that's buried under work." With that self-assurance that inherited wealth provides, he ended the discussion. He switched off the reading light, tucked his *Economist* down the side of the seat, let his head loll back, and closed his eyes.

Dicky said, "We'll drop you off first, Bernard. You are nearest." He said it in a whisper in case Bret would be disturbed.

Until now my concern for the Swede had pushed from my mind the effect his death would have upon all my other plans and ideas. Now the consequences fell upon me like an icy avalanche of wet slush. I wasn't going to Ireland or Cuba or South America. I wasn't going anywhere; I would be staying here and putting up with all the crap the Department chose to dump upon me. There was no escape from consequences; that was a fact of life.

"See you in the morning," said Dicky as he dropped me off at the apartment block.

"Yes," I said. "I'll see you in the morning."

The apartment was dark and cold when I got upstairs. Fiona had left, but not before tidying up every-thing so that the place was pristine. She'd picked up the pieces of discarded tissue paper, and washed and put away the dishes, milk pan, and a coffee cup and saucer she'd used. The overlay had been taken off our double bed. It had been made up with clean starched sheets, and the pillows were arranged ready for me to go to bed. On the pillow at my side she'd placed the fabric camellia, like a token of love. I was suddenly troubled by the thought that her tears had been shed for our marriage.

You can see right across London from the top floor of our SIS building. Today was hazy, the cloud-filled sky bruised and battered; rain was expected at any minute. Last night I'd watched the steely clouds racing across the sky. This morning they had slowed. Now they were completely still; anchored and threatening like an extra-terrestrial armada waiting for the order to invade.

I was first to arrive in the No. 3 conference room, unless you count the Welsh lady who brews the tea for such gatherings. None of the others were on time. Bret came with the Director-General. Gloria, who was now appointed to a permanent position as Bret's assistant, came with Bret's newly appointed girl secretary. Soon after, Augustus Stowe, the abrasive Australian who used to have Dicky's job, arrived. He was still trying to hold Operations together, and the black marks under his eyes and his general demeanor showed what it was taking out of him. Nevertheless, Stowe was always able to summon up energy in its bellicose form. He came in slapping his hands and shouting, "What are you idiots all sitting in the dark for? Switch on the bloody lights someone."

Dicky hurried in breathless, wearing his new Armani trenchcoat. He was the last person to arrive. He obviously hadn't even had time enough to look into his office for the cup of coffee that was awaiting him at 10:30 each morning. I could see from one glance at his face that missing his regular dose of caffeine had made him resentful, peevish, and dyspeptic.

"I wish you had reminded me, Bernard," he hissed as he hung his raincoat on a wire hanger and pulled out his chair at the conference table. Dicky hated having his precious clothes on wire hangers; he had banished them from his own office, and from his home, too.

Although Dicky, like others of the Department's senior staff, sometimes used the No. 3 conference room as a snug hideaway, the rest of us knew it only as a place where we were summoned to give evidence, or be grilled about mishaps or disasters.

Today I wasn't standing on the mat. I was among the eight important people seated at the highly polished coffin-shaped conference table and discussing "Departmental policy." Each place was set with a new notepad, a sharpened pencil, and a tumbler of water. There was also a copy of the minutes of the previous meeting, and an agenda for this one. My name did not appear on the agenda, but that did not mean anything when Bret was in the chair. And Bret was in the chair. He was seated across the table from me with a gold pencil in position; it was a heavy gold pencil that he clinked against the water glass when he wanted order, silence, and attention. His new secretary sat next to him; a dark, debby girl wearing a beige-colored twinset and pearls and an expensive watch. She was keeping a record of the meeting in longhand. It might have been an impossible task except for the way in which Bret said, "Don't minute this" frequently enough for her to catch up with the dialogue. In front of her there was an added responsibility: a tray with eight cups and saucers and two plates of biscuits together with milk jug, teapot, and so on.

On the other side of Bret sat Gloria. She had come straight from the hairdresser. I could tell, for her hair shone with lacquer, and she never used that at home. Gloria was wearing a dark, rather mannish suit. She had the official black box of documents—orders, regulations, correspondence, carbons, and even maps. She was expected to produce the papers Bret needed about two minutes before he knew he needed them. By some miracle, she managed this.

The conference room was all exactly as I remembered it, except that someone had removed the big silver-plated cigarette box that used to be on the table, and all the glass ashtrays, too. I remembered that silver box well. Like most other employees, I had often used the need for a smoke as an excuse to defer answering a question, and gone rummaging into that box for as long as possible. I felt sure Bret had banned smoking from the room. Bret was a puritan. When he gave up smoking the whole world had to get in line behind him. When he closed his eyes it was night. Bret was an autocratic do-gooder; a liberal tyrant; a crusading drop-out. The combination of opposing characteristics is what made him so American, and so difficult to understand at times.

This gathering was distinguished from meetings of lesser importance by the attendance of our Director-General, Sir Henry Clevemore. He was accompanied by "C," his beloved old black Labrador which followed him everywhere. It was the only animal permitted into the building. Once, long ago, a German visitor described Sir Henry as looking like a punch-drunk prizefighter. The venerable face, long hair, and dark complexion easily misled any casual foreign observer. But no one with firsthand experience of the British class system would mistake Sir Henry for anything but what he was: a preeminent member of the British establishment. Sir Henry's life story could be written on a postcard: Eton, the Guards, White's Club, Anglican Church, renowned horseman and foxhunting man, married into titled Scottish landowning family with Palace connections. His tall, shambling figure— and the Savile Row chalkstripes that he made look like something from an Oxfam shop—was less often seen in the corridors of the Department since his illness the previous year. But disproving all predictions, his voice was firm and unhesitating and his eyes were quick, like his brain.

Bret had grown older too, of course. But Bret was American and they knew how to keep time at bay. He was aging the way film stars age; preserving all his coil-spring energy and menace. Last night at midnight he looked like hell, but last night he'd been tired, the effects of his rowing machine and vitamins waning. Sitting in his big car, the harsh light of the tiny reading-lamp cross-lighting his face and bony hands, he was about to turn into a pumpkin. But today, having read the sports pages of the *Herald Tribune*, he was rejuvenated. I could see he was on the warpath and I feared that I was in his sights.

Contributing significant thoughts to meetings like this was not something at which I had ever excelled. I would not have been here, except that Frank Harrington was determined to hold on to the well-established tradition that Berlin should be represented. With Frank now in Berlin, and me temporarily in London, it seemed sensible for Frank to send me to attend in his stead. But I sat through all the exchanges and statistics without doing much more than hold up a hand in assent, and respond to familiar jokes with an occasional smile.

Bret had gone through the meeting at breakneck speed. He turned over the last page of the agenda while Dicky was still talking, and pushed on to the next and final item without pause or apology beyond saying, "We know all that, Dicky. We've been through it a dozen times."

I could see Dicky had brought a thick bundle of notes and references, and was only into the first of them. Poor rejected Dicky. In front of the D-G, too. Dicky wouldn't like that.

Augustus Stowe, who never passed up an opportunity to rub salt into wounds, especially Dicky's wounds, added, "You bring too much material to these meetings, Dicky. And a lot of it is time-wasting crap."

Bret waved a finger aloft to the secretary. "I don't want any of this on the minutes."

"No, Mr. Rensselaer," she said.

"So I think that does it . . ." said Bret, leaning over his secretary's notes and making pencilled ticks against agenda items which had not even been brought up for discussion. He looked round the table. "Unless there is any other business?"

With that tone of voice not even Stowe dared to have other business. Everyone could see Bret was what he called "loaded for bear," and they were only too pleased to escape.

Gloria packed up and left, having given me only the briefest possible smile. I was about to follow her when Bret said, "Could you hold on, Bernard? Dicky, too. There are a couple of things . . ."

He waited until the door was closed. "About last night: the dead man." He looked down at the neatly arranged contents of his document case. "I thought you should know that the Soviets had been dealing with that German renegade for years; at least two years." Bret said this like a sudden and surprise announcement. It was clearly something he wanted over and done with quickly.

Bret looked up at me and waited for this to sink in. I nodded and noted the way in which the Swede, who had risked his life for us countless times, had suddenly become a German renegade. I noted too that Bret had done his homework since last night, when Dicky had had to clarify the misnomer to him. "Well?" he said, waiting for me to reply. The D-G sat staring into space, as if this exchange was nothing to do with him.

"The Swede was desperately short of money," I said in his defense. There was a silence. It was of course the wrong thing to say.

"A lot of our people are desperately short of money," said Bret, and let the implication go unspoken.

"But he wasn't exactly one of our people," I said. "Not exclusively. We didn't give him enough money to get his exclusive services. He contracted. He was the best of all our arm's-distance contractors. He was dependable. He never let us down."

"No," said Bret. "He let *them* down; that was the trouble. He tried to sell them what was rightfully theirs; they don't like that kind of freebooting. That was why they wasted him."

"Could you explain that, Bret, please?" the D-G said.

"Killed him," explained Bret. "He betrayed the Soviets and they killed him."

"Ah, yes," said the D-G.

Hearing his master's voice, "C" awakened and crawled along under the table until he brushed against my feet, sniffing and snorting. Making sure it was unobserved, I gave the dog a firm push with my shoe, and it retreated a few paces along the table as far as Bret. It sank down with a groan and went back to sleep. Bret guessed what I had done and fixed me with an accusing stare. I suppose he was unhappy to suddenly have the dog resting against his legs, but he didn't complain about it.

I said, "Am I permitted to hear more detail about this?"

"They brought in a hit man from Dresden," said Dicky proudly. "We have been monitoring the whole circus for days. Two local toughs were used. Then the fellow from Germany arrived on an early flight to brief them. He took a rented car to Wimbledon, paid off his two English thugs, and was back in Berlin again before the Swede's blood had dried."

"Two thugs?" I said. "Where did they clean up?" Squeaky's reasoning had convinced me that it was too clumsy and messy for a contract killing.

"They didn't want it to look like a professional job," said Dicky. "That was specified in one of the messages we intercepted. It's new, reformed Gorby-Russia these days. They don't want anyone to know they are still doing the same nasty things they did in the bad old days."

Then Bret's words sank in. I said, "You monitored it? You're telling me . . . you let them kill the Swede?"

"We had to let them go through with it," said Bret. "We knew they were on the warpath. We thought it was a hit against one of our people from the way the messages sounded. Then we saw what it really was. To have acted on the information would have blown our source to fragments."

"And you knew all this, too?" I looked at Dicky to make it personal. "You knew last night when we were talking to Squeaky? You knew about the plan, let it happen, and then leaked it to Five so that they could find the body?"

"I thought you guessed what it was all about," said Dicky evasively. "When you told Squeaky you weren't convinced, I thought you must know something. I was thinking how well you handled it."

"No, that was the real me," I said. "Those two came looking for me. They were searching for the Swede. They wanted my help."

"What happened?" said Dicky.

"I said I'd call them back."

"You didn't report that," said Bret very quickly.

"No," I said. "I wasn't sure who they were."

"Really?" said Bret. I could tell from his face that the driver had reported my little fracas. "And yet by then you knew that the personal security alert was extended to all staff. And you knew the Swede was in town doing business. You had a meeting with him. A meeting in a bookshop on Charing Cross Road."

Bret was trying to rattle me. "Routine," I said.

"I don't think so, Bernard," said Bret. "I think it was to discuss some job you wanted done. A flying job?"

I looked at him full in the eyes. "Tell me all about it," I said. Bret was in a combative mood but I felt able to take him on.

"We've had you under observation, Bernard," said Bret. "It's no good you playing the innocent. You are up to your old tricks. You might just as well level with us."

"I have nothing to tell you," I said. "What evidence do you have? What the hell am I supposed to have done? I fought off a couple of muggers, and I met with one of the people we use. So what?"

Bret remained cool. "That's just the trouble," he said softly. "You've got the fixed idea that we are on trial—the Department. You carry on as if everyone here should be answerable to you."

The D-G spoke. It was all a little charade acted out for him to watch of course. A play for which I had not rehearsed my role. The D-G said in his deep, fruity voice, "Your brother-in-law is a mischief-maker. Everyone here knows that. But that doesn't mean we can ignore the accusations he brings against you."

"I didn't know he had brought any accusations against me." I glanced at Dicky. He looked at me and smiled nervously.

"No. Exactly. Because his wild accusations are not worth repeating," said the D-G calmly. "But what have you done to reassure us, Simmons? Very little. Admit it. Haven't you been hinting that the Department had some sort of complicity—however slight, however tangential—in the death of Tessa Kosinski?"

He paused long enough to tempt me into replying. I said, "We let the Swede die. We knew he was going to be murdered and we just let it happen. Isn't that what we have just heard?"

"That's quite different," said Bret. "There was no alternative. That's a ridiculous comparison."

The D-G ignored both my remark and Bret's, too. He said, "I have decided to extradite this American fellow Thurkettle." Sir Henry delivered this pronouncement in an august manner that made no reference to other men. Silas was not to be mentioned, let alone my conversation with Silas. "Any questions that may have formed in your mind," he said, staring at me, "will be answered at the Board of Inquiry. It's the fair thing to do. Perhaps we should have done that last year, at the time it happened." The English have an obsession about fairness, and the D-G was very English.

"Will the Americans extradite Thurkettle?" I asked.

"I have been given assurances at the highest level," said the D-G. "But once the process starts there is no telling where it will end. The Americans will protest if they think their man is being treated unfairly. Object on a point of principle." He sniffed. "We might end up in open court, with you giving evidence."

"Yes," I said.

"You saw the fatal shots fired, didn't you?"

"Yes, I did. Thurkettle killed her. I was there."

"If it came to a public trial you would be the vital witness—er ..." The D-G stared at me as if trying to recall my name. Dicky was looking at his raincoat hanging on the rack. I couldn't see Bret's face; still seated, he was bent over, reaching down to the carpet.

"I know what you mean," I said. He was reminding me that after such a public display I could not be employed by the Department.

"There is an axiom in Bengal," said the D-G. "The trackers say that by the time a hunter first sights his tiger, the tiger has seen him one hundred times."

"I know," I said. "But who can rely upon what a tiger claims?" It was a warning of course. He was telling me that any time I thought I was two jumps ahead of him and the Department, they would be three jumps ahead of me.

Outside the window the sky became ever more somber. All morning London had awaited the rain, but the threatened storm had never arrived.

"Are we going to bury him?" I said. "The Swede: what will happen now?"

Bret abandoned whatever he was bending down to fiddle with on the carpet, and sat up straight in his chair to face me. He had obviously considered the problem already. He rattled off his reply, "When the coroner releases the body, if the body isn't claimed, the Department will provide a proper church burial, and a headstone ... Somewhere quiet. We'll find a village church in the sticks. We don't let our people down, if that's the thrust of your question."

I grinned. For a moment I truly believed Bret must be trying out a deadpan joke. I thought it was only in the opening shots of TV movies that eager spooks staged pretty little country funerals to entice out the heavies of the KGB's First Directorate. "Who's choosing the hymns?" I asked.

"You may go, Simpson," said the D-G. I got up, glad to be offered an escape.

"Samson," said Bret, once again bent over and hidden behind the table.

"What's that, Bret? Speak up," said the D-G in the loud voice that is a symptom of deafness.

"His name is Samson," said Bret, in a voice that revealed his bad mood. I guessed he was trying to brush the dog hairs from his trouser legs.

"Charity. Charity," called the D-G in the low firm tenor voice with which he always hailed his dog, taxi-drivers and anyone on the other end of a telephone. "Charity, come here."

The dog groaned and shuffled towards its master. I'd always heard him call the dog "C," and believed it to be named after the D-G's august Departmental predecessors. It shows how easy it is to get things wrong.

SEVEN

Cindy Prettyman had grown older; we all had. The amusing, friendly, and attractive girl I once knew was divorced, middle-aged, and devoting all her energy to her career. This did not mean she was not still an attractive woman. In some ways the chic confidence she'd acquired with her responsibilities and her traveling had made her more interesting. The gloom of the hotel bar, lit only by a couple of tiny wall fittings, and the flickering light from the TV, flattered her.

Having greeted me, she assumed a pose. One hand held her fur-lined raincoat open to reveal her tailored outfit of black and white check. Pale fingers splayed on her hips, her nails long and red, a selection of rings and bracelets and a fashionable wristwatch well in evidence. It was a joke, and I grinned to acknowledge it.

Cindy was the epitome of the hard working and ambitious woman, fighting to survive in a man's world.

And her world was peopled by international finalists in the art of self-advancement. No doubt the ability to switch on a sexy provocative come-on was a valuable part of her repertoire.

"Cindy! What a lovely surprise," I said.

Cindy Prettyman smiled at me and I recognized that expression. She was the indulgent Mother Superior and I was the unwashed choirboy. Her ex-husband had been infatuated with her, and I'd always tried to see her through his eyes. But romantic old Jim was nothing if not a pragmatist. He had gone to other places, other people, and other things. Cindy had become a stranger.

The voice of Cindy Prettyman, or Cindy Matthews since she had reverted to her maiden name, had made me jump out of my skin. I was sitting alone in the bar of Lisl Hennig's hotel where I lived, catching up with the German newspapers while waiting for the bartender to come on duty.

"Hello, Bernard. I thought I might find you here." Big smile.

"Yes," I said, though Cindy had no reason to think I was in the bar of the Henning Hotel, or even in Berlin. But Cindy was like that: she combined the instinct of the hunter with the steady pulse of a marksman.

"You haven't changed, Bernard."

Jim Prettyman had been a Departmental colleague and pal. He taught me to play snooker and billiards, too. And helped me learn how to lose with good grace. We all used to play pool back in the old days: Fiona, Cindy and Jim, and me. We were all Foreign Office low-life, with few responsibilities and even less money. We went to a snooker hall in south London every week. Usually we followed up with a spaghetti and steak dinner at Enzo's in the Old Kent Road. The winner paid.

They were happy days but they didn't last. Jim's promotions took him up to the top floor, where he was soon rubbing shoulders with Bret Rensselaer on the Special Operations committee. Then he got a new job in America, changed his name from Jim to Jay, found a new wife and made enough money to have his teeth capped. Cindy—who was already becoming a resolute Whitehall *apparatchik*—also left England. She was offered a contract working for the European Community or the European Commission or European Parliament, or one of those well-paid jobs with first-class travel and other lush extras that every pen pusher in the world dreams about. Meanwhile my wife Fiona had completed her caper in East Berlin, returned, and got her name in flashing lights over the Department's marquee. Of the four of us, I was the only one who hadn't changed, the only one who could still be found in the same haunts that I was frequenting in the old days. And wearing the same suit.

She had got older but her salary seemed to be helping her keep time at bay. Her hair, her facial, her gold baubles, and the fashionable fur-lined raincoat that she threw on to a hanger and hung in the closet, told her story. And she had become French enough to believe that expensive outfits, fine perfume, and extravagant cosmetics were not worth spending money on unless they were kept well in evidence. She grinned. She was the picture of success. She pulled off her headscarf and shook her head to loosen dark hair that had been streaked and restyled. It was cut in a mannish no-nonsense style that meant a minimum of her valuable time spent with the crimpers.

"I might be coming to Berlin regularly in the future," she said.

"Is that a threat or a penance?"

From her large crocodile handbag she got a silver cigarette case and a gold lighter. She'd been born in a region of England up there near the River Humber where the iron-ore fields stretched conveniently close to the coking coal and the limestone flux. Her father grew up in the time when good steel was precious, and Britain's need for it seemed endless. But nothing lasts forever; not even battleships or empires. Cindy was quick to recognize that. She hadn't entirely lost her accent. Or perhaps she assumed it for my sake, to show me that her achievements hadn't made her forget that she was the same little lass with the beer-drinking left-wing dad, and the Catholic mum who worked in the laundry.

"What would you like to drink?" I asked her.

She lit the cigarette with an elegant flourish and, with the cigarette in her mouth, used both hands to close her handbag. She threw her head back and half closed her eyes as the smoke crawled up her face. Then she removed the cigarette and said, "Would it be possible to have a glass of champagne?" She wrinkled her nose in a way that Jim Prettyman once told me was cute.

On the TV screen over the bar two white-coated doctors argued in silence. "What about the house wine?" I said. "Hungarian, but not bad. They lock up the best stuff in the chilling cabinet when the barman is off duty."

I went behind the bar, helped myself to an opened bottle of wine, and returned with a glass for each of us. I poured it carefully, knowing that she was studying me to decide how much older I was looking. *"Gesundheit!"* she said, and smiled before sipping her wine. Then, as if in reaction to the taste of it, she hunched her shoulders.

"When does it get lively?" she asked, looking around at the empty bar. The Hennig Hotel had seen some notably boisterous days and nights, but overall it was a place frequented by less-successful business travelers, tourists who didn't mind going along the hall to find the bathroom, and mysterious men and women who, for reasons of their own, preferred the obscurity such unfashionable accommodation affords. Most abstemious of all there were the elderly long-term residents who eked out their fixed incomes by rationing their eating and drinking. All in all such clientele were not lively in the way that Cindy sought.

"It varies a lot," I said, sinking down on the sofa next to her.

"It would have to vary quite a lot before getting rowdy," said Cindy, and laughed, giving a hint of the sort of schoolgirl shrieks that I remembered from the old days.

"I suppose so," I said.

"Why are you always such a bastard?" she said, without much change of demeanor. She leaned forward, slipped off her shoes and massaged her feet with delicate movements of her long fingers. Through the toe of her stocking I could see that her nails were painted gold.

"Me?" I said.

"Let me see my husband," she demanded fiercely. "How can you be such a brute?"

"Jim, you mean? Jim, your ex-husband?"

"You came to Berlin with him. You brought him here. I know. Don't deny it."

I would have denied even that, but that would have brought more difficult questions, and it would have been bad security to tell her how I'd been hauled off the

Moscow Express and locked up by the Polish secret police. "I was on the same train that he was on," I admitted. "But that was just a coincidence."

"Mother of God: don't lie to old liars, Bernard." She touched her foot again. Far above us in the gloom, a muscular doctor went running athletically across a field and climbed into a helicopter with a red cross painted on it. The pilot was female and blond and young.

"I thought that was all over—you and Jim."

"It is. He bolted off with that American divorcée," she said with delicate distaste. "You don't have to be so sensitive, Bernard. You won't make me burst into girlish tears."

"No," I said. Envisaging Cindy bursting into girlish tears was something that challenged my imagination. "So why?"

She bounced to her feet in a manner that demonstrated a seemingly inexhaustible vitality. Still in her stockinged feet, she went to the bar counter and stretched right over it to grab the neck of a bottle of Scotch. She wrenched it from the rack while grabbing glass tumblers with the other hand. Then she got ice from the ice-maker and threw it into the tumblers, expertly, like a bartender. It shouldn't have astounded me that she guessed where everything was kept, and put her hands on it so effortlessly. That's how she'd always been.

"I'll have a proper drink," she announced while sloshing the Hungarian wine down the sink. "Scotch for you?"

"No thanks. I'll stick to the wine."

"I hate wine. I get too much of it where I work. The French have never heard of any other kind of drink. Wine turns to acid in my stomach." She slid back into her position on the sofa.

"It does that with some people," I said.

She poured a small measure of Scotch over the ice cubes, and kept pouring while first they crackled, and then floated. "Damn you, Bernard," she said. "I need help."

What fueled her, I wondered. Where did all this energy come from? "I don't know where Jim is," I told her. "He looked very ill when I last saw him."

"Someone is determined I shouldn't contact him," she said resentfully.

"Why? Where is he?"

"Are you listening to me, Bernard, damn you? That's what I'm asking you."

I was on the point of denying that I knew anything about Jim, or where the Department might have squirrelled him away. And that was the truth. But I was curious to discover what Cindy was after. "I might be able to get a message to him," I said, without troubling to think where I would start.

"Don't be such a monster, Bernard. This is urgent. There are other people looking for him. They come to me and ask for him, and get nasty when I say I don't know."

"What sort of people?"

"Pushy Americans from Geneva. Heavies." She pushed her nose with a fingertip, bending it to show me what sort of plug-uglies they were. "I can't get them off my back. They say they are acting with authority. I suppose Jim was a partner with them in whatever it is they do. They hinted they have money for him but they want a box file of business papers they say belongs to them. One of them is a lawyer. He says he has a power of attorney."

"What did you tell them?"

"I said I didn't know what they were talking about."

"CIA people?"

"I wondered about that at first." She sipped her whisky. "No, I don't think so . . ." She pulled a face. "Maybe."

"What papers are they talking about? You split up with Jim years ago."

"This was recent. He phoned me in my office. Right out of the blue and dumped this box file on me. Secret material, he said it was. I was in Brussels. He was on his way to Washington. What could I do? Very secret, he said. He made it sound as if the safety of the free world depended upon me. He said he'd collect it the next time he came to Europe." She made it into Yurrup; a sarcastic reference to the way Jim had acquired a slight American accent since living over there. "He never came back for it. I tried all the phone numbers I had for him, but I couldn't get through to him. Then I put the box in storage, with some furniture my mother left me. And I forgot about it. Until last month, when I got my things out; storage and insurance and all that stuff was costing me a fortune. Last week, when I heard that he'd come to Berlin, and that darling old Bernard was with him on the train . . ."

"Who told you that?"

"Never mind who told me that. Just make sure Jim calls my secretary, and arranges to collect his bloody box file from me. Or says it's okay to let his playmates have it. In writing. I must have his okay in writing. It's in the safe in my office—that's the only place I could think of—and I need the space. And it weighs a ton."

"When was this? When exactly did Jim bring it to you?"

"A few months back. When was it now? . . . I haven't got my diary with me. Back when there was all that awful trouble in Berlin; yes, last summer. When your sister-in-law got killed in Berlin."

"Jim is sick, Cindy. Very sick."

"For richer or poorer; in sickness or in health; yes, that's how I married him. But Jim had other ideas, so I was given the elbow. Jim doesn't give me money, Bernard, not a penny. I earn my own living, and it's not easy. Frankly, I don't care how sick he is, I don't want to be involved."

"I'll see what I can do."

"Otherwise I'll just throw the bloody box into the burn bag. Or give it to our security people. Perhaps that's what I should have done at the beginning. I should not have agreed to take it in the first place. The men, his pals, said Jim knew where to find them. They have an office in Geneva. Jim used to work there with them. That's what they said. You can bet it's some kind of deal; you know how keen on money Jim can be. But I'm not going to hand it over to them. If it is secret material I could go to prison."

Jim Prettyman had always been one for the big numbers. Starting with codes and ciphers, then Special Ops and secret funding. I'd never been officially notified that Jim still worked for the Department, but everything pointed that way. "Better you hold on to the box file, Cindy," I said. "It may have some continuing importance—some bearing on work Jim does for the Department from time to time."

She narrowed her eyes and said, "I wondered how long it would take for you to get round to that." She upended her whisky, looked at her watch and slipped her shoes on. It seemed as if she had decided to leave. "I should never have let him dump that box on me, the bastard."

"He knew you were a soft touch, Cindy," I said.

She didn't smile. "Phone for a cab, will you, Bernard. I've got a mountain of work that's got to be ready for my policy meeting in the morning."

I phoned and I watched her as she put on her raincoat and looked at herself in the big mirror behind the bar. So Prettyman had left a box file with her just after that night I pulled Fiona out of the DDR. I knew what she meant by a box file. It was a government-issue, steel safety box with combination lock. If it had been a normal office box file she would have been describing its contents to me, not its weight.

If the Swede was to be believed, Prettyman was due to fly out with him that night. But Cindy went instead. Did she fly? Was she in it with the Swede? Never mind all the crap about a bicycle. By my calculation there would have been room for at least two passengers. I suspected that the two seats were for Prettyman and Thurkettle. Or for Mr. and Mrs. Prettyman. How did the box file fit into the story? And what was likely to be in it; a clean shirt, toothbrush, and razor? Used currency notes? Or chopped-up pieces of Thurkettle? Jim's Diner's Club accounts? Or gold sovereigns? The trouble was that Cindy was not renowned as a selfless witness. This yarn might just be her complicated way of locating Jim to put the arm on him for alimony.

Cindy, her coat, her hat, and her hair arranged to her satisfaction, the touch of orange lipstick applied, and her lips pressed together for a moment, turned from the mirror to say: "I saw your blond bombshell in London. She was looking lovely, I must say. I chatted with her.

She worries about you; she wanted to know if I thought you were happy."

"Gloria? You saw her? What did you tell her?"

"How would I know if you were happy? I told her I never see you nowadays. She must be the only little girl in the world who hasn't discovered that you fell in love with yourself a long time ago, and will never be unfaithful." She produced a smile to soften this judgment. "The poor child is crazy about you, Bernard. So I take it that your little fling is still going smoothly?"

"I'm with Fiona," I said.

"You men!" She looked in the mirror again and flicked her hair with her fingertips. "I saw Fiona, too: in Rome; the big security bash. Chanel suit, Hermès bag. What a woman. Lovely children, desirable husband, and gold Visa card. What more could any girl ask for? She had a Commissioner on either arm but she spared a chummy word or two for little me. What a success she is, Bernard. What is it like ... to have two amazing women desperately, foolishly in love with you?" When I didn't respond Cindy turned to look at me and said, "Tell me honestly. I would like to know."

"Give over, Cindy."

"It's that shy modesty that gets them, Bernard. That and the dimples. Or is it the challenge? The challenge of trying to wring affection from the most selfish, egoistical loner in the world?"

"Are you going back to Brussels now?" I asked.

She smiled. I'd been unable to keep from my voice the heartfelt hope that she was speeding directly to the airport and leaving town forever. "No, Bernard. I'm staying with Werner and Zena in their gorgeous new home. I'll be in town for a few days."

"Oh, good," I said. I'd forgotten that she knew

Werner from our times in London together. Cindy was a loyal and conscientious friend to people far and wide. Or a calculating networker who could rally a thousand people to any cause she cared to name, according to whether you heard it from Cindy or Jim.

"And did I say male chauvinist pig?"

"Good luck, Cindy," I said as she swept out of the bar, her arm upraised in a regal farewell.

I sighed. The blond doctor had taken off her white coat to reveal black lacy underwear. Her muscular colleague was giving her mouth-to-mouth resuscitation.

Cindy was right: Scotch whisky was better than Hungarian wine.

The presentation portrait of Frank Harrington will be exactly like this, if Gainsborough gets the chiaroscuro right. Frank had pushed his chair close to the window and was reading the *Spectator*. He looked up. In that moment, as his eyes met mine, Frank was his sincere, avuncular, and gentlemanly self. His suit—that had doubtless come from the same tailor's workroom as had the suits of his father and grandfather—was in every way perfect. The room was shadowy, with Frank's bony features side-lit by Berlin's gray winter sky. Hair brushed smoothly against that elongated head that is the distinguishing mark of the English among their Continental neighbors. The tall forehead and stubby military moustache made him unmistakably a gentleman.

"I was trying to reach you," said Frank in a deceptively remote manner. "All morning," he added plaintively.

"I was doing a job for Dicky. I still haven't finished."

"I thought it must be something of that sort." Frank tapped at the glass window with his fingertip so that it made no audible sound. I followed his gaze. At the other end of the frosty white lawn, near the apple trees, Frank's valet Tarrant was talking to one of the gardeners. They were standing outside the door of Tarrant's workshop, their breath condensing on the cold air. There was a child with them; swaddled up in a white furry hat and coat. He was nursing one of Tarrant's model locomotives.

Tarrant had slowly taken possession of the small brick building at the end of the garden. In my father's time it housed the lawnmower and other tools, and was a shelter where the gardeners could hide to smoke and eat their lunch. Now the garden tools were relegated to a wooden shed, there was only one gardener and his lunch was usually no more than a currywurst on a stick. The brick building had become Tarrant's playroom. It was fitted with an elaborate workbench with a lathe, drills, and power tools and everything needed for building and working on his extensive layout of scale model trains. Tarrant took his loco back from the child, and went back to his bench. He spent a lot of time there: he always referred to it as "the workshop" and claimed to be doing household repairs. Frank called it "the gingerbread house."

"I am never quite sure who it is I work for," I said, becoming defensive when Frank didn't even turn to look at me.

"No one here is," said Frank. "Berlin's always been like that. It was the same when your father was doing my job."

"I wish it could be settled," I said. It was bad enough to be running around town on one of Dicky's fool's errands without coming back to face Frank's consequential icy mood.

"Now is not a good time," said Frank, still staring out of the window. He meant of course that Dicky was not yet confirmed in his job, and reluctant to make decisions. While Frank was too old and too near retirement to be picking new fights with anyone in London. Meanwhile I would have to try and work for the uncoordinated wishes of both of them. "Where do flies go in the wintertime?" said Frank. "Did you ever wonder about that? In my young days there was a song about it, a music hall song."

I didn't know what to make of this quaint entomological digression. It might have been a rhetorical question. Frank was one of those exasperating people who reveal their true feelings only after wrapping them into protracted anecdotes and labyrinthine parables. "No," I said after a long silence.

"They end up in these empty spaces between the double-glazing. Look, I'll show you, there are dozens of them here. Dead." He tapped at the window again. He hadn't been looking at Tarrant and the gardener; he'd been looking at dead flies. Frank was like one of those grand actors who, having devoted time and many performances to understand and assimilate a role, then claim title to it. It was playing the role of quintessential Englishman for a lifetime that enabled Frank Harrington to be convincingly himself. But now, like any great actor nearing the end of his career, his technique had nowhere to go but parody.

"If it's urgent I can put Dicky's little job on hold," I offered.

"How do the little blighters get in there? That's what I can't make out. Must be the devil of a way to go.

Sheets of glass on each side of you, but no way of escape. No way in, and no way out."

"Do you want me to tell the housekeeping people? The windows all need cleaning up here. The snow dumps all the smoke of that filthy *Braunkohl* down on us."

Frank ignored my suggestion. Perhaps he thought I was being sarcastic. Perhaps Frank's little one-way-in, but no-way-out, was intended to have some subtle meaning for me. "What exactly are you doing for Dicky?" he asked.

"One of the German scientists who defected last month has got them all going with talk about uranium mines."

"Uranium mines in Germany?"

"About thirty k's south of Chemnitz. Schlema, it's called."

"It's true then? Uranium? I've never heard of it."

"Tons of it. In the foothills of the Erz mountains. Ore mines. The 'ore mountains' the Germans call them. There are ski resorts and lots of thermal springs, too. I suppose the spa was a way of getting tourists there when the snow had gone."

"Uranium?"

"There's a mine there. It's no big secret. Back in the days when it was a fashionable resort, it was called Oberschlema and it was advertised as a *Radiumbad—das starkste Radiumbad der Welt*—guaranteed to lower your high blood pressure, ease your rheumatism, and make you feel young again if you had enough money to stay there. And didn't mind glowing in the dark."

"What's Dicky's angle?" said Frank, in a voice that suggested that he didn't much care. But I knew Frank better than that: he liked to know what London was doing on his patch.

"There's uranium there all right, and what they dig out all goes to the USSR. At least it used to go there." I shrugged. "It might be difficult to confirm what's happening right now. We don't have anyone reliable anywhere near there, as far as I can remember. I'm checking it now."

Frank sighed. "Are our masters back to their brawling about whether the Russkies are still manufacturing atomic weapons? I thought all that was settled last year."

"That was a dispute about bombs; this is a dispute about artillery shells."

Frank looked at me and nodded as if he was thinking of something else. "Keep London happy," he said vaguely. Ordnance was among the things he tried to keep away from. Frank got on well with the army, but he didn't think that providing that sort of intelligence was our province. He called it "assessment" and maintained the army should be able to deal with that without our help. They had their military attachés and liaison officers sniffing around the Russian army all the time.

"What was it you wanted, Frank?" I said.

"Wanted?"

"You said you were trying to reach me."

"Oh, that. Yes, I was thinking about that business in London . . . that poor devil of a pilot who was killed. Your friend."

I didn't respond to the "your friend" but I could detect some underlying disapproval in Frank's voice.

"The funeral was yesterday," said Frank. "We arranged it. No one claimed the body."

"So I heard."

He went on, "You saw him immediately after it happened? You chatted with Squeaky?"

"Chatted with him? Have you ever tried chatting with Squeaky?"

"Ha!" said Frank mirthlessly. "I know what you mean. He's always been like that: abrasive. I mean have you been chatting with anyone at all?"

"At the scene of the crime?" I said. Frank nodded. I said, "Is this something Dicky has been saying?"

"He said you hung on there for a few minutes afterwards."

"I didn't go striding out holding Dicky's hand, if that's what you mean. I know the doctor. I was intending to see him again in some other place in the hope he might be more forthcoming."

"But you didn't see him again?" Frank opened a brass and ivory marquetry box he kept on a shelf under the windowsill. From it he got his battered Dunhill pipe and his yellow oilskin tobacco pouch. He had reduced his smoking to three pipefuls of his special tobacco per day, and I was going to be on the receiving end of one of them if I didn't get out of here soon.

"No I didn't," I said.

"London Central has received an official request for us to clarify what we are doing with George Kosinski. Five want him. They are furious."

"Oh, Jesus! So that's it."

"I told Dicky that it couldn't have been you who let the cat out of the bag."

"The doctor is not a part of Five, he's just the doctor. We use him, too."

"Five's official letter went to the D-G, of course. So Dicky will have to go into the fire and flame, and explain things, so the D-G can cobble together some sort of servile groveling explanation."

"Dicky is good at that sort of thing," I said.

Frank filled up his pipe bowl with the dark brown muesli that he liked to burn. There came the sudden flare of a match as he set light to it while making little spluttering sounds. Once it was alight, he exhaled smoke, and with a contented smile asked, "Dicky? Servile groveling? Or taking the blame?"

"It's no good Dicky trying to dump this one on to me, Frank," I said. "I submitted a report after being sent down to see George Kosinski. It's on file. It recommends his immediate release. We won't get anywhere with him by locking him up in Berwick House. You know George."

"No, I don't know George. Tell me about him."

"Reflective, self-righteous, single-minded, and with more than a touch of the Old Testament."

"So why won't locking him up and interrogating him get us anywhere?"

"Because he's sanctimonious. Devout. He goes to Mass early in the morning whatever the weather. Forgives his wife all her many sins. And goes on forgiving her when she sins relentlessly. He won't become anxious or angry or repentant. He'll see Berwick House as a chance to live the cloistered meditative life he's always secretly hankered after."

"Is that really what you think?"

"Of course it is."

"I don't know George Kosinski. He's almost family for you of course."

He was smoking happily now, poking at his pipe bowl with the blade of a penknife, and attending to every strand of burning tobacco with all the loving care of a locomotive engineer. Or a dedicated arsonist. He looked at me. "This is off the record, Bernard. Strictly *sub rosa*. You tell this to anyone and I'll deny it."

"Okay, Frank."

"If you want my theory, it was George who arranged the killing of his wife."

"George? Had Tessa killed?"

"I didn't mean to upset you, Bernard."

"I'm not upset. I just can't follow your reasoning."

He nodded. "You are too close to it, of course. But George had the motive, the opportunity. And we know he had money enough."

"To pay a hit man?"

"Of course. You told me, you saw her shot. You said it was some mad American who did it. A professional killer, wasn't he? Or is it your theory that the American killed her for some personal reasons that we are not party to?"

"I don't know," I said. For a moment I considered telling him about my conversation with Uncle Silas. But it was better kept to myself.

"I've shaken you, I can see. I didn't intend that, old lad."

"It was certainly a contract killing," I said doggedly. Then I admitted, "It could have been something between Tessa and the American. If they were having an affair. I think she might have been getting drugs from him. But . . ." I couldn't get my thoughts in order.

"Come along, Bernard. Forget all those might-have-been excuses. When are you going to start looking soberly at the facts? She had betrayed her husband on a long-term basis. Lover after lover. You've told me this, and it was common knowledge. On the weekend of her death she was betraying her husband with another man, wasn't she?"

"She was sharing a Berlin hotel room with Dicky Cruyer," I said, to see how Frank responded.

Frank ignored this reference to Dicky. He said, "How must George have felt? Ask yourself that. Humiliated beyond measure."

"George is a Catholic."

"That doesn't make him a saint. It only makes him someone who can't be released from a nightmare situation by means of divorce."

"No, not George." And yet . . . could George have found a way of contacting Thurkettle and paid him to go a whole lot further than Silas wanted?

"No, not good old decent George. Will you start using your brains, Bernard. Your brother-in-law has been deeply involved with Polish spy agencies for years. You saw the effortless way he made contact with that ex-CIA hoodlum Timmermann, and employed him to go prying into the KGB compound in Magdeburg. God knows how much money he paid him."

"We don't know that George sent him there," I said, without putting much spirit into it.

"All we know is that Tiny Timmermann died there. We also know that Timmermann was the sort of ruffian who will do anything for money, and we know that George admitted to paying him money . . ." Frank paused. "You told me that, Bernard. George said he was employing him."

"Yes. To investigate. To find out what had happened to Tessa."

Frank took the pipe from his mouth and gave all his attention to the smoldering tobacco. "I wasn't at the meeting between Timmermann and George. And neither were you, Bernard."

I didn't answer. I sat there and let Frank blow tobacco smoke across the room at me.

Finally Frank said, "Reflective, self-righteous,

single-minded; and a touch of the Old Testament. Exactly right for someone who would plan a premeditated killing of an unfaithful wife by a third party. The killing to take place during the weekend she was sinning."

"Yes, Frank. You don't have to draw a diagram for me. Very Old Testament. You are right. It is possible." I said it in a way that meant I thought it was extremely unlikely. He knew I was unconvinced, but my concession satisfied him.

"Are you thinking of going there?" Seeing my puzzlement, he added, "To this place, Schlema? For Dicky. The radium place?"

He had put a finger on what was still pushed far into the back of my mind. Dicky was devious. It was only a short step from "What do you think about Schlema?" to "Why don't you step across and take a look at it, Bernard, old boy?"

"No," I said firmly. "I wasn't thinking of going there personally."

"It's always bad luck to be good at something you don't want to do." He looked out of the window. "Or to be good at something dangerous. My brother-in-law Alistair suffered like that. He was a pilot in Bomber Command in the war. Pathfinders; showered with medals. God knows how many bombing raids he did. He was the best, so they kept sending him. Again and again and again, long after he was worn out. He didn't enjoy it."

"I don't remember meeting your brother-in-law." I'd known Frank almost all my life, and yet I'd never heard about his brother-in-law until this moment. How strange it is that some intimate aspects of those we know so well remain a firmly closed book. And yet perhaps in this case not so strange. Spending your life here in Berlin with German friends would not encourage anyone to recount stories about close relatives who had excelled in bombing their cities to rubble. "Is that why your son wanted to fly?" I asked. Against Frank's advice his son had become an airline pilot. His promising career came to a sad and dismaying end some years later, when he failed his medical.

"Yes. My boy lapped up all those flying yarns he read at school. It was my fault as much as anyone's. I was always telling him stories about Alistair. Alistair was a lovely man. No, you never met him, Bernard. He bought it in that big raid on Nuremberg—March fortyfour. A massacre for Bomber Command. My sister married again within the year: a man from the same squadron. She was only a child; she lived only for Alistair. When the telegram came she almost died of grief. I think she was trying to find some fragment of Alistair in the man she married. Perhaps she found it, I don't know. They are still married."

"How can you be sure your brother-in-law didn't enjoy his bombing? Some men enjoy being heroes."

"Not Alistair. He left a diary in a locker in his room. His batman had the key: he sent the diary to me. Thank God he didn't send it to Emma. It was a chronicle of concealed torment. Not just for himself, but for the men he sent out each night. Poor Alistair. I burned it eventually."

"If someone has to go over there, it had better be me," I said as I reflected upon the alternatives. "At present there is no one else I'd feel happy to send."

"You'll stay here," said Frank. "I'll make that clear to Dicky, and anyone else in London who argues. You are more useful here. I don't want you schlepping around their bloody uranium mines. It's too dangerous and you've done your share—far more than your share—of those jobs."

"There is no one else to use. You know that."

"What did that wretched woman want?"

"Woman?"

"In the bar at Lisl's last night. Come along. No one is spying on you. I just happened to be passing as she was coming out. She didn't recognize me, thank God. I know everyone says she's hard-working and amazingly efficient, but I simply can't stand her."

"Mrs. Prettyman?" It was something of a relief to know that Cindy's networking didn't extend into Frank's office.

"She's been sniffing around Berlin for almost a week. What is she up to, Bernard?"

"She wants to talk to her husband."

"What husband? Ex-husband? If you mean that fellow Prettyman . . ."

"Yes, she wants to talk to him. She says she has a box of papers belonging to him."

"I'd treat that with a certain amount of reserve. She has a reputation as a troublemaker. And this is a domestic quarrel." He pursed his lips. "What the devil is she doing here?"

"She said she was sent here to work," I said. "Only for a few days." I could see that Frank was getting worked up and I wanted to defuse his anger. I didn't tell him she was staying with the Volkmanns. Werner had enough trouble fitting into Frank's domain without that.

"You know she went to the funeral of your pilot friend?"

"No, I didn't know that," I said.

"In England. She talked to everyone there. Asking questions and making a nuisance of herself. Dicky sent someone along to make a video of all the mourners . . . everyone who attended. She was the only surprise, Dicky said."

"I see."

"You persist in thinking that Dicky is a complete fool. You made a joke about him setting up a funeral to discover who would attend. But sometimes such obvious devices prove valuable."

"Yes," I said, feeling deflated.

"What was her motive? What could be her interest? Was she close to the pilot? Is there a security aspect?"

"As I say, she is very keen to make contact with her husband. I suppose she heard about the Swede's funeral—she always seems to know what's going on—and was hoping Prettyman would turn up there, too."

"I don't like the sound of it. I don't trust that woman. Find out what she's up to."

"I'd rather go after the *Radiumbad*."

"Of course you would," said Frank. "So would anyone."

"What about the report for Dicky?"

"Dicky's uranium mine can go on hold for the time being. I'll get Werner on to it. We have other tasks more urgent. I shall tell Dicky that."

"Yes," I said.

"My son has decided to go and live in Melbourne."

"Has he?"

"Australia."

"Yes." I looked at Frank. He doted on his son. To be told he was planning to go to Australia must have been one of the worst things that had ever happened to him.

"I'll miss him." It was the ultimate understatement. Frank's relationship with his wife had dwindled to a point where she was spending most of her time in England. He lived only for his son.

"It's a small world nowadays," I said. "People fly across the world, backwards and forwards all the time."

"My boy told me the same thing." Frank opened a brown file and looked down at the letters that were waiting to be signed.

Thus dismissed, I went back to my office to check my incoming afternoon work. The dark skies of Berlin's winter were oppressive. I switched on the desk lights, the overhead fluorescent lights and every other light I could find, including the ones in the corridor. My secretary watched me do this. If she was surprised she gave no sign of it.

"Don't you ever feel like going off to live some place where the sun burns the skin off you all year round?" I said.

"Oh, no, Herr Samson. That would be carcinogenic."

She had opened everything already. When I sat down, she came and stood by my desk to make sure I didn't toss the difficult ones into the pending box. She was very German.

I went through it quickly. At the bottom of the tray there was a bulging brown manila envelope. It was not internal mail. It had been posted in London using a long strip of Christmas commemorative postage stamps. The cover was already slit open, so I tipped the contents out. A shower of rose petals fell upon my desk. They were crisp and brown and dead, and there was a brittle piece of stem and a curly leaf with charred edges. I looked inside the envelope. There was nothing else. Just the remains of my roses. They had not died a natural death; there hadn't been time enough. These were petals from red roses that had been scorched, or perhaps rescued at the last moment from an open fire. I wondered what my German secretary thought of this tacit message. I looked at her but she gave no sign of what she was thinking.

I dictated my way through the daily stuff from London. When we were finished I said, "Did we ever get the police reports I asked for? The ones for the night Mrs. Tessa Kosinski died?"

"I thought you had finished reading them."

"Was that all?"

"I will bring the file," she offered.

"Don't bother. There was almost nothing. I'd like to spread the net wider." I went to the map on the wall of my office. "Look at all these jurisdictions. . . . The shooting took place here. Assume someone left the Autobahn at any one of these exits. Here, here, or here."

"Each jurisdiction? Towns and villages, too? Every one?"

"Yes."

"May I ask you what we seek?"

"I don't know exactly. Drunks. Dangerous driving. Trucks illegally parked. Accidents. Wrecks. Property lost and found on or near the highway. Anything unusual in even the smallest way."

She wrote it down.

I thought about Thurkettle's possible movements. "What would I have done had it been me?"

"I don't know, Herr Samson."

I had spoken aloud without realizing it. I wouldn't drive eastward, would I? It would be too dangerous to go east after a shoot-out that had wiped out a couple of important Stasi men. What fugitive would head towards a land brimming with cops, and endless demands for signed papers with rubber stamps? No, I would drive along the Autobahn westward. It would be cold and dark. How do I feel? I feel lousy. I'm driving fast, but not fast enough to get a ticket or to get noticed by other road users. I'm hyped up but I feel lousy. I stink of fear and sweat and dirt and spilled blood. I need somewhere to hide for five minutes while I collect my wits. But there is no one I can trust. So I want an empty house, not an apartment, a house, an isolated house. Because I like to do the hard bits first, I would want to get across the border before stopping. I would choose a lonely spot just across the border in the Federal Republic and near an exit from the Autobahn. Why near an exit? Because I might choose to get back on the Autobahn. It's night; I might decide to put as many miles behind me as I can. But then another thought came to me. If I was dirty and bloody and conspicuous I might want to have somewhere to clean up before going through the checkpoint.

There would have to be a rendezvous with my paymaster. I will be paid off and change my clothes and my ID and pick up my tickets or whatever I needed. Hits were always like that. There was always someone waiting at a rendezvous. If not a someone, a somewhere, a place of refuge. I had never heard of a hit man working without back-up. And I'd never heard of a hit man being paid one hundred percent in advance. Somewhere that night there had been a contact. And that meant the chance that some cop or nosy neighbor had seen it happen. There had to be some clue somewhere, but I had no idea what it might be.

And then a likely solution came to me. "It's got to be one of those camper vehicles," I told her. "That's the sort of thing I'm looking for." That could be placed wherever it was wanted. He could use it to wash and change. Then he could use it as a vehicle in which the journey could be resumed under a different name, and with all the necessary papers. "A camper," I said aloud. That's why he used a motorcycle to get to and from the killing. His plan was beginning to make sense to me.

"I will require a person to help."

"Parked overnight on some isolated stretch of road near one of the exits, but not on the Autobahn where a cop might stop and check it." Stopping on the DDR's Autobahn was verboten. "Talk to all the West German cops who were riding in cars that night, riding anywhere in the vicinity of the exit ramps. Asking for written reports was the wrong way to do it. Talk on the phone. Talk to them in person." I would have to tackle the DDR side myself.

"How near to the Autobahn? One kilometer? Five kilometers?" she asked.

"I don't want to extend it too far or it will give you too many cops to contact. Tell them we are after a serial killer, I don't want them to think we are chasing up parking tickets."

"I will require help."

"Five kilometres. Start right away. It's the night-shift cops you want. Take anyone you need . . . within reason," I added quickly in case she did something crazy, like demanding help from Frank's secretary. Or Frank.

EIGHT

HORRIDO CLUB, BERLIN-TEGEL

Tegel, West Berlin's third airport, was built in a hurry. In a vindictive attempt to squeeze the Anglo-American armies out of the capitalist "island" that defaced their communist domain, the Russians suddenly blocked the road links with the West. They cut off everything, even the long-standing delivery of Swedish Red Cross parcels for hungry Berlin children. The U.S. Air Force, the RAF and a varied assortment of civilian fliers supplied the city by air. In that feverish climate of resentment and hatred a new airport was built. It materialized here on the flat land of Tegel on the edge of a sector of town that the Americans and British had given to the French so they could play conquerors. The airfield was operational after little more than eight weeks, built with American engineers directing German laborers, almost all of whom were female. Without notice, two Red Army radio masts in line with the approach were blown away. Angry Russian generals demanded an explanation. The French Commandant disarmingly replied that it was all done with dynamite.

That was in 1948. Now, almost four decades later, we were sitting in what had been the site-manager's office during the construction work. At least we were sitting in a hut of which one badly scarred wall, and the concrete base block, had been its final remains. The old hut had remained abandoned and neglected on the edge of the Tegel runway until Rudi Kleindorf came and preserved it. Rudi was an oddball, a one-time professional soldier and self-advertising patriot who declared a sentimental attachment to this place. He'd put up a notice on the wall claiming that it was the last remaining trace of a miracle of construction work. Now, said Rudi's notice, it was almost completely forgotten, even by those who came here.

"So what is going on in Frank's mind?" said Werner, after I'd told him about Cindy, and about Frank's reaction to her sudden intrusion into what Frank always considered his own personal fiefdom. When I shrugged, Werner rephrased it. "What was the implication? Does Frank think she's going to kill Jim Prettyman?" Werner's heavy irony seemed to be as much directed at me as at Frank. With Cindy as his house guest he felt defensive on her behalf. He got up and went to the refrigerator to find a bottle of carbonated water. He held it up: I shook my head. It was clubby enough, and German enough, for that sort of self-help and payment on trust system to survive. Perhaps that was what attracted Werner to this large prefabricated shack, half hidden in the trees of Jungfernheide.

"Kill Jim? Good God no," I said, pretending not to notice the little dig at me. "Why do you say that?"

"It was a joke," said Werner.

"Yes, well Jim Prettyman knows where all the bodies are buried," I said. "And there are not many people left who might know the true story behind what happened on that night Tessa died."

"Is that what Cindy says?"

"Cindy? She knows nothing about it, except that Jim left a box of papers with her the next day."

"So what did she want then?"

"She wants more space in her office safe. I think she was hoping that I would ask her for the box file, and pay her a reward or something. You know what she's like."

"Why didn't you?"

"Not with Cindy," I said. "Nothing is simple with her. You can bet it was some kind of baited trap. I take the box file from her, and she hits us with a demand for official recognition as Jim's wife."

"Jim remarried."

"In Mexico. Cindy has been advised that Mexican marriages are not recognized under English law. She would like to see it annulled. It would give her the green light for a legal action against the Department."

"Yes, I remember now. And where would that leave Prettyman?"

"Exactly. She's a devious woman," I said.

"You used to like her."

"Did I?"

"You were always saying how clever and attractive she was. You used to say that she was the brains behind everything that Jim Prettyman did."

"Not Cindy," I said.

"You don't like any of your old friends these days, Bernie. What's happened to you? Why are you so caustic? Why so suspicious of everything and everyone?"

"Am I? Well I'm not the only one afflicted with that," I said. "There is an epidemic of suspicion and distrust. It's contagious. We are all in its grip: you, me, Fiona, Gloria, and the whole Department. Frank has got some crackpot idea that George had his wife killed because the Church wouldn't give him a divorce. Even when my father-in-law's superannuated moggy rolls over dead, I have to listen to some half-baked conspiracy theory."

"Yes, but cats have nine lives," said Werner. "There must have been eight other serious attempts."

"I must tell him that," I said. "It would be something more for him to worry about."

The conversation stopped while a British Airways jumbo trundled along the perimeter and revved its fans loudly enough to rattle the bottles on the bar counter, and shake the moths out of the fur collar of Werner's ankle-length black overcoat. There were soft thuds on the roof as the snow was shaken out of the trees above us.

I suppose all airports have hideaways like this: places where staff on duty can escape from work for as long as it takes to swallow a drink or two and smoke a couple of cigarettes. But this prefabricated cabin was not content to be a ramshackle refuge for airport staff. It pretended to be a club. The décor was contrived to make it seem like a private and exclusive spot for intrepid birdmen to gather to exchange stories about Richthofen. Its name was enough to tell you what it was—The Horrido Club. The word Horrido had gone into German folklore as being the word used by old-time Luftwaffe fighter pilots to proclaim an enemy aircraft shot down. Children's comics and romantic military historians endorsed it. So did Rudi, who enjoyed nothing better than reading books about the war. But as I told him, none of the Luftwaffe fighter pilots I had asked could remember anyone ever saying Horrido: they simply said *Abschuss*! Rudi had just grinned. Like so many people who had fought in the war, Rudi had developed a possessive attitude towards it. He was apt to dismiss anything I said about that period as an example of the English sense of humor, which he much admired.

Rudi had decorated the "club" with all kinds of junk. There were model aircraft, baggage labels, and sepia reproductions of old photos and posters. On the ceiling there were tacked two large sections of fabric bearing RAF roundels and one with a black German cross insignia.

Sitting in the corner, nursing beers, there were two policemen and two engineers from Lufthansa. Rudi was there, too. They'd been arguing about the football game they'd seen the previous Saturday. Now the argument ended with that suddenness with which such conversations can become exhausted. They downed their drinks, looked at the clock—an old RAF Operations Room clock with colored triangles—and left.

Rudi came over to say hello to us and offer us a drink. He was at least one hundred years old, a craggy-faced giant, with broken nose and battered cheekbones. His hair he could call his own, and his upright military bearing went well with the card he gave me advertising his new club. Since he had not yet decided upon a name for it, the card just had Rudi's name on it—Rudolf Freiherr von Kleindorf—and the address and phone number. Small type under his name claimed him to be a retired Colonel of Infantry, *ausser Dienst*. Many times I had vowed to check up on the old rogue, and blow away these pretensions to aristocratic title and military rank.

But Rudi was very old: one day soon I might be glad that old men are so often indulged in their petty vanities.

We listened to Rudi's extravagant description of his new club, the hard sell message being larded with amusing gossip and the scandals that were a permanent part of Berlin's high society. When Rudi finally departed, the club was empty, apart from me and Werner.

"How often do you come here, Werner?" I wondered if it was somewhere he came to take refuge from Zena; and from Cindy, too.

"You come here, too," said Werner.

"Not often. I've never liked this part of the city." Through the window I could see the forest. At this time of day in winter there was always a white mist threaded through the trees.

It made me remember that day long ago when, as a schoolboy, I came here on a trip. One of our teachers, Herr Storch, an unrepentant Nazi, told the class about the vast dump of artillery shells that had been hidden under the trees of Jungfernheide during the final weeks of the war. It must have been a misty winter day exactly like this one. The dump was guarded by a dozen or so Hitler Youth boys. They were in their uniforms, and proud of the new steel helmets they'd got from the Spandau army clothing depot, together with ten *Panzerfaust Klein 30* antitank rockets that were effective only when used as close as thirty meters. Accompanying the boys there were three elderly brothers named Strack. They were local men: foresters who had been given Model 98 rifles and Volkssturm armbands. Ruined by rifle–grenade training, the guns were virtually useless for shooting.

Also here that fateful day, there was a broken-down three-ton ambulance—an Opel Blitz. Its transfer lever had jammed halfway into the four-wheel-drive position, and the vehicle had become inextricably stuck in the overgrown ditch from which the driver had been trying to reverse. The driver was a female civilian volunteer. Herr Storch described her vividly: she wore a fashionable hat and coat and chamois gloves, and was distinguished only by her *Im Dienste der deutschen Wehrmacht* armband. Standing round the ambulance, there were eight nurses of a surgical unit, none them warmly clad.

At this point in his story, my teacher Herr Storch kicked the ditch at the place the Opel had stuck as if to convince himself it had all happened.

The nurses were on their way to a *Feldlazarette* of Busse's 9th Army at Storkow. It was all futile, for Busse's men were no longer there: tanks of Koniev's First Ukrainian Front wheeling north had flattened and forgotten the Mobile Field Hospital. Storch had never been the sort of man to take orders, or even suggestions, from a woman. So there was little chance of the unit's nursing sister—a gray-haired woman, long past retirement age—commandeering Storch's own vehicle, a six-wheel truck that he was loading with rations and rifle ammunition. Storch was, at the time, a lieutenant of a Luftwaffe signals regiment that had been pressed into service as infantry. He wouldn't let the nurses have his truck. To take such a step would have been to invite execution at the hands of the "flying court martials" that were to be seen roving the streets, interrogating the old and the young, the high and the low, with equal ferocity.

While Storch was arguing with the nurses, unwelcome strangers stepped out of the mist. They were the "point" of an armored reconnaissance battalion of the

12th Guards Tank Corps. This was the other prong of the attack: Marshal Zhukov's army heading south to cross the canal and descend upon the industrial complex of Siemensstadt. A large proportion of the foot soldiers were fighting drunk on plundered schnapps. Some were injured and others burdened under incongruous assortments of looted domestic treasures. They were all hungry, and now they pounced with glee upon the unexpected bounty of German army rations. They also pounced upon countless tons of munitions hidden under camouflage netting. And with even greater glee they pounced upon the nurses.

Storch had jumped down into the ditch to show us how he had survived. From there he had watched the killing of the Volkssturm men, the cruel deaths of the Hitler Youth boys, and the repeated brutal raping of the nurses. He told the story with an intensity that horrified me and my classmates. "Defeat is shame," he yelled at us as the tears rolled down his cheeks. "And shame is having to watch barbarians defile your women while you do nothing—nothing—to defend them. Shame and fear. I did nothing, do you hear me: Nothing! Nothing! That is defeat."

What was he trying to tell us? We schoolboys watched Storch with consternation that did nothing to aid our understanding. I was the only foreign barbarian in the class, and his wet, wide-open eyes stared at me for so long that the boys who had at first turned their heads to look at me turned away in confusion and embarrassment. I never did fully understand what motive he had for inflicting upon us the emotional trauma we all shared that day, but for ever afterwards even the name of this place was enough to bring upon me an ache of apprehension and misery.

"Are you listening?" Werner said loudly enough to bring me out of my reverie.

"Yes," I said as the voice of Storch echoed in my memory and faded away.

"I like airplanes," admitted Werner. "Remember all those models I built?"

"I thought you bought them from that woodcarver," I said.

"Black Peter?" said Werner, showing great agitation. "What are you talking about? My models were immensely better, and far more detailed than those Flying Fortresses he made. His crudely carved models were just for selling to the American soldiers."

"Were they?" I said innocently.

"Don't be stupid, Bernie. My Dornier X had all the engines in it. You could lift up the cowlings and see the details inside." He was passionate now, his voice quivering with indignation. It was so easy to crank him up, but I always felt guilty afterwards. It's only our very closest friends who are so immediately vulnerable to our teasing.

"The big flying boat? Yes, that was a good one, Werner. I remember that one. You kept it for years."

"What are you going to do about the Matthews woman?" said Werner, as if trying to get even with me.

"Nothing," I said. "Frank expects you to follow up on her. He'll ask you what's happening."

"I can't start cross-questioning her. She's a guest, and very close to Zena. He's dumped the radium mine problem on my desk. He told me you were doing something urgent for him. I thought he meant about Cindy."

Clever old Werner. But I fielded that one. "Frank

doesn't know she's staying with you." I drank the drink Rudi had so kindly pressed upon me and then said: "Not so long ago, Werner, I looked up at the stars in the night sky, and wondered how they had come into such harmonious configuration. Everything seemed to be going perfectly. I was foolishly in love with Gloria, and I was beginning to believe—against all reasonable expectations—that she was deeply in love with me. My kids seemed to have recovered from the shock of their mother's departure. Gloria and me and the children all shared our sleazy little suburban love nest in the sort of foolish happiness I had never known before. Of her own choice, Fiona had defected. Given average luck, it seemed like I would never see my father-in-law again. My brother-in-law George was packing his bags to become some kind of rich tax exile in Switzerland, and I was happy to say *auf Wiedersehen* and good luck to him. My job seemed secure. I was in London, and that elusive pension for which I was not officially eligible was almost within my grasp. You were here in Berlin, as happy as a lark, fixing up the hotel in conjunction with your lovely Ingrid. Can you remember those days, Werner? Those Elysian days."

"The Elysian fields were the dwelling of the blessed after death," said Werner, who could always find a way of dampening my euphoria.

"I said, can you remember those days?"

"No. What did Rudi put in your drink?"

"Look at the situation now, Werner. Gloria hates me. Fiona is eating most of her meals on planes, and is too busy to stop work for five minutes to talk to me. My children have been kidnapped by my father-in-law. My job is on the line. The chance of my getting into any sort of pension scheme is zero. My father-in-law thinks someone is trying to poison him. My brother-in-law is being held as an enemy agent . . ."

"And me?" asked Werner, when my voice trailed off. I suppose he guessed I was trying to find some acceptable way to describe his reconciliation with his wife, the fiery Zena.

"No news is good news, Werner," I said.

"You're right," he said grimly. He'd given up trying to persuade me that Zena wasn't as bad as I thought.

"Where is Jim Prettyman? What have you heard?"

"Am I your friend?" said Werner.

"Sometimes I think you are my only friend."

"That would be paranoid," said Werner. "You have hundreds of friends—too many—even if they are mostly low-life specimens. And more supporters than I can count. Your wise words are endlessly quoted and your deeds recounted. Seriously, Bernard. You have many friends."

"I don't think so."

Werner looked at me, took careful aim, and then hit me in the eye with a mossy clump of Schiller:

> *Freudlos in der Freude Fülle,*
> *Ungesellig und allein,*
> *Wandelte Kassandra stille*
> *In Apollos Lorbeerhain.* *

---

* Joyless there, where joy abounded,
  Friendless and misunderstood,
  Walked Cassandra, fear-surrounded,
  In Apollo's laurel wood.

"Cassandra" by Friedrich von Schiller. Translation taken from *Treasury of German Ballads* (Frederick Ungar Pub. Co. Inc., New York, 1964).

"I don't need poetry, Werner," I said.

Werner said: "For the sort of work you do, you have an instinct that I envy. And over the years I have seen you combine that instinct with powers of deduction, and pull off the impossible."

"Now for the down side."

"But you make little effort to see things from the other point of view. Maybe that's why you bring such powers to your work: that unyielding, single-minded determination. But at times like this, it cripples your reasoning."

"Is that what I'm doing now?"

"You have become obsessed with discovering some dark secret about the death of Tessa Kosinski. At least, you seem to be obsessed with it. You drag it into the conversation every time I see you. But who was present at that shooting? You were."

"Not only me, Werner."

"Fiona has repressed her memories of that night," said Werner. "She remembers nothing. A hundred analysts working day and night wouldn't dredge it up into her conscious memory in a hundred years."

"Who says so?"

"The shrinks said so. You said so. You told me that Bret said exactly that to you in California after one of the debriefing sessions."

"Oh, yes," I said. "I thought I recognized Bret's flowery syntax. I remember now. But you've got to allow for the way Fiona was traumatized at suddenly finding herself in the middle of a shoot-out. She's worked behind a desk all her life. She wasn't ready for that especially nasty little bloodletting."

"No one is ever ready for it. But you handled it with your usual superhuman efficiency. You wrote out a detailed report and answered questions about it for weeks."

"I don't see what you're getting at, Werner."

"It was dark. Chaos. You were worried about Fiona, and about Tessa too. There was a lot of shooting. Men were killed. You shot and killed that KGB man Stinnes, and the man he brought with him."

"Kennedy; Fiona's lover."

"Kennedy, yes. And then you pushed Fiona into the van and drove away and escaped. But no one, not even you, comes out of a shooting completely unscathed. When you arrived in the West you were in a state of shock. You told me that."

"There was a lot of blood. Fiona was covered in blood. Having Fiona there was what made it terrible for me. You are right, I wasn't prepared for it."

"The British army doctor sedated you?"

"I was hyped up. He said I needed some magic pills if I was to fly across the Atlantic."

"So you remember the pills?"

"Of course I do. Didn't I tell you about them? How would you know else?"

"Where's the gun you used?"

"It was my dad's Webley Mark VI."

"Yes, where is it?"

"I don't know. I'd never used one of those old wartime guns before. The rounds come out in slow motion, and tip on impact. They land like an artillery shell and tear a big hole in a man, Werner. It worked okay, but it was pretty damned grim to watch."

"How many rounds did you fire?"

"I can't be sure."

"One? Two? Three? Four?"

"I said I don't know!"

"Don't get excited, Bernard."

"I know what you're thinking."

"What am I thinking?"

"You're going to pretend I shot Tessa."

"Well, isn't it possible? It was dark: just the headlights of the cars. And then someone shot the headlight out. Dark and muddy. People running. Confusion . . . try and remember."

"You weren't there, Werner. Thurkettle shot Tessa. I saw him."

"Slow down, Bernard. Play let's suppose. Many shots were fired that night, but we don't know who fired which. You fired, Thurkettle fired, and maybe the others fired, too. You depart in the van with Fiona. Thurkettle leaves on his motorbike, and goes to London and tells them what he saw. How will his account fit to yours?"

"Is Thurkettle in London?"

"He might well be. I'm playing let's suppose."

"Jesus Christ, Werner! I don't care what Thurkettle is telling them in London. No one is going to railroad me into confessing that I killed Tessa. I loved Tessa. She was always wonderful, supportive and full of life. When Fiona went, Tessa helped me with the children. I wouldn't think of killing her."

"You wouldn't think of it? Couldn't think of it? Never? Not even if she died as the result of a perfectly understandable accident? We are talking about an accident, Bernard."

"Is this what Thurkettle said?"

"Tessa was stoned . . . drugged to the eyebrows that night. She was dancing through the mud, twirling around in her silk dress and singing. These are your words, Bernard."

"I'm not sure . . ." I said.

"You took Tessa there in that van," said Werner. "But for that, she wouldn't have been there for anyone to kill."

I jerked as if I had taken a slap in the face. It was true. Tessa had climbed into the van I was using that night. I had driven her to the shooting and thus to her death. It was the guilt that came from that fact that gave me no rest. She had come to Berlin with Dicky, and shared his bedroom at the hotel. But I could not free myself from the feeling that her death was my responsibility.

"Bernard. If you killed Tessa, you must come to terms with it. No one is going to charge you with anything. London would give a big sigh of relief. Everyone knows it wouldn't have been done intentionally."

"Who's got my Webley?"

"I don't know."

"But someone has? It was my father's gun. Have the DDR been playing games with phoney ballistics?"

"I heard that Thurkettle brought your Dad's Webley back with him," said Werner.

"Why the hell would he do that?"

"You used it to kill Russians. It was a British Army pistol with marks leading straight back to your father. Leaving it at the scene of the shooting would have been madness."

"Is this what the Department think happened? That I killed them all?" I looked at Werner; he often got to know what people were saying long before I did.

"I don't know what they think," said Werner. "Probably they are as puzzled as I am: they don't know what to think."

"Where is Thurkettle now?"

"I don't know."

"The Department is going after him. They want to bring him face to face with me."

"Bernard. If Thurkettle is in hiding it's because he's frightened."

"Frightened of me, you mean?"

"Of course. See it from his point of view."

"That I killed Tessa?"

"And he is the only witness. Yes. What chance would he stand, with you challenging him in a Departmental inquiry? That's how he will see it."

I sat back and rubbed my hands together. My palms were sweaty and I could feel that my face was flushed and burning. I must have looked as guilty as hell. "It's bullshit, Werner. I don't know who you've been talking to, but it's all bullshit. In any kind of inquiry I can clear up all the details. I remember everything as clearly as if it happened yesterday. Everything important anyway. When they bring Thurkettle in I'll tackle him. I'll show you what is really what."

"I wouldn't count on finding Thurkettle," said Werner. "When a man like that wants to disappear, there is no finding him again."

I sat there for a long time.

"I was going to run away," I said finally. Werner nodded. "I was going to grab the kids and Gloria, too. I had planned everything. The Irish Republic and the Aeroflot connection: Shannon to Cuba. From Havana a ship to . . . I'm not sure where."

Werner stared at me. "Have you gone mad, Bernie?"

"It would have worked," I protested.

"Did you ask the children?" He didn't wait for a

reply; he knew I hadn't taken them into my confidence. "It would have been a fiasco," he said softly.

"I don't think so," I said.

"And what about Gloria? Did you talk it over with her?"

"No," I said.

"That's all over, Bernard. I saw Gloria in London. She's happy. No men in her life. Sometimes she has dinner with Bret; I suppose they both get a bit lonely sometimes. But I could tell she's content living her own life on her own. She brought you into the conversation. She said how pleased she was that you were working in Berlin. She said you were brilliant and that she hoped you would make a big splash. She meant it. There was no bitterness, no ill-feeling in her, Bernie. But you are not a part of her life any more. And not a part of her future. You'd better face up to it."

Werner's words drained the life from me. I felt sick. "You don't know her, Werner," I said desperately. "And anyway . . ." I sipped at my drink and recovered my composure. "Gloria and me; yes, that's all over. Very much all over. Now tell me something I don't know."

"So what is it all about, Bernie? This madness of yours. Is it some deep-down resentment and envy of Fiona's success?"

"Envy? Really, Werner."

"Or hatred? Do you hate Fiona? Perhaps without even really understanding that you do. She loves you very much. She's like me, she's not good at saying things, but she loves you, I know."

Werner's calm voice and considerate tone made me cautious. This was Werner the world famous children's psychologist. I answered him in the same calm manner, "I don't think she does," I said. "Fiona is in love with

her work. She would be happy to see me run away with
Gloria and the children, too. It would give her more time
for meetings and writing reports."

"Frank guessed you were going to run," said
Werner.

"Frank did? How do you know he guessed?"

"He sent for me. And you know what a surprise that
must have been. Frank and I have never got along.
Frank said he'd be wanting me to go over to London
and talk to you. He didn't say what about. Then, when
he heard from Bret that you'd been meeting with the
Swede, Frank told me to be in Leuschner's Café next
morning. I got there early and Frank was waiting for me.
I don't know how long he'd been waiting, he had
already downed a couple of coffees and bread rolls and
stuff. He was very agitated: filled his pipe with tobacco
and put it away without smoking it. You know what he's
like when he's jumpy. He said the Swede was dead, and
that there was no need to talk to you after all. He said
you'd be okay."

"Frank's known me a long time."

"That's the trouble," said Werner. "We all know
each other too well."

"I'm not going to sit still for this one, Werner," I
said. "I didn't shoot Tessa. And you can go back and tell
anyone who asks you about it."

Werner stood up, huge and threatening. I'd never
seen him like this before. He didn't raise his voice
above a whisper, but for the first time in my life I found
him intimidating. "Very well," said Werner. He made it
sound like the final curtain to a Chekhov play.

I didn't move. Werner walked across the room to a
photograph of Richthofen standing amid a group of
scruffy pilots in front of an Albatros biplane. Werner

took his time studying the picture, as if trying to recognize which one was Göring. Werner was walking with a limp. Long ago he had his leg broken by some thugs from the other side of the Wall. The leg bothered him sometimes: in cold weather like this, or when he was emotionally unsettled. I said nothing. Werner stood with his back to me, looking at the photo and bending his leg slightly, as I'd seen him do when it pained him. It was better to let him calm down.

Eventually Werner turned to look at me. Perhaps he'd been counting to ten. He said, "You spoke with Silas Gaunt?" He spoke in a casual voice, but could not conceal his interest in the meeting. "Did he add anything?"

"Yes, he added to my confusion," I said.

Werner continued quietly, "Well, perhaps it hasn't occurred to you, Bernie, that if the Department was desperate to cover up the judicial slaughter of that poor woman—bringing along a highly paid hit man who came in, did his job, and disappeared—they wouldn't be forging documents, wriggling and lying, and going to all the other absurd lengths that you ascribe to them. Now would they?"

"Maybe," I said.

"No. . . . They would simply kill you. If that's the way they did things, they'd do it to you. That way they'd get it over with neatly and quickly. And relatively cheaply."

I still didn't move. He looked at me for what seemed like a long time. I stared back at him and finally he stalked out, his terrible anger seemingly unabated. His long black overcoat, and his infirmity, added an extra and sinister aspect to his somewhat theatrical exit.

Soon after Werner had departed, a man named Joschi, I never knew his family name, suddenly appeared behind the bar. He was a small melancholy individual who had lost both parents in the war. He spent his childhood in a Silesian orphanage. In the final weeks of the war, Joschi, with the other inmates, trekked westward with the Red Army close behind. He had worked in a communist-run chinaware factory in Dresden until he escaped from the DDR two years ago. Now he insisted upon thanking me for his job working for Rudi in the Horrido. In fact I'd done no more than mention his name at a time when Rudi was looking for an honest and uncomplaining slave who would work the clock around for starvation wages.

"Schnapps, Herr Samson?" He was standing holding a glass and a bottle ready to pour.

"No thanks, Joschi. I've had enough."

"Scotch? Cognac, seven years old?"

"Thanks, but I mustn't."

"You are looking well, Herr Samson."

"You too, Joschi." I appreciated his encouraging remark, as from what I had heard from several outspoken friends I was looking decidedly timeworn.

"Can they make a handgun from plastic, Herr Samson?" I hesitated and looked at him. "The customers were arguing about it around the bar, the night before last. One of the airport cops—the noisy argumentative young fellow with the trimmed beard. The one who shows everyone his paper targets from the pistol range. I think you may know him. He bet fifty marks that it was possible to make a plastic gun. They couldn't agree. I said I knew someone who knew about these things."

"How did it start?" I asked.

"A package came for Mr. Volkmann . . . long time

ago. . . . A courier-service delivery. It was a plastic gun. I said it was a toy."

"Sounds like a toy to me," I said. "Maybe I will have that schnapps."

He poured my drink and I sipped it. He held up his glass in a toast of good health. I could see that I was being told something important. This was Joschi repaying something of the debt he thought he owed me. But I wasn't quite sure how far I was permitted to go in asking questions. I said, "A long time ago?"

"That time when there was all the fuss, and you went off somewhere to recuperate."

"This cop who thinks they make plastic guns: what does he say?"

"He says he's seen them. American plastic pistols, with triangular plastic bullets that fit tightly into the breech. They are made to get through the airport security machines."

"What would Werner want with it?" Werner had no special interest or need for a handgun, let alone a special-purpose one. I worried lest he was involved in something that would get him into trouble. There was a secretive side of his nature; I'd known that since we were kids together. But I felt sure that there was nothing he would not confide to me, just as I had no secrets from him.

"We get a lot of funny packages behind the bar here, Herr Samson. The boss looks inside sometimes; he likes to make sure it's not drugs. Of course Herr Volkmann's name was never spoken."

I nodded. Any of the arriving airline crew members could walk across the airfield, and come through the same broken wire fence that all the on-duty engineers and office staff used when they dropped in for a furtive drink. In a way I had played into Joschi's hands. He now knew that the gun had not been handed on to me, or gone to Werner with my knowledge or blessing.

"Don't mention it to anyone, Joschi," I said. "It's a toy I'm sure. Talk about it and you might spoil a nice surprise for someone."

"I'll say it's impossible then?"

"Yes, you can take my word for it. The poor fellow has lost his money."

NINE

COLNBROOK, ENGLAND

It was a strange place to find the grievously sick Jim Prettyman. Jim was rich. He was an unnamed "exceptional business and financial adviser" according to an article about one of his clients that had appeared in the *Wall Street Journal*. Jim liked numbers, and his mathematical talent enabled him to adjust effortlessly to computerized management. He was a sought-after man nowadays, a consultant to half a dozen international companies, as well as condescending to occasional jobs for the Department. I would have expected to find a sick Jim Prettyman hidden behind diagnosticians, pretty nurses, and grim-faced specialists in white coats. I would have looked for him in a big private suite of the Mayo Clinic, the top floor of a Harley Street infirmary with three-star cuisine, or one of those fancy hospitals in Switzerland where the best rooms have a view of the Alps.

As it was, he had chosen a suburban house in Colnbrook, not far from Heathrow, London's major airport. Heathrow's claim to be the world's most active airport was disputed, but surely its role as the largest must be uncontested. Aircraft hangars and repair sheds, service areas, high-security car parks, transport depots, and freight warehouses, and offices for the legions who flew the word processors, sprawled for miles in every direction.

Not so long ago, the airport's vociferous neighbors were continually staging demonstrations protesting about the noise and inconvenience they suffered. But eventually they discovered that their houses had become very desirable as accommodation for well-paid airline employees. Soon specialist rental agents took interest in this area, conveniently close to central London, where houses could be made available on short leaseholds for wealthy foreigners. Now Jim Prettyman—born a Londoner—found himself in this wealthy foreigner category: a weary, wealthy visitor looking for a place to rest his head.

His rented house was typical of those built in southern England between the wars, but it had been furnished and equipped to meet the more stringent requirements of foreigners. The house was served by a heating system that dispensed warmth. The furnace could be heard somewhere in the cellar, roaring like an antique jet engine and shaking the whole house. The other facilities included two German dishwashers, a gleaming chest freezer, and a two-door refrigerator with ice water dispenser. The kitchen was like the flight deck of a spaceship, with an array of whippers, mixers, and blenders, a coffeemaker that dispensed steam for frothy milk, and a complex of ovens that would microwave, turbofan, or radiant heat your dinner at the touch of a button.

"I'm so glad you came, Mr. Samson. Jay needs cheering up." From some unseen speaker system there came a soft but spirited performance of *The Merry Widow.*

I had seen photos of Mrs. Prettyman. I remembered how "Jay" had large colored portraits of her in expensive frames around his Washington, D.C., office. The photos had always shown her smartly dressed in simple shirt-style dresses that were right for Washington's hot summers. In the pictures she had a wide, film-star smile and athletic pose. Her wealthy family and her father, who was something important in the State Department, had taken Jim to their heart and helped his career. No wonder that in the photos Jim was always smiling, too.

As she took my coat and hat she said, "Of course he's doped up. I have coffee brewed; will you take some?"

"Is he? Coffee? Yes, please."

"He has to be on medication. I have a nurse come in three times a day. She's a lovely person: Australian. The clinic wouldn't discharge him to my care except on condition a real good qualified nurse attended him."

"But he's on the mend?"

She frowned at me. "No, he's not on the mend, Mr. Samson—may I call you Bernard? I thought you knew that."

"No," I said. "I mean yes, do call me Bernard."

"And my friends call me Tabby, it's short for Tabitha."

"Tabby. That's a pretty name. So he's not on the mend?"

She made a movement of her hand to invite me to sit on one of the high padded stools that were alongside the breakfast counter. An "open-plan kitchen" was the sort of amenity estate agents like to mention on their prospectus.

There was a glass pot of coffee sitting on the hot-plate of the coffeemaker. She took two decorative mugs from a shelf and poured coffee into both of them. My mug had a brightly colored pre-Raphaelite woman drowning in a pale blue river. Ophelia I suppose. The coffee was watery, too.

"He's not expected to live above three months," she said.

"I had no idea. I knew he was sick of course. . . . I was on the train with him."

"He wanted to be in England again. North London, he said, but this was the best I could do at short notice."

"Three months?"

"At most. Jay doesn't know that of course. He thinks he's recovering strength enough for his treatment to resume. But I think it's better that you should know the score."

"Thank you. Are you telling all his friends?" I wondered if Cindy was a party to this alarming prognosis.

"He hasn't seen any friends. Few people know where Jay is." She gave a little chuckle, as if hiding him away was good fun. "I was surprised when you tracked us down and said you wanted to come."

I smiled and nodded. We drank coffee.

"Jay goes up and down," she said. "Today seems to be one of his good days." She was very restrained, very understated: no makeup, no ornaments, not even a watch; cotton dress, and hair cut like a schoolgirl. Yet she had a natural effortless elegance that gave her authority and importance. It was, I suppose, a product of her affluent background. Bret had the same sort of aplomb.

"The nurse will be down in a moment," she said. "She goes through a routine. She takes about twenty minutes usually. Tell me about yourself, Bernard. Are you married?"

"Yes, I am," I said.

"That's wonderful," she said. In theory—and on paper—the second Mrs. Prettyman was everything I usually ran fast to escape, but I have to admit that I found her both clever and charming, the way Werner told me I used to see Cindy. I decided that Jay was lucky to find such a loyal and generous lifetime companion, for Tabby told me that, despite two failed marriages and grown-up children, he was "the real thing at last."

"We understand each other, you see," she told me. "My previous husbands were not too particular about telling the truth: to me or anyone else. But Jay is just wonderful. We tell each other everything."

"Do you really?" I said. Jim Prettyman was entrusted with some very dark Departmental secrets. It was hard to believe that Tabby had been made a party to all of them. And in any case Jimjay was not noted for his unwavering veracity.

She leaned over to see that my coffee cup was empty and poured more for me. "I'm not saying it wasn't the religion that did it. But Jay says that has nothing to do with it."

"What religion?" I said.

"He went back to the Church. You didn't know that?"

"The Catholic Church?" I remembered the rosary he clutched constantly on the train.

"Yes, I'm not a Catholic. I was brought up a Presbyterian. What are you?"

"I'm not sure," I said. "It depends what sort of trouble I'm in."

"Jay felt bad at discouraging his first wife from attending Mass. He was born a Roman Catholic. His folks were Catholic. Catholic childhoods seem to take a grip on people, don't you find?"

"Yes, I suppose so."

"It's a comfort. It has helped him endure this terrible sickness. He can't go to Mass, of course, but the local priest calls in frequently. He's a lovely Scotsman. Jay looks forward to the visits, and the father likes a glass of whisky. They chat for hours."

"That's nice," I said. But it wasn't nice. I didn't like anything I was hearing. I didn't enjoy the idea of Prettyman confiding secrets to his wife, nor chatting for hours with his priest over a glass or two of whisky.

Perhaps my reservations showed on my face, for she said, "Have you seen Jay's first wife recently?"

"As a matter of fact I have."

Tabby seemed distressed at this. "You are not here because of her?"

"No, I'm not."

"She's blackmailing Jay, you know that, do you, Bernard?"

"Blackmail is a serious accusation, Tabby. I hope you know what you are saying."

She smiled. "I should, Bernard. I have a Ph.D. in International Law and ten years' experience as an attorney in Washington."

Touché. "So what kind of blackmail?"

"You'd best level with me, Bernard. What's your angle? You say you are not acting for the first Mrs. Prettyman?"

"I certainly am not," I said.

"But you have spoken with her. Is she seeing you again?"

"Not if I see her first."

"Okay. I'm convinced. I was all prepared to be friendly with her. I'm sympathetic. But she's nothing but a troublemaker." She held up the coffeepot and I shook my head.

"So what kind of blackmail?" I asked again.

"Maybe you should ask Jay," she said. "It's his ex-wife."

Tabby had warned me that the injections, and whatever other dope they were feeding him, left him in a euphoric mood, but I wasn't prepared for the transformation. I'd last seen him on the Moscow express stretched out like a corpse and only half as lively, but I found a Jim who was full of fight.

"Bernard, you son of a gun. Where have you been?"

"Trying to find you," I replied.

"England is wonderful, Bernard." He had a plate of grapes by his side, and he was popping one into his mouth between every few words. "Green and fresh and friendly. I didn't realize how much I'd missed it until I came back this time."

I looked out of the window. It didn't look so great to me: too many bricks and cars and not enough trees and grass.

"We are not bothered by the planes," he said. "They take off the other side; unless the wind is that way we hardly hear them." He offered me his grapes but I shook my head.

The bedroom was equipped with an assortment of expensive medical equipment of the sort that glitters in the windows of medical suppliers in London's Wigmore Street. Jim was not in bed. He was dressed in a striped, cotton dressing-gown and sitting in a chair, a soft, cream-colored blanket draped over his legs. Despite his lively manner his complexion was, as always, chalky. On his knee he had an open notebook, its pages covered with scribbled numbers. He saw me looking at it. "I can't seem to concentrate on reading these days, Bernie. I started doing number games ... it started me off remembering old times." He tapped the notebook. "I was thinking of the way we cracked the one-time pad," he explained. "That was the high point of my days in the Department." He stared at me. His eyes were bright and unnaturally active. I suppose it was the medicine.

"I heard about that," I said.

"They all said that the Soviet one-time pads were unbeatable, didn't they? No one wanted to know. I said it was worth tackling, but no one wanted to know."

He held up his notebook so that I could look at the lines of numbers he'd written, but it was difficult for me to understand what he'd been doing. Was it gibberish or genius? I couldn't even read it properly. Perhaps his scrawling writing was also something to do with his drugs.

"Consider the problem," said Jim, as if to the world at large, rather than to me. "Forty-eight five-digit groups. Every page of every pad different, with the sole exception of the corresponding leaf of the pad at the other end. Impossible to crack. Bret told me that. He said, 'In two words, Jim, Im possible.'"

"Yes," I said. "Bret has always had a great sense of humor."

Ploughing on without pause, "Where do one-time pads, and all their clever constantly changing codes, come from? I asked them that. They are not handwritten, are they? They are all printed, and if they are printed that must be done on a printing machine. They don't have thousands of Russian machinists standing there, turning a handle to change the numbers one by one, do they? They use a printing machine that automatically changes the numbers or letters. That printing machine has to be programmed. And that order—the sequence in which the machine changes the ciphers—can be cracked, just like any other code can be cracked."

"It was quite a triumph," I said. There was no way of stopping him; it was better to let him go on. While he talked I looked round the room at the electrically controlled bed and the stainless-steel bedpans, the medical trolley, and racks for medicines and syringes. It all made me wonder if Tabby was that kind of woman who, late in life—after charity committees, piano lessons, and the history of Renaissance painting—discovers a need to play Florence Nightingale with any relative within reach. Well, maybe that's the way it was, and maybe it suited both of them.

"And later on I found that it had been done before; back in the war," Jim was saying. "Of course I went back through the *American Mathematical Monthly*. I found the copies published in the summer of 1929 when the idea was first being mooted at Hunter College in New York. But then a chance remark from one of the old-timers put me on to what our own Denniston and his Diplomatic Section had done in Berkeley Street, Piccadilly, right here in London in the war. The German pads had eight lines of six five-figure groups. Of course that set me thinking." He gave me a quizzical stare.

"Of course," I said, trying to look like someone who would know how many lines of six-figure groups a German wartime one-time pad always had. And figure it the way Jim had figured it.

"It was obviously using 240 wheels," he said.

"Yes," I said.

"When I went to the old man and showed him the way that the diplomatic OTPs had been cracked in the war, he wouldn't believe it at first. When I talked to him about it, he gave in."

"I can imagine," I said.

"The old man was ecstatic: he gave me everything I asked for."

"It was a triumph, Jim."

"It came together neatly. The Americans went wild; Langley opened a whole new department to handle it. Millions of dollars went into it."

"It restored their faith in us," I said.

"I would have got an OBE—maybe something even grander—had we not been so covert. The old man told me that, and later on Bret told me the same."

"Maybe even a K," I said.

"Not a K, Bernie," he said, coming to earth with a bump. "You don't have to overdo it." He looked at me. "Now what did you really come here to ask me?"

"Does there have to be anything?"

"Come along, Bernard. You don't pay social calls and you don't like grapes. When you come out here, to the wrong side of the airport, it's because you are after something." Perhaps he felt he was being a shade too offensive, for he added, "No one in the Department pays social calls. It's not in the training manual, is it?"

"Cindy dropped in on me. She said you left a box file with her. She wants to get rid of it."

He swallowed the grape he was chewing and pushed the rest of them aside. "Get rid of it?"

"She says she's looked after it long enough," I said.

"Is that what she told you?"

"Yes. That's what she said. It's not true?"

"She's a lively one, isn't she?"

"Yes, she is," I agreed emphatically.

"She stole it. She stole that box file. I gave her a lift to her apartment in Brussels, and when I helped her carry her bags from my car boot into the building she took the box file along with her other baggage. I didn't notice until I got to the airport. I called her from the transit lounge but her line was busy."

"You didn't do anything about it?"

"What am I going to do? Tell the Department that I let my ex-wife steal a secret box file? Jesus, they would have ripped my balls off. If they find out what's happened, they still will. You've got to get it back for me, Bernard."

"Okay. You think she will just hand it over?"

"Not Cindy. Nothing comes free with Cindy. Where is she keeping it?"

"In her office safe, she said."

"In Brussels?"

"How many offices does she have?"

"What did you think? When you saw her, what did you think of her?"

"She looked fine," I said cautiously. Experience told me that no matter how much men criticized their ex-wives, it was not an invitation to join in. "Very glamorous; very attractive." And yet making ex-wives sound too attractive also held its dangers, so I added, "Of course, we are all getting older."

"Is she still using all that makeup? Fluttering those false eyelashes; rouged cheeks like a tart. And dousing herself in scent? I told her she was overdoing it: she smelled like the perfume room in Harrods."

"You told her that, did you?" It sounded like a dangerous conversational ploy.

"We've got to get that box back," he said.

"What's in it?" I asked him.

"I'm not sure."

"You're not sure? I thought it would be something you wanted and needed."

"I was told to open it only after getting the order to open it. I figured it contained orders of some sort."

"It's big and heavy," I reminded him.

"And maybe a gun or something. I had the key and the combination but I lost both. And then I thought what the hell."

"I see."

He looked at me. "Have you reported this?"

"Reported what?"

"Don't be dumb, Bernard. Have you reported what Cindy told you? That she has the box file."

"Of course I haven't. I wanted to talk to you about it first."

"I always said you were the smartest one there," he said. "More cunning, more devious, and more far-sighted than any of the rest of them."

"Spread it around," I said. "Or maybe not."

He was smiling, and perhaps there was some margin of admiration in this trenchant description but I don't know how much. He was resentful. Indignant in the way that I would have been if he had tried on me the trick I was pulling on him. "No," he said. "If you had reported it you would have nothing to threaten me with, would you?"

"Don't be that way, Jim."

"So now I've got two of you twisting my arm. You and Cindy: the two who were closest to me in the old days."

"Oh, sure. *Et tu, Brute.* But Caesar hadn't mislaid a

box file, old buddy." I gave him back his notebook and his numbers. "I'd get that box back from her, Jim. If I were you, I really would get it back from her. Even if it means paying her some alimony. In the long run it might prove cheaper. The Ides of March are come, Jim. This is a bad time of year."

"But not gone. Yes, well I don't give a damn. Go back and tell them all you know. And tell Cindy to go to hell. I don't work for the Department any more. I don't give a damn what happens to any of you."

"Cindy said two men came to her asking for it. Americans from Geneva, she said. Business associates of yours."

"And you believed her? Jesus Christ, Bernard. How can you let her make such a fool of you? That was my lawyer and his partner. I sent them along to talk with her, but she played little girl lost with them. She is too cunning to say anything that a lawyer might use."

"I wish you two would get your stories straight," I said. "Surely you don't enjoy all this hassle."

"I've got no money to spare for Cindy. Do you know how much it costs to be sick nowadays? A fortune!"

"You should have taken time out to be sick back when we could afford it."

"Yes, that was my big mistake," he said ruefully. "Why are you so interested in that box file? What are you expecting to find inside it? Give it to me straight."

"Once upon a time there was a man named Thurkettle, a rent-a-gun who killed my sister-in-law . . ."

"Hold it . . ."

"No hold-its, Jimmy. I was there; I saw it. He shot Tessa Kosinski on the Autobahn, and then came to meet you and catch a plane to safety. Knowing the way the Department do things, I know that he must have been debriefed by someone. . . ." Seeing that Jimmy was about to start interrupting again, I quickly added, "And that someone was you."

Jim wet his lips. I thought he was going to say something interesting but he picked up a glass of water and sipped some. "Go on."

"Cindy drove to the plane and got the box from the Swede. Meanwhile you paid off Thurkettle and helped him do his disappearing act."

"No, Bernard."

"Don't tell me no. You gave him his money and his new ID. He was so pleased that he made you a present of the sapphire brooch that he had ripped from the dead body of Tessa Kosinski."

"You've got it wrong."

"Oh, sure. Well, you'll be able to explain how wrong I've got it to a Board of Inquiry. Washington has agreed to extradite Thurkettle. So don't imagine you will be able to run back to America and escape their clutches."

"Extradite Thurkettle!" He laughed scornfully. "How are they going to do that? Resurrection? Thurkettle is dead. Very, very dead. Yes, I went to the rendezvous— the Ziesar exit ramp—and saw Thurkettle. But he was dead."

"If Thurkettle is dead, you killed him. Where did you get Tessa's brooch? You must have stolen it from his body after you wasted him."

"I didn't steal anything from him. I didn't touch him."

"Let's play it your way, Jim. You arrive to find your contact is dead. Of course you would touch him. You'd have to be crazy not to check his pockets. London would want proof that someone had hit the right target. You would need to know if he had a gun in his pocket. A gun could get you into a lot of trouble in that jurisdiction. Or get you out of it."

"Okay, I looked in his pockets."

"And found the sapphire brooch?"

"Yes. Yes, I did. In his pocket. That was a silly mistake." Prettyman suddenly stiffened. Sometimes throwing a scare into a suspect makes them freeze like that. "I've got the brooch here," he said in a whisper. "You didn't say anything to Tabby, did you?"

"Say anything? How would I start? You are such a complicated, double-dealing crook I wouldn't know how to tackle it."

"I didn't know the brooch belonged to your sister-in-law. I swear I didn't."

"That would have made a difference, would it? You are the bastard who had her killed. And then killed her hit man."

"I tell you no."

"No, not you. You just waited for Thurkettle to arrive at the rendezvous and have heart failure."

"I was just a contact man. Let me explain. The first I heard was that Silas Gaunt wanted to talk to some sort of hit man. It was not such a surprising request. The Department often use me to make contact with hard-to-find people or esoteric institutions. So I set up the meeting. I didn't know what it was all about."

"Silas Gaunt actually talked to Thurkettle? When? Where?"

"How was I to know that Silas was going nuts? No one told me he was a crazy man. His name was whispered like he was about to be canonized. They told me he was an infallible old hero. They told me that nothing important was decided until word had come from this oracle in the Cotswolds."

"How do you know he's going crazy?"

"Right! It came as a surprise to me, too. Everyone said it was the D-G who was going nuts, didn't they? Now it becomes clear that it was Silas Gaunt who was running out of control: the D-G was just on a damage-limitation exercise."

"What is out of control?"

"All the signs were there ages ago but no one would face up to it. First I heard that Silas Gaunt was sick and bedridden. Then he gets some sort of brainstorm because the local district council tells him to chop all his elm trees down. Maybe there were other signs of physical deterioration. Who knows what was hatching in his brain? All we know for sure is that now they have locked him away."

"Silas is alive and well and living at Whitelands," I said.

"They are keeping it very need-to-know."

"You say Silas briefed Thurkettle? Are you sure?"

"Sure? Sure? I arranged it. I took Thurkettle to the Hilton Hotel in Park Lane. I wasn't allowed to sit in at the meeting of course."

"Silas Gaunt would never have revealed his identity to a hit man."

"What did he have to lose? He was arranging for Thurkettle to be killed, too. And anyway, as I say: Silas was crazy."

"I don't believe you. I've known Silas Gaunt all my life. I saw him recently . . ."

"I don't care what you believe. If you go chasing after him, like you chased after me, you won't get to him. Because they finally slammed him into some special funny farm the Department uses for people who have State secrets in their heads."

"It shouldn't be difficult to check out," I said.

"Not difficult at all," he agreed. "Check it out. And you'll find I'm telling you the truth." He craned towards me and stared. "I swear to God."

"Look, Jim. Thurkettle killed Tessa Kosinski; I was there, I saw it. But you killed Thurkettle. You took the gun that Werner Volkmann delivered to you; a special plastic gun. You waited at the rendezvous for Thurkettle to arrive on his BMW motorbike. No one pays a hit man in advance, so he would have had to meet you somewhere to collect his payment. You wasted Thurkettle, grabbed the money, abandoned the motorbike, dumped the gun and drove away. My guess is that you drove away in some kind of camper vehicle."

"This is your theory, is it? It's not something you saw on late-night TV?" Prettyman narrowed his eyes. Perhaps he wasn't staring; perhaps he was in pain.

"And that's not all of it," I said. "Your Cindy was there. I sometimes suspect that this knockdown, drag-out brawl the two of you like displaying to everyone is a cover-up. I think you two have been in cozy agreement until now. She took you to your rendezvous with Thurkettle in a car. You had to have someone drive you there, because after killing Thurkettle you have to drive his car away somewhere. Cindy maybe helps you with your murder and then drives on to meet the Swede and his plane. She collected the box file from the Swede and took it away with her. Now you have some kind of fight about who owns it. Or maybe you don't have a fight; maybe that's a scam, too."

"Maybe there's not even a box file," he said.

"The thought had occurred to me," I agreed.

"Very good, Bernard. Very logical, but too baroque for a Hollywood movie. Cindy help in a murder? Are you serious?"

"You took the payoff money to Thurkettle. A lot of money, because professional hits like that cost a lot of money. You would have had to bring back some kind of receipt, however disguised that paperwork might have been. There would have to be a piece of paper, for some cashier somewhere in Whitehall to do his sums. And somewhere too there would be a debriefing report."

"And is that what you think you'll find in the box file?" He forced a little laugh. "You're a card, Bernard, you really are. You'll be sorry you ever started this nonsense."

"Let's not play truth or consequences, Jim. Threats leave friendships in tatters."

"So you've noticed that, have you, Bernard? It took you a long time, didn't it? And cost you a lot of tattered friends."

"Too late now to worry about that, Jim old pal. Right now I'm more interested in the box file Cindy wants to sell you."

"Are you? You are very clever, Bernard. And very nearly right. But no cover-up. Cindy and I don't get along and that's for real. Your biggest error is thinking that I killed Thurkettle. You're right too about him leaving a camper in place. I was told not to let him drive off in it, so Cindy was with me to drive the camper away. But when I found Thurkettle dead I sent her to the plane instead. Wrong about the money too. I didn't have any money for Thurkettle, I had an arrest warrant. Thurkettle had been told we would fly him to a spot he'd chosen in Germany. But my orders said I was to fly with him to

England, to a military strip in Dorset. They were going to put him on ice. I had no money for him: that was how I was going to get him on the plane instead of letting him drive away. And I wasn't told to debrief him. In fact I was told not to talk to him about any work he'd done, or let him tell me anything about his operation or his orders."

"Why try to wriggle out of the Thurkettle killing?" I asked him. "It's got your prints all over it."

"Of course you don't believe me. The truth doesn't fit into your theory, does it? Well, you can go on disbelieving for as long as you like. The truth is that I was fooled. We were all fooled. Thurkettle was more fooled than any of us: fooled to death. But Cindy knew nothing of it: she was waiting back on the Autobahn. I didn't tell her I'd found Thurkettle dead. Yes, I searched Thurkettle's body to get his car keys. I took his VW camper and went through the checkpoint and drove all night to a safe house I knew in Düsseldorf. I went to earth and waited for instructions. I think that's what the manual says is the right drill." He smiled. How these bloody office people always liked to play field agent. "Two days after that, the alarm bells started to ring in London. With me sitting in Düsseldorf, and the Swede arriving in England with empty seats in his plane, Silas Gaunt knew his pet scheme had fallen apart. Nothing had gone the way he planned. From the Department's point of view it was a total disaster."

I nodded as I ran it through my mind. Prettyman's story would have a strand of truth woven into it. Good cover stories always do. But I noticed that Cindy could not be called in to corroborate his version of the Thurkettle death.

Was it a cock-up or a triumph of concealment? Never mind the way he now wanted to bend the truth. Prettyman was concocting a story that got him off the hook. I suppose he didn't want to go along to Mass and explain that gunning down a colleague in cold blood was a part of his misspent past. But look at it another way and Jim had done more or less what he was told, and the Department had got more or less what they wanted out of it. Silas had fixed it so that no one knew the whole story. Only a maniac or a genius could have programmed such a complex operation, and Silas was a mix of both. Congratulations Uncle Silas. Disaster? A couple more disasters like that and they'd be giving Jim the medal he so desperately craved.

Perhaps he saw what sort of doubts I had. He said, "Maybe it was all planned that way."

"Was his payoff waiting in the camper?"

"No. I went right through it the next day. The camper was obviously arranged by Thurkettle himself. He planned to take the money and run, but I had no money for him. Inside the camper I found a wallet with an Amex card and Visa and some other plastic, small change and odds and ends. It was all in some Scandinavian name—not Thurkettle—so I guess he was going to change identity. No passport; he must have hidden that somewhere else. He'd made all the arrangements to escape, but he had reckoned without the arrangements that someone else had made for him."

"You're a cold-blooded bastard," I said. "You go through his pockets, and you steal a brooch and give it to some girl you take a fancy to. It stinks; you stink." I wondered what else he'd stolen from the body and I would never know about. I couldn't help wondering if Prettyman disobeyed orders and killed Thurkettle in order to steal the payment for the hit. I wouldn't put it past him if he became desperately short of money. And the fee for a tricky and dangerous job like that might have gone into six figures.

"The stink comes from the Department," said Prettyman. "And it didn't even work."

"Didn't it?"

"They thought they could foist off the burned body of Tessa Kosinski as being that of your wife, while you two escaped. That was a stupid idea. I could have told them that if they had consulted me. You can't burn a body properly in a car fire with a few gallons of petrol."

"Why?"

"You need a temperature of about one thousand degrees centigrade to reduce the big bones to ash."

"It doesn't have to become ash to be beyond identification," I said.

"No it doesn't, but that wasn't the problem. They wanted a corpse that *was* identified, a corpse that would resemble another specific person. What Thurkettle did was useless. It didn't burn properly. You've got to take into account all the water in the guts of a human body. I saw the East German report on the Kosinski body."

"Where did you get hold of that?"

"The Department. Did they never show it to you?"

"No," I said.

"The skin and flesh was blackened, the legs were burned, but the abdomen and the internal organs—lungs and liver and so on—were virtually intact, and that had prevented the upper body burning properly. . . . Is this affecting you, Bernard?"

"No," I said. "Go on."

"It's your sister-in-law, I know."

"Go on, I said."

"The failure of the upper body to burn meant that the skull was too preserved to fool them. The top of the skull had gone, but the frontal sinus was intact. Fiona had been treated for a sinus problem. They had X-rays of her skull."

"A substitute skull was burned with the body. The prepared skull had had its dentistry specially done to be like Fiona's."

"It wouldn't fool them for a moment. The sinus cavities are just as identifiable as teeth. And anyway, much of that clever dentistry was a waste of time and effort. The lower jaw detached from the skull and was burned away; the upper was less easy to match." He rubbed his hands together. "No, it was all for nothing."

"What happened to you, Jim? Back in the old days you would never have considered becoming a part of a dirty business like this."

"That was the old days," he said, looking at his hands. They were bent and pale and spotted; the hands of a sick man. "We live in a different world now, Bernard. In the old days it was all an amusing game, and we were good at playing it. But the world has gone professional, Bernard. You tell me I stink, and maybe I do. It's because the Department called me in to do their dirty work. I do it so that people like you, and Bret and Sir Henry and Silas Gaunt and all the rest of the sanctimonious timeservers, could keep your hands clean, and keep your conscience in good shape, by telling me I stink."

"You can't rationalize murder," I said.

"I've never killed anyone," said Prettyman. "I draw the line at that. And at the drug dimension, too. I never knew that Thurkettle was supplying Tessa with dope to keep her under his spell. But I'm through with all that. I have made my peace with God. I will meet my maker and I will be free." He reached into the top pocket of his dressing gown and found the sapphire brooch. "Take it; give it to Fiona or to George. I don't want it." He passed it to me. It was carefully wrapped into a white silk handkerchief. He must have already decided to give it to me, and put it in his pocket before I arrived. I suppose he'd been sitting here all morning rehearsing his story. I wondered how much he had changed in the face of my questions.

I unwrapped the brooch and looked at it. The sapphire was scratched but its faint blue cast was luminous and liquid, like a glass of mountain water. The sparkle from the diamonds was quite different; a very hard light, like the beam from a carbon arc lamp. It was easy to see why people became obsessed by such stones. The brooch suddenly reminded me of Tessa and I could hear her voice. I wrapped it up and put it in my pocket. "I'll send it to George; he's next-of-kin I suppose."

"The pretty little Canadian nurse told me what you said to her."

"She thought you'd got it out of a bran tub."

"I didn't know it was that valuable. Or where it had come from. I just wanted to empty Thurkettle's pockets. I don't know why I didn't just throw it away at the time. I wanted to give the Canadian kid something. She was a nice little girl."

"They all are, Jim. But don't tell Tabby, is that it?" I said.

He gave me a man-to-man smile. I was sorry for him, in the way I would be sorry for anyone living out his final days near London's airport. But he was a creep and he was using me as an anvil upon which to beat his newly heated memories into a shape that suited him. I'd had enough. I got up and said goodbye. From the downstairs hi-fi a soprano was singing exuberantly. Under the circumstances, I'm not sure that Tabby's *Merry Widow* was a felicitous choice of background music.

"Was that all?" he said with evident relief. Despite my denials, he still thought the Department had sent me to check him out.

"You've told me all I need to know, Jim," I said. "You did okay. You are well on the way to a medal."

He smiled suspiciously.

How much of it could I believe? Was Thurkettle really dead? I wasn't even totally convinced that Jimjay was sick. If next week I happened upon Jim and Thurkettle playing a strenuous game of squash, Jim would just give me a shy smile and another long explanation.

TEN

AN AUTOBAHN EXIT.
THE GERMAN DEMOCRATIC REPUBLIC

The best way to test Prettyman's story was to go to the exit ramp he'd specified and see what could be found there. It was forbidden to leave the Autobahn, so I didn't tell Frank what I intended.

I took Werner with me. I hadn't told him about my meeting with Prettyman, but he knew I'd been pursuing every lead I could find. By the time we reached the Ziesar exit ramp I had formed a clear idea of what Thurkettle would need for an inconspicuous rendezvous.

"This would be good, Werner," I said as I lowered the window and looked around. This was Germany at its most rural. There was the smell of freshly dug lignite on the air. Since the oil crisis of 1973 the Soviet Union had become more possessive about its oil. The German Democratic Republic was producing its own energy and paying the price in dozens of opencast *Braunkohl* workings. They scarred the landscape, and this low grade, solid fuel polluted the air, both before and after being burned.

Werner didn't reply. He seemed to think we were engaged on a wild-goose chase, although he was too polite to say so in those exact words. But this was a perfect spot for a secret rendezvous of any kind. The junction was wide and hidden from view, protected from the weather and yet very close to the Autobahn. I ran the car—it was Werner's ancient Mercedes—up on to the grassy verge and used my binoculars to scout the surroundings. Two or three fields away I saw two farmworkers forking over a manure heap. "Let's go, Werner," I said, getting out of the car. I buttoned up tight against the steady downfall of wet snow that had continued ever since we left Berlin. It was better to walk over to the men. Until I had sniffed out the situation in this sleepy little backwater, I preferred that they didn't see the West Berlin license plates on the car.

The temperature seemed to be below zero, but that was hard to reconcile with the sleet. It fell steadily and was whisked into little tempests that whipped my face painfully, like shaving with a rusty razor blade. The wind was from the north, the most unkind wind, for north of here the world was flat; as level as a vast sea-bed, which it had once been. From here to the Baltic Sea there stretched the north German plain. This was Europe's battlefield, an arena where invading armies had maneuvered and fought since Germans stood firm against the Slavs, and their recorded history began. Little wonder that the wall dividing the Soviet Empire from the forces of NATO was so near to this place.

As we walked towards them, the two men stopped

work. They rested upon their long-handled forks and watched us approach, viewing us with that cool suspicion that country dwellers save for visitors of urban appearance. Werner's long, black overcoat was not the sort of garment to be encountered frequently in the German countryside unless he had been the proprietor of a traveling circus—a few mangy lions, a zebra, and a trapeze act—the sort of family enterprise still to be found touring round Eastern Europe from one small town to the next.

"Good day," I said. Both men nodded with an almost imperceptible movement of the head. Reaching into my pocket I brought out a half-bottle of schnapps. I twisted the cap from it and offered them a swig. Only after they had drunk some did I gulp at it myself. It warmed my throat. I gave it to Werner, who pretended to drink some. Werner was not keen on booze and particularly hated apple schnapps.

Taking my time with some preliminaries about the weather and the changing seasons, I asked them to remember the previous June. Had they seen a car or any kind of van or camper . . . left parked in the next field? Or anywhere near the Autobahn. Some time last summer. I didn't give them the exact date; it was better to reserve one known fact against which to test the information.

"Yes," said the elder of the two men. "Dark green: a sort of van."

The younger one added, "It was there two days and nights. There was no one inside it. We went and took a close look at it. It had a cooking stove, and a soft bed inside. No one went near it. Then, a couple of days later, it had gone. Gone in the night." The younger man's voice was keener and he seemed more accommodating than his father. They looked alike, except in stature. The elder man was short, his unshaven face deeply lined, and his manner resigned.

The younger man was freshly shaven, his hair cropped in a style that Germans thought was American. His clothes, although equally old, were cleaner than his father's. Under his waterproof jacket the boy had Western-style denim pants. He said, "We thought it might have been damaged on the Autobahn and waiting for the tow truck. But it seemed to be in perfect condition." The boy was unafraid, almost defiant in his willingness to help us. The two Germans personified the history of their land. The wary old man was a typical product of wartime rationing, postwar shortages, and the rigors of the police State. The confident boy was tall and fit, a beneficiary of State welfare but restless and discontented.

"It sounds like what I'm looking for," I said.

"Are you the police?" said the young man. He had been studying my English trenchcoat and waterproof hat with the close interest that comes from living in a society where imports are virtually unobtainable. He was about eighteen, and strong enough for the toil of a farm with few mechanical implements.

"I work for an insurance company in Stuttgart," I said. "I'm a claims adjuster. I make sure my company doesn't get swindled by false claims." That explanation seemed to satisfy them that I wasn't dangerous. The most dangerous visitors were of course the avid communists from the West: trade union officials and activists and busybodies. These were the ones that were likely to report any lack of enthusiasm they encountered in citizens lucky enough to live in a workers' paradise. "I'm a capitalist," I said. It was usually the best way of being reassuring.

"That's where it was," said the boy, pointing a finger.

So Thurkettle had parked his camper under the trees. He'd pulled off the feeder road to where the silver birches sprang from the unruly gorse. This was a land of sand and birch and beech; the sort of landscape in which I had grown up and felt at home. "A Volkswagen. Not new. West Berlin license plates." The younger one sensed there was money in it; I could tell by the way he looked at me. He was trying to introduce the subject of payment. In the West he would have asked directly. Such reticence here was not only a legacy of the socialist State, it went right back to the old Germany where any mention of money carried with it a stigma. Nowadays such niceties had long since been forgotten by hotel staff, and others who came into regular contact with Westerners. But here in the countryside such manners remained.

"Did you see anything else over there?" I asked. "Anything at all?" They looked at each other and then said no with rather too much emphasis. I let it go. "He's claiming for a wristwatch, an expensive wristwatch," I said. They nodded but seemed unconvinced. I suppose they were wondering why the insurance company had waited so long before investigating the claim. Fortunately there is a prevalent view in the East that Western-style capitalism moves in strange inexplicable ways.

"We don't go over there near the road," said the younger man. He smiled, revealing uneven and overcrowded teeth. He might have been a handsome youth but for that. Eastern Europe had not yet discovered orthodontistry. With no proper elections to contest, its leaders did not need teeth and hair. "The land is the property of the State," he added. At one time it would have been the "property of the people," but now only party members were clinging to such starry-eyed notions. All pretense had gone: land and people were the property of the State, and woe betide anyone who forgot it. Soon the State would make a more immediate claim upon the boy. He was obviously waiting for the summons that would take him for the compulsory couple of years of military service.

I nodded. The three long Autobahnen that linked West Germany to Berlin were subject to complex laws and international agreements. Westerners were permitted to use them, subject to checks at each end of the journey. But even to wander a few yards from the road was a serious offense. The sort of offense that I was now committing.

"We keep away," said the old man to further endorse his son's statement. It was apparent that they were tenant farmers, which was as near to capitalism as the German Democratic Republic was likely to get. The State remained the sole owner of the tiny plot of land they farmed, while they were permitted to work it and sell its produce for gain. But one had only to look at them to see that, after taxes and rent, the gain was very small. The government wanted to ease the food shortages but they didn't want anyone to start thinking that such capitalism was widely desirable.

"Oh, yes," I said, as if searching for something to say. "I forgot to mention it: there is a reward."

I passed the apple schnapps to them for a second round, and we stood there looking at the endless flat land, at the occasional truck and car that went whizzing past on the Autobahn, and at the smoke rising from the chimney of what must have been their lopsided little brick farmhouse. There was no shelter. The sleet stung my face and reddened my hands. I blew on my fingers to get the circulation going but the two men seemed hardly to notice the wind or the wet ice that dribbled down their faces.

"Reward?" said the son.

"Two hundred West Marks," I said.

"For what?" said the father, his caution signified by the way he laid his hand upon his son's arm.

"For any material thing . . . for any piece of solid evidence that will convince my company that the thief came here."

The two men looked at each other. I got out my wallet and flipped it open casually to reveal a lot of West German paper money.

"There was a motorcycle," said the son. "The remains of one . . . it is badly burned, so not much of it is left."

"Find me a piece of it, and one hundred marks is yours," I said.

They took me to a ditch near where they said the camper had been parked. It would have taken hours, perhaps days, and a properly organized search party to find it. "We saw it burning," said the boy.

"We found it after it was burned," said his father in flat contradiction to his son. "It was just like this when we found it."

I could see why the old man changed his account. The bike had been stripped. It was bereft of any valuable part that could be carried away and concealed. Perhaps the burning had been a way of disguising the extent of the theft.

"Have you got time to help me?" I said. "I pay twenty West Marks per hour." Neither man answered me. By that time we all knew it was a rhetorical question. "I want to search the ditch."

The two men used their potato hooks and began to stab into the hidden depths of the ditch to find anything that had broken free from the bike.

"Now do you see what happened, Werner? Thurkettle came here on his motorbike, dumped it here and left in a camper."

I looked down into a drainage canal to see the motorbike better. Over time it had settled deeper into the earth. I climbed down to examine it more closely. Although its remains were damaged to the point of being virtually worthless the frame was not old. I pulled some brambles away to see the engine; all the electrical accessories had been stripped out. The motorbike was wide and squat-shaped: one of those high-powered BMWs. And it wasn't the costly sort of Western luxury that citizens of the DDR would be likely to spend their precious hard currency on. Or abandon by the roadside.

"It's a beauty," I said. The two men looked down at me without changing their dour expressions. Werner smiled. Despite the way I was trying to remain cool and composed, I suppose he could see how pleased I was. Werner liked to tell me that I frequently behaved like a schoolboy. No doubt at some future time he would quote today's doings as evidence of it. "A beauty!"

"You're getting mud all over you," said Werner.

When new it had been an impressive machine, its chrome bright and paintwork glistening. Its engine must have made it as powerful as many a small car. Now the frame was twisted and blistered with burning. Its fuel tank had held enough to make a ferocious blaze. Both wheels had disappeared, and every part of the engine not caked in mud was ravaged by fire. Only the tiniest pieces of heavy plastic remained to show where the rivets had fixed saddle and panniers to the frame.

I took out my Olympus camera and took some photos of the wreck. The camera was tiny, and over the years of using it I had found that pictures could be taken, and the camera hidden again, before anyone really noticed what you were doing. That's how it was now.

"Probe the ditch all the way along to the ramp," I said.

"Let's get out of here while we can," said Werner softly in English.

It made me angry. Although he said it in English the tone of his voice was enough to create anxieties in the two locals. Luckily the thought of the money seemed to keep them going.

Each man carried a three-pronged *Kartoffelhacke*, which they had been using to turn over the manure. They dragged the prongs through the drainage canal, twisting them to disentangle the roots and brambles and dislodge clods of sandy earth. They knew about clearing ditches and automatically assumed positions as a pair: the old man in front and the boy behind digging deeper. To account for the need for such meticulous searching, I explained to them again that we were looking for the wristwatch. Werner grunted. He was about to say something but changed his mind, and smiled instead.

Any more sardonic remarks from Werner were silenced when the old man's fork struck the leather case. By now the two farmworkers had caught the fever of finding buried treasure. "Fifty marks," I said as he pulled it up for me to inspect. I handed the money over.

It was a Samsonite metal-framed document case. The frame was only slightly corroded and its imitation leather exterior was little affected by the months it had spent in the ditch. Apart from a long gouge and a bad dent on the underside, it could have been cleaned up to look no worse than the average item of luggage seen on commuter trains every morning. It was not locked but there was enough corrosion on the hinge fittings to make it stiff to open. It was slimy inside with a coating of fuzz. All kinds of grubs, worms and squrming animal life had made a home in it. I ran my hand around the rotting cloth lining. Werner watched me. There was nothing there until I scratched at the lining with my fingernails. I peeled a label from where it had stuck, tearing it as I pulled. The "label" was a small piece of a U.S. fifty-dollar bill. I held it under Werner's nose. "How does that grab you, Werner?"

"You did it, Bernie," said Werner with as much enthusiasm as he could muster. "How did you know?" Then it clicked. "You talked to Prettyman?"

"Yes," I admitted.

"How was he?"

"Too late for sweets; too early for flowers," I said.

"Is there something wrong?" said the elder man, who had been trying to follow our conversation in English.

"This gentleman is my business associate from Dresden," I said. "We had a disagreement and a small wager about the solution of this mysterious business. Now he is angry to find that my theory was right. He is a bad loser."

"Look," said the younger man. He had continued prodding into the ditch while I examined the document case. He was about ten meters away from me. He held up the hook. On the point of the prongs there was a large section of rotting fabric: striped like shirt material. "There is something here! *Gott*!"

Farmers are used to life and death, but none of us were prepared for the human remains that he found at the tip of his fork. Dump a side of beef into a ditch on a warm day in June. Within a week it stinks. Flies descend upon it, and so do rats and all the other scavengers of the countryside. Eventually the worms move in. "It is Thurkettle," I said. He had been there a long time.

"How do you know who it is?" said Werner.

"We'll get him out," I said. "And you'll see."

"No," said Werner. "It's too risky."

I ignored Werner's caution. It was very heavy. An old dried-out cadaver like that would normally have been as light as a feather, but Thurkettle was heavy. His coat had become one with the earth, so that a massive weight of mud was clinging to him. Had the corpse not been clad in tough ballistic nylon coveralls we would never have lifted it intact. But the heavy-duty nylon had defied the attacks of the rodents, and the degradation of nature. The woven plastic was as stout and intact as the day the coveralls were made. With all four of us combining our utmost efforts, we gripped the plastic of his arms and legs, and lifted Thurkettle's earthly remains out of the ditch like a sack of coal. Puffing with the exertion we dumped it on the embankment. The two locals looked at each other and then they looked at me. The elder man made the sign of the cross. I kneeled down. In places the body had been gnawed to the bone. Half of one arm was missing entirely; little was left of the face, so that the teeth were bared.

Closing my mind to the disgust that human remains

always bring, I pushed my folding knife into the body to locate the spine. I'd seen such remains before, but always on a properly drained mortuary slab, with hot black coffee and a cigarette not far away, and a pathologist to do the tricky bits. Now I had to do it on my own. The juicier parts of the internal organs had long disappeared. The rats had gone first for the delicacies: the liver, kidneys, and stomach, and for the eyes, too.

The position of the body was that of a man cowering from a blow; that defensive posture that some bodies assume in death. Now I could see what time had brought. Some of the muscle was still intact; dried and as hard as granite. Muscular contractions had distorted the skeleton. I probed deeper. What a way to go. No man deserves to be reduced to such a horrifying bundle of old bones and leather.

"You have found what you were looking for," said Werner without pleasure. "Let's go."

"I must know the cause of death," I said.

"It wasn't old age," said Werner.

"No," I agreed. "And if he was shot, I might find evidence of that on the skeleton." I looked up at the farmers. The discovery of the dead body had frightened them. What had started off as an amusing way to get their hands on some Western currency had turned into a nightmare that was likely to end with them facing interrogation by the Stasi. I could see what was going through their minds.

"Give me one more minute," I said, closing the knife and putting it away. I shut my eyes and thrust my hands right into the remains. It was hard and bony. My fingers found and felt the spine, and the pelvis and the shoulder blades. "Yes, Werner. Yes, Werner, Yes." I said. I could feel what I was searching for: the rough edges on the bones. It wasn't the gnawing of rats. "He's been hit by a fusillade of bullets," I said.

When I examined the coveralls again more closely I found the bullet holes in corresponding positions. There were at least six of them, very close together, the surrounding burn marks still just visible. "I'll settle for that," I said. I got to my feet.

"Gunshot?" said Werner.

"Six rounds, maybe more: two of them probably high enough to find the heart." With my foot I rolled him over. Nothing would have persuaded me to touch the body again except with the toe of my shoe. I was about to give it a final shove that would roll it back into the ditch when I spotted there at the bottom of it what looked like a bright green patch of patterned fabric. "What is that?" I said aloud. But even as I said it I knew what it was. The corpse had been resting upon a fortune in dollar bills. Dozens upon dozens of fifty-dollar bills. Protected by the weight, and by the nylon coveralls, the money had remained fresh and new-looking. I glanced at the others. No one wanted to grope through the worms to get the money. We had all had our fill. With no more hesitation I kicked the corpse gently. It flopped back into the ditch with a squelching sound, a protest that seemed to come from the dead man's mouth.

"All gone. All finished," I said to the two men. I gave them the rest of my West German money: three hundred marks. "Go home," I said. "Don't go spending the money and attracting attention to yourselves. You understand? Forget everything. Don't tell your wife. Don't tell your neighbor. Don't tell anyone. We will drive away now. And we will never come back."

For a moment they stood there transfixed. I thought they were going to make trouble for us. I invented a story for them: "It was his wife who did it," I said. "She is not a bad woman. He beat her. Now she is trying to collect his life insurance. Go home and forget it all. In the West this happens sometimes."

It seemed ages before the two men looked at each other and without speaking turned and began to walk back to their home and their fields. I had a feeling that they were going to walk until we were out of earshot and then discuss it. While I was still trying to decide what to do, Werner went after them. I watched him as he stopped and talked with them. I couldn't hear what he said but they both nodded assent. When Werner returned he said, "It will be okay."

By that time I was so hyped up that I didn't care about anything except the proof of my theory. "Look, Werner," I said. I had already spotted the most conclusive discovery of all. "I didn't want the farmers to see this." I climbed down into the ditch again and used a twig to hook up my find. I wanted to show Werner what it was, but I didn't hold it up high in case the farmers were looking back at us.

"What is it?" said Werner. "Is it a gun?"

"It's the final link with Prettyman," I said. "This is the gun that killed Thurkettle."

"Funny-looking gun," said Werner. "It looks like a toy."

"Yes, it does. We live in an age when toy guns look like the real thing, and the real guns look like toys. But a plastic gun like this is deadly. Expendable and non-ferrous so it goes through airport security checks. Hatchwork all over the grips so that no fingerprints can ever be found on one. The triangular cartridge cases fit tight, and are supplied in short strips. Rapid fire: pull the trigger and it goes like a machine gun. I should have guessed what it would be, when I saw the gouge marks in the bottom of the document case." I laid the white plastic gun alongside the document case. "When fired, the metal bullet snaps out of its triangular polyethylene cartridge casing. One round must have nicked the bottom of the case. The whole story is right here before us, Werner."

"Are you going to take the gun along?" asked Werner.

"It's evidence," I said. "You can see what happened. Prettyman came here to meet Thurkettle and pay him. Perhaps they quarrelled; about the payoff or about going to the plane instead of letting Thurkettle drive away. Prettyman holds the case like this . . . like a tray. He holds it high and with one hand to conceal the gun he's got under it. I remember you doing that, Werner, when we got into that little problem in Dresden back in . . . oh, I forget when . . . Prettyman fired the gun at point-blank range. Prettyman is no kind of marksman, but with the muzzle almost touching Thurkettle's guts he didn't have to be. Thurkettle drops instantly, and he tips the body into the ditch. Prettyman must have had it figured in advance. I think he enticed Thurkettle to a position near the ditch, so that he didn't have to drag the body over here."

"You make him sound very cold-blooded," said Werner, as if unconvinced.

"Prettyman. I know him very well, Werner. He is cold-blooded. We're talking about a bastard who went through Thurkettle's pockets and took Tessa's sapphire brooch. And then gave it to his fancy girlfriend in Moscow."

"If it was the same brooch."

"I don't make mistakes like that, Werner. I recognized

Tessa's sapphire as soon as I clapped eyes on it. And Prettyman admitted taking the brooch. He puts it in his own pocket, tosses gun and document case into the ditch, jumps into the camper, and drives back on to the Autobahn and into the West. Cold-blooded? He's cold-blooded all right."

"Very clever, Bernie. But aren't you forgetting one little thing?"

"What?"

"He drives away in the camper. What about the car he arrived here in? The farmers didn't see any other car parked here. If there was no car, how did Prettyman get here?"

"Mrs. Cindy Prettyman. That's the answer to that one, Werner. Everything has fallen into place for me. I talked to the Swede before he was killed. He said a woman came to him that night. She collected from him the box file she's been talking about. It was intended for Prettyman: his payoff, no doubt. Swede asked her for ID and she showed him a U.K. passport in the name of Mrs. Prettyman. I'd say that was conclusive enough, wouldn't you? She brought Jim here and then drove off to the plane, while Prettyman drove away in the VW camper."

"Jesus," said Werner.

"Yes, your friend Mrs. Prettyman. You think she's all sweetness and bright light, but she's always been able to look after herself."

"You can't prove any of that."

"The camper's not here now, Werner," I said sarcastically.

"The Swede is dead. You can't get anything more from him."

"I don't need him," I said. "I know just about everything

I need to know. I know Uncle Silas briefed Prettyman and Prettyman sent Thurkettle on his mission."

"If you take that plastic gun back to London I'll bet you anything you care to bet that London will accuse you of the killing."

"Me?" I said.

"Bernie, they already suspect that you are deeply involved in all this. I've told you once, and I'll tell you again: they think that your wild accusations are made to cover up your guilt. You take that gun and tell them where we found it and they will say you arranged the killing of Thurkettle. They will say that you left the gun here and planned this excursion so that I would witness the 'discovery' and so back you up."

"Frame me?"

"No, Bernie. I'm not saying that London Central would frame you. But to them it will make you look guilty. I believe your theory about Prettyman. At one time I thought you were going crazy but now I believe you. But you won't make your case any more convincing by taking this document case and plastic gun back to show them. You need people to give evidence. Failing that, you need signed and witnessed statements. A gun without fingerprints, and your story about where you found it, won't mean much. Let it go, Bernie. We know what happened. Now let it go."

Maybe Werner was right. He was sober and level-headed in a way that I would never be. He was often able to see things more clearly than I could. I dropped the gun and the document case back into the ditch and kicked them well down and out of sight. I could see another metal artifact there, too. Werner hadn't seen it. I didn't prod at it, or dig it out from where it was half-hidden in the earth. It was my father's Webley pistol.

"Let's get out of here," I said. "I've had enough of this for one day."

"You did it, Bernie," said Werner to cheer me up.

We reached the car and Werner slid behind the wheel. I got in the passenger seat and Werner started the engine. "Do you think those two farmers will report us?" I asked him.

"No," said Werner. "It will be all right." As we got to the top of the ramp, and joined the traffic on the road back to Berlin, there was a sudden fierce downpour of sleet that obscured the glass. Werner flicked the control to increase the speed of the wipers.

"What did you say to them?" I asked.

"I told them you were a trouble-making foreigner but that they could take your Western money and keep it. I told them that I was a secret policeman, assigned to keep watch on you. I told them that if they mentioned anything they had seen, I'd make sure they went into a prison camp."

"A foreigner? Did they believe that?" I looked at him. His face was solemn as he stared at the road and at the blizzard that obscured the windshield and buffeted the car.

"You think your German is perfect," said Werner. "But you have an English accent that you can cut with a blunt knife. Any German can hear it."

I aimed a playful swipe at his head. He knew how to goad me. "How can you be sure they believed you were a secret policeman?"

"Don't I look like a secret policeman?"

"I suppose you do."

"I demanded one of the fifties back and put it in my

pocket. That convinced them. They know a Stasi man's technique when they encounter it."

"Brilliant, Werner. That was a stroke of genius. And don't forget you owe me fifty marks."

No sooner had I said it than a police car with flashing light came speeding along the Autobahn towards us.

"They must have phoned," I said anxiously.

"Watch to see if it goes down the ramp," said Werner.

"I can't see. He's too far back and there's too much snow."

"I'll put my foot down."

"It won't help, Werner. If those two bastards have sounded the alarm they will be waiting to lift us at the checkpoint."

"It will be all right," said Werner. In the old days we would have enjoyed the danger of it, but the old days had gone. Werner was sweating and I was swearing. We didn't say much but we were both thinking of what kind of gruesome and incriminating exhibits were going to be produced in court before the prosecutor got his unchallenged verdict. If the guards at the checkpoint had plucked us out of the car and grilled us, I'm not sure how composed we would have been.

As it was, they waved us through without coming out of the box. One pressed his nose against the glass and made a thumbs-up sign. There was something to be said for the blizzard and the freezing cold after all.

I don't know which of the two of us gave the deepest sigh of relief as we rolled across the checkpoint into Nikolassee, so close to Werner's new home. He stopped the car near the station. "I promised Zena I would buy oranges and milk," he said. Zena was a health freak. "Why not come back to the house?" he suggested. "We'll have coffee and relax."

"I'd rather get back to my place and shower," I said. The heat in the car had made me aware of my dirt-caked hands, and the stinking offal into which I'd been groping.

He looked at me and my soiled coat and hands. "I'll run you back there," he said.

Before he started the engine I said, "You haven't been entirely frank with me, Werner."

"What's wrong?"

"That gun. That plastic gun. You had it."

"What gun?"

"Don't play the innocent with me, Werner. We're friends, aren't we?" He grinned nervously. I said, "You received a package containing that gun."

"I can't answer that, Bernie. It's official business."

"That plastic gun that you were pretending you'd never seen in your life before—you handled it. You acted as a letter box. You took the gun and delivered it to Jay Prettyman."

"Who says so?"

"I say so."

"No," said Werner.

"What do you mean, 'no'? What are you—Prettyman's lawyer? What's got into you? Why don't you tell me the truth? That plastic gun is the last remaining link that puts Prettyman there at the Autobahn meeting and killing Thurkettle."

"You know how these things work," said Werner in an unnaturally calm and lowered voice. "It's need-to-know, Bernie. I can't confirm it without breaking every promise I made."

"Screw you, Werner. You're a sanctimonious bastard."

"You've put it all together with superhuman skill," said Werner, without reflecting any of the anger I'd shown him. "Be content."

"I'll get a cab," I said, and climbed out of the car and walked away.

"You're forgetting your binoculars," called Werner.

I went back and climbed into the car. Werner started the engine without saying a word. He drove me into the center of the city and to Lisl Hennig's hotel. I didn't speak to him again, except to say thanks when I got out of the car.

I knew it was as far as I was going to get with him. I would have to be content with that grudging affirmation. Werner had a stubborn streak that was unassailable. He'd always been like that, ever since we were at school together.

ELEVEN

The SIS Offices, Berlin

Even before the First World War, the joke about "count the dumplings, and divide by ten" had been doing the rounds. The dispositions of Rommel's Afrika Korps had several times been betrayed by a "dumpling count," and no doubt all the belligerents had, at some time or other, infiltrated spies into the enemy catering arrangements to equal effect. So I suppose I should not have been surprised when London's questions about the radium diggings at Schlema were solved by means of an intelligence method even older than blowing trumpets at the walls of Jericho.

Larry Bowers, a long-term Department employee, had brought it in to me. Bowers was an enigmatic fellow. A young, good-looking Oxbridge graduate who always landed buttered side up. For a long time I had regarded him as someone on a postgraduate fling, someone doing his stint of service to the Crown before leaving to start his real career, someone who would eventually wind up with a dozen undemanding director-ships and a Rolls-Royce with a personalized license plate. But I was proved wrong. Larry Bowers fell desperately in love with Germany and stayed on. It was a fatal attraction, as I knew to my cost. And for people like Bowers, who went freely from West to East, protected by his military identification, Berlin had no rivals. Here was the only city in the world with three renowned opera houses, a dozen symphony orchestras, theaters of all shapes and sizes, countless cabaret clubs, three universities, and even two zoos.

Larry Bowers put the report on my desk on Tuesday afternoon. Some agent unnamed had reached Schlema and gained access to the kitchens of the ore miners' canteen and even survived the eating arrangements. Bowers had had the report beautifully typed. He'd bound it with a bright yellow cover, and put his name on the front in a typeface large and clear enough to be read from the far side of the office. Bound into the back of the report, there were photocopies of documents from the mine cashier: food accounts, the licenses, ration documents, and delivery manifests. The report was as comprehensive as can be, apart from not mentioning the name of Werner Volkmann, who had supplied a considerable part of the material and been the principal contact for the informant. I liked Larry Bowers, but he could be very showbiz when it came to screening the credits.

I read the report carefully. Flour, coffee, and potato consignments for the month of November were all that we needed. There were no records of beer or mineral water, but the figures were enough to convince anyone that there were no more than thirty or forty men and women eating at the miners' canteen each day, and that included the kitchen staff. The uranium mine was obviously on an upkeep and maintenance schedule. Safety men to work the pumps and the fans, keep the conveyor belts lubricated and operate the lifts from time to time. The German Democratic Republic was not noted for its labor-saving mining technology. Even if it had been, a mine like that can't be worked by shifts of a dozen or so men.

At noon Frank came steaming into my office as I knew he would. He was waving his abbreviated copy of the report. "I'll tell London there is nothing doing there?" he said, holding the paper up to his face, so he could read it without his glasses.

"That's it," I said, passing some additional sheets of figures to him.

"You file them," he said, without taking them to look at. Frank was a cunning old fox. He wasn't going to tell London that his belief that the Schlema workings were not producing uranium was based upon any kind of "cold dumpling estimate." And making sure that I filed the notes away would enable him to deny that he knew the source. Should the estimates prove incorrect, I would face London's angry questions about the source.

"Going to Werner's housewarming party?" asked Frank.

"Yes," I said.

"You don't have to answer in that guarded manner. I'm going, too. At least, I was thinking of going. I was wondering what sort of a gathering it will be. Big? Small? Very formal? Dinner suit? Sit-down? What's he planning?"

It took me a moment to digest this shattering turn-about in the always turbulent social history of the Berlin office. Frank Harrington had long pursued what I had heard described as a "vendetta" against Werner. An additional obstacle to the relationship came from the short but intense love affair that Frank had had with Zena. Not one of Frank's pull up your pants and run affairs. It had been very earnest. He'd even found a love nest for her: a comfortable house tucked away in the leafy northern Berlin suburb of Lübars. "It's not entirely a housewarming," I said.

"I thought . . ."

"Rudi Kleindorf's new club. This is a launch party for it. The decorators are not finished at the club premises. Rudi persuaded Werner to hold it at his house and combine it with a housewarming."

"I noticed Kleindorf's name in small print. So that's it?"

"Gold-edged invites with color . . . you can bet a lot of them have been sent out. I can't imagine a printer wanting to do that kind of job a dozen at a time."

"Always the detective, Bernard," said Frank, without putting too much breathless admiration into it.

"I try, Frank."

"You were right to bring Werner back, and put him on the payroll," said Frank. "I had doubts at first—especially about him having an office—but I decided to let you do it your way." He provided a significant pause during which I could worry about what was coming next. "And it's worked out very well, hasn't it?"

"Yes," I said. I was tempted to point out the way that Werner's bare, bony, and much-calloused hands had pulled the Schlema chestnuts out of the embers. And wonder aloud why his name was nowhere to be found in that report. But I didn't.

"I don't want to offend him," said Frank vaguely. I could tell he was seeking an excuse to go to the party.

Frank loved parties. He loved planning them, giving them, and attending them. He loved talking about them and hearing about them. It was an element of what made him so influential and effective in Berlin, for this was the greatest party town in the world. Forget New York or Paris or London. You had only to see the elaborate fancy costumes in the Berlin stores when *Fasching* celebrations brought party time around, to know that this was the place where the party had been refined to an art form for big spenders. Party time was always the highlight of Frank's year. I remember a German visitor to his office asking Frank what they did in England at *Faschingszeit*. Frank replied, "We eat pancakes; it's what we call pancake day." The German visitor laughed heartily. Too heartily. I knew him well: both his parents had died in the RAF firestorm raid on Dresden in 1945. I knew Germany well enough to know that for some Germans Shrove Tuesday was best remembered as the anniversary of that night.

There was another reason for Frank's interest in the Volkmanns' party. It would provide an opportunity for him to see Zena again. She'd been away in Switzerland for quite a while; perhaps he still carried a torch for her. Frank was practiced in the alchemy that transmuted lovers into friends. "You heard that Rensselaer and his entourage are in town? At least, on their way," he amended, looking at his watch. "They are finished in Frankfurt."

"Bret? You mean here, in Berlin?"

"I wish I didn't mean here in Berlin; I wish I meant there in Timbuktu. This city is packed with visitors right now. Do you know how long my secretary Lydia spent on the phone, pleading for hotel rooms for them all? Pleading."

"How long?" I said in innocent enquiry.

"Instead of returning to London directly he suddenly decided he had to detour this way and bring his entourage with him. I suppose he intends it as a display of Yankee methodology, but I call it a pointless waste of time and effort."

"He eats too much sugar," I said.

Frank nodded without hearing what I said. "The Steigenberger. Bret specified the Steigenberger; Dicky demanded the Kempi." He gestured with his pipe. "They will have to put up with what hotels they can get. And they might end up in a bed and breakfast in Rudow." Frank always saved his most caustic contempt for Rudow, an unremarkable residential neighborhood that formed the southeastern tip of capitalist Berlin. I wondered what caused this antipathy. Was Rudow associated with one of Frank's unhappy love affairs?

"Dicky Cruyer, too?" I asked. Dicky would not be happy with the sort of bed and breakfast typically on offer in Rudow. Frank nodded.

"Yes. How am I supposed to entertain such a crowd at short notice? My cook is visiting her married daughter, and Tarrant is still recovering from this damned gastric influenza that is doing the rounds. I can't entertain them all at the house."

"So you are taking them along to Werner's party?"

Frank looked at me; I met his eye solemnly. Frank said, "It would solve a problem for me."

"They will love it," I said. "Music and dancing and champagne. Wonderful food. Werner has been talking about nothing else."

"I thought he was away," said Frank, who didn't miss everything of what went on in the office.

"He went away. Only one day. He's back now."

Frank said, "Bret's NATO conference was scheduled to go on through the weekend, with a formal dinner on Sunday. But the French delegation made a fuss about the agenda and walked out yesterday morning. The Yanks released some woolly press statement about continued meetings of the secretariat—you know what bullshitters they are—and that ended the whole get-together."

"Most people will guess it was a French walkout. There was an argument with them last time," I said. "Fiona was there."

Frank sighed. Moscow's protracted political operation that levered France out of NATO was the KGB's finest battle honor. It was never mentioned without a resonance of our failure. "Yes. There must be better ways of plastering over the cracks." Frank was renowned for his expertise at patching over administrative disasters. "They will all have dinner suits and so on," he said, as if putting his case to me.

"It's brilliant, Frank," I said. "Take them to Werner's party."

When I got back to my own office there was a fax in my tray. It was the copy of another police report about traffic movements on the West Berlin Autobahn on the day after Tessa was killed. It described traffic accidents and abandoned vehicles and mysterious strangers wandering in the vicinity of Autobahn exits. Campers' tire marks and picnic remains. I had of course found everything I'd been looking for at Autobahn exits. But I didn't want to circulate a message canceling my requests. I didn't even want to confide to my secretary the fact that I'd found what I was looking for. There was no way I could call off my search without being asked questions I didn't care to answer. I put the reports and faxes in my drawer and shuffled them so it looked as if I'd been studying them.

Then I went back to my room in Lisl's hotel to change and make myself ready for Werner's party. It would be a dressy affair. Werner had moved into one of those grand old houses in Wannsee. A house of any shape or size was a conspicuous mark of success in a city where most people lived in apartments. This one was truly remarkable. From its terrace there was a view of the waters of the Wannsee and as far as the pretty little island of Schwanenwerder where Goebbels, the Nazi propaganda minister, lived during the war. I knew these Wannsee houses and I had visited many of them. I liked them. Sometimes I've thought how happy I would have been in a career such as architecture. I had mentioned that to my father during my time at school, but my father said an architect's life was precarious. To him a government job was the epitome of security. I wondered what he might have said if he were still alive.

But my interest in buildings remained with me. More than once, being able to guess where an upstairs landing emerged, or the fastest route to the roof, and where to find a fire escape back to ground level, had helped me out of serious trouble. Tonight I had no difficulty guessing the layout of Werner's new home. I drove past a NO ENTRANCE sign, and found a place to park at the back. I let myself in through a service door on the terrace.

Werner had chosen this house not just because it was so spacious and light but because of its history. Like many of the houses in that street so near the lake, there were rumors about its history. Berlin's real estate men had discovered that having a top-level Nazi as a one-time resident was unlikely to deter their prospective clients. It wasn't something to be included in the prospectus, of course, but a whispered word about some notorious blackguard of the Third Reich could sometimes conclude a sale.

The stories said this particular house had once been occupied by Reinhard Heydrich. As well as being the evil spirit behind Himmler, Heydrich was a notable athlete and a fencing champion. Support for the contention that this was his former home was to be seen in the extended room that gave on to the terrace. It was said to have been built to satisfy Heydrich's need for a fencing hall. The large room had been restored to something like its nineteenth-century origins, and could be divided in two by ornate folding doors. Or, as tonight, the whole ground floor could be made into a room into which a hundred guests could dance without knocking over the tables loaded with luxury food, or blundering into the massive flower arrangements, or getting poked in the eye by the elbows of any of the musicians. I mean: it was big.

In line with Rudi's intention to offset part of its cost against tax, the party was described as being a celebration for the opening of Rudi Kleindorf's new club in Potsdamerstrasse. There were signs advertising the club, which was now named *Gross und Klein*—"high and low," or "adults and children." It was also a reference to Rudi Kleindorf's nickname: *der grosse Kleine*. Personally I preferred the place when it was a shady dump called the Babylon, but Werner never liked that name. He said Babylon had bad associations for a Jew. I wondered what the associations were. Or how those associations could be more disturbing than living in Wannsee, a stone's throw from the place where the infamous conference was held, and living in a house where coming downstairs for a midnight snack you might rub shoulders with a natty-uniformed blond ghoul with blood on his hands.

I wondered if the club's change of name was an indication that Werner had invested money in the new venture. I hoped not. The old Babylon had gone bust, owing money to most of its suppliers. I couldn't see how the new one was likely to do much better. It was all right for Rudi: he used the club as a hangout for his cronies, and a base for his murky business activities. In the front hall there was an artist's impression of what the new club would look like. Rudi was standing alongside it, telling anyone who would listen about his new place.

I could see all this as I stepped through the terrace window, and hear it too. The five piece band—veterans of Rudi's previous excursions into Berlin nightlife—was expanded by a few white-haired musicians. They were indulging themselves by playing kitsch thirties music more in accord with their advanced age, and more in line with my dancing lessons, than their usual repertoire at the Babylon. As I closed the terrace door behind me, they were moving into the final chorus of "Sweet Lorraine."

Once inside the main room, I looked around. The decoration that had been installed for this party took my breath away. I knew that the house was wonderful. Werner had shown me the photos, and the surveyor's report, and discussed his offer and counteroffer. I was ready for the house but I wasn't ready for the decorations. They had obviously been installed solely for the party, and would be torn down tomorrow. That was what I called conspicuous high living.

The theme of the party, as stated on the printed

invitations, was "The Golden Twenties." Its ambivalence had left the German guests uncertain of whether to respond with a fancy dress suited to Berlin in the Weimar years, or simply to wear gold. Many had done both. There were plenty of gold lamé gowns, and gold jewelry was in abundance, for this was Berlin and flamboyant ostentation was *de rigueur*. There was even a gold lamé evening jacket—although that was worn by a tenor from the opera and so didn't count as a surprise of any kind—and there was a glittering outfit of gold pajamas worn by a skinny old lady who did cooking lessons on TV.

Gold wire and gold foil and gold ornaments of many kinds were liberally arranged on the walls. Gold ceiling hangings echoed in shape the antique glass chandelier that Werner had bought in an auction, so that it could become the centerpiece of the room. The moving beams from clusters of spotlights were directed upwards to patch the false ceiling with their light, and create golden clouds that floated overhead.

Looking around at all this I began to understand what the extravagant Zena did for Werner. Zena was the catalyst that enabled Werner to waste his money in the ways he secretly enjoyed. Such symbiotic relationships were not uncommon. Any number of middle-class husbands bought a big Volvo or Mercedes saying its impact-proof construction would protect their families. They installed top-of-the-range computers because it would help their kids at school, ear-shattering hi-fi equipment to play "good" music. To help their kids' history lessons they went first class to Egypt and made sure the Pyramids were still on the Nile. So did Zena provide for Werner a rationale for his intemperate lifestyle.

There was a time when I would have been concerned

at Werner spending money so recklessly. For Werner periodically confessed to me that he was on the verge of financial collapse. At first I was flattered by these confidences, as well as alarmed on his behalf. But over the years I had come to understand that Werner's measure of poverty was not like mine. Werner became alarmed when the interest on his capital was nibbled by inflation, or when he suffered some other financial malady that periodically scourged the rich. For people like me, just getting enough in my savings account to stave off impending bills gave me a heady feeling of opulence. It was not so with Werner. Right from the time he first got a car, Werner always went into a petrol station and filled his tank to the brim. And he had the oil checked, too; and frequently asked if his tires were worn enough to need changing. Werner simply didn't know there were people who bought petrol, beer, or milk one liter at a time. Or managed with tires that were down to the wire.

The dance floor was full and there were crowds arriving but I spotted Werner and Zena by stepping up on to a wooden pot in which a monster-sized fern plant was growing. I could see over the heads of the dancers to the front lobby. Werner and Zena were in the large oval-shaped hall, formally greeting the guests one by one as they were ushered through the front door. It made a theatrical scene. The second massive chandelier—in the hallway—had been hung in such a way that the wide staircase curved around it, following the wall up to the interior balcony on the upper floor.

Werner waved and bent down to whisper to Zena. She looked up with fire in her eyes. She didn't approve of guests letting themselves in by the back door. She wanted guests to arrive two by two, like animals boarding the

Ark. And she wanted them at the front door, where she could inspect them closely, make sure they had washed their hands and face, and tell them how lovely it was to have them with her.

They were both looking good. Zena had her dark hair coiled up and studded with jewels. She was wearing a simple cream-colored silk dress: long and low cut so that her diamond necklace and matching bracelet sparkled against her bronzed skin. Zena liked being suntanned. The darker she was, the better she liked it. She had grown up in the days when foreign travel was a sought-after rarity. But a complexion like a Malibu lifeguard was incongruous for someone dressed as a delicate Meissen figurine.

Werner was wearing a cream-colored, slubbed-silk jacket, black pants, and frilly evening shirt with a big black bow tie. I suppose he knew he looked like a bandleader from the sort of old Hollywood film they show on TV in the afternoons. This effect was further endorsed when the band struck up "Laura," the schmaltzy old Mercer number. Werner looked at me again and gave a self-conscious smile. I waved an imaginary baton at him.

It was while I was moving through the dancers, to the tables where the food was arrayed, that I was suddenly grabbed from behind by two hands and someone said, "You don't get away as easy as that, you bastard."

I turned to see who it was, and came face to face with Gloria at very close range. My amazement must have shown on my face, for she laughed. "Didn't they tell you? I'm with Bret. We were all at the NATO conference. Frank Harrington brought us here." She grabbed me round the waist and said, "Dance. Hold me tight and dance."

"Gloria . . ."

"Shut up. Don't say anything. Just hold me very tight. Dance . . . and don't blunder into anyone."

We stepped out on to the dance floor. If we had on occasions blundered into other couples, it wasn't due solely to my clumsiness but also because she always danced with her eyes tightly shut.

A vocalist sang in uncertain English: *She gave your very first kiss to you . . .*

"Is it supposed to be fancy dress?" asked Gloria.

"The Golden Twenties."

"I wish I'd known and had had time to dress up."

"You are the Golden Twenties," I said. It was true. Her hair against her dress was shiny gold and she was looking younger than ever.

She gave me a broad, tight-lipped smile. "I've missed you, Bernard."

"It's no use pretending any more. I must talk to you. We must . . ."

She reached up and pressed her hand to my lips. "Don't spoil it. Just for this evening let's pretend. No talking, just pretend."

"Okay."

We danced. She was soft and warm and fragrant and slim and lovely. By some miracle my feet hit all the right places at the right moments. Neither of us spoke.

I would be dancing there still, but the music eventually ended: *You see Laura on a train that is passing through . . .* I held on to her with a desperation that I couldn't contain. That was Laura but she's only a dream. As the music stopped my reverie came to an abrupt end, but I remained close to her, very close.

Bret Rensselaer gave no sign of noticing my despair as he approached us, balancing his own glass against two glasses of champagne for us. "Isn't this a phenomenal party? What a surprise. I was just telling my old buddy Werner that this has got to be the bash of the year." Bret was looking ten years younger. Those golden threads in his silver hair reminded me of the blond tough guy who had almost died after that shooting in an abandoned Berlin train station. So did the grin and the radiant self-confidence. I suppose his new Deputy's job had given him a fresh lease on life. Or maybe he was still floating on the euphoria that came after sneaking across the Atlantic for a weekend and front seat at the Super Bowl. Or maybe he was eating too much sugar.

Bret pointed towards the food-filled tables now, since the music stopped, obscured by eager guests piling up their plates. "Did you taste those homemade poppy-seed cakes?" said Bret. "Wow. Looks like they are homemade. What do they call them in German?"

"Are they called *Mohnklösse*?" said Gloria.

"Yes, but here in Berlin they call them *Mohnspielen*," I said pedantically. "Werner is very keen on them. They say they were Hitler's favorite snack."

"Yeah, well I always said he had taste," said Bret. "Werner, I mean."

"What does it mean: *Mohnspielen*?" said Gloria, childishly put out by my correction.

"*Mohn; Mond*. Moon; poppy. It's some kind of Berlin double meaning that makes it into the moon's plaything."

"You are a living encyclopedia," said Gloria.

Having no immediate ambition to be a living encyclopedia, I sipped my champagne and nodded and smiled. And marveled at the way in which life can go from heaven to hell in such short measure.

"And he's working with you now, Bernard?" said Bret, to demonstrate the way he had his finger on the Department's pulse. "On the payroll?"

"Werner?" I said. "Yes." And I perversely added, "It was all Frank's idea."

"Quite a bash," said Bret, who knew very well how strenuously Frank had opposed Werner's employment. "And the kind of old-timers' music I like." I suppose it was a nice surprise for anyone expecting an evening of shoptalk and passive smoking with Frank Harrington. But there was no mistaking the benchmark change in Werner's fortunes. Twenty-four hours ago I would have bet a million pounds to an old shirt button that Bret didn't remember that Werner Volkmann existed. Now he's Bret's old buddy, and getting three-star accolades for his homemade *Mohnspielen*.

Werner old pal, you made it, I thought. Frank might pretend this was some half-hearted reconciliation, a rehabilitation or a convenient place to dump unwanted visitors. The fact was that Bret Rensselaer— the Deputy D-G no less—was giving Werner the coveted guarantee of Good Housekeeping handwritten on parchment. And doing it in public, in a manner I had seldom witnessed.

While we were talking, Frank had approached us. He listened to Bret's continuing appreciation of Werner's party but, judging from Frank's smile and nods, he thought it was Bret's tactful way of thanking him for bringing the errant souls of Frankfurt to this golden Berlin evening.

Frank said, "I hear the Frogs were playing up again."

"It wasn't entirely the fault of the French," said Bret diplomatically. "One of my countrymen started the row."

"It was filthy weather," said Gloria with feminine insight. "They were all in a bad mood."

Bret said, "One of the London people had an Irish name, and our little German interpreter with the beard made a joke about the Irish Republic not being a member of NATO. One of the CIA crowd didn't understand that it was a joke, and got defensive. He said something about France not being a member of NATO either. . . . There was a bitter row. All bathed in smiles and nods, but they became damned spiteful. Afterwards I even heard one of the Italians saying the only way to define a Frenchman was someone who knew the difference between Hitler and Napoleon."

The music began again, and Bret asked Gloria to dance. "You don't mind me taking her away, do you, Bernard?"

"Where did you say the poppy seed cakes were, Bret?"

Gloria gave me a brief consolatory smile.

Isn't it a lovely day to be caught in the rain; I always liked that melody. Astaire and Ginger Rogers dancing in the rainswept bandstand where no one could get to them. I went to eat. I didn't waste too much time watching Gloria and Bret dancing. I didn't want to pursue her, and if I was old enough to be Gloria's father, Bret was old enough to be her grandfather. Anyway, she knew we could not go on. She knew it and I knew it. Her unexpected appearance had unbalanced me. I was frightened that I might do the wrong thing here; do something or say something that, instead of healing the wounds, would cripple both of us forever.

"Aal grün," called Werner from the other side of the table as I reached for potato salad. "Not smoked: fresh." He knew I liked eel. I put some on my plate, trying to keep it separate from the pan-fried slices of ham dumpling with wild mushrooms. It was a buffet dinner. Real plates and real cutlery, but wobbly tables and gold-painted chairs supplied by the catering company.

"Come and sit over here," said Werner. "I haven't seen you all evening."

"I was dancing." I looked around to see where Gloria was, and caught a glimpse of her golden head and Bret's white hair. They made a nice couple. They would have looked like father and daughter, had they not been dancing so close.

"With Gloria?" said Werner. "Oh yes, I saw you and Gloria dancing. Wonderful, Bernard. You looked very happy, like a kid in love."

"Any objections?" I said.

"No, I suppose not. But love is like the measles; the later in life it afflicts you, the more severe the consequences."

"Is there anything you can take for it?"

"Only wedding vows."

"Is that what Zena told you?" I asked politely.

He gave a tiny smile to show that he forgave me for my bad temper. "Zena believes in marriage," he said. "All wives believe in marriage."

"I suppose so," I said. "I don't see Cindy Prettyman anywhere. Has she gone back to Brussels?"

"She's up in her room," said Werner. "She's in a bad way. I took some food up to her but she won't eat a thing. She said eating would make her vomit."

"Why is she in a bad way?"

"Something happened at her job. A robbery. She

was on the phone to her office and suddenly burst into tears. She's been stretched out on her bed sobbing. I've given her a sleeping pill but it doesn't seem to have any effect. Zena said it's better to leave her alone."

"Maybe a whole bottle of sleeping pills?"

"You don't have to be a bad-tempered pig all the time, Bernard," said Werner stiffly. "You can take an evening off, and try being human."

"I tried it once; I didn't like it."

"If you must be your usual obnoxious self, go and be obnoxious to the soldiers sitting around in my kitchen all dolled up in shiny belts and guns. They are getting in the way, eating all the *petits fours*, and annoying the people from the caterers."

"Soldiers?"

"Redcaps. Do you think I should ask Bret to send them away?"

"Not if they are redcaps," I advised. "Bret is a top-of-the-range spook nowadays. He has to be given a military and civil police escort in this sort of situation. You probably have a busload of uniformed Kripo parked on the front drive."

"What for? Who's going to assassinate him?"

"It's not only that. They can't risk anything happening. Suppose he was picked up by a cop . . . for being drunk or something. And he's not on home ground. Your house is in the American Sector. If there was any kind of wrangle—if he got punched on the nose—all concerned might get dragged down to the barracks, and held in U.S. military custody while IDs were examined and charges drawn up, and it was sorted out. That would be a major embarrassment for everyone concerned."

"Is that why you are not going to punch him on the nose tonight?"

"Very funny, Werner," I said.

Werner led the way to the terrace.

Tonight the bitter winter weather was being defied in a manner typically *Berlinerisch*. Flowers and sunny colors recreated the outdoor parties of summer. The terrace—where now bench-style tables were arrayed—had been roofed over. It was a cleverly designed temporary structure supported by Roman columns made from hardboard faced with golden foil. From the low ceiling, leafy creepers and real blooms trailed, reaching down to table tops to become table decorations. Hidden heaters made it warm enough for bare shoulders, and hidden loudspeakers brought soft, vaguely classical music.

"Don't mention the redcaps to Zena," he said. "I promised I'd get rid of them."

"No, of course not," I said, and took a deep breath as I saw that he was guiding me to where Zena was sitting with an elegant selection of their friends.

"Bernard! How lovely!"

"You're looking ravishing," I told her, and nodded while she told everyone at the table that I was a very old friend of her husband's. It was the nearest she could get to completely disowning me.

"Beside me," said Zena. "I must have a word with you." I sat down at the empty seat that had obviously been reserved for Werner, while Werner squeezed himself on to a bench that was the seating arrangement for the other side of the table. I said hello to the other guests, who nodded acknowledgments. There was a "mergers and acquisitions man" from Deutsche Morgan Stanley and a high-powered woman dealer from Merrill Lynch. There was a bearded man who designed costumes for the opera, the wife of Werner's wine merchant, and a young woman who owned a fur shop on

Ku-Damm. I struggled to remember their names, but I am not good at the social graces: Fiona and Gloria agreed on that.

I tried the eel. It was very good. "You should eat salad," said Zena.

"I do normally," I said. "But these dumplings looked so delicious."

"That Berlin food was all Werner's arrangement," she said. Werner caught my eye and nodded. "It's not healthy—all those heavy, old-fashioned German dishes. And Werner is far too fat."

"It's a lovely house, Zena," I said. A waiter was pouring wine for everyone at the table. He looked at Zena to make sure that he was doing it right. She had them all well trained.

"You can see the water from here," said Zena.

"Yes," I said. I couldn't actually see the lake. There was condensation on the windows so that the lights in the garden became colored blobs. There were more distant lights too: lights from across the water, or they might have been boats. In daylight the view would be wonderful.

"Cindy is here," said Zena. It was almost a hiss.

"Where?"

"She's in bed." The way Zena said it, you would have thought that I knew all about Cindy and her indisposition.

"Is she sick?" I asked.

"In a way. She's very angry, Bernard. Very, very angry."

"I'm sorry to hear that," I said. Perhaps this expression of condolence was marred by the overlarge mouthful of *Schinkenknödel* I was chewing. Or perhaps Zena wasn't listening to my replies.

"Yes, I know all about that," said Zena. She gave me a look of fierce dislike before smiling at everyone around the table and asking Werner to go and get another plate of lobster salad for the elderly banker. Turning to me again she said into my ear, "She's upset about what you have done."

"I haven't done anything," I said. "At least not to Cindy Prettyman."

"Her name is Matthews. She's not married to that ghastly friend of yours any more."

"Matthews, I mean . . . Look, Zena, I don't know what Cindy has been telling you," I said.

"When Cindy is angry . . . really angry, she is likely to do something desperate."

"Yes, I can imagine that."

"You must go up and talk to her. Say you're sorry. Make amends. Give her back whatever it is her husband stole from her office."

"I'll take her some eel."

"Finish your food and I'll show you to her room," said Werner, who had come back with a plate of sliced wurst instead of the lobster, and now looked as if he was keen to escape being asked about this failure.

I abandoned the rest of my meal and got to my feet. As we went across the crowded floor, Werner said, "Rudi was looking for you."

I said, "You haven't put money into that damned club, have you, Werner?"

"Only pennies," said Werner. "Rudi said he wanted a bigger number of shareholders this time. He said more people would come along and support the place if they had a stake in it."

"And did he find people?"

"They all bought shares in the club," said Werner,

waving his arm in the air. "Almost everyone here tonight bought at least one share. The invites went out only to special friends and to people who bought a share."

"You're a genius, Werner," I told him as he was waving and smiling to his appreciative guests. "Is that why Tante Lisl isn't here?"

"You are in a filthy mood tonight, Bernie. You know I wouldn't leave Tante Lisl uninvited. She wasn't feeling well enough. And it's her evening for playing cards."

A string quartet had been playing Mozart while the meal was eaten. It had provided a change of pace that relaxed the eaters, and encouraged them to chew every mouthful twenty times before swallowing. But now the dance band were returning from wherever they'd been to eat dinner. There was a riff on a trumpet and it was every stomach for itself.

While the musicians were settling themselves down for an evening of hard work, the waiters were clearing the trestle tables and folding them up to make more room for dancing. The guests stood around talking and laughing and smoking and drinking and planning all kinds of other things that are bad for you. Several times Werner was buttonholed by guests who wanted to congratulate him on the party, so it took a while to cross the dance floor. With a drink in my hand, I followed Werner from the large ballroom to the brightly lit front hall, and its wide and curving staircase. Understandably reluctant to hurry in his visit to Cindy, he frequently stopped to talk, but eventually he started ascending the main stairs and I followed him.

From halfway up the staircase I looked down. I spotted Frank Harrington near the band. He was standing with Zena: she looked ravishing tonight, her dress and jewelry transforming her into a fairy princess. Not a real princess: Berlin was well provided with such nobility, and none of them looked like Zena. Zena had all the glitter of Hollywood, and she had the imperious bearing of a film star that made her the center of attention. Frank was laughing with her. She was showing him the palm of her hand as if it was something to do with fortune telling. I wondered what she was telling him. Frank didn't usually laugh like that.

"What a crowd," said Werner.

"It's like the last reel of *Sunset Boulevard*," I told him in a meaningless attempt to think of something to say to someone who is watching his wife so obviously enjoying the company of another man.

"What?" said Werner.

"Nothing," I said.

Then, as if in fulfilment of my remark, a woman started down the staircase, stepping with the slow and deliberate manner of someone under the eye of a movie camera.

"*Scheisse!*" said Werner.

Then I recognized her. Her hair looked like hell but it was no more untidy than hair I'd seen coming out of expensive hairdressers. Her nightdress was thin and frilly and filmy with an elaborate pattern of orchids. It could easily have passed as the most expensive of evening gowns. She was barefoot but I'd seen at least one guest dancing without shoes. Even the sleepwalking manner of this woman's movements was not unique to her. The only thing that distinguished her from the other guests was the shiny pistol she was holding high in the air as she came down the stairs.

"Cindy!" said Werner.

"Get out of my way," called Cindy. Her voice was croaky. She waved the gun at him. It was a Walther. I recognized it as a Model 9 that Werner had bought for Zena but never given to her. That model was always in demand because the smart alecs in the Ku-Damm bars sold them to credulous tourists together with all kinds of cleverly forged documentation to prove that this one was the gun that had once been owned by Eva Braun.

"Put it down," Werner called to her.

She was at the top of the stairs. Beyond Cindy's shoulder I could see guests standing along the upper-floor balcony. Sensing danger, they began to move back out of sight. Below, in the hallway, guests were also alarmed at the sight of Cindy brandishing the gun. From the corner of my eye I saw the crowd crushed back upon one another, as they sought the protection of the wall or doorways.

I halted and froze. So did Werner. Cindy brought the gun to eye level with care and precision. It was only a handbag gun, but I've looked down more gun barrels than the Lone Ranger, and I knew that a hole measuring only 6.35 mm could, at this range, end a promising career. "You, and that damned husband of mine, got together, did you?" Cindy yelled at me.

Werner moved closer to the wall, trying to get to the side of her, so that he could grab the gun. But she wasn't going to let that happen. She put her back against the wall and was moving down the stairs a step at a time. I moved down a step too. Werner did the same. We all moved together. I would have thought it comical had I not been almost scared to death.

Without warning she pulled the trigger. I had hoped it wasn't loaded but it fired, and there was a crash of broken glass somewhere below and behind me.

"You've got what you want now, have you?" Cindy shouted hoarsely. Her eyes were red and bloodshot. She looked ferocious now that I was closer to her. She had lots of makeup on her face but the paint job wasn't completed. Tears had made the mascara run, so that her lower face was marbled with gray and black wavy streaks. "You thief! Are you satisfied now? You swine. I'll kill you."

"Listen, Cindy . . ." said Werner. She swung round to him and pulled the trigger. He was close to her but she was too hasty and the shot missed him. The round hit the wall alongside him and broke off a large chunk of molding. The plaster shattered and its pieces went spinning away to land with loud noises on the marble floor of the hall below. I heard a distant scream, a man's shout, and the soft sounds of a woman sobbing hysterically.

Without taking proper aim, I threw the glass in my hand at her. My action was completely instinctive, and like most completely instinctive actions it was ineffective. The ice cubes bounced out, and the whisky came splashing over me. The glass didn't cut Cindy, but that was because she saw it coming and ducked to avoid it before firing again.

That next shot still scored. It hit Werner in the head. He cried out and grabbed at his skull. His cry was very loud, and very close. The impact knocked him backwards. He lost his balance, to fall full length. He curled up and went head over heels down the stairs past me. "Werner!" I tried to grab him as he tumbled past but it was all happening too fast for me. Foolishly I turned my head to see him falling. His eyes flicked open wide as he fell, his face was clenched in pain and I saw anger in his eyes. His cry was shrill. It ended in a choking sound as he landed at the bottom and kicked his legs in the air.

Realizing that my back was exposed to this mad-woman's marksmanship, I swung round in time to see a big man in a khaki uniform leaping down the stairs. His red-topped cap fell off, and went bowling down the staircase. The cap created a diversion: everyone's eyes followed it as the soldier jumped. With arms spread wide apart, he tried to grab her and pinion her arms. But Cindy was too quick for him. As he came towards her she jumped aside, smashing her back against the wall with an audible slap. She brought the gun up and fired again. Having misjudged his leap the soldier's arms were flailing, his hands trying to grab carpet or banister to save himself from falling all the way down the stairs, as Werner had done. But what he grabbed was Cindy's lower legs. He held on to her. He was a heavy man and he held on tightly. His weight was enough to pull her with him as he continued his fall. Her legs dragged from under her and Cindy buckled at the knees. Letting out a yelp of pain and fear, she toppled like a tyrant's statue.

She could not escape the policeman's grasp as, twisting and turning, they grabbed at stair carpet, and at each other, in the panic that free fall produces. They came bumping past me, crashing against the wall, against the wrought iron and against the stairs, until they both ended heaped upon Werner. They were still; the three of them dumped at the bottom of the stairs like a big bundle of laundry waiting to be ironed. Werner's head moved, emerging from the confusion of limbs and bodies. He was still holding his head in his hands; his hair, face, and fingers so bloody that it was difficult to distinguish between them. Blood was everywhere on the soldier's face and all over Cindy's nightdress.

For a moment the whole house was silent. Then everyone began talking at once. Two agile waiters ran to help the injured, while a couple of quick-thinking soldiers ushered others away. As more soldiers crowded around the bodies they were hidden from view. The band started playing "Mister Sandman" very softly. The lights went down to a glimmer so that the only illumination was a spotlight trained on Frank Harrington. He came sauntering across the floor, cigarette drooping from his mouth, clapping his hands in a warm, appreciative way. Others joined in the applause. Then the music stopped with a little drumroll and Frank was standing on a chair making a speech saying that the "most original entertainment" was a truly splendid surprise but typical of Mr. and Mrs. Volkmann's imaginative gala setting. There were calls of approval and more scattered applause. An English voice shouted "Hear! Hear!"

Frank seemed to enjoy his improvised role of master of ceremonies. He looked around, beaming at the upturned faces, for by now he was the center of attention. He continued talking. Frank was good at after-dinner speeches, and now he used fragments from ones I'd heard many times before. It was all delivered in Frank Harrington's version of German. You couldn't exactly fault the syntax, but his old-fashioned German had the flavor of years long past. If there was anything that could persuade the guests present that they had really witnessed a charade, rather than a shooting, it was Frank doing his spiel in his weird *Kaiserliche* German. Then someone propelled Zena forward, and Frank told everyone how lovely the hostess looked and Zena smiled with grim satisfaction and everyone applauded.

Some of those present knew of Frank's affair with Zena, and I had the impression that most of the jocular cheering came from them.

By the time Frank had finished his eulogy there was no sign of poor Werner or Cindy or the injured military policeman. The band was playing louder and faster than they had ever played before; the waiters were pouring larger measures than before, both activities probably done at Frank's instigation. The guests were dancing and laughing and flirting. Only the broken section of molding was there to prove that the evening's "most original entertainment" had ever taken place.

They didn't let me see Werner until past one o'clock in the morning. He was in the Steglitz Clinic, in the hospital of the Free University. It was dimly lit and silent and there was that unmistakable smell of anesthetics, antiseptics, and disinfectant that mingles and hangs on the air in all such medical establishments. By that time, I was the only one in the waiting room. Frank had squeezed an optimistic prognosis out of one of the senior medical staff, and then taken Zena back to her home before going to the office to phone Bret and other people who would expect to be kept informed. Frank would be blamed for this silly fiasco. It was not his fault, but that was how the system worked. It could even hasten Frank's retirement.

I waited. The surgeon finished his needlework and finally took pity on me because I had been there so long. He came out and gave me a detailed account of the surgical job he'd done on Werner's skull. Bad concussion, extensive cuts, but probably no fractures. Head scan in the morning: then he would have more to go on. The surgeon had the sort of unmistakable Berlin accent with which Bavarian comics get laughs in Munich night-clubs. Hearing his accent I responded using the soft gees and clickety voice I had acquired as a streetwise Berlin schoolboy. He responded with a more pronounced accent as he told me that Werner's upper body was badly bruised and that he had damaged his ankle, too. Perhaps a tiny fracture there. After another exchange of ever-broadening dialect he smiled and said, "Five minutes; no more. He's a lucky man to be alive."

Werner was sitting up in bed. He'd had a local anesthetic while they stitched up the furrow that the bullet had torn above his ear. Now that they had cleaned away all the blood from his hands and head, he looked much better than I had dared hope when I saw him at the bottom of the staircase. But his face was seriously bruised and beginning to swell. According to the doctor it would be some time before he was allowed out of bed. They had shaved the hair from the side of his head to get to the wound. Half bald, he had his stitches covered with no more than a small rectangular dressing, secured by strips of pink tape.

"You had me worried, Werner," I said. "I didn't know whether to bring the girlie mags or a wreath."

"When I go, it's not going to be from a handbag gun."

"Don't be macho, Werner."

"What happened to Cindy Prettyman?"

"She's here in the Clinic. Asleep. One of the soldiers gave her a hefty sedative in the ambulance and forgot to write it down for the hospital reception. The doctor who examined her gave her another dose. She's well away. The doctor says she won't be fit enough to question until late tomorrow. Maybe the day after."

"I blame myself," said Werner.

"You couldn't have known she was going to run amok like that."

"She thought you and Jim Prettyman had organized the robbery in her office. She thought you had the box file."

"No, I don't have the box file," I said. "Jim Prettyman must have organized it. He played it very cool but it was his box. I shouldn't have told him she had it in her office. My fault. He must have got on the phone right after I left him. Jim knows where to find hoodlums and thieves. Seems like it's his speciality."

"Jim has it?"

"I'm sure he does. But I can't help wondering if it was official. I wonder if he talked to someone in London about it. It's an official box and the Department must have an interest in it." I looked at Werner quizzically. It took a long time for him to respond. "I went to Brussels. I stole the box file from her safe."

I smiled blankly.

"Did you guess?"

"It took time. But when Cindy started shooting I could see what had really happened. And you were the one who knew where Cindy was all the time. You knew that while she was in Berlin she would not be in her office. And you had a perfect opportunity to take an impression from her keys."

He gave a grim smile. We knew each other too well. "Why lead me on about Jim Prettyman stealing it?"

"I wanted to see how good you are at telling lies."

"What do you mean, you could see it when she started shooting?"

"Cindy was on the stairs. At that point maybe she thought it was Jim Prettyman who did it. Then she saw you and me together on the stairs in front of her. She had told me that the file was in her office safe. You'd been away from Berlin for a day. She figured that I had told you to go and steal the box."

"She intended to shoot me?" said Werner, frowning as he tried to decide whether he preferred the role of injured innocent bystander or target. He touched his head with a fingertip. I suppose the frowning had caused him pain; or maybe it was the thinking.

"She aimed that shot at you. Sure she did," I said cheerfully. "That's why I am still in one piece and you have a hole in your skull. She was going to plug me. But then all her anger was redirected . . . at you. You'd actually invaded her office and stolen her nest egg. It was personal."

"What will happen now?"

"If it was left to Frank she'd be locked away forever."

"I know. He hates her," said Werner and nodded.

"That is something of an understatement. Frank regards the shooting fracas as a personal affront. But you know how Frank works. He won't let her be charged with attempted murder, or common assault or party-pooping. He'll pull strings in Brussels and try and get her fired. Frank feels he was humiliated by it happening while Bret was here in the city."

"They won't get away as easily as that. Those people who were there last night will work out what really happened."

"Maybe. But it will take time. And news editors spike timeworn stories."

"Is that redcap in one piece?"

"He won't be going back to the gymnastics team. A bad compound fracture of the ribs and mild concussion.

He'll be all right. They will fly him home tomorrow. The surgeon thinks it will be a straightforward job. Military policemen are all bone."

"And Cindy Prettyman, too?"

"Drunks bounce like rubber balls, Werner. She was lucky. For security reasons none of those redcaps had been told who they were guarding. They were just told that there was a political VIP in the car Bret was using. They figured that any kind of shooting was likely to be an attempt on the life of the man they were guarding. If that cop's flying tackle had not done the trick, there was a sniper lining her up, and about to shoot Mrs. Prettyman dead."

The door opened and the surgeon came in and said I mustn't make his patient tired. He was taking a personal interest in Werner's well-being. I wondered what Frank must have told him.

"They wouldn't let Zena in to see me," said Werner as I was putting on my overcoat.

"Yes, well, Zena doesn't speak Berlin German as well as I do," I said in my heaviest possible accent.

The doctor nodded. I think he was beginning to think he was the butt of my humor instead of a part of it.

"You haven't asked me if I got the box open," said Werner as I moved to the door. "You don't know what might be inside it."

"Don't try opening it, Werner. I know what's inside it, believe me."

"Tell me."

"That would spoil the fun," I said.

"What fun?"

"The fun of seeing if what you hand over to Bret fits my guess."

Werner looked at me and said, "It is the same box file. I haven't substituted it for another. Take the keys of my desk. It's in the office; in my big filing cabinet."

"Let it stay there," I said.

"I'm sorry about what happened . . . and tearing you away from the party," said Werner. "I know you wanted to take Gloria back to her hotel."

"She had Bret and *Mohnspielen*," I said. "You can't have everything."

"It's over, isn't it?" said Werner. I only wish I could always see into Werner's head with the ease with which he sees into mine. "You and Gloria: it's all over."

"Try to get some sleep, Werner," I said. "That crack on the head is making your brains rattle."

It was very late by the time I got back to the hotel but Lisl was still awake. She was sitting up in bed in a frilly jacket, reading newspapers and playing her old records. She seemed to like sleeping in the downstairs room to which she had moved. It not only saved her going up all those stairs to bed, it was a way of being at the center of everything, of all the hotel's comings and goings.

Even while I was coming through the main door I heard the immortal Marlene singing, "Das war in Schöneberg." Lisl's new record player had revived all her nostalgia and enthusiasm for the music she grew up with. Werner had bought the player for her; it was becoming too difficult for her to wind up by hand the ancient machine she preferred. He had searched everywhere before finding an electric machine that would play her scratchy old "seventy-eights." I went in to her room to say good night. No matter how much her hearing deteriorated, she was always able to hear me tiptoeing past her door should I attempt to go upstairs without paying my respects.

"Was it a good party, *Liebchen*?"

"They missed you, Lisl. Everyone was asking where you were."

"You tell lies not so well, my darling. Perhaps it's better you stick to the truth. Give your poor old Tante Lisl a proper kiss, not one of those English pecks." She puckered her mouth and closed her eyes like a child.

"A big band and dancing and real German food," I said as I took her bony shoulders in my hands and bent low to give her a kiss. "But without you it was nothing."

"I let him borrow Richard, my clever young cook."

"That was very kind, Tante Lisl," I said. "Everyone was talking about the food."

"Zena wasn't sure about it," said Lisl. "She wanted to get prepared dishes from Ka-De-We. But lovely food costs lovely money. Werner should be more careful with his money." She looked at the time. "Did it go on so late?"

"Werner tripped on the stair carpet," I told her. "They had to take him for tests."

"Oh, my God. The times I've told him not to drink. When you are the host, Werner, keep a clear head. I've told him that over and over again."

"Calm down, Lisl. He wasn't drunk. You know Werner; he never drinks. Almost never. He stumbled on the stairs. He twisted his ankle. It's nothing, but Zena wanted to play safe so she made him go for an X-ray. He's in the Steglitz Clinic overnight. That's all." I thought I should mention Werner's condition rather than risk her hearing it from elsewhere.

"The Steglitz Clinic? I must go. Get my dressing gown from the door, there's a darling." She twisted in bed so that she could inspect her face in the mirror, and decide if her makeup was suited to a visit to the hospital in the middle of the night.

"He's asleep," I said. "They gave him painkillers and something to make him sleep. You wouldn't be able to see him. Anyway, it's nothing."

"If it's nothing will he still be coming for coffee and *Kipferl* tomorrow?"

I didn't know Werner had promised to visit the next day. I tried to think of a reason he wouldn't be here.

She said, *"Nit kain entfer iz oich an entfer."* The Yiddish proverb—No answer is also an answer.

"I'm sure he'll be here tomorrow," I said without much conviction.

"I can always detect when you tell me lies, *Liebchen*. It's something I can see in your eyes. Your Lisl can always tell. Why didn't the foolish boy phone me? When it happened: why didn't you phone me?"

"He's all right, Lisl. It's just a little sprain. Zena makes too much of a fuss about Werner. She worries about him too much."

"He should have phoned," Lisl said petulantly.

"He made me promise that I would tell you as soon as I got back here."

"Even one little drink can be too much. And Werner can't drink; he knows that."

"I must go to bed, Lisl. Good night. See you at breakfast."

"Yes, I know it must be boring for you to be talking to an ugly old woman."

"You are a darling," I said. I gave her another kiss and started to make my escape.

Lisl looked at me. "Very well, then. I shall phone the hospital first thing in the morning."

"Good night, Lisl."

"Oh, I'm forgetting, Bernd darling. There is a fax message for you. The telephone went during dinner. The girl was serving some people who came late so it was difficult for her. The people calling spoke no German. I had my friend Lothar take the call, and deal with them. He speaks the most beautiful English. We were playing cards here. Was that all right?"

"How is Lothar?"

"Not so wonderful, darling. He has had to stop smoking."

"That's too bad," I said. But since Lothar Koch was about two hundred years old, a prohibition on smoking seemed a minor restriction and long overdue.

"He gave the foreign lady the fax number here. I know you have told me never to give that number as a way to reach you, but Lothar said this was an emergency."

I took the printed message slip from her. As was to be expected of a man who had loyally served in the Nazi Party's Interior Ministry, Lothar Koch had neatly entered the date and time and his initials on the covering sheet and written "Herrn Bernd Samson" in the appropriate place. DEAR HERR SAMSON, THE ATTACHED FAX WAS SENT TO YOU THIS EVENING AT 21.30 HOURS. YOUR CALLER SAID IT WAS AN EMERGENCY. I HOPE THIS IS IN ACCORD WITH YOUR WISHES.

The fax consisted of one sheet. It was from Mrs. Prettyman, and handwritten in a good firm hand with big looping schoolbook letters that were characteristically American.

Dear Bernard,

I have to tell you the terrible news that my darling Jay died yesterday morning. The doctor and the priest were both with him. It was a peaceful end to his pain, and in some ways for the better. He so enjoyed your visit with us. I think it made him recall happy times you had spent together. He wanted to see you again very much. I told him you were coming back to see him and he died with that thought. He made me promise that I would send this message to you without delay. He wanted me to tell you that you were right in what you said. You guessed what happened. He was all alone that night in Germany. He did everything as you described: there was no one else with him. I hope you understand this message. I have written it exactly as Jay asked.

Would you also please pass news of his condition to any of his friends or relatives with whom you are in touch.

Yours truly,

Tabby Prettyman

I read it through twice. "Thanks Lisl." Until now I had felt certain that Prettyman had killed Thurkettle. But this deathbed confession to it jarred me. It made me wonder if this was Prettyman's final gesture of earthly compassion: pleading guilty to a killing he hadn't committed.

"A friend has died?" Lisl was rummaging through her precious collection of records, her fingers flicking against the corners of the dog-eared paper sleeves.

Finally she found what she was looking for. She looked up at me. "Is it someone I know?"

I had no doubt that together with Herr Koch she had given the fax message her earnest scrutiny.

"Yes, a death. He was very ill. No, it was no one you know."

"Was he very religious?"

"As religious as only a repentant sinner can be," I said. She nodded sagely. I held her tight and kissed her again. I loved her very much. I said good night. As I went upstairs, Marlene began singing "Durch Berlin fliesst immer noch die Spree." All those unforgettable Berlin cabaret songs had an underlying melancholy. I wondered if that's what Berliners liked about them.

TWELVE

THE SIS RESIDENCE, BERLIN

"This is not going to become an inquest," said Bret, standing at the end of the dining table in Frank Harrington's residence. Bret rested his fingers lightly upon its polished surface, so that the reflections looked like big pink spiders. Behind me I heard Frank Harrington give a deep sigh. Werner, across the table from me, shrank a few inches into his collar. He looked like hell. The clinic should never have released him. The others also looked glum. We all suspected that an inquest was exactly what Bret intended that it should become. "It's not official, and nothing anyone says will be on the record." Bret smiled grimly. He had his jacket hanging on the back of his chair and his waistcoat was unbuttoned. Experience had taught me that such dishabille was a bad sign: a warning that Bret was restless and belligerent. As he looked round at us all he added, "Or even remembered. You'll notice that this is a need-to-know gathering."

Bret sat down. Dicky Cruyer fingered his wrist to look at his watch. Dicky had remained in Berlin to attend this meeting at Bret's request. Dicky wanted everyone to know that he had urgent and pressing business elsewhere. Dicky's attire had lately taken a nautical turn: a dark blue Guernsey seaman's sweater and a red-spotted kerchief tied at his neck. He sat well back from the table, a sharpened wooden pencil in his hand. His head was tilted and his eyes fixed, like a sparrow listening for the approach of some distant predator. Augustus Stowe was there, too: swollen to bursting with impatience and importance. Rumors said that he was trying to arrange that he swap jobs with Dicky. There were notepads and pencils at each place. A small table behind me held a tray with glasses and a bottle of fizzy mineral water for those who wanted such Spartan refreshment. No one did. At the center of the table there were two potted plants that had been brought indoors for the winter. There were no blooms on them; just dark green leaves. It was going to be one of those sessions that Bret called "informal" because he honestly didn't know that for everyone else these rough-tongue exchanges, with Bret in the driving seat, were white-knuckle rides.

As if Bret had arranged it in advance, the tension created by his serious mien was relaxed for a moment while the coffee was poured and a plate of digestive biscuits circulated. An essential component of the Englishman's diet, various brands of digestives, the coarseness of their oatmeal content, their thin or thick coatings of plain or milk chocolate, are a subject of animated discussion at almost any Departmental gathering. And sometimes the most memorable one.

"We are looking at ongoing success," said Bret, continuing his leadership role from the seated position. No one spoke. Bret continued, "We are all party to some aspect of the long-term plan in which Fiona Samson played such a vital part. Maybe none of you know the full story, and that's just the way it should be." Bret waved away the biscuits, poured cream into his coffee and drank some. His offhand self-assurance in respect of digestive biscuits revealed his transatlantic origins. "But there were hiccups . . . hiccups and tragedies. I won't name names, and I don't want to apportion blame. But I know that some of you have glimpsed ugly episodes. Many others may have guessed at them. Some of you have encountered questions to which you have no answer. I want to say how much I appreciate the trust and dedication you have provided to the Department in the face of painful doubt."

The gathering remained silent. It was an opportunity for private worry. Dicky began biting his nails. I took another couple of biscuits, reasoning that the plate might not come back down the table again.

"Things went wrong," Bret continued. "In the field we contend with disaster and learn to live with it. But when flaws are traced to London; when catastrophe is built into any operation due to faulty planning, and even fundamentally wrong strategy, we have to put the blame right where it was born: London Central."

Bret drank some coffee, and let us all catch our breath, clear our throats, and wonder which way he was going. Frank reached out to push a coaster across the table to where Augustus Stowe was about to put the hot, antique silver coffeepot down on the polished surface. It was all right for Bret to talk about London's disasters. Bret had been resident in California—debriefing me and

Fiona—long enough to stay out of the firing line. He had chosen just the right time to return and assume the role of prosecutor, judge, juror, and probation officer, too. But no one said anything like that. We all chewed on our digestives, and guzzled our coffee, and thought our thoughts in a silence broken only by murmured rituals of coffee drinking.

If Bret hadn't started speaking again I think we would all be sitting there still. "I know that there is no one in this room who can truthfully deny owing a debt of gratitude to Silas Gaunt. Silas was never a glory hunter. Nothing better shows his character than the way he left the Department without recognition of any sort. No knighthood, no CBE, not even the standard letter of recommendation that we give to lower ranks. And yet, with a little lobbying, there is no question that he could have obtained the recognition he deserved. But as you may or may not know, Silas Gaunt asked that he be given nothing, so that he could continue to be in close association with the Department. And for obvious reasons connection would have to be severed with any ex-employee the Department permitted to be honored in any way."

There were noncommittal noises from the assembled party while Bret took a deep breath. "And so Silas worked at arm's length for us. And continued to work at arm's length even when he was old and unwell. It is everyone's fault. Dozens of people were in regular contact with him. Any one of them could have shouted stop. Any one of them might have pointed out that Silas was no longer the omnipotent, far-sighted strategist he'd once been. But Silas was never content with past glories: he was always looking to the future. In hindsight it's obvious that Silas Gaunt thought the Department was languishing and slipping ever further back in our war with the Soviets. He said we hadn't kept up to date. He said it to me, he said it to everyone he could influence. Unfortunately he didn't sufficiently distinguish between being up to date and becoming more operational. Our traditional role of intelligence gatherer—and nothing beyond—became in his eyes an unendurable restriction. He wanted the Department to be more assertive, even if that meant sometimes being more violent."

Bret put his hands into the praying position and sat back for ten seconds to let us think about it. Bret had gone as near to the brink as I'd ever heard a senior official go in personalizing the Department's shortcomings.

"I've now put into play checks and balances that would preclude this ever happening again," said Bret. "Even senior staff will no longer be able to give off-the-record briefings to anyone engaged in a task that could go operational. Silas Gaunt's contacts with the Department are now severed . . . a thing of the past. We have now cleared up the remnants of every stratagem that Silas Gaunt had access to. Now we start afresh."

Bret looked around to see how this monologue had been received. Augustus Stowe moved about on his chair, as if suffering a cramp. It was difficult to be sure how many people present fully understood what Bret was telling us. Werner looked half-asleep; probably as a result of all the painkillers he was taking. Frank was anxiously fingering the leaves of the potted flowers that had been brought indoors for the winter. I think he'd noticed black spot. Dicky sat with both hands in his trouser pockets, as if in a resolute attempt to stop nail-biting. Bret said, "Bernard has had personal involvement in this whole episode. No one blames him for breaking a few rules in his need to find out the answers to questions that kept him awake at night."

Bret looked at me and said, "When you went out to the Ziesar ramp last week, and found Thurkettle's decomposing body, you fitted into place the final piece of jigsaw puzzle."

They all turned to stare at me. "Who told you I went out there?" I said, keeping my voice pitched in a way that reserved the right to deny that it was true.

"Don't blow a fuse, Bernard. It's standard procedure. Werner is under strict orders to keep me informed of any serious development. . . . No, no, no. He's a loyal friend of yours, I'll tell you that. But he's also a loyal employee of the Department."

Werner looked at me and shrugged. Bret knew I could hardly go ape right now. This wasn't the moment to beat Werner over the head, or start arguing the finer details of the Tessa killing. And Bret had set it up so well. He had us all convinced that his only desire was to come up with the truth. And here he was inviting me to say anything I wished.

"Prettyman killed Thurkettle," I said.

Bret hesitated for a long time. Then he said: "Yes, I see. But can you tell us why he did it?"

"Prettyman did what Silas Gaunt ordered him to do."

"But . . . even killing?"

"Not so long ago you sent me out to Washington, D.C., to sweet-talk Prettyman into coming back to London to face an inquiry . . . money had gone astray and Prettyman knew the score."

"Afterwards . . ." said Bret.

"Sure," I said, interrupting him. "Afterwards it was all smoothed over. No money had gone missing. It was a slush fund. It was just some creative accounting to kosher away money for Fiona's operations in the East."

"But I can see that you don't believe that," said Bret.

"I'm guessing. I think Prettyman made sure that a few pennies ended up in his own pocket. I think Silas Gaunt faced Prettyman with evidence of his crime, and used it to blackmail him into doing whatever the Department needed doing."

"Hold the phone," said Bret. "Are you hinting that Prettyman was stitched up? If that's what you think, let's hear it." Bret knew all the tricks of chairing a meeting, and the number one trick was to remain on the side of the angels.

"That Prettyman was tempted, deliberately tempted, into stealing so that he could be trapped?" I said. "Yes, that's what I think. Prettyman was perfect for what they wanted: intelligent, quick, unscrupulous, and greedy. Yes, I'm sure he was targeted. But there had to be a cut out point. Blackmailers have to give their victims a look at the light shining at the end of the tunnel."

"And what was that?"

"On the instructions of Silas Gaunt, Prettyman sought out Thurkettle—a hit man he'd heard his CIA friends talking about—and set up the killing of Tessa Kosinski. Prettyman arranged to pay off Thurkettle in person. But Prettyman was waiting out there with a gun; he killed him instead."

Bret made a noise. "Sounds like a damned stupid hit man who gets killed by his client. Wouldn't a contract killer suspect that his employer might try to kill him? And take precautions?"

I said, "Prettyman made it clear that he was no more than the go-between. It wasn't Prettyman's money and it wasn't Prettyman's chosen target. Prettyman was just the middleman. That way of working would reassure a hit man like Thurkettle. Remember that, as far as anyone knows, Thurkettle had always worked arm's length for organizations. That's how Prettyman heard about him in the first place. He'd always been paid, and always found himself dealing with an intermediary. You don't go off and make a hit for the CIA, or the British government, and come back worrying about being gunned down."

"Don't you?" said Bret.

"If Uncle Silas is running wild, maybe you should," I agreed. "But you know Prettyman, he was quite a wimp, and looked even more feeble than he was. It's not easy to think of a white-faced penpusher like him gunning down a hit man in cold blood. It took me a little time to adjust to that idea. But of course that's just what made it all so easy for him."

"So for you the story is complete, Bernard," said Bret.

"Almost," I said. Bret made a movement of his hand urging me to continue. "There was always the mechanism of getting Tessa Kosinski to the place on the Autobahn where she was killed. From the party in Berlin, she went in the van I was driving. But how was she persuaded to get into it? I did all I could to make her get out. The second mystery is how she came to be in Berlin in the first place."

"She was with Dicky," said Bret. "That's correct, isn't it, Dicky?"

Dicky came bolt upright in his chair and said, "Yes, Bret" in a whisper.

"But why?" I persisted.

Bret said, "I'll save Dicky the embarrassment of revealing all the details. Tessa was given two free round-trip air tickets London to Berlin: first class. They were supposed to have come with the compliments of British Airways. In case more inducement was needed a friend of hers, called Pinky, was told to send her some desirable opera tickets. At that same weekend Dicky was told to attend a meeting in Berlin. Dicky was spending a lot of time with Tessa and it all worked out."

"Was Dicky ordered to take Tessa to Berlin?" I persisted.

Bret looked at Dicky. Dicky's face went a bright red. He said, "Yes." I suppose he couldn't say anything else; I'm sure Bret knew the correct answer already.

"That still leaves the question of why she got into my van," I said.

Dicky, pleased to move on to something other than the hotel room he'd shared with Tessa, said, "That was a coincidence. She was pretty high by the time she climbed into your van. I tried to get her out but you punched me in the face, Bernard."

"I'm sorry about that," I said. "The van started and my hand slipped." Dicky had never mentioned my one and only assault upon his person until now. There were times when I even thought he might have forgotten it.

Dicky decided not to pursue it. "But soon after you left, the Thurkettle man arrived at the party. He was looking everywhere for Tessa. He'd arranged that she should ride on the back of his motorbike. When he became convinced that she was in your van, he got on his bike and raced off after you."

"Okay," said Bret. "Now tell us, Bernard. What was Prettyman's light at the end of the tunnel?"

"The Swede was waiting at the plane with a box

that would solve all Prettyman's problems. This was to be Prettyman's final job for Silas Gaunt. And it was."

"The evidence of his malfeasance; the accounts or whatever?"

"I've got my own theory about what was in the box," I told him.

"I sent Werner to get it for us," said Bret.

"Steal it from Mrs. Prettyman, you mean," I said. "And use Cindy Prettyman's own keys. That was neat, Werner." Werner smiled. He didn't mind how sarcastic I was, he knew it was a successful operation. And he knew that, measured in need-to-know brownie points, he outranked me.

"Bernard knows what's in the box file," said Bret with an edge of sarcasm. "The rest of us mortals have to guess. I asked London to look up the reference number in Registry but they say there is no record of that box file ever having been issued."

Never been issued. Clever old Uncle Silas. "How are you going to look inside it then?" I asked.

"We are cutting the lock off," said Bret. "Then we'll settle what's inside. Good old Yankee know-how; isn't that what I'm noted for?"

I had said something along those lines from time to time to all kinds of people, so I wasn't in a position to deny it now. "I wouldn't cut into that box, Bret," I said.

"I already have," said Bret with a smug grin. "Tarrant has it in his workshop. I'm waiting for him to bring it up here and show us the contents."

"No, Bret, no," I said. I jumped to my feet so hurriedly that I knocked my chair backwards, and heard it hit the little table holding the tray of glasses. Everything fell to the floor with the sound of breaking crystal.

"Where are you going?" shouted Bret.

Like all such old Berlin houses this one had a staircase at the back so that servants could move about unobtrusively. Access to the stairs was through doors without doorknobs or locks; doors designed to conform with the wall decoration and be unnoticed by the casual observer. I knew this house well, and I went through the door to find the landing at the top of a narrow wooden staircase. I wasn't expecting to find an elderly man sitting there in regal style on the draughty upstairs servants' landing. Neither was this tall stranger ready for my sudden eruption through the wall. "Oww!" he shouted as he sprang to his feet, responding to the way my booted foot had landed on his arthritic knee, and the jolt from my outstretched hand when it steadied itself upon his neck.

I didn't stop to strangle him. There was no time. I ran down the stairs, and was at the next landing by the time I realized that the man I had stumbled over was the Director-General. He had been seated on an antique chair, with a woollen blanket over his knees and headphones clamped over his ears. Listening of course to everything that Bret and the rest of us were saying. We were being bugged by the Director-General in person! So that was how it was done; and no one had even been told the D-G was making one of his rare excursions to this outpost of Empire. That bloody Frank and his potted plants. And I thought he was finding black spot on them.

From above I heard a distant yell as the D-G recovered himself from where he had been sent sprawling across the floor. But by that time I was going down the stairs as fast as I could run. My brain had become alive. What was I doing, I asked myself. Why was I running frantically through the house, so concerned about Tarrant? I hated and despised Tarrant. He had always shown aloof hostility to me and everything I did and said. But how could I stop right here on the stairs, go back up to the others, and tell them I'd changed my mind? I remembered Frank's words at an earlier meeting: It's always bad luck to be good at something you don't want to do—or something dangerous. Well, Frank old daddy, you said it all.

I rushed down the final flight of stairs, pushed the door open, and emerged into the hall. I slid on the loose carpet so that I almost fell full length across the floor. Then, recovering my balance by grabbing the hall table, I ran through the drawing room and burst out of the garden door and into the long conservatory. Rows of potted plants were lined up near the light and the whole place smelled of the onions and apples that were stored there in winter. I pulled the outside door open with such force a glass pane cracked. Then I was out into the biting cold air and the garden. I ran along the path, skirting round a wheelbarrow, the ice and gravel crunching and cracking underfoot. "Tarrant, stop!" I shouted as I ran.

I wrenched open the door of Tarrant's sanctum. He stood at his workbench. One hand was raised as he brought the lever of a power drill down to make another hole in the steel box file that was gripped in the vise.

I grabbed Tarrant's shoulders to spin him around. Then I used both hands on the small of his back to propel him through the door and out into the garden. He went flying, his feet scarcely touching the ground. I was following behind him, thinking all the time of what a fool I would look if my calculations proved wrong.

But I had no need to worry on that account. As Tarrant and I hit the frosty lawn, and rolled over in the snow with Tarrant shouting his objections, the bang came.

Tarrant's brick-built playpen was just what the Semtex needed. It constrained the force of the explosion enough to make sure it really went with a noise that echoed round the neighbourhood. The workshop door was already open, but the force wrenched it off its hinges and sent it bowling across the grass like a rectangular wheel. The window disappeared in a red flare and became broken glass and firewood.

"Oh my God," shouted Tarrant. "I'm dying."

I stayed where I was on the cold ground. Now that it was over I was shivering, and it wasn't entirely due to the weather. I also felt an almost overwhelming need to vomit. Getting angry and screaming abuse at Tarrant enabled me to overcome these symptoms.

"How did you guess?" Bret asked me after I'd had a stiff drink, and been checked over by Frank's tame doctor. It was just Bret and me. And we were not sitting near any of Frank's potted plants.

"There was no other explanation."

"Ah, yes, Sherlock Holmes; when you have eliminated the impossible, the remaining improbable explanation must be right."

"Something like that," I said. Bret was not a Sherlock Holmes fan: his favorite reading matter was the sports pages of the *International Herald Tribune*.

"But why wait so long before confiding it to us?" said Bret. He was distressed. He was good at hiding his emotions, but Bret was always dismayed by the cadenzas of violence that brought discordant counterpoint to the formal harmonies of office life in Whitehall.

"I needed to know who else was in on the secret," I explained. "I had to see how you and Werner and Frank saw it all coming undone. And I wanted to see how you all reacted to the prospect of opening the box file. I wanted to find out who was in this with Silas."

"And did you find out?"

"Well, I bumped into the Director-General," I said.

Bret acknowledged this joke with one of his well-known flickering smiles. "Did Prettyman know what was in the box?"

"I wonder. He must have had some strange sort of worry about it. But what could he do?"

"He could hope his wife forced it open," said Bret.

"It's tempting to think that he wanted her to steal it and break into it. But when you see how difficult it was to open without a key it's clear that if someone got blown away opening it, it wouldn't be Mrs. Prettyman but some poor bloody technician in Brussels. And I'm not sure Prettyman would try that on his ex-wife. I was surprised that he found the nerve to kill Thurkettle."

"Well, ex-wives sometimes generate considerable motivation along those lines," said Bret, who had suffered chronic ex-wife angst. "What made it explode?" he said. "Tarrant had been struggling with it for half an hour."

"Some sort of composite fuse. A trembler wouldn't have been suitable. It had to be a fuse that could take rough treatment. My bet would be a light-sensitive fuse: a photoelectric cell, set so it would be triggered by light."

"I've never heard of a gadget like that."

"The Luftwaffe used them on time-delay bombs dropped on London during the war. They were put into the delay circuit as a back-up. If the time fuse failed, the light-sensitive one would explode when the bomb disposal team dismantled it to look inside."

"A secondary fuse?"

"Two fuses would be in keeping with the purpose of the device."

"Would it?"

"It was designed to make sure the Swede, his plane, and Prettyman would disappear forever. With Thurkettle already dead, that would have eliminated any possibility of the truth ever coming to light."

"Silas Gaunt," said Bret sadly. "Don't let's be mealy-mouthed about it. Silas Gaunt set up the Kosinski killing and the Thurkettle killing. And then wanted to make certain the killers were all dead too. It was almost the perfect. . . ."

"The perfect crime?" I supplied.

"The perfect solution," said Bret.

"What will happen now?"

"No one was hurt," said Bret. "What do you want to happen? Do you want to sue Silas Gaunt?" he asked caustically.

"He wasn't the only one," I said. "He is simply the one who will get all the blame. They will dump every mistake and crime the Department committed on to Silas Gaunt. They did the same with my father."

"He'll never be released." Bret didn't argue with my verdict.

"I think he knows that," I said.

"He is seriously disturbed," said Bret.

"He seemed quite rational when I saw him."

"I know. Sometimes he seems absolutely normal. No one suspected the truth for a long time. He simply lost all sense of right and wrong. I blame the D-G in some ways. He put far too much on to Silas's shoulders at a time when Silas should have been resting and having counseling."

"You said you wanted to see me, Bret," I reminded him. "Was there something else to tell me?"

Bret looked at me in a very solemn way and said, "Last weekend I asked Gloria to marry me."

"Congratulations, Bret."

"She told me yes."

"That's great." So that look in his eyes hadn't just come from eating too much sugar.

"This is it, Bernard. No fancy weekends in country hotels. Nothing sneaky. I want this to be the one thing I do just right. Love and cherish; for better or for worse; happy ever after, and all that." He looked at his hands. In what was probably some significant signal of what was in the deepest recesses of his mind, he twisted his gold signet ring round, so it looked like a wedding band. "Freud said that a man can be in love with a woman for many years without realizing that he's in love."

"Yes, well, when you read those books of his, you can tell he had a lot of things on his mind."

"I figured I should clear our plans with you first. Gloria thought the same. One of the reasons I came here to Berlin was so that I could see you and make sure it was okay by you."

"I'm not your prospective father-in-law, Bret. You do it the way you want. She deserves a break."

"I told her that I didn't want a wife who was yearning for some other guy. I had one of those wives the last time around. Gloria said there was no one else."

"She's right as far as I'm concerned. It was obvious from the start. I knew it would never work: we both knew." I gave a sincere smile and reached out and shook his hand in a grown-up, calm, and dignified way.

"Congratulations, Bret. It will be just fine. You're a lucky man; she's quite a girl."

"Whatever she is, I love her, Bernard. I need her."

"I'm a married man, Bret," I said, to stem his confession.

"I know. It will all work out for you too, Bernard. Fiona's something special. All marriages go through a really bad patch some time."

"How long does it last?"

"If it's any help, I can tell you that the Department plans to offer you a proper contract . . . pension and so on."

I nodded.

"The Department owes you that at least. And I owe you a great deal, too."

"Do you? What?"

"Have you forgotten that night I came to you at the Hennig place? That night when Five sent a K7 man to caution me and put me under house arrest. I phoned the D-G . . ."

"And the D-G just happened to be on a train to Manchester," I supplied. "Yes, I remember. The D-G becomes conveniently restless when a bitter row is in the offing."

"I was desperate. You were the only one I knew wouldn't turn me in, Bernard."

"You were taking a chance," I said.

"No, I wasn't. I knew you would go out on a limb for me, Bernard. You are your own man. I've cursed you for that many times. But I admire it, too. That's why I want to do everything right by you."

"Okay, Bret."

"I'll pull out all the stops to get Frank's job for you when he goes. Not because I owe you a favor but because you are the best man for the job. My guess is that he will resign, and go out to Australia with his son. You know how Frank feels about him."

I nodded my thanks.

"I can't promise of course. They might have bowler-hatted me by then. I'm on a handshake arrangement. When they get someone younger and more suited for the Deputy's job, I will go back to California."

"With Gloria?"

"Oh, sure. I will always have my home there. She's never been, but I know she will love it. There's a real big age disparity but . . ."

"Forget it. You'll be very happy together," I said. "Gloria likes older men."

"You have all the answers, Bernard."

"Us people with all the answers always get a few of them wrong."

"You don't have to get all of them wrong. You are the luckiest man in the world, Bernard. You're married to Fiona."

"She's married to her work," I said.

"You two just don't communicate at all, do you? You couldn't be more wrong about Fiona. Look, I have spent a lot of time worrying about this . . . worrying whether I should show it to you. But I can't see any alternative."

Bret took a sheet of writing paper from his pocket. The letterhead was La Buona Nova, the California estate where Fiona and I had spent so long being debriefed by Bret. The note was creased, as if it had been read, re-read, folded, and refolded many many times. It was Fiona's handwriting:

Dear Bret,

I can't go on day after day of talking about
my past. At first I expected it to become a
sort of therapy that would heal me and make
me whole. But it's not like that. You are
considerate and kind but the more I talk
the more dispirited I become. I've lost
Bernard. I realize that now. And when I
lost Bernard, I lost the children too, for they
adore him.

It's not Bernard's fault, it's not anyone's
fault except my own. I should have known
that Bernard would find someone else. Or
that someone else would find him. And I
should have known that Bernard was not the
sort of man who can jump into bed and out
of it again. Bernard is serious. Bernard
would never admit it but he is a romantic. It
is what made me fall in love with him, and
stay in love. And now he's serious and
romantic and madly in love with Gloria,
and I know I will never be able to compete
with her. She's young and gorgeous and
sweet and kind. And clever. She loves our
children and from what I hear, she says only
complimentary things about me. What can I
offer him that is better? Bernard hungers for
her all the time, and perhaps he's right to
love her. I know him so well that I can see
every thought that is written in his face. And
it devastates me. He's desolate at being sepa-
rated from her. He gave me some money the
other day and there was a tiny photo of

Gloria folded inside. He keeps it with his money so that I never see it, I suppose. I placed it on the floor in the dressing room and he found it there and thought I'd never seen it.

It was my affair with Kennedy that destroyed our marriage of course. I was a fool. But Kennedy could never have become a "Gloria" in my life. He was in love with Karl Marx. I soon guessed that he was spying on me, and that everything was secondary to his "duty." And I knew that if he discovered that I was still working for London Central he would turn me in without a flicker of hesitation, or a moment of remorse.

I learned that life's unendurable tests come in the shape of memories, not experiences. That night when Tess died and when I saw Bernard shoot Kennedy . . . the confusions and the shouting, the dimly lit roadside and my fears. These all anesthetized my emotions and feelings. For a few days I felt able to deal with it. But when the memories of that night visited me I saw it for the first time. For the first time, I felt the warm blood that spattered upon me. For the first time the hatred and despair was so evident that I could smell the emotion. And each time the memories return they are more fearful. Like all intruders they come unexpected in the night. They drag me slowly from deep drug-induced sleep, to an interim state of half-awake nightmare from which I struggle to awaken.

After the nightmares started, I saw Bernard in a new way. Bernard gave me everything he had to give. Throughout our married life I had blamed him for not being demonstrative, at a time when I should have been thanking him for never burdening me with the hell he'd been through. Bernard has spent all his life doing a job for which he was never really suited. He is not tough. He is not insensitive. He is not violent. His brain is quicker and more subtle than that of anyone I've ever met. And this is why he decided he must keep his nightmares all to himself. Now I have discovered how much it costs to be alone with such terrors. But for me it is too late.

How can I ever make Bernard love me again? Don't say I can't. Life without Bernard would not be worth living. No one will ever love him as I have. And do. And always will.

Good night, Bret. Thank you for more than I can ever say.

Fiona

I folded up the letter and handed it back to Bret. It had disturbed me very much. "I'm grateful, Bret," I said.

"You still don't understand, do you?" said Bret. "Can't you read?"

"Yes, I can."

"When I got to her room she had taken a whole load of tablets. She got them from the doctor two or three at a time, and saved them up. And she drank half a bottle of vodka."

"Fiona had? Vodka and pills?"

"You were away in Santa Barbara that night. I pushed her into the car and got her to the hospital. They were great. They did all the things they do, and they saved her. I knew the director there. We told everyone she was there for tests."

"I remember when she was having tests. Jesus Christ! Why didn't you tell me the truth?"

"I promised her I wouldn't. She left a note for you; I burned it. I promised I'd never tell you. Now I'm breaking that promise. But how can I stand by and let the pair of you tear each other apart? I'm too fond of you both to permit it without doing something."

"I love her, Bret. I've always loved her."

"You are a callous brute. Forget all that stuff about you being a romantic; that's just a measure of how much she loves you. You are brutal."

"Towards Fi?"

"Can't you see what you do to her? She's not married to her work, Bernard. She'd give it up tomorrow if you gave her the kind of love and understanding she needs. She's a woman, Bernard, she's your wife. She's not a drinking buddy. She works non-stop because you drive her out of your life. Can't you see that, Bernard? Can't you see that?"

"How do you know? . . . know what she feels?"

"She talks to me because she can't talk to you. You're a smart talker, Bernard, a *beau parleur.* You can talk your way through any situation if you have a mind to. Fiona is not like that. The more important it is to her, the more tongue-tied she becomes. She can't express her deepest feelings to you. She would love to have the children with her all the time. But you've got to be with her, too. Not time-wise but with her in spirit. How can you expect her to commit herself to you, while you are still sending long-stemmed red roses to Gloria?"

"I hope you're right, Bret," I said. "Last night I wrote to Fiona: a long letter. I want to start again."

"Good! That's good, Bernard. Let's make at least one good thing come out of this mess."

"I asked her to come and live with me in Berlin. And send the children to a German school. Have them grow up the way I did."

"She will jump at it, Bernard. I know she will."

Fiona was right: happiness too comes more often from memories than from experiences. My happiness came in the shape of a perfect day long ago. I was with my school-friends, Werner and Axel. We were running down to the canal, and then along it to Lützowplatz. I ran and ran until I got to Dad's office on Tauentzienstrasse. What a hot sum-mer day it was: only Berlin enjoys such lovely days. I opened Dad's desk and found the chocolate bar, his ration, that he left there for me. He always saved it for me. Today there were two bars: that's why I remember it so vividly. We shared the chocolate between us and then climbed up the mountain of rubble. It filled the middle of the whole street, as high as three floors. From the top—sitting on an old piece of box—we went sliding down the steep slope, bumping in clouds of dust. The next stop was the clinic where the salvaged bricks, bottles, and pieces of timber were cleaned and sorted and arranged with a care that only Germans could give to such things. We worked there for an hour each day after school. Then we would go swim-ming. The sky was blue and Berlin was heaven.

"I hope she will," I said.